# ADEN

# ADEN

Barry Stewart Hunter

*Barry Stewart Hunter* (signature)

This edition first published in 2017 by
Martin Firrell Company Limited, 26 Red Lion Square,
London WC1R 4AG, United Kingdom

ISBN 978-0-9931786-6-5

Main text typeset in 10.5pt Baskerville.

*For Rob,*
*and in memory of ERH*

# ❧ Contents ❦

## 1 | Jacinta

Indigo | Pretty Flamingo | Call Me Ishmael |
The Gully-Gully Man | Radio San'a | Red Sky at Night |
The Language of Loss

## 2 | Ben

Four Hundred Whispers | Shirley Bassey Very Good | The
Witness Table | Rice Krispies | The Coastline of Integrity |
Beautiful Civilian | A Handful of Sand

## 3 | Hildegaard

Hello, Darkness | Regardless of Che | Chits with
Everything | Ruby Tuesday | The Ceremony of Innocence |
Crater | Tears of Blood

## 4 | Basim

Wadi Hadhramaut | Diary of a Son-in-Law |
Song for Someone | The Look of Love | True Stories |
The Verdict of Failure | Monsoon

## 5 | Callum

The Society of Men | Blue Murder | Every Good Boy
Deserves Favour | Regatta | No Smoke Without Fire |
Exodus | The Colour of the Sky

## 6 | Sulaiman

Dog Eat Dog | The Letter 'K' | Interregnum |
Funeral of a Friend | Requiem for a Donkey | The Silent
Valley | Kingdom Come

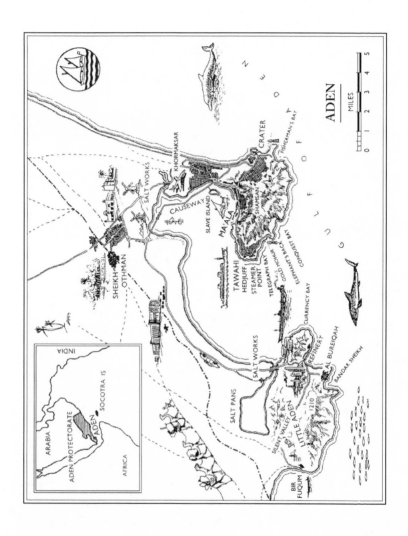

# Victory celebrations in streets of Aden

*From our Middle East correspondent*

ARAB celebrations in the port of Aden today marked the end of 128 years of colonial government and the creation of a new People's Republic of South Yemen.

Britain has struggled for four years to counter a bloody insurgency in the former Crown Colony, and peace talks with the Moscow-backed National Liberation Front – which is widely tipped to form the start-up republic's first administration – were concluded in Geneva two days ago.

The East India Company first seized Aden in 1839 to halt pirate attacks on ships sailing to and from Bombay.

*Daily Express, London, 30 November 1967*

# *1* |
# Jacinta

'I know, I know – that's what I had to find out.'

REMEMBER THIS. The young *memsahib* undid her dress of towelling, a cuttlefish bone gripped tightly in her free hand, and raised her eyes to the horizon. The sea was perfectly calm. There was nothing else between her and the edge of the world – no siren sunset to draw her on, no secret lover to call her back. There was no breeze at all in the Gulf of Aden just before dark.

Jacinta lowered her dress towards the wet sand. She felt the dress slide from her hips and pile up around her feet. As she stepped from the hoop of cloth she re-knotted the lace at the side of her polka-dot bikini. Again she heard the little avalanche of surf and felt the foam course one more time between her toes. She felt everything. When she looked, her dress had gone.

She turned to left and right. Only the pinkish dunes on one side and, on the other, the lovely lights of Gold Mohur – all the coloured bulbs in loops like smiles around the bar, with just now the shimmer of a match, surely, or the sudden glamour of a menthol cigarette.

The young Englishwoman hesitated beside the Indian Ocean. She broke into three pieces the cuttlefish bone she had picked up for its comfort, gliding barefoot from the beach club gatehouse and the wire curtain of the shark net. Now she let the bleached pieces fall as she waded into the knowing sea. Beyond the surf's tug the water was dusk-thick, dusk-warm. How it buoyed Jacinta up. Using measured strokes she set course for a horizon she could no longer see, a screw-kick action scraping the surface behind her and sending forth shock waves of pressure in regular pulses. Then it came to Jacinta in her lonely freedom – the horizon was here. She had reached it already. All the lights went out. Sill Jacinta paddled on. Her raised head was lost in the desolate merger of sea with sky. Her hair was gathered up tightly in a leopard-skin clasp. Just below the surface, her foot lashed out again in a sheath of bubbles, bequeathing shy eddies behind her as she breasted the long night in front.

TWO STOREYS below the horizon, the tiger shark circled the young Englishwoman and mapped the contours of her leg. The great fish apprehended the arc described by her hands as they cupped the sea and swept it away on this side or that. The woman had an attractive perfume that alerted in addition at least two adult bull sharks and an immature blue, eager as a puppy. As she splashed on, tired now and sickened finally by the fateful workings of her imagination, Jacinta trailed in her wake little posies of scent.

The thuggish tiger shark circled closer, then dropped deeper. It shed the loyal remoras that had picked clean its teeth since they quit together the noisome dock at Mogadishu. The shark was hungry as hell. It came up rapidly from the deep and smashed Jacinta's femur with its snout before veering off and thinking. And she was thinking too. She was very tired now. It was exactly how she had imagined it would be. She lay on her back and tried to recall the faces of those she had loved. She couldn't picture them – she couldn't see anyone. As she sculled herself towards the Horn of Africa she looked at the sky for the last time and thought – this is what we mean when we say indigo. A jet plane climbed overhead with its tables stowed and its seat backs in the upright position. And still Jacinta couldn't see what she had done wrong. She eased a wedding band from her finger and, eyes shut now, pushed the ring away from her. Ordinarily, she was the least melodramatic of young women. She actually wanted to be naked, to leave behind as little as possible of herself. A slack-jawed tiger shark on its ascent from seven fathoms swallowed her wedding ring without really noticing it, but Jacinta could hardly be expected

4

to know about any of that. She only floated at the surface while, in her mind's eye, her ring was sinking.

REACHING FORWARD to light a lamp at the prow, Sulaiman looked up and saw the wings of a Comet 4C blink red and green from the darkening sky. He rinsed his hands and feet in a bucket and lowered his forehead towards a square of clean white cotton on the thwart. As he prayed for a full sea, his bared back to the outboard engine, a small *qud* bucked on the wet planks with a hook lodged in its cheek, splashing the plastic bag that had in it the transistor radio.

Each day at sundown, the Adeni fished the deep waters of the gulf and improved his English steadily in the patient sight of God. Now he closed the door of the lamp. He took up his son's Pye radio and raised the volume to catch a reading of *Greenmantle* broadcast to Her Majesty's forces in Aden and the wider Protectorates. The net lay ready in a modest heap. Sulaiman hammered the drowning *qud* against the boards, tossed the fish into the pail, and wiped his hands on his checked *dhoti*. Then he heard the far screams.

He rubbed his pewter stubble, peering urgently across the water towards the dark presence of Shamsan. He glimpsed a knot of foam, locally intense, in line with Telegraph Bay. He jerked the cord of the outboard, opened up the throttle, and crouched at the tiller. When he reached the woman she was no longer alive – he had to club the sharks with an oar as his platform rolled and pitched in the bloody spume. When he pulled her inside, there was little left of the woman except her torso and head. It was very hard to look at her face – the tiny muscles flinched at the back of Sulaiman's eyes. He propped up what remained of the *memsahib* in the bow, draping a length of dry netting over her body, then turned his boat towards Steamer Point. To the west, the sky above the refinery was livid, inflamed. East, the

5

night sat softly on the sea. In the lurid light of the lamp and through her salt-stiffened shroud, Jacinta shone like the Venus de Milo.

But that was later.

## ❧ Pretty Flamingo ❧

SEATED ALONE AT THE cocktail bar in the Shalimar ballroom on B deck, Oona Durbridge impaled a maraschino cherry on a toothpick and tried to ignore the music of the band.

Behind her on a parquet square, their men grinning gamely and perspiring into fancy dress, daughters of the empire gave themselves over to energetic dancing with a wave of recognition here or a smile of self-knowledge there. A special few were Liz Taylor – or Marilyn, even – while others were more like Sandie Shaw in respect of their peek-a-boo hair-dos and the way they eschewed shoes. It must have been eighty degrees or more in their floating pavilion, and the night air carried top notes of toilet water and aftershave above the alluvial perfumes of the Nile.

Oona eased her foot from a white stiletto, hooking the shoe over the rung of her bar stool. She sensed, rather than saw, the muscular waiter as he shuttled to and from the service counter, undressing her routinely with his Adelaide eyes. Bruce doubled by day as a poolside lifeguard with a whistle on his chest, and trebled after midnight as a croupier in the Casablanca Club on C deck. Now Oona swivelled in spite of herself and watched the Australian circumnavigate this tipsy Tarzan and his Jane and all the covered tables coming and going in her head like flying saucers among the smoke-filled columns of light. As he moved effortlessly through elements of the playful scene, tray lifted up towards a heaven of red, white and blue balloons corralled festively in a net, Bruce's jacket rode high on his tanned stomach.

'Freshen that one for you, madam?'

Oona turned back towards the mirror, hitched up her shoulder strap, and discovered again the pretty bartender she had down as a Siamese. He was smiling with a universal disdain and drumming his dainty forefingers on the Formica counter in professional sympathy with the band.

'My husband manages them, don't you know?' Oona explained fiercely, a little protective in spite of everything.

Her eyes explored the long mirror, seeking out the dais beyond the dance floor and a sea of tables stretching behind her. She found Jimmy first, of course. Then she watched Philip crane a young neck tough with tendons towards a microphone set above and to one side of the flashing cymbal.

'Okay, okay – we're talking Pretty Flamingo, right?'

The bar boy motioned towards the stage. He too was still young enough to be someone's precious son, Oona told herself, setting out on a high tide of longing or regret to imagine, not for the first time, a mother's unconditional love. She raised her empty glass in a kind of toast to herself – to her childless self.

'He says they're likely to go all the way, as a matter of fact. My clever husband believes they're going to be big –'

'I know – bigger than Herman's Hermits. You said so last night.'

'Did I? Oh, shit.'

'Don't worry, lady – not a problem for me.'

Now the song's chorus arrived, soaring. The bar boy drenched her tired ice with gin and then slid the Angostura bitters across the counter, bored already and no longer chasing tips, and it seemed to Oona, herself bathed in the fickle aura of mirrors and bottles, his sly beauty went out like a light. At last the number ended. Oona drank once, twice, and swung her stool until she faced the platform from which Jimmy was making his announcement in a signature Scottish accent all the broader for straying so far from home.

'We thank you, pirates and gorillas. We thank you, harlequins and cowgirls and *sheeks* of Arabia, and the wives of *sheeks* –'

Polite applause, generous in tone, broke out in the area closest to the stage and spread rapidly towards the bar.

'We'd like to lower the tempo now before we take a wee break, but we'll be back as per usual to take you right through till midnight here in the Sh-Sh-Shalimar ballroom on B deck. That's the deck of your dreams, good people – and of ours.'

Jimmy, Jimmy – his falsetto was gorgeous. So what if he was a rough diamond from Glasgow's east end with an outsized quiff that had burgeoned, like resentment itself, across the troubled years? He tossed the lock of hair from his forehead and accepted an acoustic guitar from the boy who played bass and embarked on a tremulous version with Philip of You've Lost That Lovin' Feeling. It brought the couples closer together on the dance floor, kindling in Oona the desire for fellowship, which was her simplest and strongest impulse. Her pupils dilated. She felt the acquiescence of the room in what was good. She watched as Philip stroked a cymbal, heard him pedal the bass drum with its Pretty Flamingo legend and croon in a voice that was low and unselfish. Sweat flew from his hair and sparkled in the path of an upturned spotlight. So what if he insisted with pretentious youth on the need to direct every ballad of love or loss to someone most deserving in the audience? Oona tracked his pained gaze to the woman sitting alone at a table strewn with overflowing ashtrays and cigarette cases and brightly coloured drinks in which the ice had long ago melted. Behind the abandoned cocktails the young woman's fan opened and closed like a complex gill, now acknowledging and now rejecting, as Oona saw it, the possibility of happiness.

In fact, Oona recognised the young woman straight away. She slept solo in the next-door cabin. She was popular with Bruce at the poolside – it was here in the shallow end shade he demonstrated, for the benefit of the more active ladies in the course of these warmer Levantine mornings, the aerodynamic idiosyncrasies of deck quoits. There was about the young woman something fully formed but not yet fulfilled, Oona decided for the third or fourth time, getting down now from her stool – a quality of waiting calmly for life's test. What test of life did she await? Because her self-possession was so evidently without self-regard it was, Oona concluded, both sexy and demure.

'You know you look like that damned Hepburn woman, don't you?' Having commandeered a stray chair, Oona parked her latest drink carefully on the white cloth and dropped her handbag to the floor. 'Terrific actress, mind you –'

On the other side of the table the young woman lowered her fan and sipped what might have been soda water and smiled.

'Would that be the Audrey or the Katherine variety, I wonder?'

As the Hepburn girl raised her eyebrows in support of a feigned confusion demanded by a conventional modesty, Oona thought – I shall befriend this singular gamine whose floral dress is rather more deck-class than dinner-dance.

'Oona Durbridge. Seventy-eight. As in the number on the cabin door, not the miles on the clock.' She drew her glass through the air in a gregarious arc. 'You're right next door to us, aren't you?'

'Am I? Yes, I think I must be.'

The young woman discarded her fan and extended a hand, and Oona saw the wedding ring and heard her pronounce her name in her cool, clear accents. It was a beautiful name.

'Oh, Jacinta's nice – Jacinta's lovely. I just hope you can't hear my husband's world-beating snores, Jacinta.'

9

'Actually, I've been sleeping like a log. Sea air, I suppose –'

The glass – it was empty of gin. Oona gripped it with two hands. There was a real possibility immoderate thirst might motivate her at any second to take the ice into her mouth and suck it. She looked at her new friend – was it too early to call her that? No matter. Oona looked at her new friend and she thought she saw in Jacinta's open regard the natural licence that offers one heart unexpected access, in the hour of need, to another. 'Thank goodness for air-conditioning – that's all I can say, Jacinta.' Oona pushed her glass away. 'Hides a multitude of sins, don't you think?' she went on, drawing up the nearest cigarette case and rummaging inside it distractedly. 'Do you feel it terribly?' she continued, nodding at Jacinta's fan. 'The heat, I mean?' Now she cast around for a light. 'Goodness me –' she chided, barely laughing. 'You don't even smoke, Oona Durbridge.'

Then Bruce appeared from nowhere to do the honours, identity bracelet gleaming in the flare of the proffered match. Oona sat with her cigarette held at arm's length to one side of her chair and waited until the Australian had picked up the empty or abandoned glasses and backed away again, clinking.

'Please don't mind my saying, darling –' She leaned closer then to her new friend, reaching out across the table and laying her hand on Jacinta's. That was when she decided what to do. 'Only, I get the strongest possible feeling you're – you know – in the family way.'

IT WAS ON FRIDAY afternoon shortly before closing time that Jacinta Nolan handed in her notice at the London department store where she was both a conscientious employee and a worker without special commitment. She thought she might take in *Dr Zhivago* in Leicester Square. She used her outstanding staff credits to buy a cotton dress with a small poppy design and picked up a two-piece swimsuit in an end-of-line sale. Pleased though she was with her purchases, Jacinta didn't actually *know* whether or not pregnant women wore polka-dot bikinis at the beach in these uncertain times. She knew she would be called upon to swim, of course. She knew some things. She decided against going to the pictures.

In her tidy bedsitter in an unfashionable part of the capital, she ate her last few English suppers beneath an old empire map of the world. As Jacinta picked at her chop or cutlet, contented children of a colonial family beamed down at her in faded illustration from the rubber plantations of Malaya or the cocoa concessions of the Gold Coast. It was an inspirational world in which a stream of resourceful women from British Honduras to Bechuanaland balanced vessels on their heads as they went about their business. Jacinta considered the extended family on the wall above her at more or less the same hour each evening, wondering if she too might be as happy as the day is long. Mostly at these times she thought about her husband.

Exactly two months after he went out there, Jacinta sent a short letter, care of the Port Trust, informing him she planned to join him, notwithstanding the deteriorating security environment on which he insisted, just as soon as she could arrange passage. She told him not to worry about the money – she would take care of that herself. They ought to be together, she suggested calmly. She had a small surprise for him, she promised. She crossed this sentence out and told him she was expecting their first child. She said the man at the Ministry had assured her everything was very much under control in Aden, sun-struck outpost of empire. It was here only she lied.

She cancelled the milk and sent a secret message to her mother in a salubrious suburb of the city, thanking her for the money. She asked her landlady, so fearful of change and hostile towards Harold Wilson, to set aside her things until she wrote with instructions from

11

out there. Then she packed her Helen Shapiro 45s and embarked at Southampton on the *SS Oriana*, a P&O liner bound via Gibraltar and the Suez Canal for Aden, Bombay and ports beyond. She hid from her father as he saluted her from the outermost sanction of the quay with deerstalker raised above his enormous car, like an admonishing Liberty, martyred and moustached, his gabardine raincoat over his arm. His head was bowed. He was Anthony Eden beside a Bentley. Did his hat tremble in his hand? Jacinta experienced a brief episode of guilt or regret before she forgot about her father. All the coloured streamers settled on the sea. As the English coast slipped below the horizon, Jacinta said a prayer for the promise inside her, crying on her bunk bed under a porthole with her back to the rivets and the throbbing bulkhead. This child must bring us together, she thought, hugging her tummy under the sheet. Yes, a plane would have been too quick, she told herself again, full of dread in the Bay of Biscay –

'Jacinta, this is my husband Adrian. Darling, please say hello to my new friend Jacinta. She's going to have a baby.'

There was a man in a tuxedo leaning palms down on the table with a lighted cigarette clamped between his stained fingers. A pale silk scarf, worn but clean, hung limply from his shoulders. Above his watery eyes the delicate fronds of his brilliantined fringe drooped as from an exotic plant. He was rather older than Oona, Jacinta saw – still handsome in a used way. He stepped behind his wife and eased the unlit cigarette from her mouth and discarded it, bowing almost imperceptibly above her.

'I'm so very happy for you, Jacinta, my dear. And you certainly look most charming tonight.' He patted Oona's shoulder, his hand slipping down finally to caress her upper arm. 'But now, my darling, I must see to our marvellously talented boys. You'll be all right here with Jacinta until the second set, won't you?'

12

As Oona reached up and squeezed her husband's hand, Jacinta watched her and held her fierce gaze.

'Yes, of course you will be, my dear –'

Adrian Durbridge kissed the air above his wife and withdrew his hand and smiled at Jacinta with a world-weary indifference, oriental in its exquisite modulation, before backing away through the chairs as the winners of tonight's fancy dress contest were announced. Now the good-natured catcalls and ironic wolf-whistles held sway.

'You know – I don't think they realise how fortunate they are to have *the* Adrian Durbridge as their manager,' Oona said at last. The first tears welled up in her eyes, picking up sooty traces of eyeliner before making headlong for the tablecloth waiting patiently below. Oona reached out one more time and seized Jacinta's hand again and waggled it loosely from side to side. 'Will you do something for me?' she said. 'I mean right this minute?'

JACINTA GOT UP FROM the bed and closed the air vents above the basin. In her cabin it was doubly silent now – the engines too were at rest. Attended by tugs and supply vessels of umpteen flags, the big ship waited at the mouth of the Suez Canal to join the next convoy voyaging south and east via the Bitter Lakes and the Red Sea itself. Through a misty porthole the sumptuous scene revealed itself mostly by suggestion to the young Englishwoman – the crowded anchorage of lights in vivid motion and, beyond the blazing wharfs of Port Said, Upper Egypt in a storm of nameless stars.

Jacinta turned away from the porthole and watched as her new friend first clipped her earrings back on with a wince then examined her fresh make-up in the cracked mirror of her compact. 'Why are you telling me all this?' she said, as if revisiting an earlier thought she had failed to throw off, although there was really no need to ask.

13

Oona snapped shut her handbag and sniffed decisively. 'Why? Because you've got to tell someone, haven't you? I mean someone like you. Otherwise, how would you believe it yourself? It wouldn't quite exist. It would be like a mirage, pet – the product of too much sun. And I do want to believe it, Jacinta – really. I must. Can you ever forgive me, though?'

'Don't be silly. Of course I can.'

'Only, if just one other person believes you – just one – it seems to me it might as well be a thousand, or a thousand thousand, souls.'

'I believe you, Oona. I heard it. We both did. But isn't it better not to know sometimes?'

'Oh, I don't think so – best to know everything, probably. Then you can put the perfect gloss on it, can't you? Like that magician up on deck this afternoon. Did you catch his show at all, Jacinta? The hurdy-gurdy man, Adrian calls him. All got up in his fez like Colonel Nasser himself. Perhaps he'll visit again tomorrow. Beautiful, it was. The sky was dark above the faraway palms – dark with the smoke from the funnels of ships. The sea from here to Port Said was alive with dhows and feluccas stuffed with hand-knotted rugs and papyrus scrolls and knick-knacks of lapis lazuli. You could watch the whole thing from the promenade deck at around four. The hurdy-gurdy man stood bolt upright in his boat with his tiny suitcase in his hand. He made an impression, even at a distance, on account of his purple suit. Very striking, it was – extremely affecting. There was the fez, of course. Did I mention the red fez? Then he came on board and sat cross-legged on deck under a huge black umbrella Bruce held over him as he performed his tricks with all the rapt children kneeling in a great semi-circle around him. Sheer sleight of hand, Jacinta – he drew those adorably fluffy little chicks from the scrubbed ears of the nippers as if it were second nature.'

14

She stopped there finally. From the next cabin – from her cabin beyond the metal bulkhead – came the sound of the two men again.

'If it were me, I'd pick Philip too. He's a nice kid, Jacinta. Only, you do sometimes begin to wonder – you know – who does what to whom.' Oona closed her eyes tightly as if to banish or fix forever an exceptional motif. 'I don't mind, really,' she went on. 'I mean –'

But Jacinta in that instant opened the hissing air vents again. It was the least she could do under such awkward circumstances. Now she sat down on the bunk beside her new friend. 'Are we just about ready for the second set?' she asked brightly. 'All the magic of the Shalimar ballroom awaits us. And those balloons will have to come down at some point, won't they?'

Oona shook her head before changing tack, nodding resolutely as she stood up. 'I mean, if it were another woman,' she said matter-of-factly. 'Now, that would be a different kettle of fish altogether.'

## ❧ CALL ME ISHMAEL ❦

'HELLO, NOLAN SPEAKING –'

Barefoot, naked, he dragged the cord of the telephone across the tiles towards the verandah and the harbour view. Beyond the deep shadow of the interior the afternoon glare seared the air above the Port Trust apartments strung in walled compounds around the hill at Hedjuff, draining all colour from the sky, making glass of the sea glimpsed below.

'Ben – it's Hildegaard. Were you asleep?'

On the threshold of appalling light he shrugged off the image of his father – legacy of a recurring dream.

'It's Friday, Hildegaard. Half day, and all that –'

'I know. I'm sorry. Are you alone?'

He hesitated for a second. It was unlike him to lie. Which course of action he chose from one hour to the next seemed to matter more and more to him.

'Not any longer,' he said, fighting to picture her at the other end of the line, to isolate those features that were hers and hers only.

'Are we still on for tonight?'

'Don't you want to go?' he said, and he heard her laugh briefly.

'Sure, I do. Nothing I enjoy more than being bitten to death in a broken deck chair while the ants crawl up and down my straw and the projector jams every five minutes. Why – what is it this week?'

'I don't know. Oh – *From Russia With Love.*'

'Yum, yum –'

'What? As in Sean Connery?' He heard a siren come and go in the background. 'Are you still at work?'

'Can't you hear the music? Another car bomb just went off on Murder Mile.'

'Jesus Christ.'

'You know – you really shouldn't swear like that.'

'I'm sorry.' He waited for the siren to die away. 'Hildegaard?'

'Soon Aden will be all amputees, Ben.'

'Are you OK?' he said.

'Of course,' she said. 'Pick me up at six –'

The line went dead. Nolan put down the telephone and turned his back on the glare. On the tiles outside the bedroom was the tray bearing the single cup and saucer and the thermos flask of coffee left there for him very early that morning, in accordance with an agreed routine, by Ali. In the bedroom it was cooler and darker. The door creaked, just a little, in the draught from the air-conditioner. Nolan pushed the door closed with his bare foot. He slid the tray onto the bedside table and slipped below the sheet.

16

'Who was that?' Megan said, playing her allotted part now. 'As if it's any of my business, right?'

She rolled towards him and fanned his throat with a paperback.

'Nothing to worry about, stewardess –' Nolan sat up and eased the stopper from the flask. 'Just another car bomb in Ma'ala.'

She pulled him down again and sat on his stomach with her fists buried in the pillow next to his head and her breasts skimming his chest. 'Boom,' she said. 'Tick, tock, tick, tock – boom.'

Now he could smell Ali's coffee, so reliable and reassuring – or was it? Nothing was guaranteed. Nolan saw the windscreen implode and heard the hubcap trundle across the dual carriageway and spin endlessly in a gutter somewhere out on Murder Mile. After he drew her head towards his and rubbed his nose against hers Megan rolled off him and pushed the sheet away and sighed.

'Can only be a matter of time before they target a BOAC plane, wouldn't you say? Either on the ground or in the air.' She turned to face the wall and curled up in a ball. 'Don't you agree? That's what I'd go for if I was them.' A little later she added a postscript. 'Is that possible, Ben? In the air, I mean?'

He laid his arm across her form, abstract and pale, and waited for her breathing to subside. 'That's enough,' he whispered. He had the stopper of the flask in his hand and, in his head, all the images. He had the picture of his pregnant wife gliding closer on a blinding sea. Into the sea's unknowable depths he plunged willingly – then he surfaced, triumphant, clutching a parrotfish to brandish above the swell. He did this for his father, but his father looked away under a sky black with migrating insects. 'What time is your flight?' he asked Megan sweetly as she turned towards him.

She didn't say anything. Instead she brought his hand up to her face and took the stopper of the flask into her mouth like a baby's dummy, and he laughed at her and rolled on top of her and pinned her wrists to the sheet above her head.

HILDEGAARD VAN KRIS skirted the plain altar in the gloomy chapel belonging to the St Stephen's Mission hospital near the marketplace at Crater. In the third row from the crucifix, stretched out on a pew with his forearm covering his eyes, the youth lay exactly as she had left him. Slowly, gently, Hildegaard peeled back his vest to examine the blood-wet dressing that clung to his stomach on the heart side of his spare frame just below the ribs.

'How is it with you?' she asked again in Arabic, but still the boy wouldn't speak, wouldn't look.

Outside the administration centre adjacent to the chapel, Nolan leaned against his battered Land Rover, arms crossed, and waited. It was just before six o'clock. At the edge of the lengthening shade in front of him the gatehouse sentry raised the barrier – now a Queen Elizabeth Hospital ambulance veered off the road and entered the Mission compound, tyres squealing. There was no siren, no flashing light. Nevertheless, the vehicle seemed to accelerate as it drew level with Nolan, its gaunt driver hunched over the steering wheel, before slowing finally and halting abruptly in a ramshackle A&E bay below a canopy of corrugated iron hung with tattered Red Crescent flags. The driver jumped down, birdlike, his white coat fanning out behind him as he landed in a puff of dust. In the instant before he vanished he half turned and shot a glance at Nolan. Why? Nolan couldn't be sure. He couldn't be sure, and that angered him. Hadn't he come all this way – he meant all this way *east* – in order to be sure of himself at long last? There were no guarantees. Nolan blamed the dream – the return of his dream with its prospect of locusts.

'Can we go, please? I mean right now?'

There was a suggestion, increasingly familiar to him, of practical urgency in her voice. Nolan turned towards the recessed doorway of the chapel – Hildegaard stood there in her uniform, her feet planted together, shoes caked with shoe milk. Her hair was closely cropped in boyish tufts as if she had modelled it herself in the wing mirror of a speeding car. She fired a look towards the gatehouse, towards the sentry, before stepping to one side. In the deeper shade beyond her was the young Arab. His man-sized trousers were belted with string. His singlet, Nolan saw, was dark with his own blood.

'Who the hell is this?'

She was ready for him, matching his anger with something like her own.

'Does it matter?' she said.

'Matter?' he said. 'Of course it bloody does.' Nolan glared at her – at her narrowing eyes, at her lips pressed tightly together, at the rapid feeling informing her pallor. 'Inside,' he hissed, jerking open the Land Rover's door.

She sat up front alongside him, speaking only to interpret, as he directed the vehicle according to a series of instructions, sullen and laconic, from the recess behind. Left, right, left – in the labyrinth of nameless lanes and faceless dwellings somewhere behind the Shenaz cinema he pulled up finally between a tethered goat and the burnt-out remains of a motorbike. He switched off the engine and thought about what he wanted to say.

'Look – isn't this a matter for the police?'

He didn't want to speak her name – not here, not now. In the back streets of the old town the silence was total. She looked at him without disappointment. There was no quality in her look except a tired version of acceptance.

'Everything here,' she said, 'is a matter for the police.'

19

The goat began to bleat. She got out fast and reached behind, and Nolan saw her seize the boy's arm and help him to the ground.

'Don't worry,' she called out in English. 'You can leave us here.'

He jumped down angrily. 'Don't be bloody daft,' he said. 'This is Crater – remember?'

'So?'

'The curfew starts at sunset.'

She examined the sky in the meagre channel above them. From a broken streetlight high on the wall came a crackle of stray current. Suddenly the youth pushed her aside and ran for it. He disappeared immediately around the corner of a house, a drab home shuttered like the rest and unmarked except by graffiti, stark and unforgiving, daubed in Arabic at shoulder height across its flanks. Nolan started forward instinctively.

'What's happening, Hildegaard?' He took another step towards her, but she backed away from him.

'Nothing's happening,' she said. 'Please – just go and see James Bond.' She hesitated for a moment, aware – it struck him – of how foolish she might sound. Her nurse's uniform was luminous suddenly in the dangerous half-light. 'My work is here, Ben,' she said finally, shrugging slightly before turning and vanishing almost immediately like the boy between the mute cliffs.

Nolan stood in the dust with the goat. In the lane it was virtually dark. There was the Land Rover, doors flung wide, and an image of Nasser like a giant postage stamp on the wall above the shrill slogans. Not a chink of light anywhere – behind the iron grilles the shutters at the windows were like eyes stitched closed. As he reached for the key in the ignition Nolan thought he heard the *muezzin* summon the faithful, in defiance of the curfew, from the minaret out on Queen Arwa Road, but it might have been a dog in the canyons of Crater.

He quit the volcano via the Main Pass gorge. All the way from the summit he had glimpses of the Ma'ala roundabout below, of the lifting equipment and the flashing lights. At the bottom of the hill he had to slow. An MP, immaculate in white, flagged him down with the wave of a glove.

'May I ask where you plan to travel this evening, sir?'

The scorched car – an old Zephyr or Zodiac with its doors and bonnet removed by the blast – dangled from a crane above an army low-loader.

'To Gold Mohur and back, I hope.'

'Drive carefully, please, sir.'

'Thank you – I intend to.'

He left Steamer Point behind. He thought she must have used him recklessly to deliver the wounded youth – a junior propagandist or, worse, a budding terrorist – to someone waiting in the forbidden streets. As he sat, barely relaxed, in the rearmost row of deck chairs at the beach club, nursing a cold beer, Nolan decided she must have taken him for an idiot. Above the screen, a shooting star soared and then plunged without protest, making Nolan think fondly of Megan, so high in the sky every day and still so down to earth. In the beam of the projector, the trapped smoke writhed, unable to escape. Then the soundtrack wound down one more time, and the image froze all over again, and the fluorescent light began to flicker on the wall that served as the screen. As the collective groan went up, Nolan felt the hand on his shoulder.

'Telephone call for you at the outside bar, sir –'

He thought it would be Hildegaard, explaining, apologising. In fact it was Mathieson. He sounded sober enough.

'Ben? Duncan here. Sorry to butt in on Bond, but we've got a situation developing down here.'

As he pulled on his beer below the trophy jawbone of a shark, Nolan felt his pulse quicken. He pushed his drink aside.

'Are you ready for this one?' asked the Scot, very animated. 'A sick boat calling itself the *Medina* is currently two miles or so out in the company of a Dutch cement freighter, and limping towards you and me both, Ben. What's she got? A hole below the line you could push a pram through –'

Nolan heard a telex machine clatter eloquently at the other end of the phone line. He pictured the scene at the Port Trust office. He could have led – he wanted to lead, but it wasn't right.

'Duncan?'

'We're still here, son. OK – three boilers, a thousand tons plus, and two hundred and ten feet, near as damn it. Sudan Steam, if you please – a bunch of cheeky bastards, so they are, but that's another story. I've already been in touch with their insurance bods in Africa. We're talking Tyneside, nineteen twenty-three, with a partial refit in Alexandria in fifty-four.'

'What happened?'

'We're not sure. She hit something hard out there and caught fire – at least for a spell.'

'And the Dutchies?'

'Picked up the distress call somewhere off Socotra. By the time they arrived the *Medina* was dead in the water, but for some reason she just refused to go down.' Mathieson broke off again there, and Nolan heard his pidgin Arabic. Then the voice came back. 'Best get your arse down here right away, Ben. We're bringing her in.'

'I hear you, Duncan. You didn't say what she's carrying.'

'That's because I didn't want to alarm you unduly –'

The voice faded. From behind, Nolan heard the film soundtrack take up again. Then Mathieson came back, his tone bone dry.

'Not your coals to Newcastle, let's just say. And not your gutta-percha from KL, either.'

'Surprise me, why don't you?'

'Muslim pilgrims, if you don't mind. That's right – there is no other cargo. We're talking about four hundred souls from Karachi on their way to Jeddah for the *hajj*.'

'Jesus. But they're OK, aren't they?'

'As far as we know –'

'As far as we know? What about the crew?'

'That's the bit I didn't want to bother you with.'

'So, bother me –'

There was a pause. Nolan thought he must have overstepped a mark. He only wanted to be the best at it – what they did.

'There isn't any crew as such, old chap.'

'I don't read you, Duncan. You mean the crew are missing?'

'Roger that – along with one of the lifeboats.'


IN THE SPARTAN wheelhouse, Nolan replaced the radio in a holster on the wall. Beside him at arm's length, Mathieson stood with legs planted wide behind the wheel, eyes fixed on the offing. There was no moon to speak of, and a veil of night cloud hid all but the keenest stars. Kneeling on the foredeck of the tug, Ibrahim threaded the eye of a two-inch rope with a weighted painter in readiness for the toss. Half a mile out from Prince of Wales pier, the *Shearwater* ploughed a sombre sea towards a distant speck of light.

Nolan raised his hand to the humid ceiling and let the vibration from the engine run through his tired frame. As he lowered his head and wiped his damp chin on his Port Trust boiler suit, he examined the colleague to whom, in theory, he answered. Duncan Mathieson said he was fifty-five, and there was no reason to doubt him. He had knocked about in ships with a complete works of Shakespeare in his locker for nigh on forty years, he said – a regular dose, as he put it, of the east. His white hair, worn too long, roamed unchecked from below the tanned clearing on the roof of his head. His eyes, when he humoured you with his penetrating gaze, were generous, always, but hungry. He had an unsettling habit of smiling for no good reason, as if he had long since come to terms with his own obscure failure. As he let go of the wheel and pushed up his sleeves and jerked a metal hip flask from his boiler suit, an open-jawed serpent, acquired half a lifetime ago in some tattoo parlour of the orient, appeared to uncoil beneath his watchstrap and rise from wrist to elbow. The senior Port Trust pilot threw back his head and drank deep and long from the flask and roared at the night. 'Call me Ishmael,' he decreed harshly, and it seemed to the young Englishman who watched him a cry of benediction on the eve of a desperate adventure.

'The crew –' Nolan said, no longer weary, and obliged more or less to shout in the confined space. 'Any news?'

'What crew?' Mathieson shot back. 'Don't shed too many tears.'

'Callous bastards, you mean?'

'I mean I haven't told you the best part of it.' Here Mathieson rapped the cracked glass dome of the binnacle as if to encourage or censure the instruments inside. 'The crew of the *Medina* were picked up by an Adeni pearling dhow and brought to Steamer Point earlier this evening – an English skipper and four Sudanese. All five were a bit thirsty, as I understand it, but otherwise none the worse for their harrowing ordeal.' Mathieson flicked a series of overhead switches one after the other, bathing the tug from outside in its own brilliant light. 'Their story is an absorbing one,' he went on, 'if you happen to be a student of ethics or morality, let us suppose, or the lengths to which one human heart will go to betray another.'

Something, or someone, haunted him. As he eyed his colleague with a qualified recognition that fell short of respect, Nolan decided it was impossible to know him. If the notional target for Mathieson's irony lay outside, he reserved the fullest measure of scorn for himself.

'In any event, the crew reported the *Medina* as having sunk in a blaze of glory off Socotra at o-three-hundred, local, with the loss of all hands – all except themselves, that is. Unfortunate for them, then, that the old girl didn't go down as demanded by the script –'

On the surface of the sea the light was ravishing now. The tug crawled towards its embrace. Through the wheelhouse glass Nolan saw Ibrahim take up position with his bare foot on the gunwale and the painter in his hand. Above the tug the Dutch ship loomed like a whale lanced by cranes and derricks and lit up as for an unspeakable rite with, two or three-deep in a ghostly ribbon that ran from bow to stern on the near side, the rescued pilgrims at the rail.

*Port Trust one-o-one. Port Trust one-o-one. Do you read me? We have you directly below us now looking bright and beautiful. It's a wonderful world –*

As Mathieson brought them gradually closer, the chopper from RAF Khormaksar hovered above the scene. Now the night was torn apart by noise and light. The tug issued a profound lament – once, twice – as it rounded the towering stern of the cement freighter and went wider. Then they saw what they had come here to see. Inching towards Arabia, the Dutch ship carried the smaller vessel roped in tightly on the starboard side. The half-drowned *Medina* wallowed in the swollen water at a forty-degree list. Aft of her funnel, the girders of her burnt-out superstructure plucked at the night sky. Above the decks on either side, the blackened shells of her remaining lifeboats hung higgledy-piggledy from distorted davits on hawsers tangled or twisted by the force of extreme actions or events.

*Port Trust one-o-one. Port Trust one-o-one –*

25

'Respond, man, respond.' Mathieson yelled. 'We're going in.' As he pulled the flask from his pocket and offered it, arm outstretched, to Nolan, the young Englishman yanked the radio from its holster on the wall and stared at the hip flask, fascinated by its potential. 'If you've got something to say,' Mathieson concluded, 'let's hear it.'

He had nothing to say. It was simple – he knew exactly what to do. He was thirsty. The water was on fire. Nolan accepted the flask and drank from it and returned it. Then he opened the transmitter.

'Port Trust one-o-one calling interested parties – it's a wonderful world, to be sure. We're going in now. Repeat – we're going in.'

'Are you familiar with the works of my old mate Joe Conrad?'

The Scot was enjoying himself. All was for the best, his eyes said as they met Nolan's, in the best of all possible worlds. Well, wasn't it? Now the two pilots braced themselves side by side at the wheel.

'You mean the writer of the sea?'

'Aye – and the hearts of men.'

First Ibrahim swung the weighted rope and hurled it high –

'No, I don't believe so,' Nolan said.

'You will be soon,' Mathieson told him, grinning wildly.

Then they went in all the way.


## ↦ THE GULLY-GULLY MAN ↤

MOTIVATED BY A POWERFUL creative impulse, Philip laid his sticks on the snare drum, dried his hands on a P&O towel, and dragged his stool towards a baby grand that squatted at the edge of the stage in the Shalimar ballroom on B deck. It must have been mid-morning – eleven o'clock, say – and the *SS Oriana* lay at anchor at the head of a convoy preparing to enter the Suez Canal. From a mile upwind, their juices evaporating fast in the vaulting heat, Port Said's sewage basins informed the coastal breeze with their vernacular accents. In the Shalimar ballroom, the tables and chairs were stacked carpet to ceiling against a wall. With the shuttered cocktail bar behind them, uniformed stewards moved in a ragged rank towards the stage, some vacuuming, others polishing the parquet dance floor, or emptying pedestal ashtrays into sand-filled fire buckets.

As Philip raised the lid of the piano its stained keys leered up at him, daring him to invent or imagine, around a middle C missing its ivory cladding. He let go a tentative arpeggio, then another, major and minor. A steward in a mint green waistcoat flicked at the piano with his orange duster, but Philip ignored him. He was alone with his song, a self-penned ballad that set out to wed the nonchalance of Michelle to the insouciant charm of If I Fell. As he closed his eyes and lifted up his voice, Philip pictured a definitive face in the crowd, a face so hopelessly ideal it lacked any, or all, sexual identity. This androgynous oval floated somewhere above the imagined audience at a London theatre during the encore to a sell-out concert coming hot on the heels of Pretty Flamingo's successful tour of the east. Still the face failed to take shape. As a muse it was without useful gender – in his mind's eye, Philip was obliged to visit it with certain formal attributes or physical features. That was the trouble. Of the male or female options routinely available to him, the young composer knew already which inspired him the more. Nevertheless, he kept testing himself to see if he had changed.

He quit singing. At the same time he heard the whistles of favour coming from behind. In the cavernous ballroom he turned from the keyboard and saw all the stewards clap like penguins in a row. Their cleaning had ceased. One of them glided forward now as if to confer a prize or an award. It was the Siamese bar boy of the Shalimar late shift. From the pocket of his waistcoat he drew the familiar pack of

27

Senior Service cigarettes, which he opened for Philip, revealing the dark nuggets of hashish within.

'Want some more chocolate, my friend?'

Philip hesitated at the edge of the stage. He felt his heart beat a little less rapidly at long last – the narcotic anxiety of ten o'clock had been replaced by an overwhelming hunger he ascribed to the bitter fudge. He wiped his fingers on his shirt.

'That really is terribly sweet of you,' he said, leaning forward to select a lozenge from the cardboard tray.

'Small piece, small piece –' advised the Siamese shrilly. 'If you like it so much, mister, next time you pay.'

CROUCHING AT THE SHALLOW END of the pool, Oona Durbridge lowered her chin to meet the shiny water, watching for a moment as a bare-chested Bruce intervened on a point of order at the play-offs that brought to a friendly climax this latest deck quoits tournament. From deep inside the anchored ship a series of dismal belches found expression without obvious meaning, provoking in today's seagulls a raucous demonstration of feeling. The sky was superbly blue. From above the bickering birds a colourless sun beat down on the deck, sculpting Bruce's torso with a striking effect of bas-relief. Compelled by an approval that was far-reaching and general, Oona turned to confront the landward perimeter of the pool and paused admiringly – how perfectly judged were her young friend's modest expectations of happiness. At the edge of the water, her newly shaved legs dipped to the shin, Jacinta sat in a parallelogram of shade, leaning back on the palms of her hands with her sunglasses perched on her head.

'Are you thinking what I'm thinking?' Oona asked humorously, wading closer to her friend.

Jacinta smiled politely, sitting up now and hugging her knees.

'If I were ten years younger – that's what I was thinking.' Oona stood, rather plump, in the water and hitched up a strap. 'Whereas you – you definitely are ten years younger, Jacinta. You have every excuse, it seems to me.'

'To ogle Bruce?'

'Goodness – what else are lifeguards for?'

There was an impossibly pale lady wearing a red swimming cap making her way to the ladder. As Oona waited, Jacinta paddled the surface of the water with a toe.

'Oh, give me brains, not brawn, any day,' she protested happily.

'But, my dear –' countered Oona. 'I do believe we may even be in the presence of the celebrated alpha male.'

'What? Reeks of aftershave? Hates to lose at backgammon?'

'Reeks of youth, one hopes – doesn't actually *know* backgammon. Triumphant *derrière*, though.'

'And not too much between the ears?' suggested Jacinta kindly, lowering her sunglasses on her nose before seeking the lifeguard out once again in keeping with the spirit of the exchange. As she shifted her bottom sideways, one tile at a time, from the enclave of shade, a fat little girl squealed close beside in a yellow rubber ring in the sun.

'I was thinking more of between the legs, chuck.'

'Oona, please –'

'Well, I mean to say.'

'You know –' Jacinta said. 'I begin to see there's a bow-legged quality to the man after all.'

'I rest my case.'

'It looks like he's left-handed into the bargain. Had you spotted that sympathetic detail which might count as a redeeming feature – a sign of hidden depths, perhaps?'

'Oh, no, darling – I don't think we want any of *those*.'

They sat wrapped in beach towels at the rail, looking out across the anchorage. They saw boats at work and boats at rest. Here and there between the tethered hulls the sea rose up in oily hillocks, but mostly it was hard and flat all the way to the Egyptian shoreline.

'So –' Oona continued, rather business-like. 'Tell me honestly.' She set down her tanning lotion and shielded her eyes with a hand. Behind the shapeless warehouses of the wharfs, the dun residences of Port Said sprawled like discarded boxes in the sun. 'Was it a love match made in heaven, or did you consciously marry beneath your father's legitimate aspirations in order to spite the old boy?'

'Oona –'

'Well?'

'Oh, I loved Ben all right –' Jacinta said, peeling the towel from her lap and shaking her head at some far memory. 'Here we come – ready or not.' She pressed a hand against her stomach and sighed. 'I suppose he'll just have to love me now.'

Oona leaned back in her deck chair and closed her eyes. After she found Jacinta's hand she squeezed it and then let it trail in hers. 'He's a man, darling,' she said at last. 'I wouldn't bank on anything.' She felt the comforting heat from the sun in the old wood where the deck made fleeting contact with their knuckles. 'Because I expect he can do whatever the hell he wants in this world.'


UNDER A LOW-HANGING LAMP in the Old Havana lounge bar, one deck below the swimming pool, Jimmy waved a tumbler in the face of his manager.

'I'm telling you, Adrian –' he insisted, as if the conversation had reached a turning point. 'It's either him or me.'

Durbridge lit his umpteenth cigarette of the day and smothered the beginnings of a yawn. Nodding carefully as he tapped a book of matches against the table, he let his eye wander from the portrait of Hemingway posing with a marlin in the Cuban sunshine towards the slicked-back hair of the young Scot. Jimmy's anachronistic *coiffure*, Durbridge concluded idly, sent out entirely the wrong message in a universe of calculating signals. It was important to master the arts of presentation and disguise precisely because it was so easy to be taken in by appearances. To belong – that was both the key and the prize. To see others as they saw themselves in the mirror at night, naked and alone – it was the only sensible basis on which to flog them an ideal of who they most wanted to be. Wasn't the isolation of human hearts the very engine of market forces? That he had failed thus far to exploit for profit such an insight was a source of pride and regret to Durbridge, impresario of loneliness and longing. All his life he had counted himself a stranger.

'You know, Jimmy –' he came back. 'I can quite enter into your feelings.' Blue smoke swirled between them in a funnel of artificial light. 'And no one rates your contribution more highly than I do.'

'I'm the lead singer, right?'

'You most certainly are the lead singer.'

'I pick the songs, don't I?'

'We do need more songs, Jimmy.' There was a silence. 'What is it you want, son?' Durbridge swept up the young man's empty glass and waved it in the general direction of the bar. 'Is it, by any chance, a bigger slice of the action? A bigger slice of what, I wonder? Of not very much, as a matter of fact.'

'And that's another thing –'

'What's on your mind, Jimmy?'

'Your cut, Adrian – I'd like to know what you get out of this.'

'Oh, I hardly think I'm likely to get rich off the back of Pretty Flamingo.' The pop group manager smiled his most indulgent smile as the bar boy came and went wordlessly. 'One day, maybe – if you start to enjoy some success with your own material.'

'We do covers – remember? It was your idea, Adrian.'

'I know – but I don't think we want to be trotting out California Dreamin' until the end of time, do we?' Durbridge extinguished his cigarette with a fastidious stabbing action. In the resentful silence he leaned back in his armchair, then brought his fingers together in a thoughtful steeple. 'Look, son –' he went on with renewed intimacy. 'Can I ask you to do something for me? Try to get along with him, will you? There's a good chap. At least until we hit Sydney. Because I couldn't do it without you, Jimmy. No lead singer, no group –' He pressed forward then. 'And he really is a perfectly decent drummer.'

'Is that a fact? And how would you know, exactly?'

'Indeed.' The manager scooped up his scarf and draped it over his shoulders. 'Look –' he picked up smoothly. 'If a musical Martian dropped in right now I'm certain he'd express the same view. Philip is a capable drummer, Jimmy. He can sing a bit, too. And if you're worried by any writing ambitions he may harbour, I suggest you try to work with, not against, him.' He stood up then and buttoned his jacket as if to signal the end of their chat. 'No one is indispensable in the formative stages of a group's career.'

Jimmy whistled approvingly. 'Is that a threat, pal?'

'Listen, Jimmy –'

'No – you listen, Adrian.' The young Scot was on his feet. 'I'm the lead singer, right? Forget the drums and the bass guitar and all that shite. I'm the one they come to see –'

Durbridge surveyed the near empty lounge. 'Who, exactly?' he enquired casually. 'It's a team effort, Jimmy. We've all got to pull our weight, including me. Songs, son, songs – that's what it's all about, surely.' He drew a pen from his breast pocket and bent down and signed the chit and waved it at the bar. 'Have you boys thought any more about growing your hair longer?' He patted Jimmy's shoulder like a favourite uncle and winked at the young Scot. 'Is it just me?' he said. 'Or is the world turning?'

AROUND THE DESERTED POOL the deck chairs grouped themselves in twos and threes, advertising a deferred ownership with towels and personal effects and sun products. It was lunchtime – there was the desultory fluttering in the breeze of pages belonging to open novels or magazines. Above the pool the awning was rolled back tightly on its wooden spars. Under a flawless sky the water danced itself slowly to a standstill against a shifting backdrop of turquoise tiles.

'Aden, Jacinta – I don't even want to think about it yet. We'll be losing you before we know it.'

As she watched her husband approach, Oona Durbridge raised herself up from her deck chair between the sheltering curves of two lifeboats. Now she stood before Jacinta in a trouser suit of pale blue linen, her lips painted cherry red, her sunglasses riding on a canary yellow headscarf.

'Last chance, last chance – are you sure you won't join us?' She let her husband take her arm. 'Anything to get off this old tub for an hour or three, we say – don't we, dear?' Durbridge was dabbing his forehead with a handkerchief. Now he folded the white square over and over with his stained fingers. 'Adrian it is, really, who wants to go. His close friend died here during all that unpleasantness back in fifty-six. Still in his parachute, wasn't he, Adrian?'

'That's right, my dear.'

'Dreadful business,' Oona concluded.

'Thanks anyway,' Jacinta said. She might well have chosen to go ashore with her new friend, but not with the husband of her friend.

In fact, she thought she might have seen too much of the sun. She had a sudden idea the ship was an infinite hotel whose every wall or door was a mirror – you could roam its corridors for years and never find what you were looking for. Every smile was an invitation, every glance a secret or confidence. And it seemed to Jacinta she had only ever existed in relation to others – as someone's daughter, or wife, or friend. How tired she was of that. She really wanted to discover who she was, and what her life meant. Now the afternoon light was so brilliantly clear – Jacinta even thought she might be seeing it in her own right for the very first time. 'I believe the gully-gully man's scheduled to appear,' she explained brightly.

'Like the face of God?' suggested Durbridge quickly. 'Step up – the great prestidigitator revisits the scene of his cleverest work.' As he steered his wife around the hip of a lifeboat he relented. 'Uncanny stuff, Jacinta – you almost expect him to vanish in a puff of smoke.'

Later, from behind a well-attended rail of the promenade deck, she watched the magician traverse the harbour – ambassador of the unknown on a chauffeur-driven barge. In a purple suit he stood tall at the prow with a fez for a hat and a small valise to hand. Jacinta's eye followed the line of spectators to a gate in the rail around which Bruce marshalled the smaller children in the committee of welcome. At the bottom of the gangway the gully-gully man stepped from his boat and seized the rope banister, glancing up for a moment before he began his ascent. Up on deck, the excited chatter gave way to an expectant hush as Bruce raised his big umbrella above the steps. It was then that the conjurer's suitcase exploded below with sufficient force to open up the purser's office and the deluxe accommodation aft of the muster station on C deck. The umbrella was wrested from Bruce's grip. Jacinta watched it surf the billowing smoke and land, handle up, on the water. She had the unscheduled aroma of singed

34

hair in her nostrils and, on her tongue, a bitter taste – as if she had just licked the bonnet of a burning car. Directly below her she could see the late magician's fez. It had the look of a giant throat pastille as it floated, marvellously red, among the hissing jetsam scattered around the gangway's stump. Into an amazed silence plunged the indignant commentary of birds. Jacinta saw the scarlet fez begin to sink before she herself fell down on the promenade deck, her eyeballs rolling up behind her eyelids. That was when she lost her baby.

## ❧ RADIO SAN'A ❦

'WHAT'S WRONG WITH THE PICK-UP?'

'The Chevrolet?' Aziz asked, as if there might be other options.

'Our pick-up –' she insisted. 'The St Stephen's pick-up.'

As Hildegaard looked on from the rear doors of the ambulance the doctor stacked the serum phials in their polystyrene trays on the floor of the vehicle. Now she gave him the immunoglobulin pouches and the insulin sacs – Aziz stowed these in twin cabinets above the wheel arches.

'What's the problem, nurse?' he said finally, patting the cabinets meaningfully. 'We have ourselves a couple of little fridges today.'

Surveying the unfamiliar interior with something like suspicion, Hildegaard invoked her usual mental checklist, ticking off typhoid, cholera, yellow fever and polio. She pointed to two wooden packing crates stacked one on top of the other behind the driver's seat.

'What's in those boxes?'

The gaunt Lebanese followed her gaze and shrugged. 'Who can say? Sugar lumps for the polio vaccine, perhaps? They were in here already.' The doctor consulted his watch. Hildegaard stepped back to let him out of the ambulance. After he closed the doors he twisted their chrome handles decisively and rapped the rear of the vehicle below the peeling letterforms of its Queen Elizabeth Hospital livery. 'Appropriated by virtue of considerable personal charm,' he noted, pushing past Hildegaard towards the front doors of the ambulance before hopping up, birdlike, and turning his head back pointedly. 'If nurse van Kris is quite ready at this time –'

They drove in silence, Aziz behind the wheel, Hildegaard with her knees tucked up and her bare feet on the dashboard. Having left behind the Khormaksar roundabout they made their way north on the causeway road, quickly overhauling Slave Island with its wall of unfinished dhows on stilts. From out of nowhere on the airport side of the causeway came the roar of a jet plane, followed presently by the dispersal, unhurried and impressive, of fifty flamingos from the marshes at the end of the runway. From the reclaimed land around the shimmering airfield rose an intoxicating miasma of natural gas, crude oil and aviation fuel – the jet plane hung in it for ages before touching down with a little squeal.

'You know they build them by eye.' The traffic on the causeway was light. Aziz steered with just a finger on the wheel. 'Arab dhows,' he explained. 'There are no plans as such.'

Hildegaard drank in the colourful harbour scene on her left and considered the idea, championed locally, that Noah's ark had been built here. 'I know,' she said. 'They make it up as they go along.'

'And yet nothing is left to chance. Every boat built becomes an act or expression of faith.'

'Manufactured in heaven?'

'With Allah as underwriter.'

'Underwriter?' she said.

'Insurance,' he told her.

'Ah, you think of God as a type of insurance salesman.'

He flashed his thin smile – the Christian one he informed from day to day with a bitter irony. And again she almost asked him why he laboured alongside her at a mere mission hospital. Of course, she knew the story in outline. The gifted surgeon of Beirut had bungled a high-ranking hysterectomy in Syria, falling rapidly from grace via the state hospitals of Damascus.

'In fact, I think little of God these days,' he remarked casually, dropping down through the gears to negotiate the roundabout at the end of the causeway. 'One might be tempted to see the Kalashnikov rifle as a more reliable form of insurance for our times –'

How did he do that? How did he manage to direct a seemingly harmless conversation from boats to God and then to guns beneath what looked like a perfectly innocent sky? It was a kind of ideological skirmishing, decided Hildegaard, all the while harbouring her own fierce version of faith forged in the fire of personal and, increasingly, professional experience. As they skirted the windmills of the salt farm she saw the crusty booty ranged in dazzling hills around the lagoons and drying in the sun. Must he continue to test her loyalty and her commitment – her nerve, for that matter – like this? Yes, it must be a test, Hildegaard concluded – no more and no less. As they passed the mosque on the outskirts of Sheikh Othman, Aziz spoke again.

'We'll be going upcountry after we finish our clinic here.' There was a definite tension in his voice – Hildegaard couldn't fail to detect it, and Aziz couldn't fail, in turn, to notice that. 'Look –' he went on. 'It's nothing to get excited about. We're simply making some routine medical deliveries to the more remote townships.'

'In this thing?'

'It's an ambulance, isn't it? What could be more fitting under the circumstances? I'm the doctor and you're the nurse –'

They had passed the zoo – the unlikely zoo at Sheikh Othman.

'How far upcountry were you thinking of, doctor?' Hildegaard slipped her shoes back on, planting her feet side by side in readiness for what might lie ahead.

'Oh, not too far, nurse. I don't think you'll need your passport.'

THE DAY AFTER ENGLAND beat West Germany by four goals to two to lift the football World Cup, Callum Kennedy sank to his knees in the Aden Protectorate, encircled by bits of pottery. The young man of foot with the Argyll and Sutherland Highlanders scooped up the nearest fragment, cupped it in his hands, and let the sands run away through his fingers. He blew hard on the shard a few times to clean it. Then he heard the Jeep's horn and, immediately after, a shout.

'Oi, Kennedy –' The churlish tone of voice belonged to Taylor, the normally patient private who sat in the Jeep with pants riding up towards the steering wheel under a copy of *Parade* magazine made brittle by numerous unaudited handlings. 'Don't you know there's a war happening around here somewhere?'

Callum peeled off his beret, then filled it carefully with pottery fragments. He pulled a pencil stub and a folded sheet of paper from his shirt pocket, spreading the paper on his thigh. He looked around for a landmark – nothing. The location was roughly half a mile west of the road about ten miles south of al-Hauta in Lahej, the ancient sultanate and federation ally that straddled the desert plains between Aden and the Yemeni border. Callum marked his sketch map with an X and drew a solitary tree beneath a radiant sun – his reference points – to describe the site. He heard Taylor sound the horn again. He set off in the glare with his finds, cresting a rise, leaving behind the shallow pit of his excavations with its finer, redder sand. Now he was back at his landmark. In the shade of the lone Christ-thorn tree he emptied his beret piece by piece onto the bonnet of the Jeep.

'Can't say it strikes me as *antique*, exactly, boyo —' Taylor tossed the magazine over his shoulder, then stood up and peered over the windscreen. 'Looks about three years old, you daft bugger.'

He sat down and fired up the Jeep. Immediately the fragments of pottery began to migrate on the bonnet until certain pieces were in danger of falling off. Callum watched, hands on hips. He stepped back, folded his arms, and waited for the engine to die. 'Thank you, Taylor —' Now he began to gather up his samples. 'What would you know about it, anyway?' he asked quietly, distributing the elements among all the available pockets of his uniform.

'I know a load of old bollocks when I see it.'

Callum Kennedy smiled without looking up. 'Oh?' he said. 'Did you know Arabia used to be joined to Africa near here?'

Taylor hung his hands over the windscreen. On his wrist beside his watch he wore an off-duty bracelet of elephant's hair picked up in the *suq* for less than one East African shilling. 'So?' he said with an exaggerated indifference.

'See that tree above us?' Callum said, climbing into the Jeep as Taylor sighed ostentatiously and shook his head. 'I think you'll find they sell its powdered leaves in the market.'

'I know that, smart arse. They chew on them and then swallow the juice and it makes their dick go hard.'

'Wrong —' Callum said. 'This stuff's got nothing to do with *qat*.'

'So why are you telling me about it?' Taylor restarted the Jeep's engine and crashed into first gear and drove.

'If you must know — they use it as a shampoo.'

'If I must know?' Now they reached the firmer ground, Taylor laughing. 'I think I'll stick with the army carbolic, thanks.'

No further talk as, behind them, the orange dust started to thin. After they rejoined the al-Hauta road Taylor accelerated, glancing at Callum and grinning in a way that said everything was all right. Everything was OK between them, his look said. As the dust trail behind them fell away Taylor checked the mirror – immediately his foot rose from the gas pedal. He swore and hit the brake and pulled up hard at the edge of the track.

'Too busy discussing bloody shampoo –' he complained.

He turned from the wheel and hauled a .303 rifle from beneath the discarded *Parade*. Beside him, Callum scanned the horizon to the south, eyes shielded, kneeling on his seat. Now he was on the bonnet of the Jeep. Soon the air began to clear. There were five camels. At the vanishing point of the road Callum spotted their cloud of dust, a tiny knot in the ribbon of the heat haze. He grabbed the binoculars, focused calmly, and watched the hobbled beasts cross the road from east to west behind their herdsman. Then he picked it up as clear as day. 'Civilian ambulance heading north – two people up front.' He jumped down and dumped the glasses.

'Ammo, please, private,' yelled Taylor, swinging the Jeep across the track. 'Prepare to receive uninvited guests.' He got out with his rifle. 'Best raise the sarge,' he barked, nodding at the radio.

'It's an ambulance, Taylor.'

'Exactly – so, move it, please. No, wait up. Here we go –'

Head on, it was hard to gauge the vehicle's approach rate. In the end they stood beside each other without speaking and waited for it to arrive. The ambulance halted on its own shadow. Taylor stepped forward. Now he approached the door on the driver's side. Callum, eighteen years of age, drew himself up with boots set wide apart, his rifle held diagonally in front of his chest. There was a pretty blonde, older than him, beside the driver. What was she – Swedish, maybe, or Dutch? She looked so fresh to Callum in all the heat, coming and going in white behind the dazzling glass. She raised her cup to offer him a drink, but he shook his head, and she nodded as if to say she understood. How thirsty he was suddenly. His scalp itched below his beret. He had the dust from the pottery under his beret, the broken pieces in his pockets. Did she know he had all the pieces? Of course she didn't. She could have been his big sister.

'I'm Dr Aziz, and with me is my colleague, nurse van Kris.' The driver handed over some forms and opened the ambulance door.

'Stay where you are, please, sir,' Taylor said, eyeing the papers.

'We have an injured man in the back.'

Taylor returned the forms. 'Let's have a shufti, shall we, doc?'

The driver got down beside Taylor. Callum made to join them, but just then she leaned out and asked him a silly question.

'All alone in the burning desert, soldier-boy?'

Was she flirting with him or, worse, teasing him? Callum started forward, then stopped. 'We're up from Aden on a tour with the feds – the Federal Regular Army.'

'I know who the feds are,' she said. 'And will you be chasing all those nasty insurgents back to Yemen where they belong?'

'We'll be doing our best, miss.' She was mocking him. Why do that? It was so unlike her, he decided. Was she trying to arouse or to allay suspicion? She must have been playing a part, Callum decided intuitively – a part she couldn't quite accept or believe in. Her role was to distract him, surely. 'Is everything all right here?' he said.

She nodded, smiling, but Callum didn't believe her. Even so, he trusted her. She felt things the way he did. He knew that. When she offered him her cup – that was what she was like. This conviction the young soldier held instinctively. He heard Taylor call his name.

'If you're sure everything's all right, miss –' he said.

At the rear of the ambulance, a stretcher on wheels was half in and half out of the shade. The injured man turned out to be an Arab in his early thirties as Callum saw it – in his late twenties, even. His arm was hooked up to a drip. His cheeks were unshaven, his eyelids purple. Around his head was a bandage stained brown with blood in the region of the left ear.

'Who's this, then?' Taylor was asking. 'And where are you taking him in Lahej?'

The doctor returned the stretcher to the shade. 'He's an Abdali tribesman. Some VIP or local bigwig – a cousin of the sultan.'

'What happened to him?'

'Oh, he went shopping in Aden.' The doctor smiled indulgently before closing the ambulance doors. 'There was an explosion at the *suq* – a modest car bomb, I dare say. This chap was picked up at the side of the road in Crater with a bolt of Egyptian cotton in his arms – a gift for one of his many wives, no doubt. The poor fellow hasn't regained consciousness since.'

Callum followed the conversation to the front of the ambulance. Now the doctor climbed up.

'OK, Kennedy – let's raise the sarge and see what he knows.'

It should have happened strictly by the book. Later, as he stood beside his comrade and watched the ambulance vanish in a storm of dust, Callum hefted a triangle of pottery in his hand.

'You do know I didn't get through,' he said. At the same time he saw himself skimming stones on the shore of a lapping loch with the Scottish mist hanging low above the water.

'I guessed,' Taylor said. 'Did you try?' he added after a pause.

'Of course I tried.'

'Don't worry – it probably wouldn't have made any difference.'

Taylor climbed into the Jeep and threw his rifle on the back seat and reached below for the canteens of water.

'Did you believe him?' asked Callum, anxious suddenly.

'I don't know. The paperwork looked super official. Only – why carry a wounded and unconscious man deeper and deeper into the desert, eh?' Taylor followed up one question with another. 'Did you believe *her* at all, Private Kennedy?'

'I'm not sure,' Callum said. 'She offered me a drink.'

Taylor started the Jeep. 'Proper Florence Nightingale she turns out to be. Pretty, with it. She probably thought you were looking a bit peaky, boyo.'

Callum hurled his pottery fragment at the sun and saw it return to the desert forever. 'Wasn't this was meant to be time out?' he said.

'Drink up, and let's go home,' Taylor said. 'I think that's about enough orientation and familiarisation for one day, don't you?'

'HERE. TURN HERE AND TAKE IT SLOW –'

As Aziz issued his instructions, the meagre glow from a shielded torch spilled across the map at his feet. In the undulating scrub east of al-Hauta it was night already but scarcely any cooler. On a rutted track the ambulance inched forward without lights towards a white wall screened by clusters of date palms. The torch died. Hildegaard switched off the engine.

'Where are we?' she said.

'Please don't be alarmed, nurse.'

Hildegaard froze in the sparse light thrown off by the wall. The calm voice – it had come from directly behind her. She spun round sharply and saw the injured man rise from his stretcher and begin to unwind the bandage from his head. Now Aziz touched her arm.

'Inside,' he hissed.

She stepped across the raised threshold into a courtyard open to the night sky. A short veiled woman ushered her through a curtain of beads to a dormitory furnished with cots and illuminated from the floor by a single lamp. Against a backdrop of distorting shadows the veiled woman poured water from a pitcher into a basin on the tiles in the middle of the room. She invited Hildegaard to wash.

*Shukran.*

*Afwan.* 'You're welcome –'

The woman withdrew noiselessly. Hildegaard took off her white coat and set about washing her face and neck. It was a funny thing – she had a recollection, laughably vivid, of childhood. Here? Now? She didn't want it. She didn't want it at all. There was a farmhouse near Haarlem. Hildegaard stood naked in a zinc bathtub, her body subject to the unwelcome attentions of her brother's soapy sponge, while the lightest snowfall melted all around her in the steam. Now, as then, the steam – the idea of it, even – carried off her fear. She washed her forearms and wrists, discovering down there the actions of her own pulse. Then Aziz was beside her with a towel.

'Come and eat something with us,' he said.

She followed him into the courtyard. Two youths manoeuvred the wooden packing crates from the ambulance across the threshold. In a carpeted room with its shutters open to a grove of plantains she sat on a cushion between Aziz and a hurricane lamp that attracted five or six winged ants. Opposite her, his bandage of disguise coiled negligently at his feet, the still figure said nothing. His attention was held by a radio broadcast in Arabic.

*… and so today the British government announces it intends to grant Aden independence by 1968. Question – why fight for something that will in any event be given? Comrades, true independence is not given but taken. Let us carry to the enemy an armed revolution in which we are prepared to pay the highest price in life and blood …*

The radio fell silent in his hands. Hildegaard watched him raise his eyes slowly from the coarse rug until they met her own.

'Could you follow what was said?' he asked in English. 'I believe you speak Arabic rather well.' In the warm embrace of the lamp his eyes were red. 'Radio San'a,' he explained. 'From across the border in Yemen.' In his voice was a hoarseness that matched his bloodshot eyes. 'Let me introduce myself. Basim Mansouri – I'm a journalist, nurse van Kris.' He hesitated fractionally before adding his proviso. 'Among other things.' His handshake, when he extended his slender fingers across the carpeted divide, was light and cool. 'Please forgive the amateur dramatics of a little earlier today.' Here he pointed to the discarded bandage. 'I prefer to disguise my movements from A to B, that's all. The key thing is this – I want to thank you for your help this afternoon.' His languid gesture took in Aziz, the lamp and the insects hurling themselves at the glass. 'It seems one shouldn't, after all, underestimate a pretty girl.'

She didn't really register what he said. Instead, she was struck by the cruel fascination he exercised. As she conjured up at random the events and images of the shimmering day Hildegaard asked herself what was real and what was imagined. She made to say something conventional, but just then Basim cut her off with a clap of his hands. The veiled woman scuttled back and forth using an archway behind him and set down the bread and water and then three glasses and a metal tureen. Aziz poured from the jug. They ate in silence, tearing the sweet white bread and scooping meat and gravy from the bowl, until Basim took up again.

'I understand you're best friends with a certain Ben Nolan at the Port Trust.' For a moment there was only the pock-pock-pock of the insects at the lamp. 'What kind of man is he, please?'

Thinking, Hildegaard made him wait. Thinking, she had been able to eat little, and now she withdrew carefully from the bowl.

'I don't really see what business that is of yours.'

'Come, come, nurse – we are all friends here, surely. And, you know – you might be surprised by what is and is not my business in Aden.' There was the glance at Aziz. The doctor got up and left the room. 'The Port Trust, for whom Mr Nolan works, employs at least three thousand people – most of them poor Arabs. These are simple souls, proud souls. It takes so little to inflame their passions –'

What was his agenda? Was it about labour unrest? Hildegaard thought she saw it. 'Ben's just an acquaintance,' she said.

'Naturally. A married acquaintance, I believe –'

'I'm afraid I know nothing about his wife.'

'No? She'll be with us in Aden very soon.'

'I don't even know her name.'

'Ah, her name is Jacinta – a lovely name, don't you think? An unfortunate accident has just befallen Jacinta in Port Said.'

Hildegaard was on her feet. 'I think I'd like to leave now,' she said. 'Where's Dr Aziz, please?' As she wheeled away from the lamp she ran into him at the curtain, her coat in his hand. 'One moment, please, while we refuel the ambulance,' he said, taking Hildegaard's wrist and returning her gently to the light. Then Basim swept aside the tureen and rose easily in his loose-fitting pants.

'Hildegaard, Hildegaard,' he chided. 'Please don't imagine you can gallivant around our scenic peninsula at will dispensing aspirin and social justice like some kind of apprentice Ingrid Bergman. This is hardly a game, is it?'

She challenged him directly then. 'What's in those two wooden crates?' she said. Now she turned to Aziz for an answer.

'It's not what you think,' he said.

'Our plan,' Basim interposed smoothly, 'is simply to establish an underground printing press here with all possible speed. There are no homemade bomb kits under our beds, my dear.'

46

'I think I'd like to leave now,' Hildegaard repeated.

Quickly it was over. Basim nodded, spreading his arms in a kind of blessing. 'I beg you to be careful, nurse,' he said darkly. 'I'm not sure your British friends would look favourably on the part you've just played in the smuggling of a known NLF sympathiser through a military checkpoint – if I can call it that – to say nothing of ferrying an injured youth to his people in Crater recently without reporting it to anyone anywhere.'

Hildegaard found it increasingly difficult to breathe. She felt his touch, so delicate and dry, on her forearm, staying her deliberately as she turned away.

'God is very great,' he murmured, squeezing her arm now, as if to test her in one last area of interest. Up close, she searched his red eyes for the light of faith, or the fire of zeal, discovering instead a raw hunger for something, for everything – it burned brighter than any flame. 'We know now your heart is in the right place,' he told her. 'I do so hope your head will follow, keeping pace –'

She sat in the shadowy ambulance, rocking slightly, her hands clamped between her knees.

'Are you all right?' Aziz asked her.

'Of course,' she said. She wanted to be certain of the experience – all of it. She wanted to be completely certain about every aspect of it in order to take from it as much as she could. She felt humiliated and scared, angry and excited. Yes, that was it. She leaned back and closed her eyes tightly. 'Can we go now?' she said finally.

BEHIND THE GREAT DOOR in a courtyard open to the night sky he stood aside as the youth took a crowbar to the crate's lid. There was a long shriek as the nails left the wood. In the silence that followed, Basim heard the ambulance start up on the other side of the wall. He

reached inside the packing crate and lifted out the first rifle – an old
.22 single shot, a No 2 Mark IV, which had been reconditioned in
India. The smiling journalist worked the bolt a few times like a pro.
Then he tossed the weapon at the second gawping youth. The rifle's
butt, Basim couldn't help noticing in the flickering lamplight, was
badly split. It had cracked a few Mau Mau skulls in Kenya.

## ❧ RED SKY AT NIGHT ❧

SUFFUSED RICHLY WITH BARBITURATE in the sick bay on E deck,
and floating above the screws at the stern of the ship, Jacinta drifted
towards consciousness on a magic carpet of dreams. All around her
the air began to vibrate. She was leaning over the rail as the sea sped
north and the ship raced south – from the hull's crushing weight the
foam escaped in little doilies. Jacinta looked up and saw Arabia. Just
then a giant manta ray launched itself at the sky and glided alongside
before belly flopping into the ocean blue with a report like thunder.
Astride the fleshy mouthpart at the front of the devilfish, Jacinta's
baby rode the waves like a goblin of the deep.

The sun slipped down another notch as the *Oriana* cut through
the Red Sea towards the exit at Bab al-Mandeb. Jacinta saw Bruce
get up from the bunk beside hers. His dressing gown fell open on his
hairless chest. He lowered a mask just like the one the Lone Ranger
wore when Silver reared up on hind legs against the mesas and the
evening sky. Clouds swarmed across the plain. The Lone Ranger's
movements were jerky and grimly comical – he might have been an
officer of the trenches in a cinematic record of Passchendaele. All the
hooves rained down. Jacinta saw a woman inhabit the desert below
the clouds and the hooves. The woman was naked, running. She was
running from the horseman and trailing behind her a ragged scarf

of dust. She turned as she ran. She was crying and crying, her face bruised, her hair on fire. Then the Lone Ranger grinned at Jacinta from his jewel-studded saddle. When he removed his mask this time he looked a lot like Anthony Eden.

'Your mother's not herself today, girl –' he said.


IN THE SOUTHBOUND SANATORIUM, Oona drew up a chair and sat down beside the bed. She wore a strapless evening dress of crushed black velvet and unusual gold earrings in the form of tiny Arabian daggers. Her patent leather handbag was on her knee.

She sat there, quite still, and watched her friend's eyelids flutter, and it seemed to her the unfortunate young woman occupying the bed could see her, would see a great deal from now on, without the expedient of looking. Suddenly Jacinta opened her eyes. She twisted her neck slowly from one extreme to the other on the pillow as if to confirm or deny the contents of a dream. On either side of her the beds were empty and made up tight as a drum.

'How are you feeling, chuck?'

There was her friend's voice, very close. Jacinta could hear it.

'Look – I brought you a gift from the Harrods of Port Said.'

A gift? What kind of thing might that be? A gift for her, or a gift intended for another and now put to alternative use? Jacinta stroked the tissue paper on the sheet beside her. She thought she must have lost something vital – her confidence, perhaps. She saw the dagger flash at her friend's ear – that was what comforted her most in the excoriating light of the sick bay on E deck.

'Oh, Oona – I don't think I've ever seen such lovely earrings.'

How like Jacinta to issue a compliment straight out of the blocks like that. Oona patted the shiny scabbards jutting from her ear lobes, saluting her friend's courage. 'It's French night,' she said, as if that explained everything. She shrugged her tanned shoulders. 'The boys are on stage later. Adrian will be fussing around somewhere –'

Again Jacinta saw the clouds swarm feverishly behind her eyes. For some reason she had the chorus of Walkin' Back To Happiness going round and round inside her head. Then Oona came back.

'Listen, darling – I've had a word with the doctor here.'

'I didn't deserve my baby. I didn't want it enough.'

'Don't talk rot, dear – you've had a tremendous shock, that's all.'

There was the pretty parcel in her hand, present from a friend. Jacinta tore open the tissue paper using all her strength and held up a leopard skin hair clasp in the shape of a shield, a Zulu shield, with an ivory spear running through it to anchor it in position. 'I almost believed a baby would bring us together,' she said, closing her eyes again and turning away from her friend. She pressed the Zulu shield to her breast below the sheet, stroking the hard fur with a fingertip. 'How foolish I must seem to everyone –'

Now Oona sat on the bed and kicked off her shoes. She brought her legs up one after the other and stretched out sideways with her arm around her friend's waist. 'I'm terribly sorry, Jacinta,' she said, squeezing a little harder. 'But you're right, absolutely right, because a baby was never going to be the answer. You always knew that in your heart of hearts, didn't you?' In the unhappy silence Oona went on with her hugging and returned to her favourite theme. 'Did you ever really love Ben, Jacinta?'

'Oh, I did.' It was such a relief to say it again. Jacinta wanted so much to affirm it one last time, and now her good friend had given her the chance. 'Yes, I did,' she repeated. What was it Oona herself had once said? If just one person in this world came to believe you it might as well have been a thousand souls or more.

'Did he ever really love you?'

50

'He said he did.' She couldn't lie – she only wanted to be fair.

'Did he think you were a catch?'

'Oh, Ben was very unsuitable –'

'How, Jacinta, how? Was he too poor? Was he too ugly? Was he, perhaps, the violent type?'

'Of course not.'

'But your father regarded him as unsuitable – am I right?'

Now Jacinta said nothing.

'And that mattered to you as much as anything, didn't it?' Still Jacinta said nothing. 'Why, darling, why? Was he cruel to you? Was baby's father cruel to her?'

After a while their breathing became synchronised. At last, just as she threatened to fall asleep beside her friend, Oona stirred.

'Forget what you carried inside you, girl. It never existed, strictly speaking. I know that sounds dreadful – you've simply got to believe me. You're going to start over. Everything's going to be fine. Either love Ben or leave him, but don't carry a cross for him all your life, if you don't mind. And, you know – where love has died it might even be rekindled over time.'

Now Oona sat up purposefully beside her sick friend. 'You're so young,' she said. 'You can't quite see it. You can either walk away today or you can reach an accommodation with conditions as you find them.' She sniffed and checked her earrings and swung her feet towards her shoes. 'It's not so hard, girl. Just change the world a bit at a time.' Here she wiped her nose with the back of her hand. She was almost laughing now. 'Take my Adrian –' she suggested fondly. 'Forty-five years old and he'd never seen a proper sunset. Red sky at night, shepherd's delight – but not for him, darling. No, no, no – he always said he was colour-blind. He said he couldn't tell his purple from his violet. He claimed he didn't know what we meant when we said indigo. Yes, indigo. The thing was – he didn't give a monkey's because he knew what indigo meant to him. Isn't that beautiful? He invented his own private rainbow. Only, one day he admitted to me he'd made the whole thing up. Are you with me? He wasn't colour-blind at all. He'd made the whole business up when he was a nipper because he wanted his stepmother to love him just a tad more than she did. Imagine, Jacinta – trapped by his very own lovely lie until I finally put him out of his misery. Aren't we ridiculous?'

She stood at the foot of the bed, brushing down her velvet dress and swinging her handbag backwards and forwards. 'You get some rest, girl,' she said. 'We'll have you up and about in no time.'

'Oona?' Jacinta raised her Zulu shield above the sheet. 'Thank you so much – I think it's just perfect.'

Oona shrugged, then laughed. 'Or it will be if you ever decide to grow your hair longer.' She hesitated in the doorway, tucking her handbag under her arm before she went on. 'We're going to see a bit more of each other, after all, it seems. The old tub's heading straight back to Blighty for a refit once they've patched her up in Aden. We have the option of flying onwards to Sydney – only, Adrian's seeking compensation for loss of tour earnings. As if it makes any difference, darling, really and truly – the coffers are always near empty. In any event, the boys aren't scheduled to play down under for weeks.'

'But what will you do?'

'In Aden, you mean? Why, the same as you –'

'Me?'

'Yes, of course, you – we'll just have to *shop* for England.

Was it was their moment of maximum closeness? Already it was passing. They held each other's gaze, fixedly, knowingly, across the expanse of room before Oona went on, a note of regret in her voice now at the suddenness of experience.

'Tell me really – why did you come all this way?'

Now it was Jacinta who hesitated. She had never seen it more clearly – the starkly looming coast of Arabia with, above it, a black sun. 'Where love has died,' she said, 'it may even be rekindled.'

'But what if he lied, baby? What if love was never there?'

Jacinta smiled as a service to her tough friend. 'I know, I know –' she said. 'That's what I had to find out.'

She closed her eyes and tried to forget about everything. On the pillow beside her was a hair clasp – a leopard skin hair clasp. What was its role in life? Jacinta didn't know. She only knew it meant a lot to her. Suddenly the hair clasp took off – Jacinta thought it must be a migrating moth. The moth alighted at a near porthole on a stack of *National Geographic* magazines. As it opened and closed its wings it looked to have forgotten what it knew of navigation and flight. The *Oriana* plunged southwards towards the mouth of the Red Sea. Tiny beads of condensation formed in the spaces between the inner and outer walls of the portholes. In the sick bay on E deck it was a time for dreams – the overhead lights went out one by one.

## ❧ THE LANGUAGE OF LOSS ❧

IT WASN'T YET AS HOT as it could be in the concrete shed that had been their home these past eight years. Scooping up with his finger the condensed milk that dribbled down the tin on the table between them, Sulaiman was struck with unexpected force by the beauty of Isa, his seventeen-year-old son. There were aspects both qualitative and quantitative to the father's impression. Why, he asked himself, should Isa's looks strike him more forcibly today than, say, yesterday or the day before if not to mark some subtle shift in family relations? And was it actually reasonable to ascribe the condition of beauty to something that, until now, had been content to be just comely in a conventionally masculine way? As he licked the milk from his finger and tried to focus on his son's fluent recitation, Sulaiman reconciled himself without too much reluctance to the idea that, yes, Isa was as beautiful as his mother. But Fatima was dead.

He poured tea into two glasses, then looked up and concentrated on his son's amused or sarcastic voice as the boy read aloud with his battered book held at arm's length. Isa's white shirt was as crisp as a schoolgirl's blouse. His spectacles, restored regularly to the bridge of his nose, gave him a touching air of authority. As Sulaiman drank in the rapid English issuing dismissively from across the table, a current of sentiment shot through his spare frame and made his skin tingle. Oh, yes – he loved his only son. Each morning he watched the grave student set out from Bir Fuqum on an oversized bicycle, his trusty transistor radio retained by a hinged bracket on the platform behind the saddle. Sulaiman saw his son's shirt billow as the boy pedalled hard through Silent Valley – here, the sheer cliffs blocked his radio signal and the sweat cooled deliciously in the hollow of his back. His father pictured Isa in the front row of pressed white shirts facing a blackboard bristling with complex formulae at the technical college in Little Aden where the boy had a place – an Arab place – on BP's prestigious apprenticeship programme. How well versed the budding engineer was already in the technologies used for refining oil.

Sulaiman, on the other hand, knew nothing about distillation or blending, about octane enhancement or cuts. He looked on oil with favour principally as a source of fuel for his boat and its lamp. What Sulaiman liked most about oil was the proud satisfaction he derived from knowing his son understood so much more about the stuff than he did. Wasn't it fitting a son should travel further than his father on any road, familiar or new? In fact, Sulaiman cherished Isa's learning

54

with an unselfish regard for a more enlightened future. There was no jealousy between man and boy. To prospect for the black gold in the ground, or below the ocean floor – was it so different from hunting fish in the sea? There was a teasing but ultimately respectful quality to Isa's humorous enquiry. As he held the sweet tea in his mouth and savoured the lively English text, Sulaiman reassured himself in the sight of God – yes, he was right to prize his son so highly.

Isa snapped shut his book – his Enid Blyton book. As he pushed the volume across the table he reverted to his own language. 'But I feel completely idiotic,' he said, 'reading this children's story –'

Sulaiman nodded patiently. 'Drink your tea, son.'

'Look –' Isa went on. 'I think we can probably do better than a book for kids, don't you?' He got up and moved quickly across their living space towards the area that served as a shared bedroom. On a mattress on the floor was the boy's transistor radio, his trusty Pye. 'If you're serious about learning their language, you might as well get it from the horse's mouth, so to speak.' Now he sat down again at the table and began to tune the radio.

'Won't you be taking that with you today?' Sulaiman asked.

The boy shrugged without looking up. 'Only, you'd better pull your finger out if you want to learn their language at something like first hand. Don't you know they'll be leaving here soon?' He pushed the little Pye across the table. 'There you go – Forces Radio.'

'Why, thank you, Isa.' Sulaiman picked up the radio and peered at it from every angle. 'And where exactly does it say the British are leaving us?' He lowered the volume. 'It seems likely they'll want to keep their military bases here after independence, don't you think?'

'Then we must invite them,' Isa said, 'to give up their bases.'

It had more than a whiff in it, the boy's sly comment, of received wisdom. Sulaiman nodded tolerantly. 'Do you imagine,' he said, 'it will really be that simple to get rid of them?' He put the radio down carefully on the table. 'The British are everywhere, Isa. Why do you suppose we bother to learn their tongue – the language of slaves, the language of loss? It isn't just them. Get rid of the British and you'll find plenty more ready to lie in their beds. Even among our own.'

'Then we must get rid of these individuals too.'

'Ah.' Sulaiman watched his son slip several large books into his satchel. 'You know –' he went on. 'I'm not convinced they ought to be sharing quite so many insights with you at British Petroleum.'

'They don't need to,' Isa shot back. 'The fat cats are all over the shop.' The son rounded on the father then, his colour high. 'Look, Dad – you're either for the people or you're not.'

'The people, you say? When you've got rid of the British and the fat cats with worry beads who come after, what then? Who's next on the list?' Sulaiman watched as his son took off his glasses and stowed them in his shirt pocket. Although the boy's cheeks were flushed, his actions were measured – that was what disturbed the father most. 'Listen to me, Isa –' he urged quietly. 'Every dog has his day. Please don't kid yourself – there will always be some tyrant with a gun in his hand trying to tell you how to live your life. I mean always –'

'I'm late for class, Dad. I have to go now.'

'Don't kid yourself, son –'

'OK, OK – you've made your point.'

'Tell me – who have you been talking to?'

'I have to go now, Dad. I think we can safely assume Aden will still need its oil refinery and its engineers after the British have gone.'

*Insh'Allah.* 'If God wills it.'

'Oh, but God *will* –'

What was it that alarmed the father if not the son's doctrinaire insistence? There was a kind of godless conviction in Isa's presence of mind. No doubt the boy had shelved the whole question of divine attribution or intervention with the impatience of youth. That was as nothing. There was something else. Sulaiman got up from the table. He wanted to stand closer to his son, to look into his beautiful son's eye, but just then Isa raised his hand in farewell. Sulaiman hesitated – how could he view the boy's gesture other than as a political act?

'I love you, Dad. I really hope the fish bite today.'

It was official – change had come. Sulaiman stood at a screened window and watched as his son's bicycle got smaller and smaller on the track that linked the shacks of Bir Fuqum to each other. At last he turned away from the craggy outcrops that hung, brooding, over Silent Valley, and gazed sadly at their home. On the table was Isa's radio. Sulaiman picked it up – it was still on, very low. There was the skillet on the ancient burner with a few fish in it. There was the key to the outboard engine on the hook behind the door. Sulaiman switched off the radio and collected the key. What had he missed on the day change called at the door? Then he got it – there had been no valedictory ringing, happy and glorious, of Isa's bell.

ON THE BEACH BELOW THE village he untied his boat from a metal hoop set into the rock. He tossed his sandals, canteen and lunch box onto the net piled up inside the boat, then dragged the whole lot to the water. He pushed the boat out and jumped in at the same time, tipping the outboard until the propeller dipped below the sea. When he turned the key and pulled the cord, the engine started first time. Sulaiman sat on the rearmost thwart with his arm over the tiller. As he rounded the Little Aden headland, the fractioning towers of the refinery flashed one by one in the sun. Now he was crossing the bay. He left behind the two Liberian tankers preparing to discharge their crude. Not far below him, a solitary pipe on the seabed carried fuel from the refinery to the bunkering platforms in the busiest stopover between Rotterdam and Singapore. Lining the margins of the inner harbour were the bobbing chandlers and refuelling barges waiting to come alongside the bigger ships. Sulaiman counted nine big boats at the buoys. He overhauled a Union Jack to his right – the flag hung limply from the customs house behind Prince of Wales pier. To his left, her damaged hull listing crazily above two Port Trust tugs, the *Medina* took on three surveyors in shorts and long socks – Sulaiman saw them climb the sloping quarterdeck with clipboards under their arms. Soon he reached the dhow marina at Ma'ala, making landfall at the island of shipbuilders via a jetty that jutted out from a narrow strip of shingle. The morning light was superb – it was impossible to believe such perfection could endure, Sulaiman decided. How might the day go, he asked, which began with the death of beauty?

The sun rose higher above Slave Island. Outside the workshops of Khalil Kanoo, the master builder examined the lines of the dhow on the slipway, and manufactured, in his mind's eye, its latest plank. Behind him in a hanger made of corrugated iron, their *qat* leaves on the cement floor at their feet, his company of craftsmen and coolies sat out the fierce heat of midday in the presence of several narghile hookahs and a portable fan. Sulaiman detached himself from their languid society and took his canteen into the light. In the cut-down oil drum on the forecourt the coals had cooled. Sulaiman sieved the coral ashes gathered from the griddle, carried them up the ladder in a basket of plaited palm fronds, and lowered them by pulley into the hull of the unfinished dhow. In the cool interior he tipped the coral ashes into a bucket of mutton fat laced with date juice, and mixed a paste – protection against worms – with which to coat the spars and timbers of Persian oak and Malabar teak. Here inside the dhow the atmosphere was heavy with the vapour of waterproof unguents – of coconut, sim-sim and shark oil. As he daubed the noble planks with his prophylactic paste, a sackcloth mask pulled down over his nose and mouth, Sulaiman heard footsteps on the deck above his head, then a banging on the wood, then a shout.

'Hey, you in there – come out so we can see what you looks like.'

Sulaiman raised his mask and set down his bucket. As he poked his head through the open hatch he squinted first at the glare. Then his eyes travelled upwards from the exquisitely embroidered sandals and the brilliant skirts of the *dish-dash* to an expensive string of beads wound around fleshy fingers and from there to the *burnous* of finest Egyptian cotton that framed with its dazzling folds the bespectacled face of Khalil Kanoo himself. The boatbuilding import-export man and all-purpose entrepreneur gazed down at his squinting employee like a benevolent pharaoh. Behind him stood the grinning foreman, his hands pressed together in a show of extreme deference. Now the foreman pushed forward eagerly and spoke again.

'Sulaiman Ali Hassani, boss. Like I says to you before – this top-class mature worker is most probably of the first order or more.'

As Khalil Kanoo raised a hand to silence the foreman, Sulaiman saw in his gesture the unlikely poise and grace of the obese. *Is-sala:mu alaykum.* After issuing his greeting the fat businessman continued to study the upturned face at his feet. He nodded, apparently satisfied. What was he searching for? Some convincing quality, etched on the forehead or the eye, perhaps, which conformed to his stock notion of what a first order man should look like?

*Wa alaykum is-sala:m.* Sulaiman returned the greeting, hauled his shiny body through the hatch, and sat, looking up still, on the rim.

'Goodness me, yes –' Kanoo said. 'I see now what a *hard* worker he is.' He beamed delightedly at Sulaiman. What was it that pleased him if not the torso fashioned in the fire of life using hot bone, blood and sinew – the body useful, necessary, and so unlike his own? 'But why not chew some leaves over there with your colleagues until the heat goes out of the day? Or do you think yourself less compromised, morally speaking, than the rest of us on this absurd lump of rock?'

Was it a test, or a trap? For a moment Sulaiman examined the forecourt beyond the raised prow of the dhow. Outside the hanger, Kanoo's white Mercedes squatted in the coruscating light. Nothing moved. There was a used cloth, an old vest, on the hot deck beside the hatch. Sulaiman picked it up. 'I have nothing against *qat*,' he said quietly, wiping the poisonous paste from his fingers with the rag.

'He prefers to work while he can, boss. Like I says to you – he's just a poor fisherman whose boy goes to the engineering school over there.' The foreman's sweep took in sky, sea, and Little Aden.

'Ah, yes –' Kanoo put in smoothly. 'In that case I imagine there are books to be paid for and certain expenses to be met.'

Sulaiman eyed the dark interior beyond his dangling legs. 'For knowledge,' he said carefully, 'there will often be a price to pay.' He threw his rag at the darkness below and looked at Kanoo and came straight out with it. 'What exactly did you want with me?'

Now the shipyard owner looked up for the first time. He looked left and right along the sloping shingle, scene of his success. All the dhows were his dhows. Was that what he was saying? Yes, he could act as he pleased here, Sulaiman acknowledged – he didn't need to explain himself to a hired hand. Khalil Kanoo took off his spectacles and polished them with a handkerchief. His rosary was still wound around his fingers. 'Do you have a boat, by any chance, Sulaiman Ali Hassani?' he enquired at last. 'As in a boat of your own?'

'I think you heard the man, didn't you? I fish.'

'Naturally, naturally – and is it small or large, your boat?'

'It's big enough. It does what's asked of it.'

All the time Kanoo was nodding, pausing only to put his glasses back on. 'Then perhaps we can help each other,' he said.

'And how might that be?' Sulaiman asked.

'Oh, I don't know – let's imagine I'd like to help your son.' The fat man shrugged in the face of manifold possibilities. As he gazed at the dhow marina and the crowded harbour beyond it he lashed the palm of his hand with his beads. 'In the interests of knowledge, let's say – or for the sake of tomorrow.' He shot a glance, full of meaning, at Sulaiman. 'Some things are far too important to leave to chance, don't you agree? Some things are much too precious –'

'Why, thank you kindly –' Sulaiman countered, rising fast in the relentless light. 'But I'm afraid we simply don't need your help.'

Kanoo smiled. He turned to his foreman and jerked his head at the hanger and waited – having bowed low, the foreman withdrew. 'Tell me, Sulaiman – is it not our duty as employer and employee to honour one another as best we can? This much is the will of God, as I understand it. You know – I really wanted to take this opportunity to thank you personally for all your hard work here.'

It was no more than protocol required, Sulaiman recognised – the exchange of platitudes under the sun. 'To build your boat – any boat – must be regarded as a privilege,' he said in keeping with the formula. 'It's me, surely, who should be thanking you.'

Later, alone on the calm waters of the gulf as night fell, he went over his conversation with Khalil Kanoo again and again. What did it mean? Its effect was unsettling, its import unclear. Of course, the whole thing was linked in some way to Isa. *Let's imagine I'd like to help your son.* How exactly? And why? *Some things are far too important to leave to chance, don't you agree?* No, no – all Sulaiman wanted was to watch the boy become a man. To see his son grow, straight and true, from sapling into tree – that was it. The rest was as nothing. One day the father would sit in the shade of that tree with the dhow of his dreams drawn high on the sand. Was it too much to ask of life? Well, was it?

He stood up in his boat off the coast at Gold Mohur. From the radio behind him came a Forces Radio dramatisation of *The Monkey's Paw*. It must have been a trick of the light at that unreliable hour – as he hauled in his net, Sulaiman had the sudden and brutal vision of a severed head among the fishes of the ocean. The head tumbled eyeless from the mesh with all the frightened sprats, and came to rest between the fisherman's feet. Sulaiman steadied himself in his boat. He counted six jack mackerel and two kingfish. These prized critters fell thrashing to the boards beside a giant sponge – source or subject of Sulaiman's macabre imaginings. He heard the cry of the big ship. Looking up from his catch he saw the refinery glimmer finally in the weakening grip of evening. Then the passenger liner emerged from behind the headland with a heart-stopping declaration of lights and horns. Sulaiman watched the ship describe a glittering arc, slow or dead slow, from the headland at Little Aden to the central reach of the bay. As she turned now to face the harbour lights and the black depths of the interior, the *SS Oriana* moved the uncertain fisherman with something close to beauty, and made him believe again.

ON A PROMENADE DECK of blast-warped bulwarks and improvised cordons, Jacinta gripped the rail as the headland drifted astern like an iceberg. Now the drawing nearer was so peaceful. There was the whisper of the sea and the suggestion of music, more imagined than anything else, emanating comfortingly from the Shalimar ballroom on B deck. Jacinta's hands were sticky from the peppermint liqueur. She had put on scarlet lipstick and powdered her face just a little. At the captain's farewell supper, lively affair with a calypso theme, she listened closely enough to catch the going ashore arrangements for

Aden. Tonight the ship would berth at the bunkering station in the shadow of the volcano. Tomorrow they would disembark. The plan was straightforward in its essentials. Jacinta smiled at the room. First the passing steward presented her with her garland of paper flowers. Then she lifted the *crème de menthe frappé* from the tray. She accepted the serenading attentions of Jimmy and Philip as they wandered the bright spaces with guitar and tambourine singing Guantanamera or Island In The Sun. How their sensitive harmonies affected Jacinta. Suddenly she felt faint. No doubt she wasn't quite herself yet. As the singing receded in her head she sought out a chair – or, rather, she found herself seated at a large table. The Shalimar ballroom was a stadium of light. Jacinta's hands shook. Upshot? Her goblet betrayed her and went down. Jacinta watched, astonished, as a vivid river ran out across the cloth. Then she got up and fled.

On deck she gripped the rail more tightly, gulping the desert air. She could see the harbour lights plainly now. How super – a flotilla of small vessels was hurrying to meet and greet her. In her head the music came and went. On an impulse she turned from the rail. She imagined she saw her friend Oona emerge from the companionway. Was it her friend? Jacinta thought she might have seen a ghost. She confronted the land and waited, waited for a hand on her shoulder. When it didn't come, she turned again. Nothing, no one – she was alone with a question. Had Ben ever loved her? It was a question she had come all this way to answer. She had a strong urge, which she resisted, to take off her garland of flowers and cast it on the water. What possible good, she asked herself, would that have done?

# 2 | Ben

'You're right – I was trying to prove something'

HE HAD STARTED TO WAKE early in the grip of his dream. He was climbing fast through the ocean, his eyes bulging, his lungs bursting. He rose up rapidly with a brilliant fish, gift for his father, in his hand, but when he reached the surface his father's boat had gone. The sky turned black. If there was a flood tide of experience in the affairs of men – an hour of unrepeatable achievement or irretrievable loss – Ben Nolan imagined his time was very close. He could hear a clock ticking somewhere nearby. How had he got here?

In fact, he saw no need to look back for a turning point or a fork in the road. He had made an error of judgment, slightly shaming in its suggestion of weakness. It was unlike him – how he wanted to be. As he parked his Land Rover beside the taxi rank in Steamer Point Nolan decided a man should be permitted his one mistake without having to pay for it all his life. How to make amends now and move forward and take his chance? Jumping down from behind the wheel Ben Nolan asked himself what form redemption might be expected to take in a man whose qualities at twenty-six were largely untried – a man who, in his anguished dream of ideal attainment, fished with bare hands. When he told her he loved her, it wasn't really a lie. If it was a lie, it was only a white lie. It was how he saw himself – he saw himself *loving a wife exactly like her*. Of course, she took him at his word. Why would she doubt who so wanted to believe?

Already the sky, requisitioned by the sun, had ditched its colour. As he approached the neo-classical façade beside the harbour police HQ on Tawahi Road, Nolan could see and hear them. Blocking the imposing entrance at the top of the steps, a small crowd of men and older boys chanted in Arabic, their fists punching the air below the pediment. Nolan began his ascent. As he prepared mentally to carve a route to the doors, his own fists tightened and he felt a sweat break out beneath his shirt. Then a shout went up – the crowd dispersed within seconds as a camouflaged truck pulled up at the steps. Armed soldiers jumped out two by two. By the time they surrounded Nolan among the flaking columns he was alone.

'Are you all right, sir?' The sergeant had his face pressed to the glass pane in the doors. 'What's all this, then?' he said, turning and looking Nolan up and down.

'There's an official enquiry taking place here,' Nolan said. 'Don't you people know about it? A ship almost went down out there with a load of Muslim pilgrims on board.'

'Pity it didn't sink, sir.' The sergeant tossed his head towards the truck, and his men began to peel off. 'Fewer for us to deal with –'

Nolan pushed through the heavy doors. In a chamber pierced by diagonal shafts of sunlight a dozen fans suspended from the rafters rotated lazily with a collective sigh. The floor was a chequer board of turquoise and gold tiles – along the main axis of the chamber an avenue of lavender pillars extended from the doors towards a great table of mahogany or calamander sitting on a raised platform below a portrait of the Queen. On either side of a central aisle the bobbing heads of the dispossessed pilgrims animated the benches that made up the body of the chamber. Towards the front were the Dutchies who had rescued them. It had to be the Dutch seamen, Nolan told himself – even at this distance their shore haircuts signalled briskly from within a narrow border of luminous skin. At the same time he became aware of the balcony overhead with its further complement, as yet only sensed, of interested parties. Above the whole thing hung the presence, urgent and physical, of four hundred whispers.

Nolan started forward in the aisle below the overhang, scanning the benches, hoping for a glimpse of Mathieson. There were plenty of others here at the back of the chamber – Nolan imagined himself among newspaper reporters and lawyers and loss adjusters, to say nothing of harbour police officers and Port Trust surveyors and the representatives of Sudan Steam. Suddenly he saw them – the crew of the *Medina*. They sat behind a small table immediately below the platform and to one side of the hall, looking down at their hands, or glancing up at the Queen. A stenographer in an orange sari swept onto the stage from an unmarked door in the wings. As she lowered herself behind her apparatus Nolan followed the crimson dot on her forehead – sudden focus, he judged, of a throng. He stood aside. A crippled vendor shuffled past him towards the doors with a cigarette tray hanging from his neck. Now the journalist with the cool smile beckoned Nolan again with his notebook in his hand. Yes, there was a space beside him on the bench. The journalist waved his notebook, smiling. At his throat the dark hairs massed in tendrils.

Nolan sat down, thinking. No, he was certain – he didn't know the man making notes so assiduously beside him. Above and behind, the balcony too was packed with pilgrims in white *thobes*. Where was Mathieson? Nolan reached into the pocket of his shorts and pulled out the crumpled record of a shore-to-ship telegram he had sent first thing to his wife and smoothed it out on his knee and read it again, heart beating faster. UNDERSTAND DISEMBARKING 1200 STOP WILL BE ON HAND STOP BEN. Beside him the journo finished scribbling – Nolan decided he must be about to explain himself. A silence spread from the front of the hall. As the three wise men took their places at the great table on the stage, the stenographer rattled her keys.

'This inquest is now sitting,' said the man in the Nehru hat.

THREE FLOORS ABOVE the Ma'ala strip, Mathieson lay with Sonny on a mattress on her verandah and listened to the rush hour traffic below. Soon the sun would find them out – it always did. It was only a matter of moments, Mathieson decided, before the meddling sun jumped the balcony wall and discovered them stretched out hand in hand below a batik throw and gazing up at a yellow budgerigar.

'Back home in Penang,' Sonny went on unexpectedly, 'we used to say the secret of happiness was to become more like you are.'

She had stopped crying. Mathieson considered everything again. He saw the sun flash from the tiny mirror in the rattan birdcage.

'So if you're a damn fool you simply become more foolish,' he suggested, 'but happier at the same time. That's awfully good –' He sensed her pain. Still he insisted on threatening what they had. 'And if you're a monster, Sonny, or a psychopath, let's say?'

She ignored his question – it lacked due weight and proportion. Mathieson cursed his black heart. He no longer trusted himself to do or say the right thing in a context of intimacy.

'What's happening to us, Duncan?' she asked.

'I don't know,' he said, raising her fingers to his lips and kissing them one by one. He was thinking about his first drink of the day.

'You don't have to be there, do you?' she said.

'No –' he said. 'Ben Nolan will be there.'

'Exactly,' she said, withdrawing her hand. 'And they have your report, don't they?'

'They have my report.'

'So why must you go?'

Flitting from one side of its cage to the other, the budgerigar let out a series of shrill wolf-whistles, exactly as he had encouraged it to do, before sharpening its beak noisily on the cuttlefish bone wedged between bars. As he waited for the bird to settle, Mathieson worked hard to recall the pleasure he took in its simple virtue, asking himself why true happiness must always be deferred.

'I know you have to be there,' Sonny conceded at last. 'You do, don't you?'

'Aye,' he said.

'Please tell me what he did, Duncan.'

'He abandoned four hundred pilgrims with his ship on fire.'

'We know that.' She sat up abruptly and pulled the throw over their heads. 'His name is Lomax. He's a coward without principle – you told me all that.' Just then the sun filled their tent with hot light. Sonny sighed. 'But what did he do to *you*, baby?' she said.


NOLAN SLID HIS WATCH from his wrist and checked it again. Soon it would be time – time to collect his wife. Beside him the journalist had stopped writing. They were listening, all of them in the packed chamber, to a colourful account by the Sudan Steam representative of the *Medina*'s seaworthiness, which was also her life story. She had spent her youth in cold English waters, plying her trade at a steady fifteen knots between London and Newcastle, her cargo, even then, being pilgrims. For ten years she carried football fans up and down the North Sea coast until the advent, overnight more or less, of the long-distance coach put paid to that glamorous commerce. In 1934 she sailed gratefully for Piraeus, becoming one of precious few ships in Greek waters to ride out the war intact. By 1953 she had drifted south to Alex – her refit here prepared her for a regional trade with Arabia in which migrant labour and pilgrims played a part. All this was vividly evoked. The renamed ship's decks were modified at that time to create further steerage accommodation. Three reconditioned boilers swallowed forty-three tons of coal per day in order to supply her steam. If the *Medina* was carrying in excess of her coal payload when she put out from Karachi on her fateful last voyage, much of that payload had been consumed by the time she struck something

71

hard and unseen in the night and began to list harshly about eighty miles north-east of Socotra. Captain Lomax was fully awake when the Nubian mate burst, panting, through the curtain. The English skipper's eyes were red. His beard was three days old. The bottle fell from the stool beside him and rolled heavily across the floor. 'Ship – she on fiah, sah!' cried the mate, chest heaving beneath a singlet. He had a four-foot axe in his hands. As he turned and fled he tore the curtain from its hooks and, hollering tragically, dragged it into the night. Lomax sat up and cursed his luck. He reached, according to account, for his pants. Then the lights went out in a stinking cabin –

Nolan slipped his watch back on and stood up. Outside, he took the steps two at a time until he heard his name called. He stopped and turned. 'Do I know you?' he said, hands on hips.

The journalist leaned with arm outstretched against a column at the top of the steps. After he folded up his notebook he drew a card from his shirt pocket. 'Not in so many words,' he said pleasantly. He loped down the steps and proffered his card between elegant fingers. 'Basim Mansouri – I write for *Al-Kifah*, the Arabic daily.'

'Ugly business,' Nolan remarked conventionally, nodding up at the stone pediment and the big doors.

'Ugly times, Mr Nolan.'

'Look – I was just on my way.'

'Can I talk to you?' asked the journalist with a new suggestion of urgency and confidentiality.

Nolan returned the card. 'We filed a full report,' he said, 'which I'm sure they'll get round to discussing –'

'I mean about the Port Trust.'

'What about it?'

'These are difficult days, Ben – challenging ones for all of us, no doubt. You don't mind if I call you Ben, do you?'

'Why should I mind?'

'It's just that Aden so depends on the Port Trust. Without it, the place would grind to a halt, don't you agree?'

Nolan struggled to recall the name on the business card. He felt strangely disadvantaged – the journalist looked perfectly at ease on the first step above him.

'Can we get to the point, Mr Mansouri? I have an appointment I'm anxious to keep.'

'I know, Ben, I know. My point is simply this – we'd all hate to see any unpleasantness arise at the Port Trust.

'Unpleasantness, Mr Mansouri?'

Basim shrugged. 'Workforce unrest?' he proposed reasonably. 'Hidden agendas, crossed wires, misunderstandings? You know the type of thing –'

'No, I don't know, as a matter of fact.'

'Precisely my point, Ben, which is why I think we should have a little chat. We might consider a deft piece for my paper, perhaps, or a series, even, before things get out of hand. Public relations, if you will – prevention being so much better than cure.' Here he dropped his business card into Nolan's shirt pocket with measured effrontery, then backed off. 'I'll keep in touch if I may,' he called out from the top step. 'I think it's important, don't you?'

It was the shortest of hops from the taxi rank at Scott Gardens to Prince of Wales pier. Nolan had no time to dwell on a disquieting dialogue with its tenor of threat, its hint of privileged access. He saw the *Oriana* hemmed in on his right side and hogging the anchorage – in his imagination he had always pictured her at sea. In the surgical light her scar tissue, product of a terrorist act, showed all too clearly. Fêted now by the smaller boats she reclined on the slack water like a giantess pinned down harmlessly by hawsers, ropes and hoses.

He spotted his wife right away. It seemed natural Jacinta should stand out, still and fresh, from the tumultuous scene. He had parked as close as he could get. Outside the customs house he rose up for a moment in the doorway of the Land Rover, clinging to the roof as a human stream seethed around him. She was standing in the shadow of the livestock pen roughly half way down the pier, waiting calmly for her husband with a white suitcase planted in front of her.

Gangway! Gangway! A team of ghostly Chinese coolies hauled their shrieking trolleys across the tramlines set into the boards while all around them the smiles contorted on the faces of those who had come and those who had come to meet them. Nolan saw a houseboy cradle an expatriate's daughter in his strong arms and weep with an obscure joy as the young girl soiled his shirt with her vomit. No one else saw it. Tearful *ayahs* hugged solemn public schoolboys as sinewy porters shouldered stout English trunks bearing stout English names. Nolan let them rush past until their hubbub receded in his head and their colours faded away. All the time his wife waited for him in the shadow of the livestock pen. She stood still with her hands clasped in front of her while a young beggar, just a kid she would disappoint beautifully, staked a claim for *baksheesh*. Nolan waded closer through a tide of passengers and pimps. In his head he rejected as unsuitable or inadequate the words of greeting he had prepared. There was the suitcase at her feet on the border between sunlight and shade. She looked right through him. She gave no sign of having seen him until he stopped in front of her. Then she gave a gasp – her imagination must have prepared her as imperfectly for the truth as his had.

'I was worried about you,' he said, pulling the kid's hands away.

'That's OK,' she said, laughing. 'He wasn't really bothering me.'

'I meant on the ship,' he said. 'When we heard about the bomb.'

'Oh, yes –' she said with new gravity. 'It did some real damage.'

Then the beggar boy seized her floral dress and pressed it to his face and began to wail dismally.

'Won't you give him something, Ben?'

'He's only pretending,' Nolan said.

'How can you say that?' she said.

She sat in silence while he drove. Each time he looked at her on the road to Hedjuff he caught her staring at the sea.

'Aren't you going to tell me about the baby?' he said.

He had tossed her white suitcase on the bed. Ali had finished for the day. They were alone together on the verandah. Soon it would be time to mix the drinks. Still she stared at the distant water, hands gripping the rail as if it was something rare or wonderful.

'I'm afraid there is no baby,' she said.

She didn't attempt to explain things – not all at once. When she told him what had happened he asked himself immediately what he felt about the baby. Funny – he had been forcing it from his mind in the hope it would go away. And now it had. Ben Nolan would have found it extremely difficult to admit, even to a stranger, exactly how he felt. Paralysed briefly by relief, he watched his hand inch finally towards his wife's at the rail.

'Won't you at least say something?' she said, smiling at the sea.

## ❧ SHIRLEY BASSEY VERY GOOD ❧

SYDNEY, SINGAPORE, Hong Kong, Aden – in a seafront office hung with sun-blanched portraits of its liners in the great harbours of the eastern world, the P&O company played host to Jimmy, lead singer with Pretty Flamingo, and the group's manager, Adrian Durbridge.

With a foot on his knee, Jimmy eased the zip of his boot up and down while Durbridge spread his arms now and then in a gesture of urbane equanimity. From high above, a fan cooled their scalps and set in partial motion rogue documents on a desk strewn with corals, shells, and other paperweights with a marine or maritime theme.

'But my dear fellow –' Durbridge continued, incredulity rising. 'Surely a local manager should be allowed to manage locally?'

Across the desk, the P&O representative wrung his hands in the face of incontestable forces. 'I really am very sorry. I can only repeat – any appeal for contractual compensation will have to be referred to our head office in London.' From the harbour somewhere not so far away a big ship's horn underwrote the disappointed silence with its vulgar spondee. The P&O representative leaned forward and placed his propelling pencil in the gutter of a notebook and began to read, it seemed to Jimmy, from a prepared text. 'Only, you appreciate we can scarcely be held accountable or responsible for an act of piracy, not to say lunacy – an act of God, if you will – on the high seas.'

'Act of God, my arse,' Durbridge interposed dismissively. 'Some bloody fanatic was out to blow us all to kingdom come.' Now he got up without notice. The shipping clerk jumped to his feet behind the desk and held out his hand, but the impresario ignored it.

'I wish I could help you, Mr Durbridge.'

'I'll be at the Crescent Hotel,' said the Pretty Flamingo manager from the door. 'Or in Australia, I dare say, trying to sort this whole sorry mess out –'

It fell to Jimmy to shake the hand of the P&O man whose futile civility had touched the young Scot deep inside. The suggestive clues were there for anyone to detect – anyone who looked hard enough. There was the propelling pencil, so characteristic in Jimmy's poetic imagination of a certain quality of doomed sensitivity, and the stock speechifying, not to mention the sad shells from the sea.

'I really wish I could have done more,' insisted the agent.

'Aye, I ken, man –' Jimmy said. 'I ken just fine.'

In the back of the taxi, as he waited for the group's manager to patronise him about something, or anything, a subtle plan started to take shape on the creative side of the young Scot's brain.

'Bank –' Durbridge announced abruptly, leaning forward from the back seat and sucking harshly on the cigarette clamped between his fingers. 'We want to go to a B-A-N-K, driver. Do you read me?'

'Looks like a flight to Australia for you, then,' Jimmy ventured. He had seen the tethered dromedaries graze the arid strip between carriageways and now he spoke up, inspired. 'Maybe I should come too. I mean – as a spokesman for the group.' Here he examined the manager's face in profile, looking for a reaction. 'I've got big ideas, Adrian. I was thinking we should add keyboards. We could put out a few feelers in Sydney or Melbourne, couldn't we?' He raised a fist and nailed his six words to the roof of the crawling car. 'Progressive London group seeks keyboard wizard –'

'It's a thought, Jimmy,' the manager acknowledged negligently. 'But, you know, Philip is pretty handy on the old joanna himself –'

In the mind of the young Scot a familiar picture of loss began to form. 'Aye, that'll be right,' he said bitterly. 'Philip can play drums and piano at the same effing time now, can he?' They sat in silence at the lights while a rosary swung, clicking, from the driver's mirror. 'I mean – surely to God they'll want to meet at least one of us in the flesh. They need to put a face to a name – to feel the goods, man.'

'It's a thought, Jimmy, as I say. Of course, they'll have seen the black and whites. But, no – I think I need you here.' Durbridge met the young Scot's gaze and lowered his voice confidentially. 'I'll need someone with a good head on his shoulders to keep the flag flying at this end.' He looked down in an attitude of modesty and respect. 'At the very least I'll want you to keep an eye on Oona for me.'

'On Oona?'

'I hate to leave her behind, but business is business. Needs must when the devil drives –'

'Is that a fact?' Jimmy said, increasingly captivated. He nodded now because the picture had become clear to him. 'I get it, Adrian –' He stared, open mouthed, at Durbridge with a blend of fascination, horror and contempt. In the unsatisfactory guardian beside him he saw his father, his mother, his parole officer, his priest. He saw them all with their statue's eyes so smooth and blind. Not one of them had made table with his starving spirit. Yes, he was free. He was alone – who would mourn him, properly speaking, when he died? 'You'll be taking Philip with you, won't you?' he blurted out.

Then the driver jerked the handbrake on and looked up at the mirror, grinning, or leering, at Durbridge. 'British bank, my friend – top class place.' His pupils were dilated, his teeth yellow. 'You like nice young girl, boss? Saigon calling. Fucky, fucky. We go Piccadilly Circus and Old Kent Road. Shirley Bassey very good, yes?'

'Indeed,' Durbridge drawled. 'That can hardly be denied. Now, how much do we owe you, driver?'

'Four shillings, East African, boss.'

'As much as that, eh? Note our canny host's foresight, Jimmy, in directing his guests first to a well-stocked bank.'

IN A TWIN ROOM UPSTAIRS AT THE Crescent Hotel, Philip coaxed the tobacco from a filter-tipped cigarette, rolling the paper cylinder gently between his fingers and tapping it until the contents rested in a golden mound on the dressing table. Now he had only to crumble the warmed hashish into the tobacco to make his smoking mixture. With close attention he refilled the paper cylinder pinch upon pinch, packing the shag snugly using a matchstick before twisting shut the aperture, removing the filter tip from the other end, and parking the improvised reefer between his lips with a craftsman's satisfaction. He heard a knock on the door. In the triple mirror of the dressing table he saw Walter's head appear – head only, at great height. The third permanent member of Pretty Flamingo was a gentle giant from the north of England, a softly spoken and unassuming young musician with a special talent and affection for the bass guitar.

'Best get downstairs right now, bonny lad,' he suggested, 'seeing as how one of your drums has just been busted open.'

In the handsomely tiled lobby below, Oona was surrounded at the hiccoughing fountain by a scattered drum kit, two microphone stands, three amplifiers, four speaker cabinets, five guitar cases and a quantity of personal luggage. Her handbag she lifted up time and again in an involuntary appeal to higher forces as she remonstrated with a desk clerk.

'Philip, darling –' Now she digressed explosively and summoned the young man from a bend in the thickly carpeted stairs. 'Disaster, chuck – look. They've only gone and put their big foot through your precious drum skin – literally torn it asunder, babes – and I can't get the beggars to own up to a single thing.'

She turned again to the unfortunate receptionist. 'Oh, do back me up, Philip. Just tell him it was all right when we got off the ship. It was, too – it was perfectly in tact, sir, I must insist. Now, I suggest you introduce me to the senior manager at your early convenience because I will have satisfaction in this matter.'

She broke off there, impressed by the violence of her protective instinct. As Oona hugged her handbag and eyed the desk clerk with self-righteous indignation, the fountain's spluttering was superseded temporarily by a burst of music straying from the inner courtyard of the hotel. In the renewed quiet of the lobby, no one stirred.

'It's only a snare,' Philip said, responding to a conciliatory note in the subtly changed atmosphere. 'I expect I'll manage without it. I mean – it's not like I really *need* it here or anything.'

Oona sighed audibly. 'I know that, dear – but it's important to be firm with these people from the off. Otherwise, they'll seize every chance to walk all over you.' She let Philip clear a path between the speakers and amplifiers. 'And now, sir –' she added, louder, for the benefit of the desk clerk, the shrill music intruding again. 'The duty manager, *s'il vous plaît.*'

He led her through an almond grove studded with fairy lights – their coloured bulbs were illuminated despite the afternoon hour – towards the source of the flagrant soundtrack. As she approached the slatted doors on the far side of the courtyard Oona had the reckless notion she was living at full tilt for something like the first time. She scotched that rumour – she was checking into a three-star hotel, for heaven's sake. She was ruffling a few local feathers because it had to be done. These people were fanatical by reputation. It was common knowledge they were instinctively cruel. Of course, they were happy to smile at you when it suited their purpose. They would stab you in the back as soon as look at you, wouldn't they? Confronted now by the doors and the discordant music that leaked through them, Oona judged herself to have arrived at the threshold of life itself. She was unwilling, all the same, to cast aside gut feeling founded on practical prejudice – best defence against an opportunistic illusion. There was a dirty little war going on here, she recalled briskly, brushing down her dress and tucking her handbag under her arm. As the desk clerk opened the doors, the music hit her with the force of cheap cologne.

The performer under the lights was young – too young, Oona decided, to convey fully, despite her best efforts, the sexual intent of the dance. Still, her apprentice sensuality – even at a distance – was compelling. Her eyes were rimmed with kohl above a mask or scarf that cloaked her nose and mouth. Shy breasts, crushed by a sequined bodice that flashed readily in the harsh light, confirmed her boyish youthfulness. To the amplified rhythms of the *tabla* she stamped the boards with bare feet, flinging her fingers this way and that around the swirling axis of her passion, anger or resentment. Veiled by blue harem pants, her legs had the look of saplings glimpsed underwater. Where the knot of her belly button might have peeped out coyly, a jewelled brooch or similar clung to her like a glittering mollusc.

Oona heard, or thought she heard, a clap of hands. The music stopped abruptly – now the dancer's shallow breathing was the only sound in the room. But were they two, the men who watched? No, three. Oona could make out the desk clerk now – he beckoned her from the gloom on this side of the spotlights. As she moved towards the stage, Oona's focus shifted from the young dancer whose ringed eyes probed the interior blindly. The desk clerk leaned over a table and whispered something in the duty manager's ear. Was it the duty manager's ear? Oona could only guess. She saw them in silhouette, except for the dancer in the grip of the lights. The desk clerk glided to the edge of the room – now the wall lamps came on, two by two, in the dining salon at the Crescent Hotel, Aden. The duty manager must have been very young. He rose from the table and drew Oona closer with a courteous gesture. She nodded. She was watching a fat man wearing glasses seated slightly apart – he dismissed the dancer with a clap of his hands and a sweep of his beads. As the performer vanished behind a curtain the fat man turned from the stage.

'That girl –' Oona demanded of the manager – the one she took to be the duty manager. 'How old is she, please?'

The duty manager looked at the fat man. The fat man rose with surprising speed and extended his hand across the table.

'I do beg your pardon,' he said interestedly, 'but we haven't been introduced yet, have we? We'll just have to do the job ourselves, I'm afraid. Khalil Kanoo – at your service.'

Oona held his plump fingers briefly above the table.

'And you are Miss –?'

'Mrs –'

'Ah.'

'Mrs Durbridge, if I'm not mistaken,' put in the duty manager.

'Please don't concern yourself, Mrs Durbridge,' Kanoo went on expansively. 'The girl is like a daughter, or a niece, to me. Moreover, she is hardly, if I may say so, a girl.'

Now the duty manager dismissed the receptionist. 'You asked to see me, madam?' he said. He wasn't exactly *dark* – he was of mixed parentage, Oona decided quickly. He looked ridiculously young in his Coca-Cola T-shirt, shorts and worn-out flip-flops.

'Are you the manager or the manager's son?'

'I'm afraid my father's in Muscat on business right now. But, you know – this is a family-run hotel in the fullest sense. I'm Kenneth. How can I help you today, Mrs Durbridge?'

Did he take her seriously – seriously enough? Oona pressed on in the face of a promiscuous charm.' It really is quite straightforward, Kenneth. One of your people has damaged one of our instruments.'

He was nodding, his brow furrowed. Of course, he would have known all about it already. His whispering receptionist would have briefed him on the edge of the light.

'As you may know by now,' Oona continued, 'we are embarked on a musical tour of the east, and the item in question is central to our technical needs as well as to a young man's happiness. I mean utterly *germane*.' She spun round and added a philosophical footnote. 'Of what possible use, Mr Kanoo, is a drum with no skin?'

82

Now Kenneth reconfigured the chairs, making one available to her with a grace she ascribed to good breeding. 'Would you excuse me,' he said, 'while I make some enquiries?'

As the impossibly young duty manager withdrew, Oona slipped in at the table facing Khalil Kanoo, handbag on her lap. 'First-class English with manners to match,' she observed approvingly, nodding with eyebrows raised. 'I mean – you, too, of course.'

Kanoo, apparently amused, dragged his chair closer. Kenneth's mother is English, Mrs Durbridge – practically as English as you are, I dare say. Even as we speak, she will almost certainly be shopping at the indispensable Marks & Spencer in London or, possibly, some provincial town in the rain. Naturally, she will cut the Zionist labels from her new underwear before regaining our intolerant shores. It's the price we must all pay for quality and comfort where it matters.'

Oona looked at him with wary interest. 'So, Mr Kanoo – I take it you too are in the entertainment business.' She motioned towards the deserted stage. 'If I can put it that way.'

'Why not put it that way, Mrs Durbridge? My talented charge shows a certain promise as a traditional dancer, that is all. Were you looking at a budding ballerina in a tutu and pink tights you would scarcely be concerned about her moral welfare – am I right?'

Oona felt a rush of blood. She took a deep breath, but he went on. 'You are so very far from home, aren't you? Perhaps I can help you get back your land legs.' She eyed his bulk more keenly, despite a growing fatigue. 'You see, my spies are everywhere – I'm afraid I know all about your Pretty Flamingo and the bombs that explode in Port Said. As you rightly suggest, we are both in the entertainment business. The practical difference between us is merely that whereas you represent the interests of just one musical act, I peddle popular entertainments of any and every kind to anyone and everyone.'

'Go on, Mr Kanoo. I still say your dancer is unhappy – but go on all the same.'

He leaned closer to her. She couldn't see his eyes. She only saw the wall lights – dozens of them – reflected in his glasses.

'As you will doubtless know, Mrs Durbridge, a large contingent of British army personnel is garrisoned here in Aden. These brave young men require constant diversion, believe me.' Kanoo swept his hand and beads through the air above the stage. 'Now, if one could simply book a Bassey, say, or a Belafonte –' Here he spread his arms rhetorically. Oona saw his glasses flash – no, wink. The manager's son had returned with a bottle of lemonade. Kanoo stood up. 'Seek me out, by all means, Mrs Durbridge,' he urged, secreting his beads inside his tunic. 'You never know – one might even be in a position to procure drum skins at short notice to meet a spike in demand.'

He spoke rapidly to Kenneth in Arabic before mounting the few steps at the side of the stage and disappearing from view. Oona was left with the lemonade and the manager's charming son.

'I'm very sorry about the damaged drum, Mrs Durbridge. I've had a word with Philip – I promised I'd do everything in my power to make it up to him personally.'

'HOLD IT IN –'

'I am holding it in.'

'Hold it in and count to ten.'

'One dromedary, two dromedary –'

'Not out loud, you pillock.'

Jimmy exhaled with an exaggerated show of coughing. 'It does nothing for me – nothing at all. Last time I smoked that stuff was at a party thrown by my probation officer to celebrate his divorce. I fell asleep, and when I woke up again he was engaged to be married.'

'Yeah, well – it gives me ideas,' Philip said as Jimmy smirked at him. 'For songs, I mean.'

'For the lyrics?'

'Lyrics, melody, harmonies – I mean the whole magical process. Know what, Jimmy? I'm beginning to think I'm wasting my time on the drums. I'm not sure it suits me any more. It's all so mechanical, somehow. Half the time this stuff makes me see things –'

'You mean flying saucers, or just the top man with the beard?'

'I'm serious. Last night I saw myself looking down at me.'

'Just lie on yon couch, son, and tell me all about it.'

'I dreamed I fell head over heels in love, Dr Freud.'

'With yourself, or was anyone else involved?'

'Cynic – just wait till you hear my song. It's a hymn to beauty.'

'Sweet. I can hardly wait. Neither can the group's manager who says we urgently need to create our own material. Has he discussed it with Philip? Of course he has, stupid. He thinks the sun shines out of Philip's arse.'

'Would you like to try writing a song together, Jimmy?'

'I mean – he would know, wouldn't he?'

'Know what?'

'If the sun shines out of your arse.'

'Let me see – now you want to take me somewhere I don't want to go particularly. Is that it?'

'Forget it, man. Just chuck that BOAC bag over here, will you?'

Philip reached for the grip and passed it across the gap between the beds. 'Better on a camel,' he said. 'Isn't that what they say?'

'Better on a camel?'

'B-O-A-C. Have you ever been up in a plane, Jimmy?'

'No, Philip – but I bet you have.'

'My dad gave me that bag as a token of his limited esteem.'

Jimmy peered inside the grip, and then unzipped the pocket on one side. 'In that case, I apologise.' After he vomited into its pouch, the Scot zipped up the bag and wiped his mouth with his hand. 'Like I say –' he said. 'That stuff does nothing for me at all.'

IN A TINY ROOM NEXT DOOR, Walter slept face down on the pillow, his arm around a bass guitar stretched out beside him on the sheet. Mouth open a little, snoring lightly with feet dangling over the edge of the bed, he was quite unable to hear Oona's voice rise subtly in front of the mirror belonging to a vanity unit beyond the wall.

'I don't think you're listening, Adrian. I said no –'

'Why ever not, Oona?'

'Because I just don't want him to go with you, that's all.'

'It's only for a few weeks – a month at most. They really should see a member of the group, my dear – in the flesh. You know – I'm not sure you've thought it through properly.'

'Yes, I have. He may even be needed here.'

'What – in Aden? Don't be silly.'

'Why not? Something may turn up.'

'Darling –'

'Philip is staying, Adrian. They're all staying here with me. You fly on to Australia and pick up the pieces, by all means. That's your job, isn't it, as the boys' manager? Do try to be a man for me, won't you, darling? There's a good chap –'

'Oona.'

Silence at the mirror – the dreaming bass guitarist might have had the measure of its depth. Oona's husband placed a hand on her shoulder, but she waved his reflection away with her hairbrush. She shut her eyes. What did she see? She saw the legs of a dancer veiled by a blue mist. She saw the severed heads of seven sawfish. Hacked from their bodies one by one, the heads accumulated with outraged eye on the planks as Oona came ashore at Prince of Wales pier. She saw it and heard it. Now she smelt it — the reeking scene. When she opened her eyes, her husband was still there, watching her closely in the mirror. Again he laid his hand on her shoulder.

'A penny for them —' he offered tenderly.

'Oh, I was just thinking about my brave friend Jacinta.'

## ❧ THE WITNESS TABLE ❧

HILDEGAARD VAN KRIS took another sip of water and set the glass down among the damp rings on the witness table. Above and to her left the three wise men conferred in murmurs beneath the unseeing eyes of the Queen. At an isolated remove, her red spot like a bullet hole in the middle of her forehead, the stenographer sat impassively behind her machine, awaiting further developments. Now the man in the Nehru hat smiled down benignly from the platform.

'Kindly continue. We have a great deal to get through here.'

Hildegaard examined the disgraced English captain who faced her across the chamber and tried again to identify some redemptive quality — an appeal for understanding or sympathy, perhaps — in his demeanour. His crew conversed with each other dully at his table — Lomax silenced them now with his hiss. He wiped his stubble with the upper sleeve of his shirt — the sweat had left salty stains there in overlapping crescents as it advanced and receded from hour to hour and from one day to the next. In her dazzling uniform Hildegaard must have been a source of painful light to him — his sullen squint seemed to hold her personally responsible for his fate. As he moved his head slowly from side to side like a sick animal he regarded her contemptuously first with one hooded eye then with the other.

'There's very little I can add. I picked up an emergency request to attend the Port Trust compound at just after midnight. I'm a rota nurse at the field clinic there, as you may be aware. We did what we could and made the arrangements for transfers. I treated lacerations dehydration, burns – principally to hand and face – and shock. The most serious cases we dispatched as quickly as possible to the Queen Elizabeth Hospital. I think you have the report there –'

'Indeed we do, nurse.'

As she looked out across the crowded benches she felt her heart lurch. Basim Mansouri was standing at the back of the room. It had to be him. He waited there just long enough, Hildegaard decided, for her to notice him, then turned on his heels and vanished into the glare beyond the doors. Now her eyes failed to meet Nolan's. Was he avoiding her gaze? She saw him glance over his shoulder again.

'We thank you, nurse van Kris – you may step down.'

She didn't return to her place. Instead she joined Nolan further back – he had to make room for her beside him on the bench.

'You haven't called me, Ben.'

'Haven't I?' he said. He consulted his watch. 'Things have been pretty hectic this end –'

'I thought you must be angry with me,' she said.

'I have a wife here now,' he said, eyeing his watch again.

They all heard it – the portentous clattering of doors. Nolan saw Sonny – she was standing, feet planted wide apart, in the aisle below the balcony dressed as for a fashion shoot in a turquoise safari suit, and sucking on the arm of her dark glasses. Directly behind her was Duncan Mathieson, his white hair cropped razor short now.

'Mr Mathieson?' The question was thrown down from the front.

'I'm Mathieson –' he boomed. All eyes were on the Port Trust's senior pilot as he guided Sonny to a space in the body of the house.

'We have your report, Mr Mathieson. Now, please —'

The man in the Nehru hat pointed to the witness table below the platform. As Mathieson took himself there slowly, very deliberately, the attention of the chamber went with him. There was an iconic or heroic quality in his progress — the silence confirmed it. Mathieson sat down. Gradually he raised his eyes to confront the shabby crew of the *Medina* at the table that served as the dock. There was a fierce sadness now in his penetrating gaze — a pitying disgust in which the assembly, more and more rapt, acquiesced.

'In your report you make an extremely serious allegation against Captain Lomax — one which appears to go beyond the facts of the case. May I remind the room this inquest is tasked with establishing those facts objectively, in so far as they may be established. It is not in our remit to apportion guilt in this or any other matter, to assign blame, or to pass sentence. This is not a court of law —'

Mathieson stood up at the witness table. 'Facts, you say? Facts? Since when did facts have to do with a damned thing?' He looked at Lomax and nodded, his thin smile widening slowly as if in response to a salient image imperfectly remembered, or remembered too well. 'No, the fact is Captain Lomax has pulled this kind of stunt before.'

'Objection —' It was Lomax himself who intervened. He jumped up. He sat down. He let out a cry, or a laugh — it fought for air and died finally on his lips, a stillborn howl of recrimination or despair.

'Objection?' Mathieson let the word hang in the new silence. As he left the witness table he drew a paperback book from his pocket and brandished the battered volume above the room. 'The captain objects, good people —' He brought his book down hard on the edge of the platform, not far from the stenographer's feet. 'As do we all.'

He hesitated at the front of the room, scanning the sea of faces as a deeper hush set in. Then he saw her. Sonny had her face tilted, eyes closed, towards the rafters and the lazy fans. Mathieson watched her nod ever so slightly, almost gratefully, as if to license what came next, as if to sanction some new and necessary outburst. She opened her eyes and found him – that was Mathieson's cue. He swept up his book and hurled it towards the balcony and the pilgrims in white.

'*Lord Jim!*' he cried out. 'Because a man should stand up –'

His paperback novel descended, pages fluttering, and was lost.

'I must warn you, Mr Mathieson –'

The senior pilot had already raised his hand in anticipation of a challenge from behind. 'And because,' he went on, 'I believe it to be Conrad's pages that offer Captain Lomax his chief inspiration, or at least some poetical precedent, in respect of this cruel affair –'

'Thank you, Mr Mathieson – I'm sure many of us are only too aware of the parallels between the *Medina* case and Conrad's yarn.'

Mathieson didn't stop. He couldn't stop. He had his eyes fixed on Sonny's eyes. 'You see, good people – young Jim pays dearly for his cowardly act. He too escapes in a lifeboat with his fellow seamen when their pilgrim ship hits something hard in the night. And those pilgrims, too, are left to go down with a vessel reported lost. Does it sound familiar? Ha – every man for himself. And ain't we the lucky ones, boys? Only, their ship doesn't go down. No, no – the ship is towed safely to port and Jim spends the rest of his days in shameful exile, far from the forgiveness of worthier men. Of course, the world was a big place then, wasn't it? It was easier to hide – much easier. You see – young Jim had jumped. He was no longer *one of us*.'

'Mr Mathieson – I must ask you to confine yourself to the facts.'

'Ah, yes – those *facts*. I wanted to tell you about Captain Lomax because, as a matter of *fact*, I know the man. I knew him in Malaya a long time ago – that's how small the world is. You see – I knew the captain when he plied his tuppenny-ha'penny trade along the coral coast of Malaya, up and down, in and out of the nameless coves. A thousand islands there were – just a few dots on a chart if you really needed to know. But no one ever did, did they, captain?' Mathieson swung round abruptly and saw the other man's eyes catch fire. 'No – no one needed to know about the captain's smuggling exploits in and around those half-forgotten estuaries.'

Night – night without promise of day. Did he see it again as for the first time – the dancing of searchlights on the water? Did he hear it – a keening as of wounded whales?

'I don't want to detain you today with a sordid tale of drugs and gun running. Good lord, no – I shan't waste your time. Let's talk of human traffic, rather. Now, there's a trade for a smuggler to aspire to. Captain Lomax here ferried them up the coast towards Siam – towards Thailand, towards freedom. They were women and babies, political activists, rebels and insurgents fleeing prosecution by –'

As he spun round, Mathieson invoked the portrait of the Queen that hung above the great table and the three wise men.

'And they paid him well. They rewarded him handsomely. Oh, yes – the voyage was dangerous all right. But the captain was brave. He was an Englishman, was he not? He was one of us. Out of a still and starless night the gunboats came, their searchlights stroking and caressing the surface of the water. Can you imagine anything more beautiful and more terrifying? The captain took off with his mate – an idealistic Scot, as I recall – in the dinghy they had towed behind them, mile after mile, along the coast. And the captain was as good as his word. He divided up the cash there and then by the light of a torch. This was long after the guns and the cries had fallen off. He had been paid twice, don't you see? He was paid first by his fleeing passengers, then by the midnight police. There's a nice bit of history for you, people. History is what hurts. Of course, the brave captain was happy enough with his night's work. He even sang as he rowed. I know what he sang as he struck out that night for the shallows and the shoreline. I know because I was in the dinghy with him –'

Silence. Not enough of it. Mathieson had heard the siren – they all had. Now the insistent clamour drew nearer and nearer from an unknown source and direction beyond the lavender pillars and the whitewashed walls. In the packed chamber the pilgrims murmured and got up from their benches. Then the doors opened with a crash. A uniformed MP stood, pistol raised, in the aisle below the balcony.

'Is there a Ben Nolan in here?' he said.

HE DROVE – MATHIESON SAT beside him, one eye on the chopper keeping pace above them while hauling its shadow across the sea. As he swung into Larcombe Road behind a flashing escort and heard the sirens take up, Nolan was caught between the idea of a shameful yesterday, as embodied on behalf of all by the man beside him, and the prospect, so closely identified now with his own redemption, of a nobler tomorrow. *Is there a Ben Nolan in here?* He set aside his extreme anxiety – he had to do that if he could. It was up to him – here, now. At the same time he felt his actions, or his choices, were increasingly subject to forces beyond his control. And still Mathieson sat beside him. What to say to the senior pilot? Where lay consolation? Then it came to Nolan in its finished form – the question he had wanted to ask all along without realising it existed.

'The fire on the *Medina* – how did it go out?'

'Ah.' Mathieson turned his face from the sea and looked straight ahead, nodding as if he had expected Nolan's question and no other at this point in history. 'There was a sudden downpour,' he said. 'By which I mean there was a miraculously heavy or intense shower.'

'Are you saying it *rained*?' Nolan said.

'Four hundred pilgrims, Ben – that's a lot of prayers.'

Their police escort peeled off. At the Port Trust gates the crowd parted for them beside a waiting ambulance. As he inched towards the army lorries and the No. 3 slipway, Nolan felt the heat from the torsos pressing all around. Unseen, mostly sheepish, blows struck the sides of the vehicle. An entire shift was massing in the compound, or gathering at the upper windows, or congregating on the stairways, or squatting on the warehouse roofs. Two harassed paramedics passed the Land Rover – a coolie lay, unconscious, on their stretcher, a rib protruding from his chest below a halo of flies. Mathieson swore, and swore again. Nolan saw it too – there was something happening on the No. 3 slipway crane. They stopped finally behind an army truck – one of two – and immediately the Land Rover was encircled by a Royal Northumberland detachment bearing arms.

'Who's responsible here?' Mathieson barked, jumping down.

'Are you Nolan?' asked an excited NCO with a megaphone.

'No, *I'm* Nolan – Ben Nolan.'

'Looks like you're the man of the moment, sir.'

'Wait –' Mathieson raised his hand as if to stay the proceedings. 'What happened to the coolie back there?' he said, jerking a thumb over his shoulder. 'Where's Palmer, man? Where's Geddes? Where are all the bloody pale-faces when you need them?'

'The coolie fell through a warehouse roof, sir – no big deal in the great scheme of things.'

'Where's Palmer? He's the man in charge –'

Now the officer pointed to the No. 3 crane – to its glass cabin.

'Jesus Christ,' Mathieson whispered.

Above the main compound the No. 3 crane's boom appeared to be sweeping, inch by juddering inch, across the sky. Hunched over the controls in the elevated booth, Palmer was taking orders from a man standing stooped behind him with a scarf covering his face. At the end of the creeping boom, two more men sat astride the yellow girders, scarves at their faces, legs dangling comically.

'OK –' Mathieson said calmly. 'What is it they want?'

'We don't exactly know, sir. Same old song, I expect – Brits out, National Liberation Front in. They say they aim to hang themselves unless Mr Nolan here shins up there pretty damn quick and reads a statement from them in person.'

'Hang themselves? Are you out of your mind?'

'Got to be a bluff, sir. We could just let them swing, of course. Only, I don't fancy your chances around here of a Friday lunchtime clocking off, if you catch my meaning. Natives could turn ugly, sir.'

'Has everyone taken leave of their senses? We have to work with these people.' Mathieson seized the officer's megaphone and trained it on the glass cabin above. 'Palmer – what the hell are you playing at? Get down here *now*, man.'

The No. 3 crane's boom shuddered to a halt. The workforce fell silent below. For a moment nothing happened. Then a masked man stood up carelessly at the end of the boom and made visible a length of rope before draping a noose around his companion's neck.

'That's enough nonsense –' Mathieson hissed. 'I'm going up.'

'I don't think so, Duncan' Nolan said, and already he began to see how it might play out. 'I believe it was me they asked for.'

'So? You won't even be able to parley with them.'

'Oh, I don't expect to be making much small talk.'

After all, it was simply a question of placing one hand above the other on the hot rungs of the ladder. About two-thirds of the way up, Nolan came abreast of Palmer and the glass booth. He didn't try to speak to Palmer – there was no point, and in any case he had never really rated the man. The sun flashed from the window of the cabin,

94

spurring Nolan on as he climbed steadily towards the boom. Now he worked his way out across the noisy compound, crawling forward on hands and knees. Between rusting girders he glimpsed the upturned faces. Was that his name they were chanting? The metal was so hot – Nolan gulped down its heady perfume of paint and grease. Basim Mansouri waited for him at the end of the boom, eyes blazing coolly above a scarf. A masked associate crouched beside him with a rope around his neck, rocking crazily and whimpering like a kid.

'Sit down, please, Ben. I wouldn't want anyone to fall from this thing. At least, not without my say-so –'

'What the hell are you doing, you bloody fool?'

'We are ready to die, you see – all of us, at any time.'

'Are you out of your mind?'

'Did you know our people face torture every day in your jails?'

'What do you expect me to do about it?'

'You will read out a brief statement prepared by me, and then escort us safely from this compound with a gun at your head.'

'But I know who you are –' Suddenly, shockingly, he thought he saw how it would end for the one who rocked, jabbering obscenely, on his haunches above the expectant throng.

'No, no, Ben – it is *we* who know who *you* are. Please understand – we can reach you at any time. We are grateful for your assistance.'

'Assistance? Are you mad?'

'We know you drove an injured boy through Crater –'

'What? I can have you rounded up tomorrow.'

'But you won't, will you? If I keep this mask on, you won't even have to know who I am.' Here Basim drew a sheet of paper from his pocket. 'Think about it, Ben – this can be our little secret.'

He turned and spoke, calmly, gently, to the babbling colleague roped to a spar beside him. The babbling associate rocked back and forth as he received his final instructions from Basim Mansouri. He rocked faster and faster now, gibbering like an idiot. He must have been praying, Nolan decided later, to the patron saint of martyrs or murderers. What came next – the crowd willed it to happen.

'No –' Nolan cried out, lunging.

The swaying man tore off his scarf and fell forward in a graceful arc. He wasn't really pushed as such. The crane let out a tiny squeal when the rope bit at the end of a short descent. The hanged man's scarf floated briefly on the avid silence before it dropped, the crowd recoiling as it plunged to the ground. Then a roar went up, and the bodies surged forward again.

'And now, if you please, Ben –' Basim said, eyes expressionless. 'First you call for quiet, and then you read out this short statement.'

## ❧ RICE KRISPIES ❦

ON FRIDAY MORNING Jacinta sat on the verandah at Hedjuff with a box of Rice Krispies in her hand and a jug of powdered milk in front of her. She had precious little to do except play records and keep out of Ali's way as he toured the apartment with his carpet sweeper and a comb for the fringes of the worn rugs. Jacinta tilted her face at the sky and closed her eyes and challenged the sun, so high already, to deny or disprove her new appetite for life. Listless in the languid air, she let Patsy Cline sing You Belong To Me and actually saw certain pyramids, musically evoked, on the Nile and then pictured her good friend Oona at the Crescent Hotel here in Aden. Simply to entertain positive thoughts was exhausting, Jacinta decided, opening her eyes as wide as she could. She really needed to carve out a role, she told herself again – to adopt a point of view or an outlook on things. In a renewed effort to interact meaningfully with her surroundings she acknowledged the fascinating quality of the sea. There it was again, sparkling like a field of broken glass. It was always there, glinting in the sunshine. Jacinta turned away, dazzled. The next thing she saw was the telephone sitting on the chest behind the faded curtain. She saw the phone that never rang for her. She studied her watch – four hours until he finished work. And then? She poured the cereal into a bowl, added milk, and lifted the heavy spoon. Snap, crackle, pop – the contents of the bowl shifted subtly as the milk flushed the weevils from various nooks or crannies. Attuned to disappointment and loss, Jacinta found herself siding instinctively with the dispossessed beetles in the face of a catastrophic inundation. Her sympathy went out to them. She rescued thirteen weevils with a spoon. Just lately she had found herself crying for no good reason.

'Oh, Ali – where are you, please?'

He tipped four tins of Heinz tomato soup into a pan and rinsed the empty cans. Jacinta helped him raise the larder above the tiles – together they eased a soup tin under all four legs of the larder before Ali poured the paraffin in.

'Ants swim, ants die,' he told her, but she wasn't sure she cared.

'I'm going shopping, Ali. You can go home now. I'll take a taxi.'

'Taxi outside, *memsahib*. Compound gate waiting. Tip-top taxi –'

She packed a beach towel and put on her sunglasses and let Ali's cousin drive her to the *suq* at Crater. No one questioned her appetite for life as she priced material for curtains and searched the bookstall for *Lord Jim*, a basket swinging jauntily from her arm. On the cover of *Life*, a Viet Cong prisoner knelt in the dirt, his wrists bound with wire, a rifle at his head. Jacinta was moved by this image. Motivated to empathise, she plucked the magazine from the rack, but just then she felt something scuttle across her foot, or her sandal. She kicked out and looked down – not a cockroach to be seen anywhere. A silk tie caressed her instep on the pavement of hard-baked mud. The tie belonged to a crippled beggar. Jacinta considered him from above. Having no legs, he transported his shining body on a platform with castors, rolling back and forth with the use of his padded fists. His tie was knotted too tightly at his throat. Suddenly he reached out and gripped Jacinta's legs with his bandaged hands, and she, uncertain of her role, gave him all the money she had plus a copy, not yet paid for, of *Life*. His every dream had led him to make this artless gesture of fellowship, she told herself later, exhilarated. And she – what had she lived for if not to prepare herself for a stranger's touch?

COME FRIDAY AFTERNOON she discovered herself lying on a towel at Gold Mohur with the sunshine splintering around her eyelashes. At last she sat up beside her basket and cast around for her husband. He was stretched out on his stomach a few feet to one side, his head turned away awkwardly as if he had fallen from tremendous height. Jacinta reached out her hand and watched its shadow extend across his back. She knew he was capable of warm feeling. She didn't mind if he was seeing someone else. She didn't mind if he was holding the hand of another. If only he would hold hers too. And still it was just her shadow that made light contact with him. Night after night, for the sake of appearances and the servant, they slept back-to-back and a little apart on the cool white sheet.

'Someone called me at work from the Crescent Hotel.' Perhaps he felt her eyes on him in the sun-slapped silence. Or maybe he felt the shadow of her hand at his back. 'She was looking for you, Jacinta – if I was short with her, please apologise.'

'Why would you be short with my good friend Oona?'

'I don't know the answer to that. Things have been a bit hectic at the Port Trust of late. That's the only excuse I can offer –'

'Why did you lie to me, Ben, when you said you loved me?' She had prepared the ground for the longest time, and now it had simply popped out, unbidden. It must have been Oona's influence acting, Jacinta concluded, from afar. She decided to count all the li-los she saw between the shark net and the shore. 'You did lie, didn't you?' She stirred the hot sand with a little stick she had found – an ice-lolly stick, smooth and bone dry. She counted six colourful li-los between the shark net and the sighing surf. The message boy with his green cummerbund hurried past in front, ringing his bell and dragging his blackboard behind him in the sand. 'I mean – what were you trying to prove when you asked me to marry you?'

He sat up then and hung his head between his knees. 'Nothing,' he said. 'I wasn't trying to prove anything.'

'Oona said I must have been trying to spite my father.'

'When you married me? And were you, Jacinta?'

'I did love you, Ben.' There – she had said it. She had done the right thing. Because he said nothing to reward or encourage her, she pressed on. What she said next – it was meant to come out stronger, but now she felt she had to water it down. 'Perhaps I still do.'

'Then don't make me do it again.'

'Do what again?'

'Lie to you, of course.'

'Oh, I won't,' she said.

'You know I never set out to hurt you,' he said, shaking his head as if to discount – for his own benefit at least – the very possibility of such a possibility.

'But you did,' she said, laughing at the sea.

'What do you want me to do now?' he asked, and she thought she glimpsed his negotiating position, which was not to have one.

'Nothing,' she said, getting up fast and running towards the surf.

'You're right –' he called out. 'I was trying to prove something.'

She only stopped – she didn't turn around. 'But not to me,' she said, and she couldn't be sure whether he had heard her or not.

Now the sand started to burn the soles of her feet. She felt Ben's eyes on her back. She felt the shadow of his hand at her shoulder. In her imagination she felt a shadow. She had given him every chance. She had given him a chance to say he had loved her *a little*, but he had spurned it. If he was prepared to shoulder blame in an off-hand way he offered neither apology nor consolation. What kind of man did that? Oona was right – love was never there. Not really.

Ahead, the surf seethed. Jacinta felt a great emptiness. Now she had it – the answer to the question she had come all this way to ask. Of course, back then she had the baby. Without her lovely baby she had no cards left to play – how sad she had come to view it like that, Jacinta thought. Taking away her baby – it was like taking away her chance of happiness. She picked up the cuttlefish bone, so light, dry and smooth, at her feet. The cuttlefish bone was a great comfort to her in her hour of maximum sadness. Still the sea dazzled.

'GOOD EVENING, STRANGER –'

He found himself resenting her even after she had opened the door to him. He went to see her on Friday, reasoning she was more alluring because of, or in spite of, his resentment. Soon it would be curfew time in Crater – Nolan was certain the enduring mystery of life was present – right there, right then – in the briefest of twilights. She was unprepared for him, and he found that exciting. He didn't know which he resented more – her relish for endangerment or the self-conscious morality of her idealism. He only knew it was bound up, all of it, with her particular notion of service and faith.

'Good evening, Hildegaard.'

He sat on the settee that was also her bed, and she fixed him a drink by the warm light of a standard lamp.

'I'm surprised,' he said, looking at her modest furnishings.

'I don't think you've been here before,' she said needlessly.

'I'm not sure what I expected,' he said. 'The face of God?'

She sat down beside him. Everything was pretty much there in one room. 'So, why did you come?' she asked him. 'Does the word curfew mean anything to you?'

He heard the squeal of the crane as the hanged man's descent came to an abrupt halt. He heard the voice of Basim Mansouri. *We know you drove an injured boy through Crater.* Then he came out with it – what he needed to ask. 'Do you know an Arab journalist in Aden?'

'It's possible,' she said without hesitation. 'Do I have to guess his name? I assume we're talking about a man –'

'You're very sure of yourself, aren't you, nurse?'

'How do I know whether I know him if I don't know his name?'

'Who could really say what you're mixed up in, Hildegaard?'

'Ben –' she said, as if she was preparing to deliver a fine speech.

'You do know him, though, don't you?' Nolan said.

She looked at him with the understanding he resented the most. 'Sooner or later you have to take sides –'

'Spare me the sermon. Can't you see you're playing with fire?'

'All of us must choose, Ben – including you.'

Her clock said it was curfew time. Silence – she hadn't switched on her AC yet. Nolan heard a mournful broadcast from a mosque.

'What if I chose you?' he said. It came to him out of the blue – an urgent need to be more like her. 'What if I chose to kiss you?' It was absurd. He was a fool. Then he got it – he was punishing himself on behalf of his wife. Hadn't he persuaded himself he loved Jacinta because it suited him to do so? How could he apologise for that?

'If you chose to kiss me I would reject you and send you straight back to your wife.'

'In the face of a curfew?'

'Ah, the curfew – the curfew is a state of mind.'

'What if I told you my wife sleeps alone?'

'Then I would still reject you – my rejection has nothing to do with how your wife sleeps or doesn't sleep.'

All the way from Crater to Hedjuff he admired her coolness and her confidence. She didn't even ask him how he felt after his famous adventure on a crane. It was as if she didn't need to ask. It was as if she knew all about it. How much *did* she know? She must have been so sure of herself when she gave him the choice of staying or going.

'If you don't want to drive, you can stay here with me.'

'It would be nice to get to know you some day,' he said, picking up his keys. 'I think we'd all like to get to know you better.'

'Would you?' she said. 'That's very sweet of you all, Ben – but I'm not sure you'd like me very much if you did.'

### ❧ The Coastline of Integrity ❧

In the windowless office above his shop, Khalil Kanoo pushed a claw hammer aside on the desk and pulled the telephone towards him, propping the door open with a foot as he dialled. The fan was on, but the afternoon heat continued to dominate the stale air. With the ringing tone at his ear and a string of beads swinging this way and that around his finger, Kanoo grimaced as the shutters crashed to the ground below. Hassan, his assistant, was closing the shop.

'Is that Waterloo barracks? Thank you, yes – I'd like to speak to Sergeant Morrison, entertainments officer.'

'Who's calling, please?'

There was a brief exchange with the switchboard operator, then a click and five beeps.

'Ents office – Private Taylor speaking.'

'Hello? Yes, hello – I was hoping to have a word with Sergeant Morrison, as a matter of fact. Kanoo is my name. He knows me –'

'Sorry, no can do – I'm afraid the sarge is at Singapore barracks all day today. Can I pass on a message? I'm just holding the fort –'

'Tell him Khalil Kanoo called with a business proposition.

'Right you are, Mr Kanoo –'

'A concert, tell him – something major, something outdoors. An event, really – a concert in the sports stadium at Waterloo barracks, for example. I don't know. He may be interested, he may not –'

'A concert – as in Glenn Miller plays live for our brave boys?'

'Something more contemporary, I have in mind. A beat group, let's imagine – hot from London. Nothing radical or subversive, you understand – strictly covers and standards. No Elvis Presley. I mean a play list arrived at by mutual agreement. What can I say? A classy programme of international artistes, male and female – a night of morale-boosting sentiment built around a talent contest from within the ranks. Whatever matches Sergeant Morrison's vision –'

'Hot from London, you say? So what would they be doing here?'

Kanoo sighed, stilling his swinging beads decisively. 'You have a sense of humour, private – something I like. Perhaps that is why you find yourself seconded to the entertainments office at a time of rising civilian tensions in this part of the world –'

He rang off and dialled again. 'Hello?' he said softly, in Arabic this time. 'This is Kanoo –'

'Yes, Kanoo – I'm listening.'

'Everything is in place.'

'You have your ferryman?'

'Pretty much.'

'Pretty much?'

'Everything will be in place.'

*Tammam.*

'We have a rendezvous hour?'

As discussed, Kanoo. My client has a boat, or a yacht. He'll be waiting to collect at the agreed time and place.'

*Hala:s.*

'And Kanoo?'

'I'm still here.'

'The utmost discretion, remember −'

'Naturally.'

'This will make us all very rich.'

The line went dead. Kanoo hung up. He collected his beads, his keys, and his hammer, the steps from the office creaking under his weight as he descended. Below, the shop was still, silent, and almost dark. Kanoo glided through a pungent canyon lined with the fruits of his import-export activities, passing rugs from Kandahar, bolts of cotton from Rajasthan, ceremonial hookahs in huddles, and leather pouffes stacked in teetering columns. His immaculate skirts brushed the carved ornaments − exotic animals, chiefly − from Tanganyika, the ivory-studded camel stools wrapped in protective polythene, the cigar boxes from Lebanon of cedar inlaid with mother-of-pearl. At the back of the shop, guarded on either side by bongo drums raised one above the other, was a screened door, which Kanoo unlocked.

Inside, his eyes slowly came to terms with a profound darkness. The young dancer lay on a mattress on the floor up against the wall, facing away from the door and covered by a sheet. The harem pants and veils hung motionless from a nail above the mattress. Kneeling close, Kanoo put down his hammer and extended a trembling hand very gradually towards the sheet, then – as if to reconcile conflicting impulses of desire and shame – took back his chubby hand, getting up finally, like a camel, in articulated stages.

He unlocked the second door and closed it behind him, groping now for the torch on the wall. Yes, there – he examined the packing crates at his feet. With him in the store were eight smallish wooden boxes, each one unmarked, their lids secured carefully by little nails in rows like stitches. Kanoo selected a box. He took the claw of the hammer to the lid of the box and leaned on the shaft until the panel rose up with a squeak. Now the torch illuminated the straw packing materials – Kanoo swept them aside with his most delicate touch. He swore. He was full of admiration for what he saw. He saw the face – no, the head – of a youth, sensuous and beautiful. The youth's head filled the wooden box. Kanoo kneeled beside the box and marvelled at the bust of the boy. Caressing the cheek with a finger, he had the idea his own skin was on fire. As time slowed for him, he gazed into the blank eyes of an antique sculpture in shimmering bronze.

Quickly, urgently, he opened another box and shone the torch inside it. There was a typed inventory in there – Kanoo took it out. Below the straw packing he discovered first the incense altar, cast on a clay core. There was an alabaster mortar and the votive sculpture, complete with inscription, of a gazelle. There was the bronze bull – one of a pair, evidently – whose eye sockets were set with sparkling ores. Fascinated, Kanoo studied the typed listings by the light of his excitable torch. *Bronze ass, Sabaean/Qatabanian?* And in the margin, in a precise hand, was the note – *Alas, too late for the Q of S!* The Q of S? Kanoo's torch flickered. He replaced the sheet of paper and the lid of the box. For an indulgent moment he lingered above the bronze. The hair was plastered to the forehead in opulent curls. The smooth eyes of the youth bulged in the probing light. There was something erotic and prurient, Kanoo decided, in that vacant stare, in the full lips caught for two thousand years in the act of parting.

FREEWHEELING DOWN the slope towards Bir Fuqum, Isa glimpsed the parked Mercedes beyond the leapfrogging beam of his lamp. He leaned his bicycle against the wall of the house and peered through the open window of the car. A fat man lay stretched out on the back seat. Rising with the speed that confounded strangers, Khalil Kanoo reached out and opened the car's door. The light came on. Having retrieved his glasses from the parcel shelf behind, Kanoo studied the young face at the window.

*Masa:'il-kayr.* 'Good evening to you.'

*Masa:'in-nur.*

*Kayf ha:lak?* 'How are you?'

'Fine, thanks.' *Il hamdu li-lla:h.* 'What is it you want, mister?' Isa backed off as the fat man worked his way along the leather.

'I was hoping to speak to your father. My name's Kanoo.'

'You'd better come in.' Once inside, Isa shrugged off his satchel and lit the stove. 'Can I make you some tea? The milk's tinned –'

Kanoo took off his sandals. With two moths assaulting the strip light noisily above him he surveyed first the room then the books on the table in front of him. 'Tea would be very welcome –'

'Won't you sit down?' As the fat man pulled up a chair, Isa went on, his tone as coolly polite as he intended it to be. 'I had planned,' he said, 'to eat a bit of fish before I went out.'

'You have to go out again?'

'Just to Little Aden.'

'Ah – a night class, perhaps? You're a student there, aren't you?'

'I'm an apprentice engineer.' In the skillet Isa held out were the seared bodies of five fish. 'Well – can I offer you something or not?'

Khalil Kanoo ignored the pan momentarily, focusing instead on the comely youth who so delighted with his reluctant good manners. 'Provided,' he said, 'you don't expect me to get down and pray first. As you see, I'm far too large to *kneel* every five minutes. In any case, I take up quite enough space in the vertical mode –'

They ate in silence after Isa cleared away his books. Above the table, the moths attacked the light using an array of pointless tactics.

'Dad fishes – don't you know that? You're his boss, aren't you?'

'I know he fishes.'

'I really can't say when he'll be back. It depends on the fish –'

'They're awfully good, by the way.'

'We try to live decently and honestly around here.'

As Kanoo looked into his young host's eyes he saw fire. 'Then I must thank you, decently and honestly, for my supper.'

Isa slid the plates into a basin on the floor. 'Don't tell me –' he said, getting up. 'You've come to offer Dad a pay rise.'

Beside each other in the whispering Mercedes-Benz they swept through Silent Valley towards Little Aden, Isa's bicycle protruding from the boot. Above the sheer cliffs on one side the sky advertised its second sunset of the day thanks to the refinery's flares, with here and there the sulphurous sparks cutting loose like shooting stars.

'So – have you met a nice girl yet?' Kanoo said finally. 'I'm sure there must be lots of nice girls at your college. Modern girls –'

Isa eyed him coldly.

'Too busy studying, I expect,' Kanoo added, nodding hard.

'It might surprise you,' Isa came back, 'how few girls, modern or otherwise, choose to be petrochemical engineers.'

As he watched the insects swarm in front of them, Kanoo, light headed now and slightly nauseous with desire, gripped the steering wheel more and more tightly. It would have been impossible to look for long enough, or for too long, at the spirited passenger he badly wanted to undress and bend to his will. What Kanoo wanted was to make a woman of the young man – that was the long and the short of it. They had reached the township on the other side of the pass.

'The cinema's fine,' Isa indicated casually. 'I'll cycle from there.'

Kanoo dropped him off beside an illuminated poster for *Zulu*.

'Will you go back and wait for Dad?' the boy asked, leaning in.

'No hurry –' Kanoo said. 'I'll catch him tomorrow.'

'Can I give him a message?'

'Thanks – that won't be necessary.'

'Just the bit about the pay rise, then –' Isa mounted his bike on what passed in these parts for a pavement. 'Did you know you had a musical instrument in the boot of your enormous car?'

'It's a snare drum, as a matter of fact,' Kanoo said, ignoring an increasingly disrespectful quality he detected in the young man. At the same time he worked hard to scotch it – the physical longing he had, in his loneliness, been obliged to call love. 'Look here,' he went on. 'Just don't let them distract you from your important studies.'

'Who?' Isa said defensively.

'I can't imagine. But if you can be good at just one thing –'

'Like catching, or serving up, fish, perhaps?'

'Don't get fresh with me, young man. Just don't let anyone fill your head with silly ideas about progress, that's all.'

He pulled away with a powerful surge. As he rounded the bay the crowded harbour was spread out to his right like a chart of the heavens. The big ships twinkled at their fuelling stations. Behind the ships the lights of Steamer Point climbed from the glossy surface of the water and clung to the flanks of Shamsan like barnacles of fire. Above the black slopes of the volcano, in the deeper dark presiding over Crater and the curfew, the bolder stars declared their hand.

He drove at an effortless fifty along the causeway. Passing Slave Island he thought again of Sulaiman, the youth's father, alone in the gulf with just his lamp and net. What was it the boy had said? *We try to live decently and honestly around here.* For the tenth time Kanoo asked himself if Sulaiman was the right man for the job. His boat was not too big, not too small. He lived simply enough, all right – he looked every inch the humble fisherman despite his skilful work on Kanoo's dhows. The poor fisherman's interests and ambitions, such as these might be, were no doubt identified closely with the prospects for his pretty and precocious son. Yet every soul, humble or exalted, could benefit from a little extra cash during these uncertain times, Kanoo reasoned – that was the bottom line. No, there was no real difficulty thus far. It was, rather, on the rugged coastline of integrity the plan threatened to founder. Decently and honestly, the son had said. How decently and honestly? Would the father bridle or baulk at the idea of relieving southern Arabia of much of its archaeological heritage in one fell swoop? It was strictly an import-export opportunity, Kanoo insisted – all in a day's work. The priceless Sabaean antiquities were being removed for safekeeping in case the volcano decided to blow – as it surely would, he argued. He was merely helping the notional national museum to store its best pieces out of harm's reach. What could be more responsible and more patriotic? One day the treasure would wash up on a far shore and be returned to Saba amid general rejoicing. Kanoo smiled. He switched off his lights as he neared the Crater gorge. He searched his pockets for his cash float – the money might be needed should he be asked to account for his movements at a time of curfew. Then it came to his flexible mind – the answer to a recent riddle. *Too late for the Q of S?* The S stood for Saba, the Q for Queen. The date of this or that priceless relic was too late, Kanoo perceived in Crater's darkened streets, for the Queen of Sheba.

109

In the private room behind his shop he switched on the light. A collar of scorched newspaper barely shaded the bulb overhead. The dancer reclined on the crude mattress against the wall, the jewelled stud glittering at his navel. Khalil Kanoo scarcely looked at him as he unhooked the harem pants and the veils and let them fall. As the banknotes rained down after, the naked youth – just a boy, really – sprang up like a startled gazelle.

'Don't you want me?' he asked solemnly.

Kanoo smiled affectionately. He had known excitement, shame – now he just felt numb. It was always like that, he recalled.

IN A SHUTTERED ROOM IN LITTLE ADEN, Isa leaned forward on his cushion, emboldened by a single draw from the standing pipe. 'If we are to achieve the supremacy we seek,' he said, taking advantage of a lull in the interminable discussion, 'we must differentiate ourselves from them *now*. Immediately –'

The room fell silent at this urgent new voice.

'We must go further, shine brighter, hit harder. We must offer a clear alternative. As things stand, how can we expect the man in the street to be able to choose between the NLF and FLOSY? San'a is their sponsor, Cairo ours. Big deal. We both want the same thing – the keys to the castle. Am I right or wrong? With respect – we must talk rather less and *do* a lot more. We must seize, and then retain, the initiative. We must eclipse them totally –'

A sprinkling of seasoned diplomatists took it upon themselves at this juncture to uphold their point of view.

'We should be talking to the NLF, not plotting against them –'

'I'm not altogether persuaded the people want either of us –'

'First, we remove the British –'

'At the same time the people must be made to need only us.'

110

Isa silenced them all with a further strategic intervention. There was an uncompromising authority in his reedy voice. 'Us?' he hissed with a pointed irony. 'Us?' Cue a deeper silence. 'Why, then, do we sit on these cushions, nodding sagely, discussing and debating, while the enemies of the people, who are everywhere, grow fatter day by day? Such a specimen I met tonight – my Dad's boss, an enemy of the people, growing fatter hour by hour. Such a man should face a prolonged fast. He even asked me about girls. I know that trick. He probably wanted to fuck me in the ass –' He broke off there because various elders were laughing at him.

'Your Dad's boss, you say?'

'Name of Kanoo, by any chance?'

'Yes –' Isa admitted. 'Kanoo is his name.'

They were greatly diverted in the smoky room.

'Khalil Kanoo may well be the most prolific bugger in Aden –'

They fell silent, mostly, and let the senior spokesman conclude.

'He is also the biggest individual contributor to FLOSY coffers in the land.'

Isa felt the blood rise up and subside. He heard the gurgle of the pipe. He was conscious of something shifting inside him, helplessly, irrevocably, in response to their patronising indulgence and his own furious conviction.

'If you say so,' he conceded. 'But I must ask why you choose to accept a red cent from a *bourgeois* degenerate like Kanoo. The man acts in opposition, surely, to nature. It seems to me such a man acts knowingly against the will of God.'

'Oh? And what would you know about the will of God?'

A flurry of nods greeted this lofty interjection. Again Isa looked around him – he saw twenty old men and two hooded falcons. 'Not much,' he said, bowing his head. 'I know much less than you do, of course. And yet I know a man is judged by the actions he takes and the company he keeps. Isn't that how the people will judge us?' He let them murmur their regard for his passion, informed as it was by just the right amount of deference. 'Respected elders —' he cut in at last. 'Could it be I'm keeping the wrong company here tonight?'

'PLEASE – JUST COLLECT YOUR THINGS and get on your way.'

He peeled off more banknotes and let them fall to the floor.

'But the curfew —' whined the boy. 'I have nowhere to go.'

'Just go, please – there's enough there to bribe a small army.'

Kanoo glided through the canyon towards the front of his shop. He unlocked the door between shutters, leaving it open to the stars, then climbed the protesting stairs to his office and sank into a chair. Soon he heard the boy pad softly into the night. Kanoo went back downstairs and locked up. He sat in his office until the cock crowed. There was no more desire – only fatigue. Once upon a time he had been a boy, a lad, just like any other. That was such a long time ago. The shutters clattered up. Hassan was opening the shop. Kanoo got up, stiff. He found his glasses – he must have brushed them from his face in a happy dream. It struck him with the reassurance of a fact – there was a refurbished snare drum in the boot of his car. It was far too early to phone the Crescent Hotel.

### ❧ BEAUTIFUL CIVILIAN ❧

*DEAR MUM AND DAD,*

*Filthy hot. We are back at barracks after an uneventful tour of duty with the Federal Regular Army close to the Yemeni border. That's where all the trouble is meant to come from, but you could have fooled me. Just routine manoeuvres with the feds for a month. At least it was cooler up there. The hills – they call them jebel* this and *jebel* that – are green with crops right now. *I don't know what they grow on those terraces. I should have asked, but the villagers kept themselves to themselves when we were around. I don't blame them.*

*Have I told you about the feds? Their men are drawn from the various states that make up the Federation of South Arabia, or whatever it's calling itself today. (They change their name at the drop of a hat.) The feds are our allies in all this. They act as a buffer between us and two rebel factions that want to drive us into the sea. I liked the feds. Most of them seemed pretty easy going about us, which makes a nice change around here. Taylor says they couldn't organise a piss-up in a brewery, but I won't hold that against them seeing as most of them are likely to be Muslims etc. Taylor's a laugh. I think he likes me in a funny way. I hope so, because I look up to him, I admit. If things ever get really hot, I hope I'm with Taylor. He probably thinks I'm pretty wet behind the ears. He may not know too much about Muslims etc. but he knows the score about a lot of other things, so the chances are he'd be right about me too. Taylor is helping to organise a concert in the sports stadium right now. Yesterday he asked me for my ideas and my 'input'. I mean to give it some proper thought because you can't let your comrades down.*

*Talking of Taylor brings me to the subject of pottery. I think I said before that I planned to do a bit of digging when I got upcountry. Well, you'd have been proud of me. I filled nearly two kit bags with fragments from a site that looked promising and brought them back with me to our barracks. Since then I've pieced together the best part of a jug or some kind of vase – an earthenware vessel, you'd have called it, Dad. And Mum – I could have done with your jigsaw expertise out here. It took bloody ages (excuse my French) to put the whole thing together, and Taylor says it looks about ten years old, but I don't really care. The point is – I went out and did it, Dad, like you always said to do. Now I shall take my earthenware vessel to Dr Mafouz at the museum here, and he'll tell me how old it is without even looking. I don't know what type of doctor he is, but he just has to sniff a thing to tell how long it's been hiding from the light. I know you'd like him. He reminds me of you, Dad. He humours me about my excavations. He*

113

*says we have to keep digging because the truth is always a bit further down than we thought. (Who would argue with that one?) Dr Mafouz is on the trail of the Queen of Sheba who once lived here. I hope he finds what he's looking for.*

*I think that's probably enough about pottery. Like I said, it was just to pass the time in a constructive way. I'm writing this letter in the library at Singapore barracks, which I visit as often as I can. (They say it's the best library between Cairo and Calcutta.) I like finding things out, I think, whereas most of the lads don't give a monkey's – certainly not about history or anything like that. Taylor says he's not being paid enough to worry about those things, but I'm not so sure. Isn't it important to see things from the other person's point of view before you make up your mind? Isn't it, Dad? Taylor says – what's the point of seeing stuff from the other bloke's point of view if you're just going to shoot him anyway? As I say, Taylor usually has things pretty clear in his own mind.*

*What else can I tell you? I expect you already know the situation is getting worse here. I hope you're keeping the newspaper reports, although I don't suppose they tell the real story. We haven't lost any of our lads yet, but we heard they're going to step up our night patrols – that's when things will get more serious. Last week, two men shot the speaker of the parliament because they believed he was a stooge of the Crown. He was at the head of a big funeral procession when they gunned him down. Then the crowd killed the two men who shot him. They threw them both from the balcony of a mosque. That's the way it is here – dog eat dog. As usual, we had to go in and clean up the mess.*

*Well, that's about it for now. I have to get back to Waterloo barracks for an evening roll call, so I shall leave you now in the hope that you're both well and happy, as I am. There's a beautiful civilian in the library. She takes her book to the table by the window and sits down alone. I've sat there myself lots of times.*

*This is from your loving son, Callum.*

He put down his pencil and screwed up the pages of his letter as he watched her. She sat facing him three desks away and slightly to one side. Her head was bowed over a book she held open with both hands. There was something about her that would have set her apart in any public place – a physical reticence at odds with her presence. It was as if she aimed to make herself invisible, as small as possible. Callum didn't know what it was exactly. He only knew she was new and unexpected. She was no army wife in pink shorts and flip-flops. Her hair, cut just long enough to sweep behind the ear, appeared to be damp, as if she was seeking refuge from the lightest of storms. The clock said quarter to four – the whole world was asleep. The library achieved a near perfect quiet in the depths of the day. And still she hadn't turned a page, hadn't moved a muscle. Callum made up his mind to approach her. He didn't ask himself why. He was about to get up when he saw she was crying. She who hadn't stirred for such a long time began to rock back and forth at her table, her shoulders rising and falling until she cast off a strap of her dress. The first tears clung to her cheeks for a few seconds before falling from her face. By the time Callum got there the pages of her book were wet. He wasn't sure what to do – he wanted to restore the strap of her dress, but in the end he cupped his hands around her shoulders, close to, but not touching, her skin. When her breathing became more regular he sat on the edge of the table and waited until she looked up at him. Only then did he prise the book gently from her grasp and turn it over on the table. She was pushing her chair back, but something must have stayed her – some instinct she had never trusted before.

'No, please –' she said, reaching for her book.

'*Lord Jim* – it can't be *that* terrible, can it?' he said, laughing now to encourage her. Outside, he placed the volume between them on a low wall separating the library from the basketball court. 'I'm sure it has a happy ending, anyway.'

For a moment Jacinta watched six young soldiers improvise a game of volleyball beyond the tall mesh. Just their shorts, socks and boots they wore, joshing each other in the golden light of afternoon. Two of the soldiers held high a piece of old net, lowering their arms whenever play stopped.

'Do you think so?' she came back finally. 'It isn't actually for me. In fact –' She hesitated before rallying strongly. 'It's for a friend.'

Callum drew his knee up and rested his chin on his forearm. 'Let me see,' he said. 'A blind archaeologist is doing some research. He sends his best, his only, friend to a library, the finest between Cairo and Calcutta, where she breaks down and cries.'

Then Jacinta cut across him as if from far away. 'The friend,' she said, 'meets a sympathetic stranger, a soldier. He is younger than she is, but she doesn't mind – any port in a storm, she says, wiping away tears. Is she crying for herself or her blind friend?'

'We don't know, Callum said. 'We can't ask her. Does she know, or remember, how beautiful she is?'

Beyond the mesh, the tennis net was too heavy. Jacinta watched the squaddies give up on their volleyball game.

'Your blind friend –' Callum went on. He was poking the end of a bootlace into an eyelet already filled, and asking how he had got to this point, or this place. He had no relevant training or experience. Everything was licensed. Nothing was proscribed. 'Don't tell me – he's dying of something, isn't he?'

She regarded him then and caught him at it – he was searching the fingers of her left hand for a wedding ring, as if he couldn't quite believe there wasn't one. That's how it must have looked to her.

'My word –' she said, her tone changing subtly to acknowledge their little game had concluded. 'I'd have thought most of our brave boys exercised just enough imagination to lurch from one day to the next. Shouldn't you be cleaning your rifle this afternoon, or crawling under barbed wire with boot polish on your face?'

116

He was gazing beyond the basketball court towards a cluster of apartments that accommodated the officers and the officers' wives.

'I'm not stationed at Singapore barracks,' he said. 'I'm based at Waterloo barracks.'

'Don't tell me –' she said, and still it was there in her voice – the need to hurt everyone, starting with herself. 'You came here to the library because you wanted to get away from the others. You were writing to your sweetheart back home.' Oh, yes – she was ready to lash out and wound. She was ready at all times to damage her own interests, it seemed. 'No, let me guess – you were writing a letter to your parents. Dear Mum and Dad. Looks like I've made a terrible mistake. War is hell – your loving son Callum.'

He rounded on her then with his angry eyes. Above the officers' quarters the sky was turning red again.

'I'm sorry –' she said. 'I saw the name tape in your cap.'

He pulled his beret from the epaulette of his shirt. 'So now you have an advantage over me,' he said, looking away.

'I'm sorry,' she repeated. 'Look – my name's Jacinta.'

'The truth is,' he said, 'I don't actually have a sweetheart. I don't have any parents, either. At least – I never knew them. I have to sew those name tapes on all by myself.' He turned to face her again and grinned. 'Don't worry, though – it's not as bad as it sounds.'

'You've been very kind to me, Callum.'

'I am kind,' he said, laughing now. 'It's one of my good points.'

'Don't you feel terribly alone?' she said.

'Me? I could probably ask you the same question, couldn't I?'

She picked up the library book that, along with isolation itself, was responsible for bringing them together.

'My turn to apologise,' he said, rolling up his beret and slapping his hand with it repeatedly. 'I think I'd better go now.'

'Will I see you again?' she said, hugging her book to her tummy as two silver fighter planes swooped lowish overhead – showing off, really – with an insolent roar of jet engines.

'Would you like to?' he said automatically – a blind man could see she was preparing to forget all about him for a decade or more.

'Very much,' she said, jumping down from the wall and backing off as two more jet planes made an ear-splitting pass on their way to RAF Khormaksar and the marshes vivid with flamingos.

Could he believe her? He watched her all the way to the fence, practising her name – to say it was like biting into a pear. He heard the wolf-whistles from the gatehouse. He should have walked beside her as far as the road and hailed a taxi for her with his manly shout. What was happening he failed to challenge – he didn't know how. In all this he didn't think of himself because he had been taught not to. His first instinct was to watch over her – that was the upshot. Yes, he would save Jacinta from her loneliness. He would track her down via the library – she must have meant him to do that. He would ask nothing of her, keeping nothing from her. He would honour her and make her happy. To love and be loved – how hard could it be, after all? In Callum's pocket were the discarded pages of a letter – they made him feel foolish now. He didn't mind that because they were honest pages, true in their own way. Yes – true to him.

NIGHT. IN THE BUNK BED above his own, Innes masturbated almost noiselessly. Callum waited until he heard all the light snores before slipping out of bed. From his locker between the bunks he retrieved an earthenware vessel – he carried the object as far as the balcony. Over Waterloo barracks the night clouds scudded as Callum peered down, vest and underpants starkly luminous in the moonlight. He saw the empty swimming pool below. He dropped his vase without hesitating. If anyone – Taylor, for instance – had asked him why he did that, he wouldn't have been able to say. It was just a feeling. It was something about moving up, or moving on – that's all Callum knew. By the time his vase struck the blue tiles at the deep end of the swimming pool he was back at his bunk. There was a brief kerfuffle in and outside the dormitory below – then everything went quiet.

## ❧ A HANDFUL OF SAND ❦

NOLAN LOWERED HIMSELF TOWARDS a big chair. It was a botched throne, he concluded with a mounting sense of dread – a cushioned instrument of torture or execution. He peered at the glass screen or wall in front of him. Beyond it was a great darkness. He was staring, Nolan decided, at an empty aquarium. Again he tried to ignore his image in the glass. He could see the reflection of the adjutant at his shoulder like a monkey with a swagger stick.

'Just make yourself comfortable, Mr Nolan.'

'But this is absurd – you realise that, don't you?'

'Please – just take your time.'

'No, look – this is an absolute dead loss. It's a crazy idea –'

'I'm very sorry you feel that way, sir – seeing as it's the only lead we have to go on at this point in time. Clever bastards, I think you'll agree, sir. Still, if you didn't get to see his face as such.' The adjutant smacked the back of the chair with his stick. 'It's just the voice we're interested in, Mr Nolan, in that case. And the eyes, of course –'

'I don't actually remember what colour the eyes were.'

'I should forget about the colour if I were you, sir. Their eyes are not like ours, I think you'll find –'

'What? Just the voice, then, is it?'

'The eyes and the voice, sir – as I say.'

'But they could always disguise their voice, couldn't they? They could adopt some phony accent beyond that glass wall.'

'And why would they want to do a thing like that, sir? Unless, of course, they had something to hide.'

'But this is ludicrous, don't you see? How do you expect to know what their real voice sounds like compared to their pretend voice?'

'Perhaps that's why we asked you along, sir.'

'Look – they probably can't even speak English properly.'

'I think you'll find they speak it well enough when they want to, sir. Just try to concentrate now, please, and soon it will all be over. You want to put yourself back on that crane as far as possible.'

The lights went out as if by a prearranged signal – a wave of the baton, a flick of the stick. Nolan closed his eyes for a second and then opened them again just to check. Absolute dark. He began to panic and to perspire. He was at sea. He was inside a limitless aquarium, underwater, very far down. Above the surface, night descended. He had been diving all day, kicking deeper, scooping out water, hoping for sand. And each time he broke the surface he saw the same thing. He clawed harder and faster at the sea, heart racing, lungs bursting, until he found the bottom and seized his handful of sand. Yes, yes – he pushed off again and kicked out, contented now and hell bent on reaching the surface. He pierced the night with his fist. The air was dense with locusts – already they clung to Nolan's face and arm. He could see his father. His father was standing in the rowing boat like a scarecrow in a blizzard. Again Nolan waved. He had been all the way – he could prove it. He opened his hand. What? None left? All the little grains had leaked out. They were sinking one by one to the bottom of the ocean. No, no – he had been there. Yes, yes – all the way. There was no question about it. He could prove it this time. He opened his mouth and let the sand rush out in a dark flood.

Still his heart raced. Beyond the glass wall the lights came on – there was nowhere to hide inside the dazzling cube that confronted Nolan. He found himself looking at a man with a scarf around his face. The man sat on a stool on the other side of the glass partition, a microphone in front of him, a hardback book on his lap. His eyes were jet black and set close – they peered unseeing from behind the wall. Abruptly the man began to speak in expressionless English, his voice relayed by loud speakers from one side of the wall to the other.

'My name is Abdul bin-Zalaq al-Khalifa. I invoke *habeas corpus* – as is my right under British law. I am innocent of any crime.'

He opened the book and began to read like a solemn schoolboy. Nolan badly wanted to laugh his head off, to hammer at the wall, to smash the glass and let the water pour out. The masked man ended his recital. He stood up and bowed, his book lying open now on the stool. A couple of things really mattered suddenly to Nolan.

'That book –' he said turning to face the adjutant. 'What is it, and why did you choose it?'

IT WAS SHORTLY BEFORE DAWN in Hedjuff. Above the hills the sky was waking up. Jacinta watched the lights go out one by one around the harbour – what was visible of it. She disregarded him at first. He sat beside her on the verandah, a towel wrapped around his waist.

'I managed to track down the novel for you,' she said at last.

Nolan drew the library book towards him across the table. 'I saw that,' he said. 'Thanks. It sounds ridiculous, I know – I think I may have been dreaming about it just now.'

'You were talking in your sleep,' she said, switching off the radio.

'I was helping the military cops here to stage an identity parade, for Christ's sake. But that isn't the best, or worst, bit. I was bringing up the sand again for my Dad –'

'Poor Ben —' she murmured. 'Still bringing up the black sand.'

He looked for her then, but she had turned to face the morning.

'Have you given any thought to the idea of going home, Jacinta?'

'A BOAC VC-10 has exploded on the tarmac at Khormaksar.'

He closed his eyes and breathed in deeply. He admitted it — he hadn't thought about Megan for such a long time. Now her features wouldn't quite come together in his imagination.

'Did they give any details?' he said.

'No —' Jacinta said. 'Not really.'

He saw her shake her head — he used to think it was so pretty — against the blood red sky. It was important to look to the future, he told himself — what was left of it. He didn't press her at this time. It wouldn't have been right. He picked up his book and left his wife to greet the dangerous day without him.

# 3 | Hildegaard

'Pray for me too.'

ALL BUT ALONE, UNENCUMBERED by family or friends, the Bedouin let out a moan and died between the sheets without further protest or comment. Hildegaard consulted her watch. When she checked his pulse, the old man's arm felt as light and dry as pumice. No need to close his eyes – he had managed that all by himself. Did he know she was with him at the end? She had promised she would be present. It was a humiliation, or at least an indignity, to have a young woman sponge the flesh that had turned against him. But was she still there, the nurse? Perhaps she made the same easy promise at bedsides up and down the ward. What's that? No more light? None anywhere? Hold fast, then, and stand ready. Hello, darkness.

In a distant room a telephone rang and rang unanswered. Before she drew the sheet over his head, Hildegaard wiped the spittle from the dead man's lips. These past few days she had come to view him as a tree brought low finally not by disease but by the march of time. He was an arrangement of driftwood now – Hildegaard saw him as an old boat washed up on the shore. She had a sponge in her hand, but she was unwilling to use it. She was unusually reluctant to finish washing the old man's skin – that's how it made itself known to her, this latest loss of faith. Why bother? What difference would it make? It was something new in her, this impulse to set the necessary above the ideal. No doubt it was via a series of details or modest incidents that the crisis would develop and deepen from here. There would be no bells, no flashing lights. She who had so assiduously *believed* now balanced a bowl of water with maximum uncertainty on a clipboard and slipped through the curtain that gave onto the ward. Cowed by the afternoon's heat, the air hid below the beds before being sucked up by fans and squirted this way and that in merciful currents. Here and there the sunlight breached the shutters, splashing the floor tiles with drops of fire. Convinced of a change in her, Hildegaard walked the length of the ward as slowly as possible, inviting judgement with every step. No one spoke out against her. At the desk just inside the doors she surrendered her bowl and clipboard to the Filipina orderly before backing away towards the stairs.

'Time of death was sixteen-o-five. I'll notify Dr Aziz myself —'

In the toilet on the landing she examined her face in the mirror above a small basin. Everything was in order. Forehead, eyebrows, nose, lips, chin and ears — they were just as she remembered them. Now she searched her eyes for a mote of apostasy. She saw nothing, no speck of betrayal. She took some comfort from that. At the same time she felt a new anxiety she associated with her mission, lowering the zip of her uniform and eyeing the prickly heat rash that climbed above her chest towards her throat. Everything touched her a great deal. At the edge of her vision a cockroach raised its antennae above the plughole. Hildegaard opened both taps as wide as possible.

Dear God — give me the strength to do Your work. As she sat in a pew in the chapel attached to the St Stephen's Mission hospital she experienced an unwelcome chill — beside her was the cold store that served as a short-term morgue. No one, she assured Him, comes to this place. It's just You and me. On the cross in front of her, God's son bled from the usual injuries to hands and feet. On the altar were the two big candles, plus a box of matches Hildegaard had put there herself. Now her eye went back and forth between the candles and a great bible on a cedar rack. Only look at me, won't You? That was her opening move — it made perfect sense. Then she lit the candles and invited Him to blow them out, or at least have them flicker, but again He passed up the opportunity to make His presence known to her. Perhaps it was unreasonable to expect Him to declare His hand

126

in so trivial a way. Cue bells and flashing lights. She would have to throw herself, Hildegaard decided, from the highest tower, waiting until the last moment of her descent to feel His strong arms around her. In her imagination Hildegaard saw her body dash itself on the ground. In the chapel she gave out a little cry. Suddenly she saw it as a rip-off, or a swindle, that He would catch her only if she was ready to die for Him. Yes, it was a new crisis. In the tiny chapel Hildegaard blew out two candles – one for yesterday, one for tomorrow.

'SO, WHAT EXACTLY ARE YOU TELLING ME?'

Mathieson eased the carbon paper from the foolscap pad, then ripped out the job sheets and gave them to Nolan with his question. From the dry dock at the limit of the Port Trust compound came a clamour of worked metal. Nolan's eye jumped from the windows of the tugs, flashing in the sun at the moorings behind his colleague, to the fiery splutter of an oxy-acetylene torch high on No. 3 slipway.

'I'm telling you I know who he is, Duncan.'

He saw a coolie's arm rise and fall up there while the report of the hammer, not quite in step, hurried to keep pace with the action. The harbour breeze, when it came, was unusually rank.

'Now, hold on a wee minute,' Mathieson said, cocking his head sceptically. 'I thought you never actually got to see his face.'

'I didn't need to see his face. I know who he is because I've met him – I mean I'd met him before.'

Sparks flew from a heavy tool in a hanger. On the quay beside the tugs, Mathieson signed his own set of harbour discharge papers in the book. He tore two or three sheets out and turned, waving his papers at the sky, towards the *Shearwater*. 'Five minutes, Ibrahim –' he called. He looked hard at Nolan. There was a moaning of hulls as the two tugs rubbed up against the tyres of the jetty. 'I'll go with

Ibrahim. You take the *Kingfisher* and bring up the rear. We'll see her as far as the headland, OK? She's on her own after that −'

'You know Jacinta came out in her?' Nolan commented, folding and unfolding his papers.

'The *SS Oriana*?'

'Do you think it's possible that big tub might be cursed?'

'No theatrics, please, Ben − just keep in touch out there.'

In the wheelhouse of the *Kingfisher* Phineas sang tenor. Suddenly he leaned out, bald and grinning, with a lifejacket over his head.

'Shipshape, Mr Ben − catch a fish today for sure, *bwana*.'

'Very good, Phineas −' Nolan turned his back on the oily swell. Across his affairs stretched a series of lengthening shadows. How he wished his wife could be on the big boat waiting to quit the harbour and the bay. 'Bloody comedian,' he remarked of Phineas, very low.

'How is Jacinta, anyway?' Mathieson asked dutifully.

'Oh, she loves it here. She gets a bit bored, that's all.'

'Settling in all right − give or take the odd insurrection?'

'Shopping for curtains, don't you know?' Nolan heard Ibrahim fire up the *Shearwater*. He had to press on with what mattered most to him. 'He tried to warn me off up there, Duncan. He said he'd *get to* me − whatever that means.'

'Otherwise you'd have fingered him by now, right?'

'Naturally.'

'He's already got to you, Ben.'

'I just don't want anyone to get hurt − especially me.'

'What about the poor bugger who swung from our crane?'

And suddenly his new dream − new and improved − was in his head again. Nolan saw his father's boat drift empty or abandoned in a blizzard of locusts. Then Phineas started the engine − immediately Nolan tasted the diesel fumes rising up from under the quay.

'I didn't have to tell you, Duncan.'

'So why did you?'

'Just think – I'm the only man alive who knows who he is.'

'But now *I* know that *you* know –'

'You don't know the name, though. Shall I burden you with the whole truth – I mean in case anything should happen to me?'

'Thanks for sharing all this with me, Ben. I think we both know what needs to happen, don't we? I mean ASAP. Now, let's go fish.'

PERHAPS IT WAS INEVITABLE, or at least fitting in a perverse way, he should show up, uninvited, tonight of all nights. Far better for him, she told herself, if he had been a small continent away. As the pink sunlight flooded her room, Hildegaard stepped into a red dress and raised the zip between her shoulder blades. After she pulled on her high-heels she gauged the effect in a mirror. The look was signature fresh still, with just the right dosage of calculated allure. Hildegaard approved it. With the setting sun flashing from the mirror she swept her wet hair straight back from her forehead. Her earrings were tiny seahorses of jade. As she pressed her painted lips together she tasted the promise, bitter as ashes, of the night to come.

Nolan showed up unexpectedly. She wanted to be sure about the unexpectedness of his being there. She wanted to be certain she had done nothing to encourage him. She held a menthol cigarette above her as she leaned forward to brush his cheek with hers, catching the notes of aftershave and whisky before he pulled back to assess, or to reassess, her look. His short-sleeved shirt bore a horizontal crease as if it had come directly from a box. Khaki pants, on the other hand, hung carelessly ironed, gathering in folds on the scuffed desert boots that were his trademark. Once again Hildegaard had the impression of a strong frame loosely clothed. He was well enough put together, she noted, as if for the first time – it was important she logged every signal, or symptom, of the night. Sill he said nothing. His car keys he swung violently around his index finger.

'I'm afraid you can't come with me tonight, Ben.'

He smiled anyway. She even thought he might be a little drunk.

'If you know him,' Nolan said, 'promise me you'll have nothing more to do with him.' He watched her crush her cigarette on the lip of an incense burner. 'You look different,' he added. 'That's funny – I don't think I've seen you smoke before.'

'He's just a journalist,' she insisted.

'So you do know him?' He closed his hand around his keys, as if to mark the end of one phase and the beginning of another. She was trying to put herself in his shoes, or his *boots* – he saw that. No doubt she thought him much too simple an invention.

'Can I go now?' she asked sweetly. 'I do have other friends.'

'Let me drive you,' he said, inspired.

'I don't think so, Ben.'

'Then let me pick you up afterwards. Please –'

'Are you OK,' she said. 'You're acting a little irrationally, don't you think?'

'Let me in, Hildegaard.'

'Ben –'

'I don't care if you despise me,' he said without flinching. 'If you despise me – that's OK. I can change, I swear –'

She drove just ahead of him in the gathering dusk as the curfew descended on Crater, the street lamps, lit only recently, going out in batches. At the roadblock in the gorge four keen feds flagged down her Volkswagen. Nolan pulled in behind her. He said she was with him. He needn't have – she held up her hospital pass and told them he was with her. The boulevard of sandbags fell behind. Hildegaard

130

searched her mirror, but it was too dark now to see his face. On the dual carriageway, after he had drawn level with her, she put her foot all the way down and raced him from the shadow of the volcano to the first lights at Ma'ala.

UP ON THE ROOF, THE BIRTHDAY PARTY took hold. Nolan leaned against the low wall between two coloured light bulbs and watched the arrivals sip their drinks and nod their heads and cast around for somewhere to lose the ash from their cigarettes while Sinatra sang It Was A Very Good Year. Above the scene, the sky went from blue to black. There was no breeze – in an atmosphere of convivial languor, the music itself circulated among the guests like a charming hostess. Nolan turned his back on the do. Beyond the dual carriageway and the reclaimed land the lanterns of the dhows kissed their reflections in the shallows all at once, together, with an effortless intimacy that mocked him. Then he felt her elbow nudge his arm. Hildegaard was beside him with two tall drinks. Behind her was a birdlike man.

'Thanks – I was beginning to think you'd run out on me.'

'Ben – this is Dr Aziz.'

Nolan was sure he recognised the gaunt figure with hand held out. Hadn't he seen him jump down from an ambulance once upon a time? 'You know, doc –' he said. 'Sometimes I think Hildegaard deliberately keeps her male friends in separate boxes.'

'Like spiders?' Aziz suggested. 'For their own protection?'

'Forgive me,' Nolan went on. 'If I'd known it was your birthday I'd have brought something – a tail to pin on the donkey, perhaps.'

'Oh, I think we can forgive you,' Aziz said smoothly.

'Actually, Ben –' Hildegaard said. 'I suspect birthday presents are far too *bourgeois* for the good doctor. I kid you not – this is a man who, rumour has it, sleeps below a picture of Che Guevara.'

'As a matter of fact, there is nothing *bourgeois* about growing old, my dear. Even the most ardent subversive has been known to mark his own birthday. A few friends, a few drinks – what say you, Ben?'

They were standing side by side at the wall, gazing at the lights and the pretty reflections of the lights, with their coloured drinks in their hands. Along the dual carriageway immediately below sped a convoy of armoured personnel carriers, heading for Crater.

'Would you excuse us now, doc?' Nolan said. 'I try to find myself alone with someone of the opposite sex at around this time of night. In case the volcano decides to go up at short notice –'

He took her arm and led her from the wall and held her tightly until she stopped fighting him. The roof space was filling up rapidly around them. Someone, somewhere, had upped the volume of the music. They were alone together in the cosmopolitan crowd.

'When,' Nolan said, 'are you going to tell me why you're mixed up with these people?'

'Which people?' she said. 'Dr Aziz is a work colleague of mine.'

'You should hear yourself,' he said. 'Always the same defensive tone in your voice. Defensive and evasive and a little smug –'

'I told you not to come here tonight, Ben. I tried very hard.'

'You wanted me to come tonight. Why can't you admit it?'

'That drink – I believe it might have affected your reason.'

She slipped from his arms. He saw her eyes widen – he followed her gaze to the top of the stairs where a committee of welcome, some clapping enthusiastically, parted for the latest arrival. Acknowledging applause to left and right, Basim Mansouri edged closer and closer, his bottle of Coca-Cola rising from moment to moment in an ironic toast. Nolan laughed – he had to. He looked at her finally. Had she designed the evening's outcomes deliberately to humiliate him? Now Basim was leaning forward to brush her jade earring with his lips.

132

'Ah, yes – Ben Nolan, isn't it?' The journalist smiled, draping an arm around her bare shoulders. 'I've heard such good things about you from Hildegaard, Ben –'

The music fell off. Aziz was beside them, beating the nearby air in an appeal for quiet. Various guests murmured appreciatively.

'Dear friends – please. Gather round now, I beg you.' Ditching urbanity for a type of scornful passion, Aziz nodded, eyes shining, forehead filmed with the lightest dew. He lifted his glass as he went on. 'To a fearless journalist who simply can't stop winning awards –' Nodding, beaming, he redirected their spirited applause with a deft gesture towards the man beside him. 'What was it this time, Basim? After all, one can hardly keep up –'

The award-winner dismissed their attentions with a little wave.

'To the truth,' Aziz proposed harshly. 'And all who sail in her.'

Nolan gulped down the air so lacking in oxygen. He didn't look at her. He didn't look back. He lurched down the steps and was sick in the dirt beside the Land Rover. The music took up again above – Nolan imagined them dancing cheek to cheek to Norwegian Wood, with all the others standing back in an admiring circle. He wiped his mouth and turned the key. There was nowhere to go – nowhere he wanted to be. He hit the dual carriageway and headed for Hedjuff, his home. On the way he had to stop. Lying in the road was a dog, pretty far gone. Nolan had to decide whether to run it over or not.

## ❧ REGARDLESS OF CHE ❦

IN THE SPECULATIVE LIGHT FIRST THING she lay on a damp sheet, perspiration at her throat, her head at the wall below the brownish newspaper cutting with its profile and portrait of Che Guevara. She had been there, numb, since the small hours, unwilling to stir, while she waited for Basim to touch her. He lay on his side, arm beneath her neck, his fingers grazing her shoulder using the lightest contact. His breathing was shallow – Hildegaard began to think he might be hooked on a vision of his own success or else in thrall to a dream of his own glory. She must have dozed off finally because now she was alone on the bed. The new day hung tensely in the room. A window was open, but no breeze made it past the fly screen. For a comforting moment Hildegaard listened to the random hum of traffic from the dual carriageway below. She was about to get up and escape when she saw his head climb like a dark sun above the mattress.

'Pray for me too,' she whispered, a little appalled now by what she was doing, and by what she was capable of doing. She watched his head rise and fall like that in the thickening light until he got up finally and stretched his lean frame. 'Naked before God?' she said. 'I should imagine it's forbidden.'

'Everything is forbidden,' he murmured, apparently indifferent to her challenge. 'Everything is forbidden, nothing is revealed –'

He sat beside her on the bed and stroked her thigh through the sheet. She let him do it. She wanted him to do it – it was a necessary thing. His head was bowed, his eyes shut. It was the cool delicacy of his disregard that alarmed her, alerting her to a present danger. Her loyalty – did he judge it misplaced all of a sudden? Did it no longer flatter his ego or suit his purpose she should be there under his hand?

'What exactly are you doing here, I wonder?' he said at last.

'Don't you want me here?' she said, drawing up the sheet.

'Last night I asked you something important,' he said.

Then it came back to her – what he had said. The images – she tried to banish them, but without success. She was obliged to run the historical sequence one more time inside her head.

'You asked if I had surgical experience – as a nurse.'

'I asked if you could be relied on in future. I asked if we could count on you. Can we, Hildegaard? How far will you go?'

She was wet, dripping wet, from the steaming water in the tub – the metal tub was on the grass above the apple trees. She was giddy, too. Didn't her brother neigh and whinny as he bore her, soapy still, down the hill on his back? It was winter. How she squealed. At the bottom of the slope were the patches of snow lying undiscovered by the sun. In the wood it was darker. They were moving so fast below the bare trees. There were no leaves left to fall up there – not a one. Her big, beautiful brother laid her gently down on a carpet of dead leaves beneath a canopy of boughs. He undid his belt and pulled up his shirt and pressed a hand to her mouth. 'Can I count on you?' he asked her, his teeth reddened by the berry. And again, harder: 'Can I count on you, little sister?'

She heard a bicycle below – just a bell, disembodied, as it were, in the white heat – and felt Basim's hand leave her at last.

'Why so unhappy, nurse?' he enquired with concern, wiping the tears from her cheeks with his thumbs.

'I don't know,' she told him, laughing now.

'Do you miss someone suddenly?' he asked.

'Hell, no –' she said. 'Nothing like that.'

Time after time he bore down on her. Where was the weight of him, she asked – his penetrating heft? No doubt he carried it within him, husbanding it in muscles, bones and blood. He didn't affect her deeply. Soon he stopped, sat up, and reached for his shirt. Perhaps he didn't want to hurt her. Yes, she said – that would come later.

'Won't you tell me about your award?'

They got dressed on either side of the bed, Hildegaard seeking refuge behind a screen of lacquered bamboo.

'My dear, inquisitive nurse – is that the best you can do?'

135

'Please tell me – what did you write?'

'I wrote an article for a Beiruti journal – a regional review of our economic prospects. All very respectable and dull, you can be sure.'

'Dull if not for you.'

'Of course, I slipped in certain insights along the way. What did they expect? Because we do *need* a new high commissioner here, do we not? A man with a past but no future, let's say – a man who will draw a line in the sand and present us with the destiny we demand.'

'We?' she said, clipping on her small earrings of jade.

'First they must revoke the ban on the NLF.'

As she sat on the bed she reviewed her approach. Abruptly she peeled off her earrings. Their role in all this – it was ended. 'So are you saying you're NLF now?' she asked.

'Are you interviewing me, perhaps, nurse? Or are you pumping me for information? I said they have to lift the ban, that's all –'

'And will they?'

He rolled across the bed and zipped up her dress for her. 'They can't get away from here quickly enough. Everyone knows they can't wait to get back to their gardens and the rain.' He nuzzled her neck tenderly, and she felt his hot breath at her ear. 'Poor Harold Wilson – he so wants to bring his brave boys home, but he has to keep faith for as long as Uncle Sam prosecutes his nasty little war further east.' Now he gripped her chin and turned her face towards his. 'Shoulder to shoulder, Hildegaard, policing the globe – are we really prepared to believe they're making the world a safer place?'

'Is that what you wrote in your article?'

'Oh, no – it's important we subversives take up a wide range of positions. Ask Che Guevara up there on the wall. Ask the journalist who stopped short of having sex with a nurse – who merely wanted to learn how far she was prepared to travel in a particular direction.

Or was he, perhaps, rendered impotent at a stroke by the shocking whiteness of her skin?'

She looked into his eyes and felt something like pity for him. All was clear to her. In one sense all was clear – at least she knew how far she would go. 'Now you're in danger of offending me,' she said.

'But can I count on you, Hildegaard? That's the thing.'

'Put it this way –' she said, casting around for her keys. 'There's nothing I wouldn't do if the cause is just.'

FROM THE FLOOR OF THE LIVING ROOM in his flat in Ma'ala the Lebanese doctor watched her leave. She had to step over his legs to reach the door. Aziz threw off the blanket and raised himself up. He used a record sleeve drawn from the stack to cover his nakedness as he confronted Basim Mansouri in the bathroom.

'So?'

'You were right. She has some surgical experience.'

'And?'

'And nothing – we wait and see.'

'I don't trust her, Basim –'

'We know that already. Me – I admire her spunk. She wants to write her piece of history.'

'That's what I mean. And did you make love to her?'

The award-winning journalist shook his penis thoughtfully over the toilet bowl. 'My dear doctor –' he said in English. 'Do you want the nurse's help or don't you?'

'I was thinking of Hannan, that's all,' Aziz said, turning away to make sure it was hidden, this hint of a smirk, from general view.

'Then allow me to give you some advice,' Basim said, reverting icily to Arabic. 'Don't think of her. Not now, not ever. Is that clear?'

'Very. Thank you for pointing out the error of my ways.'

'Do try to remember, please – you're all washed up as a doctor. And you don't exist, politically speaking, unless I give the word. Am I right? So try not to fall out with me, birthday boy – not if you care to write your own little piece of history.'

In the doorway of a bathroom in a flat in the Ma'ala district of Aden, Aziz nodded. He smiled his hidden smile as he hugged Dean Martin's grinning face tighter to his groin. Funny – neither medical man nor recording artist could enter into each other's satisfaction.

## ❧ CHITS WITH EVERYTHING ❧

THE SEA WAS BLOOD WARM. The sky was the colour of water. Oona had commandeered two li-los, mauve and orange, from the Crescent Hotel. She sprawled face down with her cheek on the purple pillow, a lime green T-shirt pulled down prudently towards the backs of her knees, as, beside her at arm's length, Jacinta sculled the ocean with a desultory cupping action using just one hand.

Oona observed her friend with a single critical eye. Outside the zone covered by her bikini, Jacinta's skin was tanned in patches as if her body had mounted partial resistance to the sun. On her toes the red nail varnish had begun to distance itself from the cuticle. Was it a sign of neglect? As Jacinta's eyelashes fluttered involuntarily below her sunglasses Oona imagined her on the threshold of a dangerous dream. Just inside the shark net, floating high above the starfish and stingrays of Gold Mohur, the two drifted finger to finger – connected but not quite *together*, Oona decided. Given the lurid colouration of their respective rafts, they might have been visible from space.

'I really don't know, darling – to answer your painfully pertinent question. I have savings to draw on, of course, but I don't suppose they amount to very much. I just sign the hotel's chits – I'm signing my life away in some God-forsaken outpost of empire. Naturally, I stopped counting aeons ago. Chits with everything, chuck –'

'Has he telephoned you at all?'

Jacinta moved only her lips. It must have taken a considerable effort of will, Oona reasoned, to project the flickering recollection of someone else's husband against the curtain of her dream. What did she recognise there if not the yellowing fingers of Adrian Durbridge clamped around the cigarette at his lips? There was the suggestion, too, of contempt in his watery eye. Torn suddenly from his shoulder by a hostile breeze, his silk scarf rolled across the deck towards the rail and was lost at sea.

'You know – Adrian's not exactly flush,' Oona said loyally.

'But has he called you?' Jacinta insisted with an obscure zeal.

'He says it's rather difficult to get through. I did receive another nice postcard, though – from Brisbane, this time. I expect he's doing an audit of musical opportunities out there.'

'He really should have called you,' Jacinta said after a silence.

Again Oona felt a spark of feeling at the point where their bodies connected – a momentary flexing of the spirit in the face of a void. She had the unwelcome sensation she was attending the sickbed of her friend – only, this time it was for the last time. Into her head it popped like a presentiment of death without too much honour – this image of a silk scarf suspended forever in the stream.

'What will you do, Oona?'

'Exactly what I said I'd do, of course. I'm going to manage my boys. Someone's got to look after them until Adrian gets back.'

'I think you're very brave.'

'Ha – bravely foolish, you mean. At any rate, we have our first engagement here, I do believe. Pretty Flamingo, let it be known in all the land, are very much in business locally –'

'Couldn't you come to an arrangement with your hotel – I mean for dinners and dances and that type of thing?'

'Oh, but this is big stuff, Jacinta. The boys are slated to play at the army barracks here – doing their bit for the war effort.'

Even as she laughed, Oona felt her friend's hand slip from hers. She rolled over. There was no sky above her – only the light in layers the colour of a gull's wing. She watched Jacinta drag the sea across her stomach – now the water ran in broken streams from her hip.

'But tell me about *you*, darling –'

It was what she least wanted in life – to discover her friend was drifting beyond her reach. Looking back then she saw a leopard skin hair clasp in the form of a shield. She couldn't get it out of her eyes. It was all she could recall of their best time together. It struck Oona as the proof of beauty that it could be based on material evidence so scant. She heard a cry from the beach of a lost child for its mother. Paddling hard until she reached the orange li-lo, Oona restored her friend's hand to hers, squeezing tightly.

'Don't you miss England, Jacinta?' She badly needed someone, or something, to believe in at that time. When she didn't receive an answer to her question she was obliged to respond herself, on behalf of both of them. 'Oh, *no* –' she cried, splashing the sea fiercely with two feet. 'We don't miss it one little bit.'

IT MUST HAVE BEEN GETTING ON for noon. From the hot slopes of Shamsan Philip looked down on an empty reservoir, the geological centrepiece of Aden's municipal park. Beyond the scrub at the edge of the clearing the awnings and canopies of the *suq* threw a colourful ribbon around the heart of Crater. How exhilarating it was – the air up there throbbed with a collective suggestion of snakes and lizards, of dragonflies and softbills, of bee-eaters and fruitsuckers, of coneys and baboons. Philip looked behind him. Towards the upper reaches of the rock nothing was visible – all Philip could see was a harrowing profusion of light. Then he discovered another coiled fruit pod in his hand. He was reluctant to open the pod, to prise the white flesh from the seeds. He understood instinctively he should expect no comfort there – not from the shredding of natural tissues. How long had he been here? Seconds? Hours? It was hard to judge. Philip let the fruit fall and began his descent. Around the park at this height a collar of juniper trees offered welcome respite from the sun. Philip paused in the shade and studied the young man singled out by the glare in the arid basin below. His new friend was a son of the Crescent Hotel – Kenneth by name. Two inches tall from up there, Kenneth wore his Coca-Cola T-shirt and read aloud from a British forces orientation handbook he had borrowed from the hotel reception desk.

'Welcome to the Tawila Tanks –' He threw an arm wide as if to delimit his frame of reference. 'A collection of reservoirs within the park just south of the teeming market.' Now he scanned the line of trees above him in search of his musical friend. It was barely an hour since they had ingested the squares of blotting paper impregnated in the laboratory with a powerful hallucinogen and transported by jet plane from London in the stamp compartment of Kenneth's wallet. 'Formed centuries ago by masonry bonding to the living rock, these reservoirs can hold millions of gallons of rainwater, yet often remain dry from year to year –'

Up among the trees, Philip swallowed his saliva with a growing sense of jeopardy. The juice was suddenly too plentiful in his mouth, his hands were at once clammy and numb, and his brain had taken up a novel position inside his stomach. Was it an effect of the drug's onset he should develop a base preoccupation with bodily functions? Even now, for example, he was persuaded he was pissing himself –

he had to unbutton his pants and seek out the tiny organ curled up there as dry as any fruit pod. Although he understood it might have to get worse before it got better, Philip told himself he wasn't afraid. Someone should have advised him he was perfectly safe because he both admired his companion and loved himself without immoderate enthusiasm. An open mind, an even temper, a quiet self-regard, and an inherited respect for life and property – he had every quality for survival during the next two hours and more.

'Also in the municipal park is the Aden Museum –' Kenneth sat cross-legged on the baked earth, rocking backwards and forwards as he addressed the dark bulk of Shamsan. 'Built in 1930, it is home to rare pottery, coins, weaponry, soapstone carvings, calico and indigo dye works, frankincense, myrrh and other precious gums of Araby –'

Frankincense, myrrh – these two items sounded ideal to Philip. You could eat them, he fancied, or smoke them, or spread them on burned skin, or bathe in them if they rained down from the heavens in sufficient measure. Emerging from the trees with his hands full of coiled fruit pods, Philip approached his hotelier friend from the edge of the reservoir, flip-flops treacherous with sweat and dirt.

'Precious gums of Araby?' he enquired in a voice he struggled to recognise.

'That's what the man said.'

Kenneth closed his book. Still sitting on the ground, he hugged his shins and began to rock backwards and forwards a little quicker. Philip sat next to him and hugged *his* shins too. They both hugged their shins with the fruit pods scattered randomly around them.

'Do you think perhaps we should move on from here?' Kenneth asked, shivering, after half an hour in the ferocious light.

'I'm not really sure,' admitted Philip, curled up now on the hard ground with a forces handbook for his pillow.

'I'm not really sure either –' Kenneth said. 'I just think maybe we should move on from here.'

UPSTAIRS AT THE CRESCENT HOTEL, Jimmy lay on the bed with his hands behind his head, feeding his resentment. A man should have a plan, he told himself over and over again. The bed beside his was empty. The room next door resounded gently with a bassist's snores as Jimmy tiptoed along the dimly lit corridor, a guest towel around his waist. He didn't expect her to *want* him as such. He accepted he would have to force himself on her to some extent within the outline terms of his plan. He felt no real desire. Had you stopped him with a tape recorder in the hotel corridor and asked him where real desire lay, Jimmy wouldn't have been able to tell you.

He saw the light around the edge of her door. Turning the door handle, he imagined he might, after all, make her want him a little – she whose husband was always away. She was sitting up in a double bed reading a battered copy of *Valley Of The Dolls* as the door swung open with a creak. She took off her glasses and closed her book. She might almost have been expecting him, Jimmy decided desperately, shutting the door behind him before turning away immediately and banging his forehead twice against the wood. Because she had seen what was on his mind, Oona sat him down on the bed straight away and removed his towel and brought him off in under a minute using a deft manual technique. Still she wouldn't let him speak.

'Sssh –' she whispered. 'You're just in time.'

She covered him with her husband's robe. There was a knock at the door – after she had surveyed the room, as if to approve its status finally from a number of conflicting points of view, Oona called for the receptionist to enter. On the tray were the two champagne flutes and an open bottle that smoked agreeably from the neck.

'Champagne for two?' she said, laughing at her own managerial instinct, timing and touch. 'Always for two, Jimmy – that's the only way to do this thing.'

In a borrowed dressing gown that shamed him he watched her accept the notepad and a pen from the silent receptionist.

'Chits with everything,' Oona observed gaily, dismissing the man with a wave. 'Chits, chits, chits –'

## ❧ RUBY TUESDAY ❧

'SHUFFLE THE CARDS FOR ME, PLEASE, BEN –'

Sonny lit the candle on the table between them. She closed her eyes and drew a satin kimono closer around her throat and swayed rhythmically from side to side in her chair, and it seemed to Nolan she sank breath after breath towards a region of deep focus. Clearly she was concentrating very hard – it both impressed and unsettled Nolan she should take the whole thing so seriously. Although, as an Englishman, he was sceptical of the cards and psychologically hostile towards their hysterical lyricism, she insisted. After she had cooked, she asked if he had any questions about the path and pattern of his life, but he confessed to no special interest, looking to Mathieson to explain the range and scope of her attentions. There was no need to discuss what they all knew – one of them was increasingly subject to negative forces. Now the candle spat and its flame burned brighter. Nolan felt the urge to get up from the table and flee the room before it was too late. He heard Mathieson at the sink with the plates. What was he singing? He was singing a song on the radio – Forces Radio. Outside, it was getting dark, as quick as Rikki-Tikki-Tavi. Suddenly Sonny opened her eyes – she who so wanted to show Nolan the way. She shook her blue hair loose around her shoulders. She swept aside

144

the candle and three or four stray mah-jong tiles and laid her hands on the table with a glittering declaration of bracelets.

'Now cut the cards, please, Ben.'

'OK – I've thought of my key question now.'

'Continue to think of it, please –' Sonny drew the deck towards her and placed the top card face up on the table. 'This card is your significator, Ben. It's a snapshot of the now which shows something of who you are and where you've come from. It also suggests where you're going – depending on the other cards which will qualify it.'

Nolan scanned the picture card with its symbols, his eye darting from corner to corner in a search for positive indicators. Before him on the table, striding high above the world, a confident youth sallied forth towards a precipice, ignorant, to all intents and purposes, of the looming void and the dog that snapped its warning at his heels. The youth's gaze was raised skywards. His few possessions he carried in a kerchief on a pole. In his other hand was a rose. Above his head was an enigmatic zero and below his feet was a legend – The Idiot.

'The next two cards we call your crossing cards. These two cards tell us something about the barriers and obstacles you yourself have placed in the path of potential or happiness or fulfilment.'

Sonny laid a second card across the first. She didn't comment at that time – she waited for Nolan to react.

'The Hanging Man?' He saw a man – an old man – bound with rope suspended upside down from a tree.

'Of course,' Sonny said, 'its role and meaning are ambiguous.'

'Ambiguous?'

'It refers either to the man who is hanged or the man who does the hanging.'

'Ah, the hanger and the *hangee* – fascinating stuff.'

'Shall I continue with the reading, Ben?'

'Please – be my guest.' Yes, he had begun to resent her solicitous insights with their increasingly alarming undertow. It was common knowledge the cards lacked a definitive viewpoint, their allegorical significance subject at all times to speculation of the most dangerous type. Why – some experts held they could mean the exact opposite of what they appeared to mean depending on whether you looked at them this way up or that. 'I just hope you're going to make some kind of sense of all this for me, Sonny –'

She placed the third card diagonally across the second.

'A-ha,' Nolan said, nodding interestedly.

'The Tears of Blood,' Sonny confirmed.

'But what do they mean?' he asked her.

'Tell me –' she said. 'What do you see?'

'I see a young woman floating in a pool of her own tears.'

'The tears of blood –'

'Below a smiling sun –'

'Beneath the radiant sun –'

'But what does it all mean?'

'It means someone you know is in mortal danger, Ben.'

'Yes, I thought it might. Thanks for pointing that out to me.'

He didn't take himself to Crater immediately. He held off – he couldn't bring himself to visit the St Stephen's Mission hospital right away. When, eventually, he reached the curfew zone, his work shirt clinging to his back, no one even asked him to stop. How humid it had been of late. The roads were slick with the legacy of a light rain that must have come and gone without Nolan noticing it.

'What is your business here?' Hildegaard demanded tiredly.

They stood, arms folded, in a harshly lit corridor on either side of a wicker trolley filled with bloody sheets.

'I had a dream,' he said. 'I dreamt you were in mortal danger.'

'Ah, dreams –' she said, nodding.

'Look –' he said. 'The man is a known killer.'

'Because you saw him kill?'

'Yes, because I saw him kill.'

'Then why don't you report him?'

'Don't tell me –' he said. 'We must each of us make a stand.'

'Do you know what it takes for terror to triumph, Ben?'

'That people like me should do nothing?'

They had to make way for a porter pushing an empty stretcher on wheels. For a moment they regarded each other with something like tenderness in the harshly lit canyon.

'Do you imagine,' Nolan went on, 'I would ever have chosen to come here again unless I thought it mattered?'

'Have I ever encouraged you?'

'Perhaps only for a second when you forgot yourself at a party.'

'Ah, white lies –' she said, gripping the trolley with both hands.

'Do you remember you once told me I wouldn't like you if I got to know you better?'

'Go back to your wife, please, Ben.'

'Funny – I'm beginning to think you might have been right.'


IN A TAXI OPPOSITE THE MERMAID CLUB in Steamer Point, Jacinta tipped her driver and then hesitated on the back seat. Transfigured by the lights of the crawling cars, the rain sparkled at her window in chains of ruby and gold. Jacinta lowered the glass just an inch. The taxi driver glanced back at her, but she ignored him. She could see Callum behind a low picket fence outside the doors of the sprawling clubhouse. He stood alone in a persistent drizzle that darkened the shoulders of his shirt. Had he seen her? Jacinta saw him smile for a group of comrades seeking entry to the club. They took it in turn to ruffle his cropped hair with a concession to off-duty licence. He was configured so appealingly, Jacinta saw – it must have been difficult for the others to resist indulging themselves physically at his expense. Now he was bathed in red light, now he wasn't – above him was the winking sign that said NAAFI. He seemed to look right through her, Jacinta decided, his beret in his hand.

She gripped the door handle. If he had glimpsed her behind the beaded window it was already too late. For her part, she had only to open the car door and wave in order to seal their fate. Now he was gazing beyond her at the hissing traffic. He was willing her to drive on unacknowledged, to slip away unseen – that was how Jacinta saw it. His loneliness she perceived as an aura around him. It came and went with the neon letters above him. She heard the taxi driver gun the engine a little as she watched Callum attempt to light a cigarette – once, twice – with a book of matches in the rain. How he derided himself – Jacinta saw him shake his fist at the sky and hang his head theatrically. It was a performance. He had to have spotted her. He tucked his cigarette behind his ear and slapped his beret against his hand. Gradually, as Jacinta watched, his grin mutated in self-critical guises until, suddenly, he jumped the picket fence and ran across the road, dodging slow moving vehicles heading for this checkpoint or that, and knocked, beaming, on the jewelled window of her car.

INSIDE THE MERMAID CLUB FOR JUNIOR RANKS he directed her to a table in a recess hung with nets that had tiny shells in them. Driven by an unfamiliar emotion he was content to view as pride, Callum's blood hammered at his temples. He didn't need to look around the joint. He saw the eye of every mate or martinet trained on her legs and breasts. She had struck them momentarily dumb – that was her effect. Callum failed to acknowledge them in the heavy silence. Was it a mistake? He didn't look for Tom or Dick or Harry, each with a perfumed honey on his lap. They were all here, watching, waiting –

*Down in the jungle, living in a tent*
*Better than a prefab – no rent!*

And she was something utterly new. Under coloured lights her shoulders rose in suntanned bluffs above the sheer white of her dress. There was the pink scree over her chest where she had burned and peeled and burned again. The music took up unheralded. Behind a table beside the bar stood an unlikely looking disc jockey, a portable gramophone in front of him, a clutch of 45s in his hand.

'That's my pal Taylor,' Callum told her, wringing his beret.

Jacinta smiled, folding her arms carefully on the table around a white handbag. Her ears, neck, wrists and fingers – all were without ornament. How perfect and fresh she seemed to Callum. He had no idea what to do with her, but that was OK – he told himself it didn't matter. There was a dusting, slightly sparkling, of rain still visible in her hair and on her arms. Her lips were a colour he called coral.

'Aren't you going to sit down?' she asked him at last.

Beside the bar, Taylor was full of admiration and disapproval. 'At the library, you say? That's very romantic –' He nodded at the peppermint liqueur in Callum's hand and raised his eyebrows. 'She can read me a bedtime story any day of the week.'

'Will you look at that, Taylor? She sticks out like a sore thumb.'

'You should have thought about that before, boyo. Me – I could tell straight off.'

'Tell what?' Callum asked, bottle and cocktail glass in hand.

Taylor winked, relenting now, and pulled on his beer. 'Different class,' he said. 'I mean – what's her name?'

'Her name's Jacinta –'

'You see? What kind of a name is that?'

'I don't know – it's a bit special, isn't it?'

'Exactly, man – do you see it now?'

Then Dixon and Innes approached the bar in crisply laundered mufti and rubbed a hand each on Callum's head. 'Hey, Jock –' said the one, very excited. 'Don't you think you might be just a wee bit out of your depth there?' They nudged his ribs and knocked the wet snout from his ear and drew him closer and then pushed him away so casually. There was a part of him that everyone wanted, Callum saw then – a part that no one wanted to be.

'Jeez, Kennedy – she sticks out like a sore thumb in this hole.'

'I bet that ain't all that's sticking out like a sore thumb, boys.'

'Are you mentally handicapped?' Taylor said. 'Or just thick?'

'I'm afraid there's no ice yet,' he told her, sitting down opposite her with his back to the bar. Already it was all a mistake. She was so old. He tried not to think about that. He had only wanted to make her happy.

'It doesn't matter,' she told him, shrugging.

'Of course it does,' he said, angry with himself.

'Please –' she said. 'Don't keep apologising.'

'Sorry –' he said. 'Oh, shit.' He smacked his head and screwed up his face and when he peeked at her through half closed eyes she was laughing. 'How's your friend?' he said. He couldn't see why he had said that. It was because he didn't know what to say to her.

'Let me see, now –' she said. 'I have so few friends. You'd think I'd remember who they all were.'

'Your blind friend – the one who sent you to the library.'

Yes, it was all a mistake. She didn't comment on the status of her friend. Instead, she rose behind the table and held out her hand.

150

'I'm sorry –' Callum said, getting up fast. 'I don't think I really believed you would come tonight.' He crushed his beret and pushed it under his epaulette. 'Here – let me order a taxi.'

'Oh,' she said. 'Must we leave so soon?' She took back her hand. Her hand was trembling a little – they both saw it. 'Won't you dance with me?' she asked him. 'It would mean such a lot if you did.'

They came together under hostile eyes, Taylor himself looking on with a white handbag in his arms. After Callum grasped Jacinta's fingers and drew her near with all his fine feeling they rotated slowly beside the record player to a ballad of unrequited love. How easy it was to be a man, Callum decided. He had only to turn and turn in the face of their ribald whoops.

'I don't want to let you down in here,' he told her honestly.

'I know that,' she said, holding his shirt awkwardly. 'Should we give them something to talk about? I mean – after I'm gone?'

She led him through the open doors to where a patio glistened beside the unlit swimming pool, and they danced cheek to cheek in the lightest of rains. Nothing sexual passed between them – Callum was hopelessly aware of that. He wondered what she would think of him now. Although the music had stopped, they rotated as before.

'Will you do something for me?' she asked him.

'If I can,' he told her gravely.

'Will you take me swimming?'

'You mean here?' he said. 'Now?'

'Yes, now,' she said. 'Why not?'

'I can think of at least one good reason,' he said. 'I can't swim –'

He hung from the diving board – she swam towards him from the shallow end with her confident strokes. She invited him to let go and then she carried him on her back until she could touch the tiles again with her toes. He didn't know what it added up to, or whether he should feel happy or humiliated. He thought it must mean a lot to her. Yes, it was for her, not him. No one came. No one ridiculed him. He even began to think this was how it was meant to look and feel. They sat together, feet in the water, shivering in the rain, and listened to Ruby Tuesday until Taylor brought them a towel with NAAFI on it. When they got dressed it was an amusing thing – they had to cram their wet underwear into Jacinta's handbag.

IT WAS TAYLOR WHO TOOK THEM to Shanghai Sam's, an all-night hospitality venue located discreetly behind the Rock Hotel. He rang the bell twice at a side door and asked for Suzy Wong.

'I know it, Jacinta –' he admitted, very sincere, with the urge or need she had discovered in him to prefer right over wrong. 'Could be there are half a dozen Suzy Wongs all working these lousy back streets any night of the week, but this one is special. My Suzy – she sings for her supper while her little girl watches her alone through a chink in the curtain.' Here he made to punch Callum playfully, but stopped short of contact. 'Chinky-chink, boyo. No speaky English. Velly solly, can't string two words together.' Finally Taylor winked hard at Jacinta. 'Can she hell, girl –'

Then the sullen kid with the harelip came back. 'Miss Wong is very busy tonight. You want to wait, Johnny?'

'Too right we do, daddy-o. Just tell her Taylor is here and, yes, he'll wait –'

They stood a little apart below the ripped awning. The rain had stopped, and now the old stars stepped forward with a more youthful swagger. She saw how it was intended to be. It was Taylor's role, for example, to reaffirm certain fundamental rules of existence. So what if he had an unscheduled rendezvous with this or that camp follower in an out-of-bounds clip-joint at the foot of the slope below the high

152

commissioner's residence? Jacinta thought it the most exciting thing in the world she should be waiting in this very spot at this very hour. Yes, that was it – she was privileged to be here with Callum and his friend. She had asked for one night only. He knew it – Taylor knew it. Because he had the ability to see inside, Jacinta thought he might be a burly angel. His Old Spice reached her faintly in the cool night air. She was about to run when she felt him look inside her again.

'Come on, then, girl – I want you to meet my Suzy.'

They waited in silence on a red velvet banquette and sipped neat Gordon's from sherry glasses until the sullen kid stepped out of the gloom beyond the half drawn curtain. With him was a naval officer, very young, all in white – Jacinta watched him button up his jacket at the mirror. As he made to put his cap back on he caught her eye, forsaking the mirror as if she had cursed him with her woman's look. Already Taylor was on his feet. Now the kid beckoned him towards the dimly lit corridor.

'We can leave right now if you want to,' Callum told her.

There was a lucky gecko high up on the wall above the mirror. How clearly she saw things tonight – tonight of all nights. 'Oh, I'm not sure that would be quite right,' she said.

They sat side by side without speaking again until Taylor came back and ushered Suzy Wong proudly into the light. There she was, in presence compact, like a scaled-down version of herself, with her shy daughter just behind her. In the mother's black hair immediately above the brow was a deep silver lode, eloquent and shocking. She wore a man's dressing gown gathered up generously on the arm and belted tightly using a tasselled cord, the robe's silk plunging towards tiny feet encased in embroidered slippers that were neither old nor new. Her own age was hard to gauge. Viewed beside the young girl peeking out coyly from behind a clenched fist, the mother's quality

153

of experience was inevitable. She must have been forty, Jacinta told herself in the face of a timeless dignity much used or abused. There was a resignation in the charcoal eyes – far less a disappointment at the facts of living than an acceptance, despite everything, of life.

'Jacinta and Callum – this is Suzy Wong and her gorgeous little girl Amy.' Taylor hoisted the sleepy child and sat her on his broad shoulders. 'Amy and Suzy – this is my buddy Callum and my brand new friend Jacinta.'

And when she spoke her accent was French straight out of Dien Bien Phu. '*Va de soi* – any friends of Taylor's are our friends too.'

She had fallen, but not all the way. There was no gap, as Jacinta saw it with a fateful perception on this night of nights, between who she was and what she undertook or practised every day, every hour. She stood for life lived – Jacinta felt it as a rebuke. Forged in the fire of conviction her platitudes took on the glamour of eternal truths. All of a sudden she smiled warmly and held out both hands.

'Please, Jacinta – you come with me now.'

A single lamp lit the room from the floor between a narrow bed and a kid's cot. Beyond a window without glass she saw the torn fly screen and three metal bars. Stretched tightly across the divan was a clean blue sheet – it was very nearly the colour of a summer sky in England, Jacinta decided as she popped a stuffed koala back in the cot. She turned to face Callum, pulling his shirt up from his belt and undoing the buttons carefully from the top. As she stepped from her shoes she felt the heat rush from his skin.

'I still don't believe you came tonight,' he said, shivering.

'Oh –' she said, 'I wouldn't have missed it for the world.'

She pulled her dress over her head and discarded the white dress and waited for him to map the contours of her body with his hungry eyes. He didn't do that. His eyes didn't leave hers. If he was hungry, she thought, he must be hungry for love itself. He undid his belt and let his pants fall and collect around his boots without looking down. He wasn't embarrassed – not really. He might have been presenting himself, shaking, for his army physical. When he unclenched his fist Jacinta saw the funny little parcel there. He closed his hand around the sheath – there was no meaningful way he could make use of it at that time. After he pulled his trousers up she took a step forward and kissed him. He lay close beside her on the sheet and held her hand without speaking, without moving. At last his breathing slowed, and she began to think he must have fallen asleep. She heard footsteps in the corridor, then a knock at the door and, with it, Taylor's voice.

'Paging Private Kennedy – fall in now, please.'

When he jumped up from the bed she didn't open her eyes.

'I'm sorry if I let you down, Jacinta. I didn't mean to.'

Now he was throwing on his shirt. She imagined him doing it. 'I know that,' she murmured, her arms crossed over her breasts.

'Won't you at least look at me?' he said.

Now she pictured him buckling his belt. 'I shan't forget you,' she said, getting further away all the time.

'No, no –' he insisted. 'I have to see you again. Please –'

When she opened her eyes he was already at the door, grinning.

'And why is that, Callum?' she whispered, almost gone now.

'Because my underpants are in your handbag – remember?'

## ❧ THE CEREMONY OF INNOCENCE ❧

AT THE VERY HOUR JANE FONDA MADE her entrance on the screen during a matinee showing of *Cat Ballou*, a big American sedan with whitewall tyres made its way slowly across the car park at the rear of the same cinema in Little Aden. No one remembered seeing the car arrive. No one saw the driver with his scarf drawn across nose and mouth. The driver chose a space at the back of the clearing, parked there, applied the handbrake and checked the mirror – nothing, no one. On the seat behind, Isa unscrewed the cap of a jerry can filled with petrol before inserting a fuse of plaited cotton in the neck of the can. Fashioned for an era of gracious living, the big Buick carried a good few US gallons in its tank. There was a further gallon or so of petrol in a crate's worth of old gin bottles in the boot of the vehicle.

At the scheduled moment, the driver removed his scarf, got out of the car, closed the door and walked away through the saplings on the edge of the clearing. Inside the car now the air was intoxicating. On the back seat, Isa inspected the rope of cotton in his hands. He had roughly twelve inches to play with – enough, surely, to permit a dignified retreat without risking a failure of the fuse. He fished out a box of matches, so humble and so deadly. Yes, he really wanted to be *affected*. In fact, he felt only a mild exhilaration comparable with freewheeling downhill on his bike in the dark. Isa was certain – the danger to passing human traffic existed not at all. He himself was at risk only to the extent of his own inexperience. If he felt an ounce of doubt it was in respect of the cloying fumes. It would be unfortunate indeed if the act of striking the match were to ignite the air inside the car before the fuse itself was properly lit.

He wound down the windows to clear the air. Then it was time to put his glasses on for the doing of the deed. As soon as the Chevy with the Jackie Kennedy type at the wheel had drifted from view he opened the matchbox and selected an ideal candidate. Goodness – what a slight thing to bear such a heavy burden of responsibility. Isa scanned the clearing one last time. He closed the windows fast, then struck the match. Pouf – he was still alive. He lit the fuse, got out of the car, and retired calmly enough. It was just as he reached the fire exit at the side of the cinema that he experienced genuine doubt. It wasn't about his safety this time. No, he was worried he might have fluffed it altogether. He wasn't quite used to the terror game.

He stopped and looked back. It was strictly against best advice to look back. The first blast blew open the doors. The second ripped the boot off and hurled it through the windscreen of a nearby Ford. Isa was struck chiefly by the noise, a memorable whooshing he took to signal the rapid molecular interaction of one hot gas with another – of oxygen, say, with hydrogen or its isotopes. The glass fell down like rain. There was a foul taste in Isa's mouth. Nothing stirred but the flames, now orange with an exuberant flourish here and there of cupric green, now black as hell in the liquid light of afternoon. No one challenged Isa. As he collected his bike in front of the cinema he heard a second car explode in sympathy, then a third.

SULAIMAN SQUATTED AT THE EDGE OF SLAVE ISLAND in the shade of an unfinished dhow, his feet planted wide above the sluggish surf, his torn net piled up behind him on the shingle. In his right hand he had the bobbin of nylon thread, in his left a pair of nail clippers. He hauled the damaged net across his knees, feeding the gut first down and around and then up again with a little tug before knotting and clipping it. Each time Sulaiman tugged he thought of his son Isa who grew more distant every day and whom he loved more than the sea.

He heard a lone siren. Immediately he set aside his net and tools. Looking up, he saw Khalil Kanoo at the edge of his vision. The fat man teetered on the brink of the ocean with his beads and sandals in his hand and something else – an umbrella or a walking stick – with which he goaded the tired sea. A short distance apart, the two men peered across the near empty dhow harbour towards the reclaimed land and Ma'ala. Now a second siren took up in harmony with the first. Plumes of dust climbed like the smoke of slowly moving funnels towards the verandahs strung out in colourful terraces over Murder Mile, obscuring awnings, sullying sunshades. Headlights blazing in the fog of its own exhaust fumes, a procession of camouflaged trucks lumbered towards the roundabout and the causeway.

'Bad business somewhere, what's the betting –'

Khalil Kanoo aimed his shooting stick at the beach, successfully targeting a gap in the lattices of Sulaiman's net. Having harpooned the shore with the apparatus he lowered his bulk towards its leather seat and tucked his sandals below his skirts. Sulaiman said nothing. Instead he scanned the dirty sky until he saw them. The helicopters came out of the haze above the causeway from the direction of RAF Khormaksar, their stronghold. Within seconds they were overhead, the four of them observing a tight diamond formation and parleying with their heart-stopping stutter. At last the deathly racket fell away.

'Little Aden, I dare say,' Kanoo went on, apparently unmoved.

'Not exactly routine manoeuvres,' Sulaiman conceded.

'Little Aden –' Kanoo reiterated as if for emphasis. 'It looks like those spiteful dragonflies are on the warpath this time.'

Sulaiman watched the convoy crawl along the causeway.

'Your son will be there, will he not?' Kanoo resumed casually. 'Such a fine young man, too –'

Standing ankle-deep in the shallows with his back to the shore, Sulaiman bent down abruptly to rinse his forearms. 'I wasn't aware you'd met my son,' he said, heart beating faster.

'He didn't tell you?'

'As a matter of fact he did not.' Sulaiman stood up and scraped the sea from his wrists.

'What exactly *does* your son tell you, one wonders?' As the other man spun round sharply Khalil Kanoo lifted a hand to appease him.

'We live in difficult times, do we not, Sulaiman? Who knows? They may have to get worse before they get better.' The fat man swung his worry beads speculatively towards the causeway. 'How to predict the future, my friend? How to glimpse what lies beyond that horizon?' Here Kanoo thrust his chin towards a hidden prospect. 'There will be winners and losers, will there not? All those army trucks will go. Their ships, too, will one day vanish into the sunset. And we will still be here, yes? We will still be here.' He looked violently at the listless water, at the same time smiling sadly as if to acknowledge a hopeless contradiction within – the clash, for example, of human values with material interests. 'Do you think about the future at all, Sulaiman?'

'Look – I've already given you my answer.'

'Just one night –' Kanoo insisted delicately. 'Just one – or would you rather spend the rest of your days chasing fishes from this sea to that? The fish are so many, my friend, while you are but one.'

'I gave you my answer.'

'Then let me invite you to reconsider. Would it help you at all to discover what is in my little boxes? Or what is not in them, perhaps? Neither narcotics nor –'

'Guns? Listen – I don't give a damn about your precious boxes.'

Kanoo sighed patiently as if to humour a talented but wayward child. 'You see this dhow?' he said presently, indicating the hull that rose over them. 'Who owns it, I wonder? Why, me, of course. Have you ever imagined yourself in possession of such a boat, Sulaiman? You may wish to entertain that agreeable notion right now. Be my guest, please, because there is so much more to life than fishing. Ask your son, why don't you? You know he is already taking steps –'

'Steps?'

'Towards an uncertain future.'

'As you know – he has his apprenticeship and his studies.'

159

'Ah, yes – he's bright, that one. He's very smart. One day, he'll make you justifiably proud, I'm sure. If he lives that long –' Khalil Kanoo raised a hand sharply as if in self-defence. 'No, don't come any closer, please – I have a horror of deep feeling. You know – I do admire you, Sulaiman Ali Hassani. I admire your son, too. No – just listen if you know what's good for him. You will be familiar with the proscribed organisation FLOSY, yes? No need to explain? Excellent. Would it surprise you to learn I myself belong to that organisation? Yes, I fund – along with certain other well-placed individuals mostly from Egypt – its clandestine activities. Think of it, if you wish, as an investment on my part in all our tomorrows. Of course, your son has reasons more exalted, one feels. Reasons ideological, of principle – I could see it quite plainly in his eyes.'

'See what?' The two small words stuck in Sulaiman's throat as he stepped out of the sea.

'He is very capable of hate,' Kanoo said at last. 'Of hating.'

'Hating what? Tell me what you're referring to –'

'I wish I could, my friend. What I can tell you with certainty is this – your principled son is a member of FLOSY too.'

Into the profound silence they inhabited came the rogue reports of a hammer striking nails somewhere out of sight. Sulaiman sprang forward and locked his fingers around Khalil Kanoo's neck. The fat man made no effort to defend himself – he perched like Buddha on an English shooting stick, his eyes tightly shut, until he was released. Sulaiman picked the fallen spectacles up and returned them before looking away and spitting at the sea.

'I don't expect you to like me,' Kanoo told him. 'I know you love your son, and that's what matters here. No one need know anything of what we discussed on this beach, am I right? No one in authority need know. Now – are you ready to reconsider my proposal?'

'Why shouldn't I call your bluff?'

'But why would you call it? Why take the risk?'

'You wouldn't turn in my boy – you have far too much to lose if the balloon goes up and the truth comes out.'

'Indeed? Think about it for a moment and tell me who has the more to lose – you or me. I'm sorry, my friend. Love is probably not enough in the face of life –'

For a second or two neither man spoke. Then they heard it – the sound of three muffled explosions arriving in rapid succession from the other side of the anchorage.

'Little Aden –' Kanoo confirmed.

Immediately he was on his feet. Already Sulaiman was scanning the harbour, looking for a sign. Here and there between shore and horizon the bigger ships reposed on their mattress of silver. Side by side at the edge of the water, the two men shielded their eyes with a hand. Kanoo stabbed his shooting stick at the sky as, far away to the west, the black smoke rose unchallenged towards the sun.

HE SAT ALONE BESIDE THE STEERING WHEEL as darkness descended on the hill. It was the second time he had waited in a stranger's car that day. And what a day it had been. In his head he had the angry music of the choppers and the roar of the refinery's fires. He still saw the lovely flames and tasted the bitter fumes. Suddenly the car door – the rear door – opened behind him.

'Don't look round –'

He heard the door close quietly but firmly.

'Your name is?'

'Isa Ali Hassani.'

'Don't look at me, Isa. Do you know who I am?'

'No – I know everyone calls you the doc.'

'That's good. How did you find me?'

'I spoke with Ashraf.'

'Ashraf at the technical college?'

'Yes – Ashraf.'

'He speaks very highly of you.'

'Thank you – I'm glad.'

'Eyes front, please. Now – how can I help you, Isa?'

'I want to join you.'

'We know that – but why should we trust you?'

'Because of what I did today.'

'At the refinery?'

'I did nothing at the refinery.'

'What did you do, then?'

'I created a diversion with another man. Behind the cinema –'

'You did well, Isa. May I ask how old you are?'

'Does it matter how old I am?'

'No. Only, tell me – why should the NLF take you to its bosom?'

'Because I am ready to die.'

'And how might that help us achieve a just peace?'

'I am ready to kill –'

'Who will you kill, Isa?'

'A man – Khalil Kanoo is his name.'

'The local shipbuilder?'

'The invert that donates his dirty money to FLOSY – the queer who made a pass at me in his Mercedes-Benz.'

'But would that be altogether wise? Think about it for a second, please. After all, Khalil Kanoo is an enterprising businessman and a model employer.'

'He deserves to be punished for funding an illegal organisation.'

'Of course he does. Unless –'

It came to him then with its terrible logic and symmetry. It was as if Kanoo himself sat beside him, smiling his approval. Isa blurted it out. 'Unless he is also a contributor to NLF funds.' There – he had been hoodwinked, ambushed. He felt the rush of blood to his head.

'We don't ask you to kill, Isa. We encourage you to think. Nor do we expect you to die. In fact, we'd much rather you lived. You can turn around now if you wish.'

Isa twisted his body and sat sideways on the seat. It was virtually dark – he could barely make out the features of his interviewer. His interviewer held out a hand as he opened the rear door. 'I'm Aziz,' he said. 'As a doctor it behoves me to uphold life where I can.'

## ❧ CRATER ❧

TWO JEEPS BUMPED NOSE TO TAIL THROUGH the quiet canyons of the *suq*. In the first vehicle were four MPs, their special-issue pistols holstered where their truncheons might otherwise have hung. In the second, his adrenalin pumping at the prospect of a showdown, Ben Nolan sat beside a young Omani officer and walked himself through the encounter that lay ahead. Nolan pictured a busy editorial office in the teeming centre of Crater, a workplace modestly appointed but quick with ideas and insights. He felt a communion of strongly held views, heard the powerful hiss of the press and the ringing-out of the typewriter bell, and saw *him*, of course – the crusading journalist, so cynical and suave. It was not quite half past eight – too early, Nolan decided, for fisticuffs. Tired but alert, a tad unkempt, perhaps, next to the uniformed Omani, he saw himself descend, street after street, towards the black heart of experience.

Deeper they pushed through the narrow thoroughfares, skirting cardboard boxes and packing crates and rotting foodstuffs disdained by dogs. The shutters went up noisily on either side. Here and there a merchant marshalled his goods – his Salem cigarettes or his Lucky Strikes, his transistor radios or waterproof watches. This bystander saluted, curious. That one spat, on racial or political grounds. Nolan fixed his eyes on the number plate in front. Yes, he would point the finger, finally. It would be the end of the affair between the journalist and himself – the culminating point of his lousy existence. He would forget his wife, sleep but not dream, and start over without her. He would turn her away, direct her from unhappiness, draw down the moon and send it skimming across the sea to guide her. She should never have come here. Didn't she read his letters? It would end now – very soon. Only, first, it was necessary to unmask a killer. It ought to have been an out-and-out satisfaction. Nothing was certain. As he lurched towards a breakfast appointment with destiny, Nolan wasn't even sure whose moral conduct was under review.

Basim Mansouri, it turned out, was elsewhere. The offices of the *Al-Kifah* newspaper were located between a photographic studio with flashing Agfa-Gevaert sign and a Bata shoe shop immediately behind the gold *suq*. There was no need to break down the door at the top of the stairs. It was held wide open, retained at ankle height by a bust of Nefertiti. The four MPs followed their young officer towards the half-glassed enclosure at the back of the room. Nolan hesitated just inside the door. Now the typewriters fell silent at the big steel desks. On what were they reporting if not the refinery blasts at Little Aden? Security breached but damage limited? No single group claims credit for proportionate show of strength? Why kill the goose that lays the golden egg? As his eyes travelled from this closed face to that, Nolan imagined he saw the slaughter of truth at the hand of prejudice.

No, there was no trace of the award-winning journalist who had taken a life and then cursed Nolan's so negligently. They must have been unimpressed, these editorial others, because after a minute or so they began to type anew or to study their galley proofs. No doubt they were used to being raided here – it was an occupational hazard, the validating stamp on their rigour and integrity. Their telephones, hitherto silent, rang out loudly for justice and free speech. Although it was Ramadan, they puffed nonchalantly at their cigarettes. Now the old backroom boy limped from his cubbyhole in the company of the fastidious Omani, drew the pen from his mouth, and threw his arms wide in a gesture of helplessness. There was no Basim – it was obvious to all. Even as he owned up to the relief he felt, Ben Nolan condemned his rotten luck and the wisdom of happenstance.

'This man is the editor.' The young Omani spoke in English as Nolan approached from the door. 'It appears our bird has flown.'

'Yes, I'm afraid Basim Mansouri is on indefinite assignment.' In a voice absurdly high-pitched but perfectly calm, the editor made it sound as if his top reporter was on secondment to *Vogue* in Beirut, or *Life* in Tehran. He shrugged again. Between intelligent fingers and a thumb forever stained by printer's ink he held a set of photographic enlargements with which he fanned the curtains of loose skin at his throat. 'May I ask,' he said mildly, 'on what trumped-up charge you had planned to detain him?'

Looking into the philosophical eye of an editor, Nolan detected no anger in the newspaperman's tone of voice. Instead, he caught a glimpse of the blazing refinery in a black and white image that came and went before him. 'Now, let's not be coy here –' he said bitterly. At least, he *thought* he heard himself say it. He felt all resentment rise to the surface and saw, in his mind's eye, the editor's slack-skinned throat leap towards his bare hands. It was astonishing what he could do if pushed far enough or hard enough. In his lively imagination he had already raised a senior journalist off the floor and launched him at a half-glassed office partition. At this juncture the young Omani unfolded his arrest warrant and searched for a key paragraph within the official text.

'The said Basim Mansouri,' he announced, 'is hereby charged with illegal membership of a banned organisation, viz —'

In Nolan's imagination the shattered glass of the office partition was still falling down. 'Jesus —' he protested. 'Don't tell me you don't know what he did.' He challenged them all then, shouting for their benefit. 'Bastards,' he said. It was a reasonable outburst, more or less unrehearsed. In the *Al-Kifah* office it inaugurated a silence disturbed only by the rustle of papers and the hum of the fans. From the floor below came the muffled whine and clatter of a printing press. 'Don't pretend you don't know,' Nolan repeated. 'Because nobody — and I mean nobody — gets away with what he did.'

'And what did he do, exactly? Or is this whole business simply a case of one man's word against another's?'

It was no use. The *Al-Kifah* editor, a lifelong student of cause and effect, was amused but otherwise unmoved. The glass partition at his back was still in tact. It was really too bad, argued Nolan, crying out inside. The margin between intention and achievement — wasn't it this, or something like it, that gave his most meaningful affairs their familiar note of disappointment?

'I think you know where to find me, officer —'

'He who hesitates is lost, Mr Nolan. You see how costly a delay can prove?'

'I know, I know — a stitch in time saves nine, doesn't it? What is this — a British Council tea party?'

There was to be no satisfaction, or not for him. As he retreated towards the bust of Nefertiti, Nolan saluted the shocking indifference of historical forces. 'Fuck you all, friends — ' he cried, blessing them with raised arm from the doorway at the top of the stairs. 'Because not one of you could tell it like it really is.'

IT WAS EARLY AFTERNOON when Hildegaard installed fresh candles at the altar and lit them, then picked up her jotter pad and sat down on the front pew. She stared at the little flames until a vision formed of the woman she wanted to reach. She watched the woman smile. She watched the eyes widen at an unexpected delight as the woman covered her mouth with her hand and all her sad laughter filled the chapel. Hildegaard started to write. *Dear Mrs Nolan* – she began. She tore off her sheet of paper. She screwed the paper up and pushed it deep into the pocket of her uniform. Again she consulted the blank page with its ladder of ruled lines. She couldn't be sure why she did what she did. Was it an act of atonement? What for? Although she couldn't see what she should apologise for, Hildegaard felt strongly she should apologise for *him*. She even wondered briefly whether it might be helpful to take on a measure of guilt in order to qualify for redemption, rejecting this idea as unworthy of them all. *Dear Jacinta,* she wrote, still parading her motivation before God. *By now you will have looked to the bottom of this letter to discover who it is that writes to you on lined pages like a schoolgirl. These lines will help keep me 'straight' when I tell you my story. It's a story I must tell you – a story about you and Ben, and me, of course. Sometimes I imagine it never happened at all, this story –*

She heard footsteps approach the door – the little door behind the altar. She tucked her pad under the pew. Then the door opened and Aziz appeared behind the crucifix. He didn't hesitate. He blew the candles out. 'Quickly –' he said. 'Get your things.'

THE GRENADE WENT OFF PREMATURELY, killing its carrier, sending him packing. A wounded man fled the scene. Within an hour of the blast they had cordoned off the ghetto from Banin to Sabeel – now a house-to-house search was underway. Although Callum wasn't sure what he was looking for, Taylor assured him he would know when he found it. 'Anything commie, dunderhead – you heard him.' Thus Taylor described their quarry using his talent for communication.

'He said guns and ammo,' Callum insisted, naturally respectful and inclined to fair-mindedness. 'I just don't believe they would keep their Kalashnikovs tucked under the settee –'

*Move it! Move it!* They were rounding up the reluctant men – the men and boys. The shrouded women they ignored. *Go! Go! Go! Just move your fucking arse, Abdul –*

'Or under the bed, for that matter –'

'Forget the frigging furniture, won't you? Jesus, Kennedy – you were a damn sight smarter before.'

'Before what?'

Taylor helped an old man through the doorway with the butt of his rifle. 'Before you lost your cherry, lover boy –'

In an alley of dried mud stood Callum Kennedy, his rifle stock at his cheek, his mouth dry, his heart banging against a nearby rib. From all around he heard the slogan of the hour – *Go! Go! Go!* Again he surveyed the silent huddle of five at the business end of his rifle. Their hands were on their heads. Their drab costume was all shirts and skirts. Their feet were mostly bare. They were none of them like him, Callum said – of true fighting age, he meant. Still, they might have rushed him at any moment and seized his rifle and crushed his skull and died in the street, cut down from behind by some kid from Huddersfield or Swansea or Dundee. They were visibly frightened. Their youngest must have been twelve – too old to cry, perhaps, but crying anyway, quietly, sparingly, with eyes fixed unblinking on the muzzle of the rifle. For Callum that was the most difficult part of the whole exercise. He found it hard to choose the best face, or the most representative heart, at which to aim.

Word came through. The police informer was in a blacked-out van in Sheikh Abdullah Street. The men and boys were marched off, hands on heads, to file past the van. Rapid progress was made. The informer described two neighbourhood dwellings as being of special interest, as likely to bear fruit.

'Well?' said Taylor, deadpan. 'You never did tell me.' This was as they were about to split up again in order to renew their house-to-house enquiries. 'Did the earth move?'

And although he hated to lie, Callum understood instinctively it would probably be easier for everyone if he did. He lied just a little – not for himself, or not really. He had a duty to respect his buddy's belief system and to guard against general dishonour. In any case, it wasn't strictly a lie. 'It might have –' he said. 'You'd better ask her.'

'That's what I like about you, Kennedy –' Here Taylor rammed home a magazine and backed away, shaking his head. 'It's the quiet ones you've got to watch,' he suggested. 'Isn't that what they say?'

The first house yielded a horde of NLF propaganda, the second a mimeograph printer and a selection of ancient medicines in leaky phials, plus syringes, needles and bandages. Beneath a lean-to at the second location they discovered a modest arms cache in a brick-lined chamber, roughly coffin-sized and located two feet below the mud. Although it bore the signs of a recent excavation, the pit gave up a No 4 rifle with a full magazine of .303 rounds, a further clip of 9mm rounds, a venerable Mk 6 mine pressure plate, and several weeping sticks of plastic explosive. It was as the ragbag haul was being logged and photographed that Callum picked up a sudden movement on a nearby roof. Although the roof was comparatively close, the glimpse itself was fleeting – fleeting but none the less provocative. Yes, there was a man up there, and, yes, his movement, such as it was, might be described as furtive. It was a gut feeling, no more than that. Funny thing was – Callum was certain he recognised the man on the roof.

'Permission to speak, sir –' he said quietly.

ALONE ON THE ROOF, AZIZ REACHED a decision. He moved quickly out of sight – he had no intention of catching the meddlesome eye of any soldier below. The white Citroën waited in the lane behind the house – Aziz caught its flash of chrome as he ran down the outside steps to the floor below. It was here in a hot room that Hildegaard van Kris contemplated the above-elbow amputation of an arm – the one shattered only recently by the untimely action of a grenade.

'Diamorphine –' she called out calmly. 'Another slug of twenty-five, please. And I need suction drainage here. Hurry – in the car.'

Beside her, Aziz was equally calm. 'No suction drainage, nurse.'

'Then just give him another shot, damn it.'

There was a perfect silence then. Hildegaard looked hard at Aziz and saw it finally in his eye – the ruthless gleam that made him unfit to care. He carried a Luger in one hand and a syringe in the other.

'As a matter of fact, I've already given him a lifetime's supply. So say goodnight, nurse – this one need never know pain again.'

She heard the front door open with a clatter below. She jerked her head, and Aziz withdrew. She heard the footsteps in the hall, on the inner steps. She took off her gloves and waited beside the body. She might have expected a squad of excitable young men with boot polish on their faces. In fact, he was alone with a rifle, mouth open, breathing hard. Hildegaard watched his eyes journey back and forth across the bloody sheet between them and then climb to meet hers. She had an urge to smile and to reach out both hands, struck as she was by the beauty of coincidence. She remembered it vividly – two off-duty soldiers, one borrowed ambulance, and a caravan of camels on a hot, dusty road south of al-Hauta. She had offered him water to drink. Yes – that was it in its most condensed form.

'Where's your partner today, I wonder?' she said.

Callum nodded as if from afar – he was remembering too. In a silence besieged by flies he viewed in turn the ruined arm, a stained sheet, the bloody floor. When he hugged his rifle, Hildegaard had the impression of a lost kid at a fancy dress party. 'Dunno –' he said at last. 'Where's yours?'

Abruptly he backed off – she heard his boots on the steps going down. At the same time Aziz reached inside and gripped her arm.

'Lights out now, nurse. Time to exit stage left –'

He led her down the outer stairs to the car. When he turned the key the Citroën rose up with a hiss. Immediately, he switched on the siren. At least three squaddies waved them on their way. They got as far as Sheikh Abdullah Street without once having to stop or slow.

'In the glove compartment –'

He killed the siren. Hildegaard opened the glove compartment and took out a folded *chador*. Aziz was smiling now, his eyes darting from road to mirror and back.

'Put it on,' he said, observing her closely now. 'They're going to be looking for what – a white nurse in a blood-stained uniform?'

She looked into his mocking eyes.

'Don't be shy, Hildegaard – put it on and be one of us at last.'

Slowly, very slowly, she unfolded the black cloak and felt it glide silkily across her knee. How cool it was to the touch. For a moment there was no light, no sound, inside Hildegaard's head. Everything would change now – she accepted that. As she stared at the road and waited for the darkness inside her head to clear she understood one life was ending while another had just begun.

171

'No, not yet,' she protested. The words came out before she had formulated the plan. 'I have to go back to the hospital first.'

'Forget the hospital,' Aziz said. 'Your summer vacation has just begun. You don't even work at the hospital any more –'

'I have to go back –'

'Back? There can be no going back for you, nurse. The Rubicon – you crossed it today in Crater, wouldn't you say? Yes, I think so. You know – I never quite managed to believe in you, Hildegaard. It was Basim who insisted you might be useful to us. Bully for Basim. I'm sure he'll want to say thank you. And, after all, you know such a lot about us now. You've become rather a hot property, I'd say.'

'Where are you taking us, please?'

'Somewhere safe.'

'In the northern territories?'

'Don't fret – Basim will be there to thank you in person.'

'Al-Hauta again?'

'Why Al-Hauta? Put it on now, please.'

'Not yet – I have to go back. I can buy us time.'

'Oh, I'm sure you can.'

'Don't you trust me, doctor?'

'You? It's me I don't trust.'

After that it was plain sailing. It was as if he willed it to work out this way. Despite what he said she saw him as someone desperate to believe in her as an alternative version of who he was – as someone committed, engaged, free. Yes, free. That the doctor might actually be prepared to let her dupe him now struck Hildegaard as proof of his enormous vanity. It was the proof, too, of his humanity. She had to find a telephone and make her report. That was business, or duty. But there was something else she had to do – an act of free will.

'Just get me to the St Stephen's Mission hospital, please.'

He waited in the Citroën with the engine running. She hesitated inside the chapel and hugged the *chador* to her and breathed the still air. First things first — she reached under the pew and retrieved her pad. Her pulse racing, she added a few lines to her incomplete letter. She felt stronger then. Leaving the letter and the cloak on the altar she hurried through the morgue and along the corridor, smiling and smiling in her blood spattered uniform until she reached the sister's office opposite emergency admissions. She peered through the little window — there was no one inside. Hildegaard kicked the door shut behind her. She picked up the telephone and dialled rapidly.

'Password?' It was a man speaking. 'Identify yourself, please —'

He sounded so close — he might have been next door.

'Dutch courage —' she said. 'Dutch courage is all Bols.'

There was a silence. She heard the click of the tape recorder.

'Go ahead, please.'

'North under partial duress in an unmarked Citroën ambulance — colour white — with male client on board. Registration is unknown at this time — sorry. Pursue, please, with urgent discretion. Message ends here. In haste — out.'

She hung up, opened one drawer, then another. Suddenly the sister was in the room with her. 'Been in the wars again, nurse?'

'Gosh — I really think I might have been this time, sister. Let me see — is there an envelope in here I could use?'

At last she had on the glossy *chador*. Aziz drove them to Hedjuff without further protest. It was in more or less the right direction, he said. There was the light of certainty in her eyes and an unassailable integrity in her manner. She delivered the letter in person, by hand. For her it was the right course of action. She simply approached the watchman at the compound gates and gave him the envelope.

'Mrs Nolan's at the beach,' he said, his Arabic so colloquial.

Hildegaard didn't chat. She merely nodded behind her veil.

'You're very cool —' Aziz told her.

They were approaching the causeway at a low-key thirty-five.

'I like that — I find it rather exciting.' Now he rested his hand on the shiny garment in the region of her thigh. 'Did you ever consider an alternative career as a spy?'

She let that one go, removing his hand from her leg and peeling the veil from her face. 'What would Basim have to say, doctor?'

'Oh, I think you'll find Basim has his hands full already —' Aziz accelerated on the causeway, laughing freely at the world now. 'As a matter of fact, you'll be meeting Hannan quite soon.'

As they passed Slave Island, Hildegaard's mind raced ahead.

'Hannan is very sweet,' Aziz went on. 'They plan to get married out there as soon as possible, it seems. The girl herself comes from a charming village above al-Mukallah.'

'Mukallah?' It was a surprise. Hildegaard looked hard at the sea and tried to regroup. 'But I thought we were heading north?'

'East —' Aziz said. 'Into the real country and the rising sun.' The light was fading on the desert side of the causeway as he glanced at his watch and wound up his window. 'East of Aden —' he confirmed with an understated but palpable satisfaction, smiling his little smile.

## ☙ Tears of Blood ❧

IT WAS AFTER DARK WHEN NOLAN'S telephone rang. He was alone on the verandah at Hedjuff, an envelope on the table in front of him.

'Ben? It's Duncan Mathieson.'

'Speak to me, Duncan.'

'Look — I've just taken a call from a distressed watchman over at Prince of Wales pier.'

174

'Some people have all the luck.'

'There's been a drowning, Ben. Are you free to go down there?'

'Of course – but shouldn't it be a job for the harbour boys?'

'Too far out – a woman's body was brought in by a fisherman.'

'A local woman?'

'White – only, we have no idea who she is as yet. The fisherman pulled her out of the drink about a mile off Gold Mohur. There was nothing on her, of course. And nothing left behind, I fancy.'

'OK, Duncan – let me take a look.'

'Thanks, Ben – oh, and Ben?'

'I'm listening, Duncan –'

'Keep the *heid*, won't you? Apparently she's not a pretty sight.'

'Don't tell me – the fish got to her.'

'The big fish, unfortunately. The biggest –'

Nolan went down to the pier to confront the remains of his wife. Perhaps he had a premonition – he took with him the envelope, the envelope with her name on it, as a kind of talisman. He stood at the end of Prince of Wales pier, at the limit of experience, and opened the envelope while the big ships deployed their lights just for him in a loop around the bay. What on earth was she thinking of? Although he forced himself to imagine her in the deeper ocean, Nolan found himself unable to recall the way his late wife swam. He couldn't see her. Around the bay the lights linked arms and sang to him as Nolan focused on a letter. It was a letter, handwritten on lined paper, from Hildegaard to his wife. Too late, too late – she didn't have time to read it. Nolan was obliged to read it for her. *I know Ben would make a good and loyal friend, but it's not enough for me. I hope and pray it can still be enough for you.* There was a lovely postscript, too – a sketch, seemingly rushed, of the smiling sun with slanting eyes and optimistic rays. It was the smile that made Nolan recall the verdict of Sonny's cards. *It means someone is in mortal danger, Ben.* Who, Sonny, who? Now he knew – everyone did. Nolan saw a symbolic woman adrift on a tide of her own tears with, above her, the grinning sun. A man must know it all, he protested angrily as he let the letter fall. The words – they might as well have been written in a foreign language. They meant nothing to Ben Nolan. The letter flashed once, twice, below the oily surface of the water, then vanished for good.

# 4 |
# Basim

'So – who's in charge of this rabble?'

SHE WAS DEAF AND SHE WAS DUMB. EVERYONE knew the goatherd who drove her flocks each day from Shibam's streets towards the hill above the lush *wadi*. Everyone knew her, but few had witnessed the desolate beauty that hid behind her veil like darkness behind night. She was still very young. She was touched, many insisted, by God. It was said her eyes were the eyes of a fabulous beast that sees further than the furthest mountain, deeper than the deepest ocean, to reach the hearts of men. She moved among them every day like a promise or a curse. They hailed her at the scattered margins of her herd, but she only waved her sprig cut from the frankincense tree, or smiled at them, unseen, behind her veil. Because they couldn't converse with the girl they ascribed to her certain qualities poetic and prophetic, mythical and magical. In their extravagantly lyrical vernacular some likened her to an orphaned sparrow, others to a gifted gazelle.

She left behind Shibam's clay skyscrapers, their window grilles and fortress doors flashing in the sun. Soon the fertile valley opened up. The river rushed, unheard, down there through the palms and plantains. As the goatherd rose from rock to rock among inquisitive lizards her charges roamed freely around her – the agile ruminants led her on with a silent scuttling of hooves or scattering of stones. At last she stood at the crest of the escarpment. Behind and below her, the *wadi* was coiled like a snake around Shibam's heart. Glazed with fresh egg white, the upper parts of the tenements glowed with civic pride. Ahead was the desert plain with, all around it, the enormous sky. The young goatherd observed their vehicles grouped in clusters directly below her. At a slight remove from the vehicles, the martial ambassadors sat in a circle on the desert floor with, here and there, a raised umbrella. A saluki slunk beneath a pick-up for its shade. All this the goatherd took in. She saw, too, the man she was due to wed. Although he was just a pale smudge on a vast canvas, she knew him. He was quite literally the centre of attention, seated as he was in the middle of their circus of warlike tendencies, of ancestral oaths sworn under the midday sun and promises made in the dust. High on her hill, the girl shivered at the prospect of happiness, a hot wind tugging at her cloak. Where was love? Nowhere near here. She was his, she was his – love was very far off. Uncanny – he was looking up at her as her shadow leapt from the ledge and took flight.

SITTING CROSS-LEGGED ON A PERSIAN CARPET on the desert floor below an escarpment, Basim narrowed his eyes against the glare and surveyed the delegates – tribal leaders, mostly, and warlords of the eastern protectorate. Their aspects were fierce, their representations interminable. They had come in their lorries and pick-ups to bandy allegiances in the presence of Soviet advisers and Yemeni observers. As the latest spoke at length in his mellifluous drone, Basim felt his eyelids droop. Why couldn't they simply vote to sanction sunglasses – their use on a discretionary basis – instead of insisting, as protocol demanded, on eye-to-eye contact? Basim straightened his spine and breathed the hot air. How tired he was suddenly, tired of the game. He thought of Hannan and was instantly revived. One day soon she would be all his responsibility in a model world, and the dangerous political road would be run. Love was tender – love was sweet. Love was his to command – Hannan would offer up to it, and to him, her devoted heart. He saw a canteen flash, but not while someone drank – there would be none of that before sundown Now a hunting dog hauled itself, exhausted, into the circle. These elders were cunning, Basim knew – their loyalties and methods were circumspect. They raised their rifles solemnly and endorsed their mutual regard with a ragged salvo. The exhausted dog howled at the sun. Then someone spotted the looming dust trail. An indignant cry went up. The circle of diplomats lost its shape. The delegates stood in the sand, spoiling for a test of manhood or ideological commitment, their rifles stirring the molten air. The two Russian attachés rolled their eyeballs, shook their heads, and looked for answers to Basim. He reached gratefully for his sunglasses before rising from the rug with a fluid movement.

Leaving them to congregate belligerently around their canteens, he strode convincingly towards the advancing cloud. He had no idea what to expect. When he saw Aziz climb out of the dirty Citroën, he felt a thrill tempered by anxiety. Yes, this or that development must have taken place. The good doctor, pale with dust, smiled grimly as he spoke, tossing his hand over his shoulder for emphasis. Then the cloud thinned – she was visible beyond the streaked windscreen. All in black, she had her head tilted back with eyes closed – she might have been waiting at the traffic lights, Basim decided with an access of admiration. He was fully awake now, alert to the clamour inside him of interrogative voices. She was scarcely throwing herself at his feet – that was the first thing. What did it add up to, her presence? If she was in the deepest water, if she had compromised herself fatally, was it likely she would cut and run from her own people? Wasn't it more likely, if and when the chips were down, she would engineer a last stab at reconciliation and forgiveness? Or had she made the big switch back there? A deserted road, the transfiguring light – had her borrowed *chador* changed her for good? No, it was impossible, Basim decided – there was something unsatisfactory about her still.

'This is a mistake,' he said immediately, his eyes on the car.

'I had no choice –' Aziz said. 'She knows too much about us.'

'She always has done. What possible good can come of this?'

'Perhaps we should simply get rid of her, Basim – is that it?'

'There is nothing simple about getting rid of a white nurse.'

'Anyway – she can't go back. She's burnt her bridges.'

'So you brought her here on the eve of my wedding?'

'I had to make sure –'

'That she would come between me and my bride?' Basim shook his head, smiling at his own affinity with what was most calculating in human nature.

'What else was I supposed to do?' Aziz demanded passionately. 'We had British troops all over us.'

'Tell me something,' Basim said. 'Did anyone follow you here?' He spread his arms and embraced the throbbing air. 'Of course not – how could they? Has anyone mapped your recent progress across the wilderness from Aden? Of course not – because no one knew you were leaving town, did they? Because you didn't let her out of your sight for a second, did you?' He took off his sunglasses. He saw how it was destined to play out. He saw how it was meant to be. He even thought he saw her smile behind the muddy windscreen. 'She must be about all in,' he concluded, setting off towards the car.

IT WAS TIME TO BREAK THE RAMADAN FAST. When the famished eye could no longer discern a black thread against the darkening sky – then it was time to eat. They gathered on the seventh storey of an adobe tenement in Shibam, their feast spread before them. Hannan was the bearer, her aunt the cook. Aziz was beside Hildegaard – the doctor registered with a resentment bordering on pain the progress of Basim's satisfaction as the steaming dishes, set down in turn on a low table by the bride-to-be, accumulated in the aromatic silence. Beside the radishes and the celebration gravy was the pungent stew, served in a large jug, of fresh goat's meat prepared with onions, eggs and tomatoes. There was an appealing *hulba* of leeks with fenugreek, plus a selection of glistening vegetables stuffed with rice and minced lamb. Alas, Aziz had little appetite. He was more tired than hungry. Was it in spite of, or because of, the riches to be shared he felt it so keenly, so personally – a growing sense, implacable and brooding, of the injustice of his position in the great scheme of things.

Hannan sat down beside Basim. For Aziz, that was the cue to get up from his cushion, to seek out Hannan's aunt at the kitchen stove. His idea, he recognised, was imperfect. He had no plan as such. If it had been his intention to betray Basim's sexual infidelity, he agreed now to content himself with an *imaginary* conversation only. To have spilled the beans would, after all, have been unworthy of him, and a waste of time to boot – that hag, shrewish by reputation, harboured a powerful ambition on behalf of her orphaned niece. Nevertheless, Aziz badly wanted to have this little chat if only to punish himself for his unworthiness. It was natural to seek her out, to allow himself to be humiliated by a practical cook shrouded from top to toe. 'Eeeh – why are you telling me all this?' she asked shrilly. 'I mean – why tell me now? This is just malice. What good can come from it, and are you a man, all the same, to make mischief like that?' Big questions, adjudged Aziz. He pressed on, embittered, but she could plainly see Basim Mansouri was a suitor of the highest calibre, a man of destiny withal. Cause hopeless, case shameful, Aziz hung his head. 'Let me repeat it for the avoidance of doubt, buster,' the cook added loftily, wagging her hennaed finger. 'It is not so much your accusation that disappoints as its reckless timing and cowardly motivation.' Just so, Aziz acknowledged, his portion ignominy. 'First heal yourself, doc,' she urged aphoristically. 'Make peace with yourself first.'

AT LAST IT WAS TIME TO EAT. AS BASIM REMOVED the veil from Hannan's face it seemed to Hildegaard he presented her to a corrupt and decadent world as something perfectly unfinished or unformed. She would always be just like this – on the cusp of a mature beauty, on the threshold of adult understanding, which to Basim were fixed locations. It was here he could best exalt and possess her immutable potential. What did she know of life? What could she see? Nothing? Everything? She was like a doll with eyes forever open, Hildegaard decided with a little internal shudder. She heard Basim whisper to Hannan in Arabic as he swept the veil from her shoulders. 'We're among good friends here, beloved –'

'May I ask when you are to wed?' Hildegaard aimed her enquiry at the bride-to-be as if they had just been introduced at a summer fête. Such a question was ideal when so little was scripted or certain. It was understood between them or among them – there was nothing else to talk about here except everything under the sun. No answer came back across the table. 'My dear girl – can I ask when you're to be married?' Nothing. Hildegaard looked to Basim.

'I'm afraid Hannan can't answer your questions.' He spoke in English now, his voice sensual and low.

'Oh, I see,' Hildegaard came back automatically, asking herself whether he meant *can't* or *won't*.

'Ah, she too can *see*.' He was smiling, fascinated, at the creature beside him. Hannan's eyes were modestly averted. At her nose the two rings glittered. 'In fact, seeing is what she does best.'

Hildegaard watched him, fascinated too. His rapture when he spoke again was distasteful to her somehow.

'Although Hannan is deaf and dumb she has many gifts –' Yes, his curious relish was a type of self-love. His delight in Hannan was a regard for himself. She was all his creation. The girl was incapable of answering back. And yet she didn't have to listen – she need never hear his protestations of love. It was base. To Hildegaard it had the claustrophobic quality of a dream. She watched Hannan's eyes rise to meet hers and make their appeal. 'Careful, nurse – she sees right through you,' Basim warned, his satisfaction complete.

'What a terrible fate –' Hildegaard said. 'To see all the kindness of the world undone by ignorance and lies.'

Then Hannan's aunt came in to advise them Aziz had taken it upon himself to return to Aden without a moment's delay. She gave no explanation. Glancing at Hildegaard, Basim gestured at the food on the table between them.

'Please – the doctor's busy schedule matters not to us here.' He began to nod, speculatively, ruminatively, as he broke his bread into smaller and smaller pieces. 'In answer to your question –' he went on. 'We get married next week, after Ramadan, with or without the doctor. Naturally, we expect you to join us as our honoured guest – unless you too feel a pressing need to return to your work.'

'You know that isn't possible.' Hildegaard sought out Hannan. She was a gorgeous and necessary distraction from what needed to be said at this time. As the girl's jewelled fingers raised the moist rice towards her lips her bracelets tumbled this way and that. Surely she could hear it via her own skin, or feel it in her own swift blood – the lovely crashing of bangle against bangle. 'Just how long,' Hildegaard asked Basim, 'can I expect to be here?'

'That depends, doesn't it? It's up to you, I would have thought.'

She looked at him more keenly despite her fatigue. She had the impression he had worked it all out for himself – everything. Still, she concluded she was in no immediate danger. He was waiting for events to unfold. He didn't much care when that might be. It was as if he expected the future to be his *one way or another*. The personal and historical model he used – it allowed for no alternative outcome.

'Yes –' he said. 'It's really up to you now, nurse.'

185

She caught a whiff of the familiar arrogance. Around the lamps the maddened moths stepped up their fatalistic ballet. And she had stepped inside the lion's den. To what end? She was falling, falling. As she fell she had the image of Aziz at the wheel of a big white car with, beside and behind him, the shadow of a police helicopter like a scorpion on the sand. She saw a journalist pray, naked, with Che Guevara looking on. Hildegaard shut her eyes for a moment – just one. No longer did she think or judge – she simply heard or saw. She heard the waters of the *wadi* rush from rock to rock in the vale of her imaginings. As her head fell down on her chest she contemplated an above-elbow amputation in the presence of flies. There was a soldier in the doorway – just a boy, a kid. When she tried to warn him, no sound came out. The soldier was crying – the koala bear in his arms was haemorrhaging. Hildegaard woke up with a start. She gave out a little cry. Hannan's touch, delicate but strong, was at her neck and her forehead, bearing her up. Close to hers, the girl's eyes were like stained-glass windows backlit by an exploding star and viewed from incalculable distance. Hildegaard saw the tooth made of gold. Was she safe here? Was she safe? She just couldn't remember.

HE PRESSED HIS HAND TO HER MOUTH and felt her body first tense then go slack as if bidden by sheer will. He jerked the nightshirt up around her chin. She might have screamed the house down – in fact, the only person who mattered was just a room away alongside her snoring aunt, unable to hear a thing. In the event, Hildegaard failed even to whimper, although Basim set out consciously to punish her with the active support of his body. What was the use? He removed his hand at last. Still she failed to cry out. She didn't move a muscle until after he interrupted his dry excavations and rolled away from her, panting. Then she lowered her shirt and got up and opened the

186

shutters as if she did the same thing at around this time every night. For his part Basim listened to the waters of Wadi Hadhramaut and waited patiently to be arrested. He could have fled with his virgin bride, but he chose not to. How contented he felt. His marriage bed would be a prison slab. Basim thought of it as a timely career move. Yes, his political credentials were assured now. He would buff them and polish them one after the other by the light of a jailer's moon.

### ❧ Diary of a Son-in-Law ❧

*IS-SALA:MU ALAYKUM.* GREETING THE FISHERMAN a few paces from the water's edge on Slave Island's tarry shingle, Ben Nolan held out his hand, then withdrew it.

*Wa alaykum is-sala:m.* The Arab continued to wipe his fingers on a filthy rag.

'You pulled my wife from the sea off Gold Mohur –'

Sulaiman neither confirmed nor denied it. The shored-up dhow towered above him, its stained planks reeking in the morning sun.

'Speak English?' Nolan asked. 'I wanted to thank you.'

Sulaiman wound his rag around a rung of a nearby ladder.

'I wanted to ask you if –'

'Look – the *memsahib* was dead.' The fisherman turned slowly to confront Nolan, his words hanging in the air beside the cry of a gull. 'The *memsahib* was already dead.'

At least the words didn't judge – Nolan was grateful for that. He nodded. Naturally she had said nothing at the end. Why would she? Treading the water, watching the water turn red – she had plenty to think about, and lots to be getting on with.

'They're planning to hold an inquest. Were you aware of that?' He had meant to keep it simple and strong. He abandoned further efforts to shape his English, to make his words easier to understand. 'Did you realise you were in the running for a decoration?'

The Adeni picked up the basket of dully shining tools at his feet.

'The high commissioner intends to pin a medal on you.' Nolan smiled at himself just a little because Sulaiman's chest was much too bare for pins or medals. There was something else – he experienced a violent form of love for the laconic Arab. How else to make sense of it? 'To ease racial tensions, I suppose. To promote –'

He stopped there. Why explain it to the resourceful fisherman? It was blindingly obvious when you thought about it for the shortest time. Maybe see you, Nolan was thinking. Maybe I'll see you again. Because we'll always be *that* close, won't we? Yes, we will. I owe you, brother. Yes, I do. I'll buy you a frigging Fanta in Fanta heaven.

His second interview of the day was by prior appointment at the military police headquarters on Esplanade Road.

'Sit yourself down, please.' It was his fastidious young friend, the Omani junior officer. He had his loose-leaf binder in his hand. 'You have my deepest sympathies, Mr Nolan. Very sad – extremely sad.'

The air-conditioned room was as cool as a bank. Nolan drew up a second chair. 'How can I help you people today?' he enquired. 'No suspicious circumstances for you *here*, surely? I mean – a woman can take a last dip at sundown, can't she?'

'Indeed she can. No, it was about quite another matter –'

'So, have you found him yet?'

The Omani smiled patiently behind the enormous desk. 'Basim Mansouri?' He was turning the pages of his file. Still he didn't look up. 'There's a young Dutch nurse at the mission hospital here –'

Nolan felt the hot blood arrive from nowhere. He didn't see why it should – he saw nothing new to reproach himself for at this time. Without warning a panelled door opened noiselessly beside him. A slight, balding man of indeterminate age glided into the office with his suit jacket buttoned up.

'Call me Farquhar, won't you?' he said.

Nolan rose slightly and shook a cool, dry hand.

'Thank you, officer.' At this the young Omani vacated the big chair. Farquhar sat down in it with a small sigh. He waited until he was alone with his guest before taking up with his slight lisp. 'Let me offer my condolences, Mr Nolan. Very sad – very sad indeed.' For a moment he eyed the file in front of him, cracking his knuckles over the pages. Suddenly he glanced up, eyebrows arching. 'Hildegaard van Kris – a friend of yours, is she?'

'I wouldn't necessarily go that far. But I know Hildegaard, yes.'

'Then perhaps you also know a certain Dr Aziz? A Lebanese –'

'I know Aziz. He works with Hildegaard at the mission hospital.'

'Not any more, I'm afraid.'

Nolan shifted on his hard chair. 'Go on –' he said.

'Aziz has just been arrested as a member – indeed, the leader – of an NLF cell that is active both here and in Little Aden.'

'I'm not surprised,' Nolan said.

Farquhar spread his hands and smiled. 'Enlighten me, please –'

'They're obviously in cahoots, the two of them.'

'The two of them, Mr Nolan?'

'Dr Aziz and Basim Mansouri, of course – they've been up each other's backsides all along.'

There was a knock, very soft, at the door. A uniformed adjutant entered uninvited and slid a tray carefully across the desk. Farquhar waited until the door closed again.

'How do you take it?' he asked pleasantly, lifting a milk jug. 'So important to perspire freely in this beastly climate, don't you agree?'

'I don't take it, thanks. Not on an empty stomach –'

189

'What a tangled web we weave,' Farquhar continued, tilting his saucer above his cup to empty a spillage. 'Having been abducted – I can't really find another word for it – by our friend Aziz, it seems likely that nurse van Kris is even now in the clutches of Mansouri himself. Our search for him has become an urgent quest for her.'

'I expect you'll be having a quiet word with Aziz, then –' Nolan said. And still he was unable to picture her successfully in her latest role – as the victim of a politically motivated kidnap. No matter – he didn't owe her any special allegiance. 'To jog his memory –'

'Oh, we will. We already have. These things often take a little time, that's all. But meanwhile it behoves us to hunt for our missing nurse. We'll begin in the north, I think.'

'That's a pretty big place.'

'We have our reasons.'

'Don't tell me – Hildegaard managed to draw you a map on a mirror using lipstick.'

'Not exactly – she delivered an envelope addressed to your late wife, Mr Nolan. A watchman at Hedjuff insists she drove away in a white Citroën ambulance with a man aged thirty to forty – Aziz, of course. All very cloak and dagger, I'm sure you'll agree. You see – she was wearing the black *chador*.'

There was a silence, more curious than suspicious, which Nolan cut short.

'You have my undivided attention, Mr Farquhar.'

'It would be interesting to learn what was inside the envelope, that's all. A message of some sort that might offer a clue, perhaps, to our nurse's current whereabouts?'

'I'm afraid I can't help you with that one. Why on earth would Hildegaard deliver a message to my wife on that day or any other? I don't get it – I'm not sure she even knew my wife.

In fact, an interesting forensic possibility had occurred to Nolan. Perhaps the first letters of each sentence, or of every second or third word, could be isolated in Hildegaard's note and arranged to spell a secret desert location. If so, it was too late and too bad – the letter was at the bottom of the bay.

'There wasn't any note,' he explained calmly. 'Or, if there was, my wife must have taken it with her to the beach when she –' Here he tossed his head at a notional Gold Mohur. From this featureless room it was impossible to know where land met sea and sky.

'I'm sorry, Mr Nolan, but it does seem a bit odd. Of course, we spoke to your houseboy, Ali, too. Just routine, you understand. Only, Ali distinctly recalls leaving the envelope propped up against a shell on the verandah table to await your wife's return. It follows she had already left for the beach, does it not?'

And to Nolan it was like a nightmare recounted at breakfast – no one else would believe it. He saw the envelope and the seashell. He saw her name there, scribbled in Hildegaard's girlish hand.

'I'm sorry – I must be confusing things in my mind's eye.'

'That's quite understandable. You've had a terrible shock.'

'Look – I destroyed the letter. It had nothing to do with *anything* – no sketch maps in blood, no X marks the spot. It was a personal message. It was none of your damn business. After I read the note I destroyed it. There was no reason to keep it.' His deepest feeling ran away like water on sand. He saw the letter flash once, twice, before being swallowed by the darkness below the pier. 'I'm sorry – you'll just have to take my word for it now.'

'Oh, but that's perfectly all right, Mr Nolan. I do regret having to put you through this whole wretched business at such a difficult time. You're not on trial here. Not a bit of it. We're all after the same outcomes, aren't we? I apologise if I've upset you, that's all –'

'You haven't upset me.'

'Splendid, splendid – *cherchez la femme* it is, then. That's the game now. She's in trouble, I'm in the doghouse – dreadful bloody flap all round.' Farquhar smiled, dissembling easily – he could hardly have appeared less flappable in his graveside suit. As he rose behind the vast desk his slight body gave the impression of unnatural youth. His head was older – it seemed to Nolan to belong to a torso other than the one to which it was attached. The narrowest of ties gripped the white shirt collar using a small, hard knot. 'I had hoped the famous envelope might help us, that's all.'

'Anything else?' Nolan said. 'I really have to be off now.'

'Of course you do, of course – thank you for popping in.'

They shook hands above the desk. At the door Nolan hesitated.

'You say Hildegaard was pretty much abducted –'

At first Farquhar ignored him in favour of the notes he was busy writing up in his binder.

'How do you know she isn't, you know –' Nolan broke off there.

'One of them?'

'A sympathiser, yes.'

'Come, come, Mr Nolan –' Farquhar looked up finally, smiling encouragingly. 'I mean – is that really very likely at all?'

In the Land Rover the metal was too hot to touch. There was a delicious breeze on Queen Arwa Road. Nolan had to slow because a lorry had run over a camel. At the gorge he picked up diesel, then accelerated down the hill towards Ma'ala and Steamer Point. By the time he got to the Crescent Hotel there was only the stuffed ostrich in the lobby along with the gurgling fountain and the receptionist, a cocky youth of mixed race wearing a Coca-Cola T-shirt. The youth was ideally placed to confirm the old boy had gone ahead in a taxi some time ago. Nolan asked for Oona. She had gone ahead too.

It took him a further half-hour to reach Khormaksar. The sun was directly overhead. There was no shade in which to park. Nolan ran past the deserted check-in desks and closed concessions flanked by pyramids of Fanta until he got to a departure gate at the far end of the concourse. They stopped him finally at the double doors. He was panting and sweating. He pressed his forehead against the cool glass of the door and peered at the dazzling exterior.

'I have to be out there. Let me out. Let me out —'

The smell of aviation fuel was intoxicating. The silver-bellied jet shimmered on a carpet of moving air. Nolan saw no head turn from the shadow of the wing as he hurried across the apron. Included in their small congregation were two airport bods in boiler suits armed with walkie-talkies and an RAF chaplain pitting his words of comfort against the whine of a taxiing transport plane. The coffin sat on the runway at the centre of their huddled group. Jacinta's father stood slightly apart with head bowed and eyes shut. He had a gabardine raincoat over his arm and a paperback edition of *A Town Like Alice* in the side pocket of his tweed sports jacket. Nolan stepped between his father-in-law and a woman he felt he more or less *knew*. Oona's long black gloves were her sole concession to a sombre sentiment or outlook. There was a scent of citrus fruits about her, Nolan learned. Her dress bore a nice pineapple motif. When it was over, she turned to him and tucked her parasol under her arm.

'You must be Ben,' she said, peeling off her glove.

She struck him first across one cheek with the back of her hand and then kissed him lightly, rising up on tiptoe, on the other cheek. Without speaking again she looked to the control tower as if to end her association with local affairs, opened her parasol, and stepped into the glare. Nolan turned to confront Jacinta's father. The old boy had his coat on now, collar raised against the roaring currents.

'I have nothing to say to you, Ben,' he shouted at close range as the colossal transport took off in the distance behind him.

'I know that —' Nolan said, the toe of his desert boot pressing up against the coffin. 'Just take good care of her, please.'

## ✢ SONG FOR SOMEONE ✢

PHILIP HAD CONVENED AN UNSCHEDULED afternoon rehearsal. He wanted to practise or perfect Ken's contribution to Pretty Flamingo's repertoire before the group took to the evening stage. Seated behind his drum kit in the dining salon at the Crescent Hotel he wiped his sticks with his T-shirt as, beside him, tall Walter probed the bass riff experimentally and, at the front of the stage, Jimmy ran the chords up and down the neck of his guitar with a fluent disdain. There was a problem in respect of Jimmy's attitude – poor Philip was at his wits' end. Although Ken's song, duly rehearsed, was easily good enough to make their playlist, Jimmy remained hostile to it. In a nutshell, he resented the incorporation, unsanctioned but increasingly *de facto*, of the hotel owner's son within their group. Why he? Why now? Could it be they were no longer capable, as paying guests, of settling their hotel bar bill? It was scarcely a good enough reason on its own. But what Philip and Jimmy both recognised in their different ways was that Ken was a better vocalist than either of them, or both of them put together, that he sang like a tough angel even if the lyric he had penned was, in Jimmy's humble opinion, beneath critical scrutiny.

Philip peered anxiously beyond the Scottish guitarist towards a fascinating region in which the sunlight leaking from the courtyard showered the starched tablecloths with arrows of gold. There stood Ken, rimmed by fire. He was polishing cutlery and waiting, as if it could only be a matter of moments now, to be invited on stage. How noble was his clear-sighted faith in his own worth. To be near him was to come closer to an ideal you, Philip decided. Was it dangerous to admire your own projected identity quite this much? Beside Ken, it was reasonable to forget who or what you were, to start over from scratch. It was difficult for Philip to discuss his complex feelings with anyone for whom he had a real regard. So few candidates were at his disposal. He wished he could dive into the pool of light surrounding Ken and stay there, wet with gold. Yes, that was it – just the two of them. No one else need apply. Unpractised in the black art of love, and ignorant of dark desire, Philip understood he wanted to *be* Ken, to be under his clothes, or inside his skin. These days, he woke up pretty much as he went to sleep – with a sweet little erection.

Jimmy spoke out from the stage. He had his guitar in one hand and the sheet of paper in the other. '*Song for someone –*' he declaimed. '*Oceans of blue –*' He paused for a second or two to let his irony do its worst. '*Colours I'm singing someone like you –*' Now he looked out across the tables towards Ken. 'What the dickens is it all about, Jeeves?'

Ken failed to explain. Philip stamped his bass pedal anxiously.

'They're only words,' brokered Walter influentially. 'They don't have to *mean* anything – you just need to *feel* them, that's all.'

Then Jimmy inspected the lyric sheet theatrically on both sides as if it were a rare document, a repository of esoteric truths. It was a question of provenance, Philip accepted on Ken's behalf. What was wrong with the words, to Jimmy's resentful eye, was that they issued from a mixed-race former public schoolboy with a feeling for faggot poems, especially *The Rubáiyát of Omar Khayyám*.

'Oh, do come back, Adrian Durbridge,' bawled the young Scot suddenly. 'Where *is* that useless bugger when you need him?'

'Look –' Philip said. 'We have to make a go of this, Jimmy.' He waved his sticks at the world in general. 'I mean for Oona's sake.'

'Screw Oona.' Jimmy shook the sheet of paper wildly above his head. 'The sooner Adrian gets back the better, man. I'm telling you now.' When he slapped his strings with the wayward authority of his talent a plaintive wail emanated from a loud speaker at the back of the stage. 'My *boys* –' he cried, invoking Oona.

'Oh, my boys,' echoed Philip, catching on fast.

Now Walter laid down the bass foundations for Ken's song.

'Would you care to pluck that spoon from your arse, Kenneth, dearest, and join us for this magic carpet ride?'

Jimmy's invitation was the cue. He began to sway loosely before an imagined audience of avid diners, and soon the whole practised thing was ripping along furiously with a 12-string electrification that must have arrived from California, or west, at any rate, of London. Ken delivered his song with a fistful of cutlery and a confidence that belied his two-day apprenticeship, and when Jimmy leaned in and joined him for the chorus the effect was so powerful and emotional that Philip found himself belting out the words too, even though he didn't have a microphone and no one could hear him. He couldn't have stopped himself – that was how right it felt.

'Well?' he said finally, heart threatening to cast off its moorings.

'It's good,' Jimmy admitted. 'I mean – it has an obvious poetry.'

'You wouldn't know poetry if it bit you on the bum,' Philip said.

'I think our sound has a better shape now,' Walter commented.

'Song for someone?' mused Jimmy archly, winking at the lyricist beside him. 'Couldn't you at least have given her a name, pal?'


'PLEASE – TELL ME A LITTLE ABOUT YOURSELF.'

Khalil Kanoo clicked his fingers above his head as, around the big dining room, ripples of applause spread discreetly in recognition of the popular music group he had come to view and assess.

'Oh, there isn't much to tell,' Oona said, watching him corral a book of matches on the tablecloth with his ubiquitous beads.

'Of course not,' he said, encouraging her with a supple smile.

'What you see is what you get,' she confided, accepting a menu as Kanoo declined to take his with a delicate fanning of fingers. 'Did you ever live in a hotel, Mr Kanoo? His bulk, its inherent sadness – she sympathised instinctively with all that. 'Remarkable,' she added, 'how they come to resent you in time.'

'A question,' he proposed sensitively, 'of dwindling gratuities?' Again he broadcast his smile with its consummate weighting.

'Won't you share a menu with me?' she asked.

'But I always have the same thing,' he told her.

'The crayfish?' she said.

'The crayfish,' he said.

They listened without comment as the resident pop group gave out a heartfelt rendition of a country classic, the guitarist sucking a harmonica on a wire hoop around his neck.

'That's Jimmy –' she revealed at last.

'Perhaps Jimmy should stick to his guitar.'

'But I do think Ken gives them something extra up there.'

'Young Kenneth sings like a corrupt and corrupting angel.'

'He looks the part, too. That's so important in this day and age – don't you agree, Mr Kanoo?'

'Oh – youth invariably looks the part.'

'But do you think they have what it takes?'

Her boys. Her boys –

'Who knows? The road is long –'

'The road is long, Mr Kanoo?'

'All roads are long that lead towards one's heart's desire.'

She laughed then – his girth was anything but metaphysical.

197

'I do so value your opinion,' she said.

'I'm very happy about that,' he told her. 'It's the slightest part of me, really.'

As they toyed with their crayfish she began to think he might be romancing her just a bit. She was pleased about that – it meant the omens were good for when she came to ask him about the money. How could she know a middle-aged Englishwoman was the least or last dish on his menu of the heart? No, Oona only perceived he had some genuine feeling for her position.

'Tell me about the concert,' she said.

He laid down his fork and dabbed his lips with a napkin. 'What I have in mind is something really rather big –' He pushed his plate away and cleared his throat. 'Yes, on an ambitious scale. Actually, I find the idea of filling the sports stadium hugely exciting. You know – a programme of heightened performances, each one trumping the other in its scope and reach. I don't believe it's ever been done here. You fly in Shirley Bassey and give our soldier boys something to look at as well as listen to. They want to whistle, don't they? So, let them. You throw in some comedy to make them laugh – to take away the pain, the pain of war. You lower Bob Hope from a helicopter at vast expense. I don't know – the event is just a backdrop for the idea of shared emotion, of common experience. Only show me the shared experience and I'll show you the morale booster you seek, sergeant. And Pretty Flamingo will be perfect – *ideal*. The virtues of irony and camp have so far eluded these boys beautifully. All except Kenneth, I dare say, or Jimmy. I'm a man with a gun – so, make me laugh or make me cry, but please don't ask me to question what I do. Do you see it? Feed me feelings, feed me lies – show me how to be more like other men.' Here Kanoo drew back from the table, his beads wound tightly around his hand. 'Because I want to belong – oh, yes, I do.'

'Goodness –' Oona said, moved by the violence of his appeal. She was just about to ask Khalil Kanoo to advance her the sum of two hundred pounds sterling or equivalent. She didn't get a chance to do that. She saw a waiter point her out from the courtyard door. She watched a second man step through the parted drape to survey the lively scene. It took Oona a few seconds to understand what was happening. From just inside the door, his fingers feasting on his bow tie, her husband looked right through her towards the stage.

At the Rock Hotel she sat down to dine for the second time that night. It was half past nine. After a waiter had cleared the fourth place setting from their table she asked the obvious question.

'Is someone joining us?'

'I certainly hope so,' Durbridge said, glancing at his watch. He lit a cigarette and scooped a printed card – an advertisement – from the glass ashtray. '*Tonight at the Rock Hotel –*' he read aloud, '*Miss Suzy Wong, international cabaret artiste.* Alas, Miss Wong is not our third.'

Oona looked over her shoulder. In a corner of the smoky room the singer perched on a softly lit stool with her three accompanists behind her. There was a streak of silver in her hair, prominent even at a distance. She sat with legs crossed, one bare foot on the rung of her stool. Her dress of red satin shimmered whenever she moved or breathed. With the microphone held close to her glossy lips she sang I Say A Little Prayer, her voice deep despite her diminutive stature, to an arrangement lush with saxophone.

'Is this where you plan to stay?' Oona asked, discarding a menu.

'You should probably eat something,' Durbridge said, stubbing his cigarette out early.

'I've already eaten tonight,' she reminded him.

'You look thinner, Oona – you should eat.'

'You look well, Adrian.'

She watched him despise her slowly from behind a Martini. His skin was tauter and less sallow. A suntan had taken possession of his look. His hair was shorter. It was fairer, too – no longer yellow. Was he almost muscular now below his bow tie? He had come back, but not for her, not for her. It's better this way, darling – trust me. As the singer sang the song, Oona imagined she heard her husband betray her for the last time.

'I'm taking the boys with me,' he said.

'To Australia?' she said. 'I don't think so, Adrian –'

'The funds are in place – there won't be a problem.'

'Except for me, that is.'

'As I say –' he said, ignoring her diversion. 'Money is no longer an issue.'

'Meaning what, exactly?'

She had sighted him already. In fact, their eyes touched briefly across the smoky interior. Oona watched the young man approach between tables from the bar side of the restaurant, his hands in his pockets, as Suzy Wong embarked on I Fall To Pieces using a husky contralto. The young man stopped directly behind Durbridge, tight white polo neck clinging to his chest. He placed just his fingertips on the shoulders in front of him.

'Xavier?' Durbridge reached up and squeezed the fingers behind him. 'Xavier, this is my wife Oona.' He waited long enough for her to appreciate the physical qualities on offer at close range. 'Oona, I want you to meet my associate Xavier.' The epithet hung, surprised at itself, in the air above their table as the young man took his seat. 'Xavier hails from the Philippines –'

The new arrival clicked his fingers impatiently. Immediately a waiter in a black cummerbund approached the table.

'As a matter of fact,' Durbridge continued, 'he comes from an extremely wealthy Filipino family. No – *dynasty*.'

Xavier frowned at Oona. '*Used* to come –' he corrected. He let out a tiny sigh before he explained. 'They seem determined to cast me as some sort of black sheep.'

The waiter hovered, scratching at his little notepad.

'Oh, won't you order for me, Adrian?' Xavier said. His fingers fluttered above, and then settled on, Oona's wrist. 'So hard to know what to choose in this God-awful place, don't you find, Oona?'

She left them sitting there with one hand each on the menu. All the way to the arch beside the bar she thought she felt their eyes on her back, but when she turned around at last she saw they weren't even looking. Behind, in the distance, Suzy Wong came down from her stool with her flex trailing and crouched at the edge of the stage – Oona imagined fondly she was crouching to kiss a sleepy child in the wings. The child was clapping silently behind the curtain at the side of the stage. Oona clapped too. Everyone clapped on behalf of everyone else, leaning closer to each other now to share this or that secret in the warm light of common experience. Oona collected her wrap and passed through the arch as, behind her, a long way off, all the applause came to nothing.

### ❧ THE LOOK OF LOVE ❧

IN THE VILLAGE OF TARIM, NEAR SHIBAM at Wadi Hadhramaut, there were mosques enough for every day of the year. From a skyline bristling with minarets the raised finger belonging to the mosque al-Muhdar summoned the joyful to its cool sanctuary. It was here the formal ceremony took place. Basim exchanged vows with witnesses representing Hannan. There were a number of readings, chosen with the blessed occasion very much in mind, by the nominated principals in the presence of the *imam*, plus the handpicked prayers.

Three days later, Basim relaxed on a settee on the ground floor of a Shibam dwelling and waited for his bride to arrive. Surrounded in these festive apartments by relatives on Hannan's side, he wanted only to seal his private satisfaction with a public kiss. He himself had no local home in which to host the joyous *walima*. The bridegroom was without roots, they said. Still, they rallied round him on behalf of the deaf and dumb girl they loved like a daughter and pumped his hand and slapped his back and wished him all the happiness in the world – this world. As to the next, they could only speculate on the vexed question, keenly debated, of his eligibility for paradise. Basim thanked them all. That he was unlikely to see any one of them again in his life – this life or any other – he took for granted. Sitting on the sumptuously upholstered divan he pictured Hannan's motorcade in the clay canyons of Shibam. The nearer she drew, the more clearly Basim saw it. He would remove her to the city where a revolution – *his* revolution – gathered momentum day by day. He would rule her heart absolutely. She would be his consort of a terrible silence, the embodiment of wifely discretion. It was true he loved her in his way.

He gazed the full length of the red carpet to a place where the women gathered, chanting, around the nuptial thrones. In his head, the *qat*-fuelled chatter of the men fell away, leaving him with a quiet impression of oiled *djambias*, of curved daggers sporting ornamental hilts of ivory, narwhal tooth, rhino horn or cedar. Already in his life Basim had enjoyed certain moments of richly appointed success. All the more surprising, then, that he started to experience as part of his complacent reverie an emotion akin to doubt. It was unexpected. It was new – a type of moral equivocation coupled with philosophical uncertainty in the face of challenging historical imperatives. It came

202

from nowhere, much like a desert wind, causing the groom to sweat inside his heavily embroidered *zanna*. What if he was wrong – wrong about *everything*? How privileged Basim felt to have been offered, no strings attached, this glimpse of personal weakness, of human frailty. Suddenly a cry went up at the front of the house. Now the chanting died away. As five little girls in white satin slips began their dance of welcome at the door, the older women started to ululate.

FOR SOME TIME NOW the honking of horns had been unrestrained. At the head of the convoy of clapped-out cars as it crawled through Shibam's alleys was an open-top Plymouth bearing the bridal party. Up front beside the stoical driver and waving proudly *in loco parentis* was Hannan's uncle. Such was their progress in the narrow lanes he was able to shake the eager hand of every well-wisher who reached unknown from a door recess or window as the motorcade made its way among bicycles and scooters, between cheering neighbours and the odd uninterested bullock that pressed, throat drooping, against a wall. In the back of the creeping convertible rode Hannan, veiled in georgette of midnight blue and bedecked around the head with an assortment of silvery trinkets. Although the jubilant slapping of the vehicle's plates was relentless, Hannan heard nothing – nothing save the rushing from plantain to palm of the waters in her head. On one side sat her auntie, a *sitara* of dyed Egyptian cotton lurking demurely below her cloak. On the other side was Hildegaard van Kris, veiled without according to general custom but with a dread inside shared only by the bride. Although Hildegaard had no desire to be present, she was indispensable in key respects to the unfolding of events. Not only did she anticipate, from hour to hour, her rescue by impending forces, she had also been blackmailed emotionally into discharging a bridesmaid's role by a pushy aunt on behalf of a tragic bride. Again

Hildegaard registered the unhappy grip of Hannan's fingers inside the folds of their skirts. There was nothing she could do or say – she simply squeezed in return. She wrapped her hand around the rings and knuckles and squeezed until her blood drained away. At last she heard their chants and their wailing. Ahead, she saw five little girls. The five girls danced in a doorway, luminous in their shifts of white satin. Now they shrieked as the firecrackers took up in the street and the car horns brayed with an unprecedented fervour.

Beside the damascened grandfather clock just inside the doors, Basim offered up his arm. Once Hannan had laid her hand on his wrist he escorted her, Hildegaard following behind, through a storm of petals towards the chairs at the other end of the carpet. Everyone applauded. Basim's pulse was slightly raised. There was the familiar torrent inside Hannan's head. She stopped at his side when they got to the heavy chairs, and he turned her face gently to receive his kiss. Lifting the blue veil, he saw she was crying. Everyone saw. First the gasps went out. Then the wailing took up with fresh urgency. Basim wiped Hannan's tears away with his thumbs and discovered in her all-seeing eyes a terror that appalled and unnerved him. What if he was wrong? He had just that one question for her. She couldn't hear him. She couldn't help him. There was very little time left now – he sensed that. Deep in her eye he saw the horror soften or mutate, its ultimate guise a profound sadness. She didn't need him. She had no need of him – that was the main thing. It made Basim, swooping to claim her with a kiss, more determined than ever to possess her. He heard the shouts from outside, the banging at the big door. He took his lips from Hassan's, turned from the thrones in a chaotic silence, and confronted the guests lined up on either side of the carpet in a guard of honour. Moving slowly towards the door, Basim examined their faces. There – as he drew level with Hildegaard she lifted her veil so that he would see her. There was a ritual wagging of tongues at this provocation, but to Basim it was a tribute, a vindication. He saw the future – it was an endless succession of descending veils. The unlocked door crashed open now with an extravagant violence. The bridegroom progressed calmly along the boulevard of fallen flowers towards the MPs in their oblong of light. There were six or seven of them peering at the gloom of the interior, their pistols at the ready. Without warning the grandfather clock began to chime. Hesitating before the panting policemen, Basim took off his ceremonial jacket and hung it over the muzzle of a gun.

'So –' he said, smiling broadly. 'Who's in charge of this rabble?'

BEN NOLAN WENT INTO THE DESERT DARKNESS. He left Aden via the causeway road and drove through the advancing dusk towards Sheikh Othman. He was due next day to go on the lighthouse run – a passage unsuited, he told himself, to a man drifting metaphorically towards numberless rocks. He would have checked and adjusted the alignment of the Fresnel lenses and the impassive mirrors, then run the back-up generator for an hour and a half while Ibrahim scraped the gull shit from the glass housing and the six-foot-high letters that proclaimed the outcrop Abu Ali for all to see. As he drove and drove Nolan imagined the cunning sea. He would have had to step aboard it, to let it bear him up, to profess he loved it with his life because, if he didn't, it would find a way to punish him – now, always – for the death, at its cruel and conniving hand, of his wife. Instead of going to the lighthouse, Nolan went into the desert.

He left the settlements behind and offered himself wilfully to the night. The night was all around him, warm and dry and visible in his headlights as an endlessly enacted drama starring crazed insects and glittering dust. Nolan hadn't the faintest idea where he was going. In his self-pitying imagination he was running from the memory of one woman or another and hoping for a passing shot at redemption. To conduct his affairs *rightly*, aligning intention, action and consequence like the mirrors and lenses of Abu Ali – that was the instinct he set out to follow. He felt his failure most acutely in his bungled response to the sending of a letter, a most sincere letter, from Hildegaard to his late wife. So many deeds Nolan saw in a life. Which ones really mattered? He took another pull on his Cuervo and then wedged the bottle between his thighs. He was travelling north, that was all, and further than he had ever been. He had no estimated time of arrival. He searched for the brightest star, but there were too many stars in general. Their navigational potential was overrated, Nolan decided, drinking up. He had the idea a whole bottle of tequila might render him lifeless. To drive – that was the big thing. He was very far gone, unsighted. To voyage to the margins of the night and then some – it was an itinerary ideal, Nolan reasoned, for a man of his outlook.

He braked impulsively, pulling the Land Rover up on one side of the track. He switched off, got out, and sloshed more juice into the tank from his can. The engine clicked as it cooled. In between clicks there was a silence Nolan didn't know. The headlights illuminated a miasma of aerial plankton – the rest was a blackness punctuated by stars. Nolan switched off the headlights, then stretched out beside his jerry can and railed at the profligate beauty of heaven. He closed his eyes for just a moment. What a moment it was, though – he was driving blindly through angry tears and as he drove he prayed. The surprising thing was this – he saw a solitary figure up ahead about a hundred yards away. It was a difficult place to be angling for a lift, Nolan admitted. But if someone did happen along, they were more or less obliged to stop. The lone figure, a man, was easier to pick out now. His white suit sparkled in the headlights – the sartorial effect was of sequined pyjamas, Nolan decided. He hurtled past the figure in third gear, then braked hard and stopped. Having reversed a short distance, he drew level with Elvis Presley at the edge of the track.

'Which way you headed, pilgrim?' The spangled hitchhiker had his acoustic guitar slung across his chest.

'Straight on, I think –' Nolan said, peering hard at the blackness beyond the immediate pool of light.

'Mind if I ride with you some?' Elvis laid both hands on the rim of the passenger door and leaned in.

'How far are you travelling?' Nolan asked, interested.

'Oh, just to the end of the night – I have to get me to a wedding ceremony there or thereabouts.'

'In that case, you'd better hop in.'

They sped on, Nolan giving nothing away. Elvis said he knew a short cut. They left the road proper and followed an unsealed track towards an unseen horizon. Conversation was strictly limited at that time. They were content to enjoy each other's company, along with the occasional minor chord.

'Awkward spot to be looking for a lift,' Nolan suggested finally.

Their progress should have been more circumspect, surely – a case of tyre in the rut of watchful tyre.

'Oh, I don't know,' maintained Elvis, strumming his guitar with a thoughtful action. 'Seems to me the longer you wait, the better the ride. Ain't that the code of the road?'

Then he sang Kentucky Rain, and his voice was immediately at one with the whisper of the desert air.

'So, where's this wedding?' Nolan said when the song was over.

'Up ahead some,' his passenger explained. 'Are you in the mood for another, cowboy?'

'Look here –' Nolan said. 'Will you do something for me?'

207

The truth was he had warmed very naturally to the minstrel with the snakeskin boot on the dash.

'You want me to step inside the circle —' Elvis said. 'Is that it?'

'Yes, that's it,' Nolan admitted. 'Are you for or against me?'

At the side of a desert track he poured out the fuel from his jerry can, tracing a large circle in the dirt — a grinning sun complete with slanting eyes and radial spokes. Inside the circle of fire the two men stood shoulder to shoulder while Elvis extemporised around Always On My Mind — a haunting acoustic version of a new composition — and Nolan hit out again at the prodigal beauty of the sky.

'Ain't no one else knows that song,' said the singer as the flames died away all around. 'Just you and me and the Lord up above —'

At the end of the night they discovered an oasis of neon light on both sides of the track hosting at least two motel-diners and a drive-in chapel fronted by palms. It was at this very chapel that Elvis had contracted to marry his long time sweetheart Priscilla Beaulieu. She was waiting for him at a chrome altar wearing only white, and there passed between them a look of love such as Ben Nolan hadn't seen before. It made him screw up his fists. He himself was the best man. He emerged from the chapel dusted with confetti and clutching an acoustic guitar. When he woke up, on the other hand, he cradled a near-empty bottle of Cuervo and his shirt stank of vomit. It was still dark, Nolan saw. No, it wasn't — he was actually lying in a shallow pit directly below the chassis of his Land Rover. He heard the voices rise, interrogative and Arab. Then the vehicle began to roll away.

'Shoot —'

He gasped and fell back in his trench. The desert sun achieved an ocular penetration equivalent to a thousand daggers of light. The end of the night was apparently located elsewhere. At the edge of an unsealed track, Nolan found himself attended by three disapproving herdsmen and a handful of condescending camels. Nevertheless, he exulted, redeemed overnight by the code of the road. Honour found or restored, he viewed himself with every justification as a cowboy, a pilgrim and, not least, a friend and best man to Elvis. The first thing he did was look for a charred circle in the sand.

## ❧ True Stories ❧

HE COULD HEAR THE TICKING OF HIS WATCH. It was so late it was almost early. The dormitory snorers had fallen silent hours ago, and the pie-dogs had long since stopped howling beyond the perimeter at a swollen moon. Callum Kennedy lay motionless in the near dark below the sheet of his bunk bed at Waterloo barracks. He had been lying there so long, just breathing, he felt like a vital organ – a lung, perhaps, or a bladder – of the night. He had the sense of time itself rising, minute after minute, in a raging stream around his bunk. He chose not to consult his watch. He cared not for slumber. If he slept, it would be morning. In the morning it would arrive. There was no deflecting it – Callum didn't want to. It had booked ahead, made a reservation. Now he was anxious to meet it on schedule.

He threw off the sheet, stepped quietly onto the tiles, and opened his locker. Damn it – the locker door squealed. Callum waited, but no one stirred around him. He took his torch from the top shelf and eased a tightly folded square of newspaper from under his boots. In bed, he made a tent of his sheet and switched the torch on with his hand held over the beam. He unfolded the cutting. She was waiting for him in the picture. It must have been an old picture, an English photograph, because her hair looked shorter and she was wearing a heavy overcoat. Her husband's picture was right beside hers. There was only his head in the picture. Her husband's name was Benedict

– Benedict Nolan. What type of man had a name like Benedict – an angry man or a forgiving man? Callum had no relevant experience on which to draw. He looked into the husband's eyes until his own eyes stung. Once again, his scrutiny revealed no new fact. The third picture was of the fisherman who had answered her cries – her final cries, the newspaper called them. How proud the fisherman's family must be, Callum decided again sadly. But what was he like? Was he a Commie or not? It was impossible to know from the picture. Soon he would receive his hero's medal from the high commissioner at a ceremony recognising courage in a model universe. Again the noble words danced mockingly on the printed page. They had never done justice to the depth of Callum's feeling. After his torch failed he slept immediately. Still the stream rose around his bunk.

THE INQUEST TOOK PLACE OVER TWO DAYS in a sunny chamber off a small anteroom at the end of a long corridor. They were bent on recreating as far as possible the events leading to the death of the expatriate Englishwoman who had swum too far or too much. She had strayed beyond the shark net. Now she was silent witness to an official enquiry she would have done anything to avoid. Neither her husband nor the brave fisherman was present in person at this stage in the proceedings. Callum looked hard for them – their newsprint images continued to sear his retina. There were the harbour police representatives, and an army liaison man in the wings. At the centre of the panel of experts was a kind of magistrate – it was opposite this man Callum sat with his buddy Taylor on a highly polished bench.

'The Mermaid Club is a NAAFI establishment for junior ranks, am I right?' The magistrate aimed his question, which was more like a remark, at the air just above the two soldiers.

'That's correct, sir,' Taylor said.

'If Private Kennedy could answer these questions, please –'

Callum sat up straighter on the bench, bloodshot eyes smarting in the extreme light. 'That's right, sir,' he confirmed.

'You spent the early evening there, did you not, in the company of the late Mrs Nolan?'

'Yes, sir.'

'And then you went on together – the three of you.'

'That's right, sir.'

The magistrate wasn't even looking. He had copious affidavits to consider. His wire-rimmed glasses arched like an ornamental bridge over the delta of capillaries at the tip of his nose.

'Tell me, Private Kennedy – where did you go that night?'

Then Callum felt his short life – all of it – was open to question. If he didn't affirm or reaffirm it right now, image by image, feeling upon feeling, it might never have taken place at all. Taylor's sturdy frame next to his was very reassuring.

'We went to Shanghai Sam's, sir. It's a clip joint –'

The magistrate peeled off his glasses and looked up, engaged at last. He nodded his satisfaction – what were words if not the means by which one man might find another? 'An establishment unknown to me, I have to say –' He was sucking the stem of his glasses as he turned towards the liaison officer. 'And an establishment that is off limits, am I right?' He waggled his glasses in front of his face. 'Out, as it were, of bounds.'

No one moved to challenge the magistrate's assessment. He put his spectacles back on and consulted his papers.

'There you met a Miss Suzy Wong,' he went on. 'Correct me if I'm mistaken –'

Callum heard Taylor clear his throat beside him.

'Miss Wong is a friend of mine, sir.'

Certain peripheral panellists glanced up from their notes at this juncture, their expressions ranging, as Taylor might have perceived it, from amused to mildly lascivious. Had he expected any of them to hold his eye he would have been disappointed.

'And how are we to describe Miss Wong's occupation?'

Only the magistrate himself was straight and true. Sitting beside his buddy on a highly polished bench, Callum had absolute faith in this. It was impossible for the world to be configured otherwise.

'Like I say, sir – Miss Suzy Wong is a friend of mine. I asked her if they could have a room so they could be together.'

'Private Kennedy and Mrs Nolan?'

'That's right, sir.'

'For the purpose of what, exactly?'

'Like I say, sir – so they could be together. There comes a time in life, sir –'

'Does there, indeed, Private Taylor?' The magistrate nodded, distracted but thus far satisfied, above his reports. 'So, young man – would you care to tell us what happened next?'

'Nothing, sir – nothing happened next.'

The wall clock said quarter past ten. Official interest deepened in the form of a sceptical silence.

'Come, private – this inquest concerns itself with the facts and nothing more. You claim in your statement you had no idea Jacinta Nolan was a married woman. I believe you. I think you very naïve, but I believe you. Having said that – do you honestly expect me to accept nothing took place between the two of you that night?'

'Nothing took place, sir.'

'Don't try my patience, private. I put it to you without prejudice on this morning and in this room – would a married woman take her own life because she had somehow *failed* to commit adultery?'

Callum reviewed the magistrate's proposition. It was impossible to make sense of it. They had only danced, swum and cried. Yes, it was impossible to accept he might have *killed* Jacinta. He had to stop himself from blurting it out now. How do you know she meant to do it? Maybe she didn't – maybe she didn't mean to swim that far. Did she leave a message blaming me? Well, did she?

'Like I told you, sir –' he said, very low. 'Nothing happened.'

The magistrate sighed, nodding. Yes, his hand had been forced. The likeable but stubborn young soldier had left him no choice. He reached down, out of sight, for a moment. What he held up now for general inspection was a pair of white underpants.

'Perhaps I can jog your memory using this exhibit –' He draped the underpants, poignant and very funny, over the edge of the desk. 'Check the name tape, please,' he insisted gently. 'I understand this garment was discovered at the bottom of Mrs Nolan's handbag.'

Callum stared at the comical exhibit in front of his eyes. It was enough to make you laugh out loud. *Did the earth move?* Well, did it? Callum felt the heat now from the torso close beside of the comrade to whom he had almost bragged. Why? It wasn't in his nature. Two panellists smirked at the surprising evidence. Let them. To Callum, the laundered underpants, absurdly clean today it seemed, were an expression of true faith. They confirmed everything he felt about his short life – in particular its urge to courage and beauty. He had done nothing wrong – *nothing*. Such underpants should probably enter the history books, Callum reasoned, lashing out inside. Of course, there was still the issue to address of internal disciplinary proceedings.

'Nothing happened, sir. Nothing happened because I couldn't *do* it. I wanted to, but I couldn't. At the time I didn't think it bothered her one way or the other. She seemed much more concerned about me. She said it didn't matter. That was what she was like. She asked me to hold her because she felt cold. I felt cold too. We only danced or cried before that. We cried – not much, of course – because we both felt sad, for some reason. No, we *swam* as well – or, rather, she did. She told me she'd teach me how to swim, sir –'

LATER, TAYLOR SAT CROSS-LEGGED ON A RUG beside little Amy. He was meant to be seeing Khalil Kanoo to discuss the impresario's exciting plans for an outdoor concert. Kanoo hadn't even answered his phone – Taylor had faked their conversation on the basis he had better slip out to ask his question before he was confined to barracks for his sins. He wanted to put his question to Suzy Wong right now. Meanwhile, the daughter set aside her koala bear. Then she picked up two pieces of pottery that fitted together perfectly.

'Lucky little girl, Amy Wong – I do believe you've located the Queen of Sheba's teapot which has been hiding in the desert sands for all these years.'

'Go play now, please, Amy,' said Suzy Wong. She was standing at the small window in her belted robe, smoking a cigarette with her back to the room.

'Where on earth did you find that fine teapot?' Taylor persisted.

'Callum gave it to me,' Amy said, peeking out from behind the pink shards.

'Play outside now, Amy – Mummy can watch you from here.'

Once they were alone together she continued to smoke in silence with Taylor standing directly behind. Beyond the bars of the window was a small space, graveyard of appliances from the Rock Hotel.

'I don't think she'll be seeing Callum again for a while,' Taylor said. How to get round to asking his big question – that was what he really needed to know. There was no manual to help him – no army handbook. It was vital he set it up properly – that was all he knew.

'You know he comes here alone sometimes,' Suzy said, putting out her cigarette. 'Each time he comes he brings a piece of his vase for Amy. But that's not the real reason he comes –'

Outside, the little girl stepped into a fridge with no door.

'He asked me to teach him about sex, Taylor,' Suzy went on. I mean how to make love to a woman. He offered me money. When I said no, he begged me not to say anything about it to you.'

Taylor sighed. He put his arms around Suzy Wong from behind and touched his chin to her head. 'Look –' he said after a short time. 'Chances are I won't see you again for twenty-eight days.'

'You don't know that for sure.'

'Yes, I do. Twenty-eight days –'

'So, are you allowed to kill and be killed during that time?'

For a moment neither spoke. Instead they watched the little girl curl up inside her rusting fridge.

'Look at me, Suzy –' Taylor said, turning her around gently to face him. 'You know things can only get worse here. Much worse –'

She reached up and kissed him. 'I am not afraid,' she said.

'I know that,' he told her.

'What will become of me, Taylor? *Que deviendrai-je?*'

He drew her closer, but she pulled away from him. Beyond the bars, Amy lay down in an enamelled bathtub.

'I can get you both out, Suzy. Think about it, please. People will be leaving here in droves shortly – I tell you they will. Not everyone will have a safe place to go. Do you understand what I'm saying?'

'*Ouais, je comprends tout cela –*'

'Do you? Do you, really? Look – I'm asking you to marry me.' If it didn't happen quite as he had envisaged he no longer cared. The important thing was to get it out in the open as soon as possible.

'Ah, Taylor,' she gasped. 'Shall I marry your passport, *enfin?*'

215

'I want to take care of you, Suzy.' He badly wanted her to turn away from the window, but she didn't do that – not yet.

'*Non, ce n'est pas possible, ça –*' she whispered. Now she turned and consoled him with her smile.

From beyond the window Amy called out insistently.

'I want to take care of you both,' Taylor said, a little violently – desperately, even.

Now the young girl was crying, screaming, for her mother.

'My big, beautiful friend –' Suzy Wong murmured, reaching up to seal Taylor's lips with her finger.


THE WAXING MOON REACHED ITS ZENITH. On the reclaimed spit of land beyond the perimeter fence the mongrel dogs barked at the incoming tide. Callum Kennedy lay curled up under the sheet in his bunk bed. In his hand below the pillow was a shard of pottery of the type he held dear at that time. Dreaming, although not yet asleep, he waited for the shard fairy, but the shard fairy didn't show.


### ❧ THE VERDICT OF FAILURE ❧


'WILL YOU READ TO ME IN ENGLISH?'

His request was straightforward enough. Nothing, however, was simple any more. As Sulaiman watched his son dip the bread in a saucer of condensed milk, the words circled tightly in the air between them like a knot of flies.

'You know – you haven't read to me for such a long time I think my English must be getting worse, not better.'

Isa chewed his bread without meeting his father's eyes.

'Just wait till they pin a medal on you, Dad – then you'll know your English is plenty good enough to be going on with.'

They were having breakfast. The door was open to a cool light. There were no books on the table. The books had been set aside like childhood games.

'Will you come fishing with me today?'

It was a necessary test – nothing more, nothing less. Sulaiman had no real expectation of persuading Isa to join him that day. Nor was there any genuine likelihood of Isa choosing or volunteering to go fishing with him. For the father it was a painful rite, a compulsion – he wanted to hear his son deny him one more time.

'You know I can't, Dad. I have to finish school.'

Isa chewed on. The measured progress of his jaw, the lubricious action of his saliva – they were drivers of a hateful machine working quietly in the calculating silence to put distance between father and son. As Sulaiman watched he acknowledged for the first time that Isa had turned away for good. There could be no further delight. The wonder years were as nothing.

'I thought you didn't have school today –'

'I have extra school.'

'Extra school?'

'Advanced classes.'

'In how to construct a Molotov cocktail?'

Sulaiman stopped there in anticipation of a resentful silence. He would continue to test his son until he had satisfaction, by which he meant a retreat from lies. That the boy should open up to him at his awkward age, that he should bare his soul while respecting the will of his father – it was unlikely to happen. Sulaiman knew it – it was normal. What he couldn't or wouldn't accept was the silken deceit, the smooth deception. It was the triumph of fixed ideas, a verdict of failure on a father's unconditional love. It wasn't just the boy, either – something ugly and shameful had stolen into his own day-to-day affairs. Sulaiman didn't know where it had come from. He just knew it made him see everything differently – yes, everything. He glanced up to confirm what he already suspected at heart. His beautiful son was no longer beautiful.

'We've been through all this, Dad –'

He waited until Isa looked him in the eye.

'You still deny it?'

'Of course –'

Oh, the boy looked away. The boy turned away.

'Khalil Kanoo is a liar, then?'

'No – Khalil Kanoo is misinformed.'

A yellow bulbul settled in their doorway and began to sing. Isa swept the crumbs from the table and tossed them outside.

'Why don't I believe what you tell me any more?'

'Look, Dad –'

The son pushed his chair back and picked up his satchel.

'Wait – I demand to know what you're mixed up in, Isa.'

'Don't make me choose. I'm investing in the future, that's all.'

'Ah, yes – young men must act while old men like me sit around talking about it. Is that it?'

'Please don't make me choose –'

'Better for all of us if it were the other way round, I'd say.'

'You know I love you, Dad.'

'Then stay here with me today. Don't make me *forbid* you.'

The test – it was over now. Already Isa was in the doorway with his back to the breakfast table. In the dirt beyond him lay his bicycle – the yellow bulbul had taken up residence there. For a moment the songbird perched on the spoke of a wheel like a sign or a symbol at once blatant and obscure – then it was gone forever.

'Do you want me to choose?' Isa said, voice trembling now.

218

It was darker in the room – the boy used up far too much light.

'What time will you be home?' Sulaiman asked finally, normally, because he understood in that instant all the choices had been made.

'I don't know,' Isa said. 'Late, probably –'

'That's good, son – that's awfully good. Because today I have to be alone with my work.'

TIME WAS A SICK DOG – IT CRAWLED all day long. All day Sulaiman waited, his son's radio resting mute on the table between his hands. He didn't switch the radio on – that wouldn't have felt right. It was getting dark when he heard the tyres of the pick-up crush the stones outside. He heard the handbrake go on and a door open. Then the driver was on the threshold. Sulaiman said nothing. He lifted up the radio and turned it on for its comforting sound, its noise. What? No power? Sulaiman made a note to buy batteries for Isa. Small things, special things – in these lay deliverance. Still Sulaiman said nothing. The driver took eight plywood boxes from the pick-up. He built his pyramid of wooden boxes just inside the door while the engine ran. Sulaiman waited until the pick-up rolled far away across the stones. Then he got up, wiped his body with a wet cloth, and prayed.

He carried the first wooden box down to the water, aware now of his hunger. His hunger was a spur. Two kids with a torch picked crabs from a sewage pipe, but they didn't distract the fisherman. He pulled in his boat and dragged it onto the shingle. Seven more trips he made, stowing eight wooden boxes below his net. Although each box looked the same, each felt different – despite his own promise of indifference, Sulaiman experienced a dreadful fascination as to their content. In his arms they were like the coffins of babies.

The open sea was no refuge. He drifted in the Gulf of Aden with his net hanging below. When he pulled it up there were no fish in it

219

– not a one. Sulaiman had the idea there was none left anywhere in the world – not for him. True, his boat was already heavy, his catch corrupt, his cargo a bitter bargain. He put out the lamp and jerked the cord of the engine by the light of a full moon hopelessly scarred by pockmarks. It was a tragic orb to show its face like that. It was a moon for saints and shipwrecks, surely – there was nothing in it for smugglers. That was the whole thing, Sulaiman decided – the night had been chosen for its lunar prowess and distinction. How perverse – there would be nowhere to hide out there after all.

Two miles out from land and thirty fathoms above the seabed he turned his back on the twinkling refinery at Little Aden. He pointed the prow of his boat at a vacant horizon, steering south by the stars towards the Horn of Africa. He felt a hot breeze, anxious, irritable, on his face. It had travelled such a long way to meet him. He could taste it – its power and malice. It arrived, hounded and hounding, from India, an agent of dust storms, the harbinger of rains.

Now the wind picked up. Sulaiman held his course steady on a restive swell. He could see the white horses in the offing – they were skittish, spooked. All the time he eyed the sulking sky, the brooding clouds. The clouds massed as from nowhere in their liveries of black and grey, then marched towards the land. Sulaiman opened up the throttle, peering and peering. He had to time his run. Now, there – he was scouring a seething horizon, hunting a shape or form. Then he saw her. At first she was just a dark smudge on a ribbon of foam. Rapidly she took on substance, glinting dully at the edge of the deep water. Lethal and alluring, the open sea gleamed behind her in the sick moonlight. Then the rain came, hesitant and sporadic at first. It wasn't shy for long. Sulaiman knelt on the boards and approached the looming vessel through a silver forest. The rain filled his boat. Up ahead, the ghost ship gave no signal – Sulaiman had expected none.

He saw the squall deepen immediately behind her, ready to cut and run. He entered the shadow of the vessel from the stern. She was a converted yawl of the old school with a towering presence of masts and spars – they rose and fell directly above Sulaiman now, hurling abuse at a shrieking wind. She must have been running an anchor. Still her engine turned, screws snarling angrily above the surface as she pitched. Abruptly the rain stopped. The wind tightened its grip on the yawl. Sulaiman glimpsed the livid signature as her hull rolled and plunged. Her name was *Nan-Shan*. She was from Kowloon. The useless moon went out again.

He saw a light. He came alongside. He moved to seize the step, but it rose above him and flew away as he lunged. He made another approach. He saw a few figures huddled at the rail around a lamp. Someone threw a rope – Sulaiman felt its sting on his bare back and gripped it and passed it twice around the thwart. He cut the engine and hauled himself in. Now he was rising and falling with the bigger boat. Reason fled – he heard the mournful knock as the hulls came together. Now they moved apart. Sulaiman pulled on the rope and looked up. He imagined he saw a Chinaman there behind the rail. Yes, yes – he was sitting in his wheelchair with the lamp held above him while, behind and to one side, a flunkey wrestled for control of an umbrella. Horror – there was something new. As the hulls came together again, Sulaiman saw it. They had roped a boy upside down to the ladder above the step. The boy's eyes were ghastly, all white. Sulaiman looked inside them as he rose from below and passed the rope around a rung. Again the swell drew him off. Again Sulaiman hauled himself close to. When he reached the step this time he lifted the first box and thrust it at the terrified intermediary waiting above him. The boy raised the box high with a shriek – they jerked it from him behind the rail. Seven times Sulaiman went in like that. Seven boxes gathered at the feet of the Chinese. Then the rain returned – Sulaiman heard its spiteful hisses undercut the keening of the wind. Around him, the ocean came and went with a savage undulation. He was kneeling on the submerged boards of his boat, a wooden box in his arms. He looked up. The light went out. The rain blinded him. No matter. He stood up. No use – he was thrown back down again with the eighth box in his arms. He dragged himself up and looked for them above. No good, no good – their boat was gone, the rope was cut. The whole unhelpful sky was rain.

He pulled the cord. The engine started first time. He looked to left and right – only the hissing rain and the rolling sea. Which way to turn? Sulaiman ran with the wind, fighting the tiller, and climbed and plunged until the rain petered out behind him. It just stopped. Sulaiman saw the lights, very lovely to him, of Aden up ahead in the distance. He was roughly three miles from land with the squall over his shoulder, its dark column tracking south now towards Africa. He killed the engine and drifted for a moment, his chin on his chest.

The sky had cleared. The sea was calm. Sulaiman floated, very tired, between these two stations, observed by a shamefaced moon. He wondered what he had just done. Why was it so necessary he be present for the sake of eight wooden boxes? They could have loaded them at any time, in any place, couldn't they? No, it had to be *him*. That was how Sulaiman explained it. The whole thing was a fateful conspiracy with Isa at its centre. The boy was everything – the rest meant nothing. As he baled out mechanically with his tin, Sulaiman stared at the wooden box on the boards beside him. He drew a knife from its holster and inserted the blade below the lid of the box. He wasn't curious any more. He barely considered his actions at all. He simply peeled away the lid and tossed it behind him. Inside, the box was thinly stained – the blood had mingled there with the rain and the sea. The severed head of Khalil Kanoo fitted so snugly into the cabinet. The eyes were open. The look was of mild surprise. Lenses broken, the spectacles were bent violently around the face from ear to ear. In the eyebrows were the splinters of glass. From the mouth, which was held open by a carelessly inserted rosary, a trail of worry beads led gleaming to the purple neck stump.

For a long time Sulaiman peered at Kanoo's broken spectacles, his imagination bombarded by dire prophecy. When he looked up, the stars were back in position. Three tankers waited in a cluster of golden lights opposite the refinery for their escort. It was beautiful – the hills behind the harbour were starkly etched against a backdrop of bitterest blue. Sulaiman sealed the eighth box and launched it on the water with a little push. It took a few moments to settle and fill – he thought he might be forced to retrieve it, to weight it down with something. At last it began to sink – Sulaiman watched it disappear below the surface. He pulled the cord and turned to meet the coast.

At Bir Fuqum he ran his boat aground. He tied the rope to the rock before pushing the boat out again. The children slept, the crabs were feeding at the pipe. Sulaiman staggered across the stones until he got to the path, stumbling barefoot like a fugitive or a vagabond towards home. Home was still there, wasn't it? Everything was still there, was it not? It was hard, tired as Sulaiman was, to be certain of anything. To see his brilliant boy again and start afresh – that was the main thing now. Nothing else mattered. The light was off. The bike was gone. Funny – Isa's radio was on. Sulaiman could hear the radio from outside the house. He opened the door and lit the lamp, fighting against the sick feeling in his stomach. The room looked the same. No, the books had gone – all the big books. Wait – there was nothing left of Isa except the mattress and a few childish novels. The radio continued to broadcast in English as to an empty room. Was it a joke? Had the boy replaced the batteries before he quit the house for good? It was hard to countenance and harder to bear. Sulaiman turned off the little machine, falling forward across the table, cheek to the cool grain. In the swirling pattern of the wood he thought he saw the face of his only son. Isa's mouth was open. It was brimming with shiny beads. The beads dropped from his mouth, clicking one against the other, by way of a silky thread towards a bloody tassel.

## ❧ MONSOON ❧

POOR AZIZ. THEY CAME FOR HIM again around six o'clock. I know this now because he told me before he passed out on the stone shelf opposite mine. They came for him at sixish, having returned him to his cell only half an hour before. I could hardly have guessed he was my neighbour as I lay on my slab in the cell next door and listened to the jangle of the keys, to the slamming of his door. Mine is a cell for two persons – a twin room, if you will. Until this morning I had enjoyed a choice of berths. Now poor old Aziz is my cabin mate. He looks pretty bad, as a matter of fact. For much too long he has been deprived of sleep. That would explain the striking pallor and the red eyelids, the skin stretched more tightly across the cheeks. I say more tightly – Aziz has never been, to my knowledge, a fleshy man. They came for him early, lifting him up by the armpits and dragging him down three flights of steps to the interrogation rooms in which they hone various communication skills first developed for Palestine and Malaya. The current methodology is scarcely complex. The alleged NLF sympathiser is invited to lean hooded against a wall, his weight borne by outstretched fingers, for long periods without rest. Aziz, so he says, has thus far declined to provide satisfactory answers to their questions. I believe him. The good doctor is, I'm afraid, increasingly

224

in need of a good doctor himself. In respect of his general health, a second opinion may soon be required.

I get down from the ledge and pace – yes, pace – this cell beside the prone figure of Aziz. I must needs repeat – word for word and sentence after sentence – what I have only just said until I arrive at each paragraph's conclusion. They have refused me pen and paper, imagining, perhaps, I might jot down certain ideas and launch them in the form of a polemical aeroplane from a ground floor window. I must dictate this journal to myself, recalling and then committing to memory each word before moving forward. Even as I press on, I go back and consolidate. I sub-edit and I proofread, polishing the truth until it shines. I reach up for the bars at the window, raising myself from the floor and thrusting my face at the night sky. The southwest monsoon is with us, its heavy air sweet with a promise of rain. In the mountains, the rain is already falling. Alone on a hill with her goats, Hannan misses her husband every hour of the day. In time she will come to honour him, to forget his moment of doubt on the occasion of their wedding. She almost undermined him then with her terrible muteness. She almost moved him with her dumb appeal. Hers was a type of stage fright, entirely natural in view of her inexperience and remarkable youth. Now she waits in the surefooted company of goats for her husband to claim her while, inside her pretty head, the rising waters of the *wadi* rush from one tree to another.

They came for me yesterday around mid-morning. I fancy poor Aziz was leaning against one of their walls at the time. (Let me admit here and now to a measure of guilt. In the interests of confidentiality I had failed to enquire as to his whereabouts and his welfare.) They escorted me upstairs – not downstairs, note – in my baggy pyjamas, in the outsized slippers whose role is to encourage a kind of spiritual shuffling. They abandoned me in a small, empty room of which one wall was made entirely of glass. The room had nothing inside it but a corrosive light that pricked the eyes. One could virtually smell that light. There was no other sensory data to hand. I hardly knew how to behave in there until I deduced with quickening pulse I was being observed from beyond the glass wall. Of course – it was an identity parade of one. I need do nothing at all under these circumstances to acquit myself famously. I merely stood at attention and imagined I was posing for a passport photograph, peering straight ahead at my reflection in the glass. How to know what, or who, was beyond the wall? They might have been just one or two, or the whole gang with their clipboards and their ballpoint pens. There may have been the resourceful nurse, Miss van Kris, and the dapper little man from the Ministry whose name is Farquhar. At the very least there would be Nolan, the headstrong Young Turk from the Port Trust who had the pluck to join me on the crane above the circus ring. Ah, happy days without a safety net, Ben. Do you remember? I know you do. When a minor talent gains the spotlight unexpectedly he wins the affection of the crowd. Is it not so? He stumbles, they applaud. I see you now beyond the glass wall with your coterie. I arrange you as for a group portrait, the earnest seniors standing at the back, the naughty kids sitting cross-legged at the front with their chewing gum under their tongues. My flashbulb lights you up – you and your nightmares – as human history is made. I am fond of you all in my way.

They schedule for me another chat with Farquhar. I expect the nurse to be there again, but it appears she is no longer needed. She is somewhere else, nursing, or praying, or spying. She has certainly impressed us all with her Dutch courage. Farquhar too is what our American friends would call a tough cookie. He favours a funereal lounge suit and exudes at certain times of day the scent of Johnson & Johnson baby powder. (As the long hours pass, one's masochistic senses come to revel in these olfactory assaults.) I choose a different chair today. Although there are only two of us in the room, the seats are arranged in a circle as for a theatrical reading. Indeed, there is an element of farce about the whole set-up. Farquhar sits at twelve o'clock. I am not quite opposite – at half-past six, say, or seven. His trenchant calm I find narcotic. He would rather be elsewhere – in a wet suburban garden, perhaps, with his stamps and butterflies. His relentless grooming is both appealing and offensive to one who has barely seen water since yesterday. He smiles pleasantly and spreads his hands as if to say everything is ruled in and nothing is ruled out. I decide quickly to elevate to the top of our agenda my ablutionary stratagem. These are civilised people, I remind myself. As Farquhar parks his tiny hands in his lap, I demand the right to wash six times each day to ready myself properly for prayer. Farquhar listens with the closest attention. These sessions he has described from the outset as getting-to-know-you affairs. He agrees suavely to see what can be done. I can see him thinking – this is scarcely a hotel, Mr Mansouri. He gets up and exits the room. I am alone for all of a minute before an ancient toady appears with a jug of water in a bowl and a clean towel over his arm. I seize my chance – it would be churlish to pass it up. Then Farquhar comes back. It has been his experience, he tells me, that common prayer flourishes miraculously in a punitive realm where privilege is contingent on good behaviour. He is a perceptive jailer. We agree with a tacit consensus to leave God out of it for the time being, our conversation switching very naturally from prayer to politics. I am resolved, I inform Farquhar straight out, to embark on my hunger strike, or a sustained fast, until such time as is lifted their ban on the NLF, legitimate embodiment of indigenous aspirations. Ah, protests Farquhar, insisting modestly on the limited influence he personally exerts on the fate of nations. Still, he is impressed by my stated intention to fast. I watch him toss a speculative glance at my pyjama-cloaked physique as if to gauge how long I might last. Forty days? Seventy? He nods, reassured. No doubt he knows something I don't – one gets so out of touch in here. Perhaps he is weighing up alternative timetables, comparing and contrasting the chances of an end to the NLF ban with the likelihood of my body surviving a fast for long enough. On related political questions we agree like mature adults. The ban must be lifted to avoid further pointless bloodshed. Key detainees will be released to take up their positions at the head of a *duma* or government-in-waiting. Farquhar accepts intellectually the logic of two steps that lead inevitably to a third – the creation of a people's republic of all Yemen. Psychologically, too, he is up for it. The end can't come quickly enough for the civil servant who would rather be somewhere else. His waning interest in us is racist. There is something exquisitely distasteful to him in the prospect of FLOSY and the NLF clawing at each other's eyes like feral children. He has given up, I am cheered to note, on the dreary notion of a negotiated standoff between rival factions as brokered by the beleaguered feds. The Federal Regular Army has its tribal loyalties and divisions too, after all. Popularly discredited and compromised by internal dissent, it can no longer be relied on, Farquhar confides smoothly, to uphold the interests of the Crown. Ah, well.

These getting-to-know-you sessions will happen daily. They will continue until we two travel the shared path of mutual disdain. This path is the path of history. At first I imagined it angered Farquhar he should find himself admiring me, his historical enemy. Later, I came to believe he was just the same as everyone else – he was flattered by the attentions of his intellectual superior. Today, I tend once again to the original point of view. That he looks forward to our briefings is a source of private disgust to Farquhar. How close we threaten to become over time. Meanwhile, there will be little for me to do inside this correctional facility except wash and wait, pray and fast. Leaner but cleaner, I shall journey nearer to God during sessions I can best describe as getting-to-know-You affairs.

I reach again for the bars of the window. Behind me Aziz sleeps the sleep of the dead. I lift myself off the ground and press my cheek to the night. The air is thick with the promise of rain. I drink in the musky perfume – *our* perfume. Never falter. Never let go. No relief – still we hold on. This has been, in many ways, a dry monsoon.

# 5 |
# Callum

'Would you rather freeze to death at the North Pole
or die of thirst in the desert?'

THE PERIOD OF DETENTION had ended – he was no longer confined to barracks. Required as ever to defend the faith by day, he was free one night of the week to drink beer and seek comfort in the arms of another. As he lay on his bunk with his hands behind his head and talked his way through the important evening to come, Callum had the feeling the world was shrinking, his outlook diminishing. It was a feeling that had nothing to do with perimeter fences and restrictions on his movements these past few weeks. It recognised a far subtler limitation – the transfer like a pox from one unschooled soul to the next of ignorance likely to feed prejudice, injustice and tyranny. As a feeling it hemmed Callum in while setting him apart. Beyond his elbows, two lockers defined the limits of his estate. Above, his ceiling was a mattress with springs. All around was the banter of men stood down, and a coming and going of bodies in towels. Surrounded by voices, Callum was nonetheless isolated by and from their sociable traffic. Although in his head he matched every comrade's voice to a face, he was prevented by insidious embargo from actually looking, from looking at their bodies. He hadn't noticed their bodies before. Now they were all around him, mostly lean and hard, milk white or reddened by the sun. What had changed that he should notice them suddenly but be forbidden to look at them?

He swung his legs off the bed and then turned away, undressing quickly at his locker door. In the shower he faced the wall with feet apart and palms pressed against the tiles. There was a ritual flicking of rolled-up towels at bare skin and a raining down of talcum powder he ignored. Yes, something had changed. They had always set out to *touch* him where and when they could, to access his person, to ruffle his short hair. Now they were happy to work around him with their probing towels. Still, there was no clear malice in their indifference, Callum argued. It was a new kind of respect. A society had its rules and its rewards.

The sun dipped behind the rooftops of the barracks as he put on his kilt. As he neared the gym he could hear Miss Muir's piano. The stately Strathspey tempo stirred him as it always did, quickening his heartbeat with its suggestion of romance and melancholy. Inside the gymnasium the climbing ropes were knotted together in loops above the dance. The pommel horses lined the wall bars along one side of the room. Sitting erect at the upright piano, Miss Muir had her foot on the pedal and her handbag beside her foot. Now a faster dance was in progress – Callum took his place in a line of soldiers, one row opposite another. They peeled off two by two from the head of their columns and skipped their way down the kilted avenue and whirled each other arm in arm when the time came. They did this *physically*, passionately. They danced in long socks on the creaking floor while Miss Muir hammered out the reel, her foot working the loud pedal like a piston. Then an unlikely thing happened. It did so again and again. To Callum it was like an afternoon dream, feasible and cruel. First, he was arm in arm with Keiller at the head of the dance. They whirled around together as required until Keiller jerked his partner close and kissed him hard on the neck. Callum wheeled away, skin smarting, but no one had seen it. Soon he was met by Morton and spun around in the familiar way before being released with a savage kiss. It was the same all the way down the line. No one noticed. The music stopped. Miss Muir raised her bony fingers expectantly above the keyboard, half turning on her piano stool.

'And your bows?' she proposed tremulously.

She drew a thrilling arpeggio like a drum roll from her favourite keys. Up and down the avenue of kilts the men stood tall and faced each other, breathless, across the divide. Callum found it hard to see in front of him. His brain was busy prioritising sensory data, making choices, allocating supply of blood. Disoriented and disbelieving, he forced himself to go on as if nothing had happened. Had it? Callum couldn't be certain. When they bowed – Miss Muir demanded it of them at the end of every dance – he bowed deeply across the aisle, then wheeled away once more and fled this time, his boots under his arm. Just outside the gym doors he was sick against the wall.

Who else but Taylor would have turned them? Who else but the one who could hurt him most? Callum wasn't angry any more. He was among the pie-dogs and rubble of the reclaimed land, skimming stones at a mere slip of a moon. He knew exactly what he needed to do to restore order to the universe. He must win Taylor back. It was the easiest thing in the world, Callum told himself. He fished a shard of pottery from his sporran and assessed its powdery heft. It would have made the perfect skimmer, no question. Nine leaps? Ten? Ten was far too many to waste on a half-arsed moon. Callum tucked the shard away again. Yes, it was simple – he need only act as they did.

He abandoned the dogs. The clock tower was wrong. That was OK – time had no relevance, no meaning. Crossing Tawahi Road under the broken clock he made directly for the dark – the dark face of Shamsan. Soon he was behind Steamer Point in a nameless alley of colourless clothes strung out like flags of surrender on the eve of occupation. Callum saw no one. When he turned for a moment, he glimpsed the lights of the bigger ships below. He turned away again, climbing from block to block in his dress kilt beneath an apprentice moon. Was there anyone left here alive? Advancing with ransacked heart towards his destination, her sketch map in his hand, Callum discovered he had no need of Suzy Wong's directions. He knew just where to go. He saw a crimson gash on the east side in the form of a neon arrow. The sign directed him down half a dozen steps towards a door open to the night. Callum folded up his map. There was the music coming from inside, and the caged toucan – it laughed as he drew aside the curtain. Beyond the drape the light was stained blue with smoke. There was a jukebox like a church organ on the far side of the room. That was what Callum saw first. He stood rooted there beside the curtain in a quiet relieved by the tinkle of ice cubes in tall glasses. Then the jukebox plucked another 45 from the rack, its arm touching down at last with a gorgeous thump. Callum judged it all a homecoming. Yes, he felt at home here. At the centre of the room he detected a languorous locomotion – three couples danced cheek to cheek with their fingers interlocked, or hands joined tenderly above, according to the rules of a game played out repeatedly as if the world might end tonight. The game of love – it was easy to play here, and so cheap. Each time the music stopped, a heart must break.

Off came Callum's beret. He proceeded as rehearsed towards a stool at the bar, the fall of his steps keeping time with the song. The barman was oriental – no, universal. He was some toothless grinner with pipe-hardened eye. He had the mirror behind him. His grubby bow tie sagged on an elastic band.

'Happy hour, Johnny –' he announced. 'Drinks half price.'

As he eyed the flashing bottles below the mirror Callum saw her loom out of the smoke behind him. Already she limped. Already she was damaged – danced off her feet.

'Always happy hour here, love. Doesn't much matter what time of night it is. Or day –'

She slipped in beside him and drew an ashtray closer. Watching her strike her match in the mirror Callum marvelled at the easy way of her. She automatically knew what to say. She was old – upwards of thirty, say – with black hair, very shiny and clean, and nails that matched her painted lips. Her dress left her dark shoulders bare. On the shady hill above her breasts a silver chain plunged in sparkling streams towards a tiny cross.

'First time, is it, Jock?'

What did she mean? Did she mean first time here? Or just first time? It didn't matter – the answer was the same. She had worked all that out for herself, pulling hard on her cigarette. Callum thought she might be drunk. Not drunk – tipsy. The best of her smoke rose and fell in a pillar of light above her.

'Give me a beer, please,' said the young soldier.

'We get them by the busload here, Jock. Lost virgins in kilts –'

'My name isn't actually Jock. I have my own name, believe it or not.' Then he got it. His name – she had no use for it.

'Ah, good – someone's feeling sensitive tonight.' She rapped her knuckles twice on the bar. 'Better make mine a large one, Charlie.'

Callum opened his sporran. There was the fragment of pottery in there with the cash and the credits. As he got down from the stool he felt her hand, very light, on his arm.

'Do you want to go upstairs?' She took her hand away. Callum looked up and met her eyes in the mirror. 'Well, do you, Jock?' she whispered, lowering her gaze now.

He watched her drag her leg across the dance floor towards the curtain and the caged bird. She hesitated there, half in and half out of the room, as if to make him completely aware of the moment, of its implications and its ramifications, while her cigarette continued to smoulder, lipstick on its filter tip, in the ashtray at the bar. Upstairs, he watched her unfasten her cross, saw her breasts come down with their sad eyes of blue. She sat on the edge of the bed and removed a caliper plus two leather straps from her leg. Then she slipped below the sheet and waited for him beside a smoking candle.

He took his clothes off slowly. His eyes never left hers. He knew exactly how to act. Below the sheet he held her hand, his breathing steady, his hipbone against hers on a narrow divan, until she rolled away to blow out the candle. Its flame wavered and came back.

'No – leave it on,' he said.

'Are you sure?' she said.

He threw off the sheet and sat astride her stomach, his weight on his knees. He took her breasts in his hands and brought them close together, kissing their sad eyes before taking them inside his mouth, one eye and then the other eye impartially. When he looked up, she was crying. He rolled back his head, laughing silently at the world and everything in it. He could see his shadow up there somewhere, very big. He moved over her and blew the candle out.

UNDER THE TORN CANOPY AT SHANGHAI SAM'S he knocked three times and asked for Suzy Wong. Held in a short queue, he sat on the velvet banquette beside a French sailor whose cap bore the name of his ship. Callum spoke again to the kid with the harelip. This time he asked for Amy. She was half way down the corridor below a naked light bulb with her koala bear under her arm and her paintbrush in her hand, an open picture book and a jar of dirty water on the tiles in front of her.

'Shouldn't you be tucked up by now, princess?'

The girl smiled, reaching up to explore the coarse material of his kilt. After he knelt, Callum let her examine the tassels of his sporran with her sticky fingers. He turned the paint book towards her on the tiles – she had been looking at it upside down. Callum wrapped her fingers gently in his and dipped the brush in the water, guiding her towards a printed picture on the page. They painted together – first the sky, then a house, then the family under the tree with their dog and cat – and watched the planted colours come up magically. Amy squealed. She must have been only partly satisfied with her painted world because she wriggled away. Callum tapped his sporran.

'Guess what I've got in here?'

'Maybe you should keep that to yourself, soldier boy.'

'Mummy, Mummy –'

In the harshest possible light, Suzy Wong's smile was warm but tired. As she leaned back against the wall she knotted the belt of her enormous dressing gown. 'Well – they set you free again, I guess.'

'I guess they did. Look – I wanted to thank you.' As he watched Amy turn the pages of her book, Callum glimpsed an ideal world in which dogs played with cats and boats met trains on time.

'*Mais pourquoi ça?*' Suzy Wong said. 'Did I get something right?'

She drew a cigarette from a gold case, exploring the case briefly, as if she didn't quite recognise it, before she pocketed it. It was a gift from an admirer, Callum decided – one of many, high ranking and powerful and rich. He watched Suzy Wong light her cigarette and then hold it shoulder high and to one side.

'I bet people thank you all the time,' he said.

She looked at him as if from tremendous distance, at the same time reaching down towards the tiles with the fingers of one hand.

'Come, Amy – time for bed now.'

'Hang on, wee girl –'

With the child reaching up beside him, Callum fished the piece of pottery from his sporran, wiped it on his kilt, and pressed it into her little fist. Immediately the girl brought the fragment down to her lips and sucked its corner doubtfully.

'What do you say, Amy?' Suzy Wong said.

'It goes with all the other bits,' Callum said.

'*Bien entendu* – everything is connected.'

Then a little girl offered her threadbare koala to a young man – he smiled with pure pleasure. He was about to decline her precious gift graciously, but the girl changed her mind anyway, hugging the stuffed animal to her as she ran shrieking down the empty corridor, and waving her piece of pottery in the air.

'I thought Taylor would have been here, that's all,' Callum said, getting up off his knees and twisting and untwisting his beret.

Suzy Wong tapped her ash into her cupped hand. 'Oh, but he's already been and gone.' She dropped her cigarette into Amy's jar of water and brushed her hand. 'Why?' she went on playfully, kneeling down to collect her daughter's things. 'Did something so important happen tonight you couldn't wait to tell him?'

They stood very close together in the corridor and listened for a moment to a distant siren. Callum was about to back off when she rose up, her hands full, and kissed him noisily and laughed.

'What is it?' he asked anxiously.

'Nothing,' she said. 'You'd better wash your face now.'

It took him a few seconds to relocate his position in the world. If she liked him, that was good. Everything was good. Everything was OK. 'Maybe I will,' he told her, grinning, 'and maybe I won't.'

She was ready to leave him now, amused but tired. 'You don't have to be like Taylor, Callum – you understand that, don't you?'

'I don't know what you mean,' he said, pulling on his beret.

'No? Just don't waste your time trying to be someone else –'

### ❧ BLUE MURDER ❧

THESE WERE DIFFICULT DAYS FOR SULAIMAN. It was all a question of the eighth box. Still he went about his work in the belly of a dhow as if nothing had happened. But something *had* happened, something malign. There was no longer just a presentiment of mayhem. It was here like the risen tide. As he sealed the stout timbers above the keel using a suspension of quicklime in lamb's fat, Sulaiman aligned his dread feelings metaphorically with what he knew best — the ocean. It would try to get in. It always did. There were the seafaring worms to consider, too. Their principal role in life was to penetrate the timbers below the line. Meanwhile, the police enquiry had begun. They had photographed Kanoo's headless corpse on a blood-soaked mattress in the room behind his shop. In his arms, which were folded across his chest like wings, was found a selection of pornographic journals bagged in polythene and imported from America. Of his trademark rosary there was no trace. His blood was black, the stump of his neck the sweet staging post of migrating insects. Policemen themselves had swarmed, in pursuit of their investigation, across Slave Island and its unfinished dhows. They had climbed the scaffolding and tapped the hulls. They gathered statements and made terse notes. Yet they left without the severed head they sought. It was a mystery. These were dark days indeed. The worms had found the wood, they admonished proverbially, exiting by the causeway in a caravan of white jeeps.

Sulaiman surfaced for some air. He heard the hammers fall and the chisels grate. All around him was a metallic symphony of moans and groans. Their daily labours — they were desultory and resentful. Having no idea what the future held, they grimly pictured their late employer stretched out headless in a drawer of the overspill morgue at Crater. In death, as in life, Kanoo's mythology was the subject of invidious gossip. His frozen indignity, it was widely held, had been insured against power loss by means of an emergency generator. Yet he had made no special provision for them, his loyal workers. His business plans had been largely *ad hoc*, they said. The pattern of his entrepreneurial affairs they condemned with hindsight as willy-nilly.

241

In short, he had made no credible arrangements for his succession. Now they consoled themselves at the indolent pipe, taking frequent breaks and making much of the idea that life in its living was a good deal like building dhows. It must be done, so to speak, by eye.

'Hey, old man – ahoy, there.'

It was approaching the hottest period of the day when Sulaiman heard his son's voice. He had listened to it many times in his head, examining its tone in search of clues to the boy's intentions. Now he heard it again, and it made a mockery of his hopes. Isa had chosen a good time to come. The men were gathered at their *qat* – the boy would have despised them as he entered their warehouse to ask icily for the model worker who shared his name. As it was, Sulaiman was very visible. He was about half way up a dhow's mast with a harness under his legs and a double pulley over his head. The sun flashed on his shoulder blades. He carried a pail of shark oil using his teeth. His brain was busy up there compiling a short visual history of plywood boxes. There was a sudden storm. Sulaiman went over it again. His unwritten contract had been to deliver just eight wooden crates, no questions asked. In the eighth, however, he had discovered Kanoo's severed head. What should the eighth box have contained by right? How long before someone came looking for it? There was a shriek. Sulaiman glimpsed the ghostly *Nan-Shan* as she rolled and pitched, a squealing coolie lashed to her ladder. Seven boxes they had. They had anticipated an eighth – without its bloody calling card. It would hardly have been them, would it? Sulaiman went over it again as he stabbed the dhow's mast with his loaded brush. Why kill Kanoo and then take possession of his head in a storm? No, it would hardly have been them. Again and again the lone conclusion presented itself like waves on a shore. Sulaiman couldn't say why. He didn't know why he should think the way he did – not for certain. In his imaginings it

242

was impossible to forego it from now on – the association of Kanoo's brutal murder with the cold-blooded calculations of his own son.

'Is that you, father?'

He looked down and saw Isa's upturned face. Could a son fail to recognise his father either closer or further away, at any angle, with or without the glare? Or was it a coy ploy? Blood racing, Sulaiman returned to his prophylactic stippling. The next time he looked, Isa stood on the cluttered deck peering up through his fingers.

'Won't you come down and embrace your son?'

Although it had been mere days, the father approached the very idea of his son as if from the longest exile. Isa's reconstructed tone of voice – it had in it a tendentious mixture of intimacy and formality, which Sulaiman disowned instinctively.

'What happened to your glasses?'

'My glasses, father?'

'Your glasses – their job is to help you see things more clearly.'

True perspective was dead. Around the harbour, across the bay, Sulaiman had an uninterrupted view of assorted vessels, the nearest of which spread themselves out like stepping-stones towards Ma'ala. Suddenly he saw them as a lost fleet, an armada scattered by storm and scuttled by order to obviate all risk of cannibalistic hunger and predatory thirst. Right then, the father felt as low as it was possible to feel. From his psychological funk arose certain practical questions.

'Where the hell are you living, Isa?'

No answer. He dropped his brush in the bucket before gripping the handle of the bucket with his teeth.

'Are you still going to school?'

In a silence fascinated, almost amused, the especially alert might have discerned a further breaking of close family bonds. Sulaiman's words had emerged imperfectly formed. His mouth was full. After he hung his bucket angrily on a nail he winched himself to the deck in a heated rush. Wiping his hands carefully on a towel at his waist he had plenty of time to revive all tender feeling for his gifted son.

'What is it you want, Isa?'

'How are you today, father?'

In the boy's eyes he saw a kind of valedictory longing. What was it – the yearning to go back, an urge to stop all the clocks? It was an appeal Sulaiman resisted. He had to hold fast now, to run with the wind, or the storm, until he knew everything.

'Tell me, Isa – what did you want?'

'I wanted to talk to you –'

'Then go ahead – talk.'

'About the medal ceremony.'

'What about it?'

'Are you planning to attend?'

'What do you think?'

'I think you want to go, but not to collect their award as such. I honestly believe you have no interest in badges of that sort.'

'Really? What else do you believe?'

'I believe you'd show up at their garden party simply to honour a dead Englishwoman's memory. It's admirable, father. It makes me extremely proud –'

Sulaiman threw down his towel, a sudden nausea threatening to overwhelm him. He tried to wake up from it, this nightmare of love drowning, but neither rescue nor release was at hand.

'What's on your mind, Isa?'

'The award ceremony is at Government House, isn't it? I mean – the high commissioner will be there, won't he?'

'As a matter of fact he lives there. Or *did* the last time I looked.'

'There will be guests, won't there? VIPs –'

'Would it surprise you to learn they didn't consult me about the guest list? VIPs? Yes, I dare say.'

'All of them fiddling –'

'I beg your pardon?'

'While Aden burns.'

'If you say so, Isa.'

'We want you to take them a present, father.'

How finely modulated the accent of modern terror. There was nothing crude enough or base enough to undo its perfect poise.

'Oh? I understood they would be giving *me* a present.'

'No one will get closer than you – you see that, don't you?'

'Yes, I do.' He hesitated then. He would happily have looked at the sea for the rest of the day – or the rest of his life, for that matter. On his scattered fleet it had already set in – the inconsolable urge to hunger and thirst. Meanwhile, it was important to find out who had come up with this shocking little scheme in the making.

'Was this your idea or theirs?' he asked with the lightest touch he could manage.

'Listen, Dad – they know what you did all alone out there in the Gulf of Aden. We know all about your smuggling jaunt with those wooden boxes in the wind and the rain.'

We? They? Ah, yes – it was all one. The father nodded, bitterly vindicated, at the incoming tide.

'You'd better go now, Isa,' he suggested quietly. Then it came to him with a new coldness he endorsed in himself – now was the right time to learn *everything*. 'How did you know?' he said, feigning a type of bemused wonder at the way things sometimes turned out in life. I mean – how could you possibly know about the wooden boxes?'

'Because he told us, of course.'

'What – Kanoo told you?'

No, please – don't say it. Only hold, resist. An egregious disdain for life – why confess to something like that at the end of the day? It does you no credit, this pathological bent – no credit at all.

'Yes – Khalil Kanoo.'

'But when?' The fisherman turned his back on the sea – the sea and all the fish in it. 'When did Khalil Kanoo tell you, Isa?'

As he looked into his son's shining eyes he began to see how the world would end – with a smile of satisfaction at a job well done.

'When? Oh, just as he was about to die –'

How was he to live? Sulaiman sank to the deck on his knees and found sanctuary there among the coiled ropes he respected.

'You know –' he said. 'I still don't believe I did anything wrong. I ferried a few small boxes out to sea, that's all. So what?'

'Did you look inside those little wooden boxes, by any chance? Weren't you curious or interested at all? Or did you avert your gaze as usual from what you didn't care to confront?'

'I did it for you, Isa. I did it for you because I love you, as I must. Did you honestly think you could come here today and impress me as a man, like a man, by threatening me and blackmailing me? You should go right now, son. I won't be delivering any presents for you or your friends. Don't you understand that? Not today, not ever.'

Still no breeze arrived to do its refreshing work on Slave Island.

'Goodbye, then, Dad,' Isa said, backing off with a disappointed shake of his head and a little shrug.

Because the sun was literally *everywhere*, there was nowhere dark enough to hide. Sulaiman had to be content with closing his eyes as tightly as he could. As he gripped the comforting rope he let it taunt him – the image of a boat drawn high on the sand. It was all he had ever asked for *of things*. Was it too much to ask? Hadn't he discussed it with Kanoo right here on this very beach? Was it too much in one lifetime? Now the sadness within Sulaiman was intolerable – it had the effect of sucking, or driving, the breath from his body. He threw down the rope and rose up and shouted it out for all to hear – the name of his son, the name he could no longer bear to say. It was no use. There was no reply. The overhead sun cast no shadow.

## ❧ EVERY GOOD BOY DESERVES FAVOUR ❧

THE SEA CHANGED ITS COLOUR ALL THE TIME. Because he wanted to entice them and win the day, Durbridge waited until the coastline slipped below the horizon behind them and the engine's note made them contemplative, receptive to his marketing message. They were two hours out of Aden. Their picnic items and bottles of Coca-Cola sat in an icebox in a shady part of the deck. Having issued them all with floppy hats, Durbridge rubbed sun oil into their shoulders and watched them pull funny faces for Xavier as the Filipino insinuated himself smoothly with new cine camera, Bermuda shorts ballooning like spinnakers in the salty breeze.

And this is how it looked to Adrian Durbridge, sheltering behind the flapping canvas as the camera made an objective record of their bodies against a Kodachrome sky. Ken was their man-boy, tall and dark. On his chest, dead centre, hairs sprouted in a black diamond. He was quick and alert – his athleticism was there for anyone to see. Philip was golden and lightly muscled. His drummer's arms were a key feature – Durbridge had certainly regarded them favourably at various times. And Jimmy? Jimmy's abdomen was a bad boy's, milk-skinned, hairless. His appendectomy scar was an angry slash above the tight knot of his trunks – the black trunks ill fitting and graceless.

These physiques were now a matter of cinematographic record. After Xavier put his camera down they sat with him on deck, side by side below the rail with bare feet in the spray, as the hired launch took them further into the Red Sea. They saw flying fish. The foam was hypnotic. Behind the canvas outside the wheelhouse, Durbridge opened a tin of beer and prepared the ground, sipping thoughtfully. After all, it was a terrific opportunity for a new-era Pretty Flamingo. A mini-tour schedule with provisional concert dates was more or less in place. They had themselves a new Filipino promoter of unlimited means. And there were no beat groups worthy of that description in all Australia – not yet. What were they waiting for – surely not the chance to entertain Her Majesty's armed forces in an amphitheatre of sand? Come, come, gentlemen – forget about Oona. Forsake the lovely woman. Onwards and upwards, I say – just like old times. It felt as shameful as ever, but for once it didn't seem to matter. Here, on the high seas, natural instinct was true to itself. The very air was immodest. Durbridge breathed in, exhilarated, and appreciated the sinewy curves of their arching backs from his shade. He assumed he could still count on Philip, having compromised him so thoroughly in a liner's cabin and elsewhere. Jimmy was a different kettle of fish, a loose cannon, highly suggestible. As for Ken – the songwriter with the hotelier parents and the much-admired voice was, admittedly, an unknown quantity. But the question could be put to him. Ken could always be made an offer. He was either in or he was out – and that gormless bassist, too.

'Are you with me, lads?' Durbridge called out, excited by their prolific youth in its near naked prime. He tossed his empty tin over the side and summoned them to a powwow.

OONA TOOK A TAXI FROM THE CRESCENT HOTEL to the business premises of Khalil Kanoo. Although to the outside observer it might have seemed a needless or futile expedition, there was a real sense in which Oona wanted to honour the memory of the late entrepreneur whose energetic vision had been her bulwark against delusion. She had dressed – it wasn't the first time – for a funeral in the sun. Very simply, there would be no Bassey and no Belafonte, no Bob Hope in his flak jacket winched down from the sky. She had relied on Khalil Kanoo, and he had let her down badly. Now she stood on the rough pavement in front of the shop's shutter and scanned a notice printed in Arabic with a helpful translation scrawled below. Some freelance armed with blue biro must have done that small service. *Closed due to death of prop*. She might, Oona herself acknowledged, have picked up the trail that led to an army barracks, to an entertainments office, to a sports stadium. In fact, she had no further investment to make in such a musical cause. To pursue or promote it without her creative mentor would be an act of bad faith. As she reread the notice taped to the shutter, Oona found it difficult to escape a feeling its message was addressed to her in person. Although she was aware to left and right of the pedestrian throng, it seemed the apron of Kanoo's shop was hers alone. She had the strongest desire to peel the notice from the shutter, to clutch it to her, to run off with it. Doubtless it would have been difficult to account for such an action at a cocktail party or on the deck, say, of a yacht. Never mind – to Oona, it presented itself as a necessary affirmation of *her*. As she hummed and hawed, she could scarcely have coveted a keepsake more. At the same time, she recognised she wasn't alone in her obscure desire. There was a handsome beggar next to her – his legless torso rose naked above a wheeled platform from a nest of old rags. For some reason he wore a tie, immaculately knotted in the absence of shirt and collar, of silk, or what Oona took to be silk. Although he was much too low down to read the words of the notice, he seemed to have some inarticulate claim on it. He banged his bandaged fists on the shutter. He was the sometime beneficiary, Oona told herself, of Kanoo's philanthropy. Her heart went out to him. She even contemplated lifting him up by the armpits in order to let him read. Suddenly he wrapped his arms around her legs and clung on and squeezed until she cried out. No one looked – she was invisible. She had to kick his chest finally with her shoe in order to escape. As he chased her through the crowd on his wheeled platform, all the people scattered. It was very clear – he wanted something from her. Off came her shoes and fell behind. It did her no good – after all, the cripple was without feet. It was only when she dropped the notice of death ripped from Kanoo's shutter that Oona began to put distance between her and the awful trolley. She slowed down then, sobbing. She sank to her knees in the streets of Aden and retched, hugging her own body tightly. As she wept for love lost or abused, all her illusions crowded around. Then someone returned her shoes, and for one incandescent moment of gratitude and pain she thought the atom bomb had gone off inside her heart.

THEY HAD CUT THE ENGINE to a murmur. Above the bow wheeled the excited seagulls. Beyond the gulls, the Blue Grotto rose from the sea like a giant igloo made of extruded lava. It was exactly why they had journeyed all this way. How impressive to come upon a citadel of bats in the middle of the ocean like that. They approached it for a long time. As they approached it, it grew bigger and bigger in their imagination. In terms of its relative size there were no good reference points available to them – neither tanker bound for Suez nor navy gunboat nor Somali dhow. They were alone on the mirror of the sea with only an igneous cavern to appreciate or admire.

'We're going in. We're going in. Onwards and upwards, right? Just like the man said –' Jimmy's voice was a hoarse whisper. It was impossible not to be impressed by their situation, by its extravagant

250

topology. Directly in front of the launch, the dome was the head of a prehistoric beast come up to breathe – where its mouth should have been was a gaping hole without tongue, without teeth.

'No, wait –' Philip said gripping the rail tighter. 'Can't you see what's happening here?' He heard Jimmy laugh beside him. The air was suddenly colder as they neared the cave. The sky overhead – it was dark with squealing bats and squawking birds having only Latin names. 'I mean – did you ever have a bad dream that turned out to be real when you woke up the next morning?'

'I'm dreaming now, man. Jeez – will you look at that?'

'Listen to me, Jimmy. We're not going to make it. I'm telling you now – we're not going to make it.'

'Like hell, we're not, pal. It's Australia, right? Land of plenty – as in plenty for us.'

'But what about Oona – what happens to her? What about his frigging *wife*, for Pete's sake? Don't you see what's happening here?'

Philip turned away from the looming cave. Peering aft, his hair whipping his face, he saw Ken under the canopy next to Durbridge. Their confab was over – now Xavier joined them for a laugh. Ken had his arms folded as if in consideration of a proposal. Durbridge's hand settled on his shoulder. Then Xavier stepped out of the shade and raised his camera to his eye. Again Philip confronted the cave of dreams. Beside him, Jimmy swore with wonder. They were at the edge of the grotto, between sunlight and deep shadow. Philip looked over the side. At first he saw nothing. Then his eyes got used to the light. All around, colourful fish played in an emerald garden. They were in – the launch was inside now. The floor of the cave was pure sand, the draught shallow. As the engine went into reverse there was a cool splash. The Arab boy was swimming towards the back of the cave with the rope between his teeth. As the boy slid forward on the

251

rocks, the engine note died. The boy tied his rope to a heavy ring set into the wall of the cave. The ring fell down with a resounding clang. Immediately after came the salutation of bats, then silence.

SHE DREW HER CURTAINS against the afternoon glare and stretched out in her underwear. The hotel room, which had been home for so long, took back its offer of intimacy. It was just another station on the line, the repository of random furnishings. There was no further comfort of familiarity – only the subtle contempt of things. Oona lay on her side, her hands between her knees, and watched the cunning sunlight enter and retire and return around a shifting curtain. Where once she might have experienced a quiet joy in the everyday triumph of light over dark, now she glimpsed only a reef, blinding to the eye, of dashed hopes. Still, she told herself not to mind.

She shut her eyes. She was about to let go completely when she heard it – a bass guitar riff that descended rapidly to the lowest reach of her feelings. It was barely amplified and rather dignified. It came from beyond the wall. Oona had heard it before. Although it struck her as contented by and large in its spirit and outlook, it had in it a quality of disappointment she recognised, understood and shared.

She pulled on her robe and stepped outside. In a corridor of the Crescent Hotel she didn't hesitate. She didn't knock. Inside his room too the curtains were drawn at the open window. When he saw her he propped his guitar up against a wall and smiled without prejudice from the bed. Although, in theory, it was a simple enough project he took on, Oona acknowledged few things could be harder to bring off successfully in practice. He stood up and kissed her tenderly, with a light contact, about the face, and when he took off her robe she had the idea she was beautiful. She sat beside him on the edge of the bed and removed her bra with a series of quick, practical movements. As he peeled off his T-shirt she noticed for the first and last time he had a leaping salmon on his arm an inch or so above the puckered circle of his smallpox vaccination.

'Dear Walter – didn't you want to be with the others today?'

'Oh, no –' he said. 'I can't be doing with all that sun, me.'

IT WAS A YOUTHFUL STUNT that was also a sexual ploy. It ought to have been easy to swim from cool shade towards dazzling light, but in the event it proved otherwise. There were mitigating factors. The sandy floor dropped off alarmingly at the margin of the cave. Philip stopped there, treading water on the cusp of the glare with his flip-flops in, or on, his hands. His flip-flops he used as paddles. A lone seagull sat calmly just a stone's throw away on the surface of the Red Sea. It made Philip consider his own flailing limbs. Suddenly he felt the overwhelming need to be flatter in the water. The seagull's legs must be tucked up, he decided. How easy it would be otherwise to rise from below and pull the bird down into the dark depths. Philip brought his legs up quickly. He filled his lungs and spread his arms and tilted his head back until his toes bobbed at the surface. There he floated, searching the massive sky for portents. How hard it was to stay there, merely floating, once the danger had been mooted. It wasn't just a case of what might rise up hungrily from below. There was also the outside possibility of drifting, unreported for three days and nights, as far as Djibouti with its pearling dhows. Philip forced himself to dilly-dally outside the cave because he was determined to show Ken he could do it. It was imperative he pass each test of love. Love would prevail. He was ready to share the workings of his heart. Just then there was a change in the prevailing conditions, as when a cloud passes in front of the sun. Philip sensed it, but he didn't know what it was. He sat up immediately in the water. The gull had gone.

There were only the splashes, thrilling beyond words, of a swimmer approaching with powerful strokes from the cave.

'I didn't think you'd come out this far,' Ken admitted excitedly with his mask and snorkel held high above the sea.

'Oh?' said Philip, legs thrashing wildly below the surface. 'Why ever not? It's so peaceful out here, don't you think?'

As they swam close together towards the outer wall of the cave, Philip thought his heart must catch fire, wet ocean or no. He even considered reaching out to touch Ken's body, as if in error, beneath the surface. For a few perfect moments his friend was a passing seal.

'Did Adrian give you any more detail about Australia?' he asked casually after they got their breath back.

They were lying side by side on a smooth outcrop blasted by the sun and lapped by the warm sea.

'He must be crazy —' Ken said, laughing. 'How could I possibly up sticks just like that and go to Australia?'

'He must be mad,' Philip said, rolling over to hide his erection.

'Actually,' Ken said, 'I think he was probably more interested in trying to get into my pants.'

'I beg your pardon?' Philip said.

'I said — I think he was trying to get into my swimming trunks.'

'Really? And does that bother you?'

'What? Are you kidding?'

'I just thought you might be — I don't know — cooler than that, if you know what I mean.'

'*Cooler*? What is it with you these days, anyway?'

And, after all, it was only a youthful stunt or dare. For Philip it was also a necessary punishment for various thoughts, if not acts, of transgression. They climbed the outer flank of the Blue Grotto, one behind the other and in silence, until they reached its topmost rim.

254

'Your foot's bleeding,' Philip said. 'I don't think you should go back in like that in case you attract any unwanted attention.'

'Kiss my ass,' Ken said, letting his mask and snorkel fall.

He jumped off right after. By the time he hit the water his mask and snorkel were sinking close beside – he rescued them, advertising them triumphantly from the surface, and then disappeared below the overhang. Philip looked out across the ocean. In every direction the horizon was uninterrupted. For a moment he considered a descent on foot. It was out of the question. He threw his flip-flops down, saw them scattered by a spiteful breeze before they landed, then watched them drift slowly apart on the sea. Now he too was committed. How he wished he could have dived straight in – dived in cleanly between his flip-flops and struck out for the horizon without looking back. He couldn't dive. It wasn't his strongest suit. In any event, he was really too high up for all that. He waited as long as he dared – there was the urgent need to rescue his drifting flip-flops – before jumping. All the way down he debated the nature, meaning and value of love.

IT WAS ALREADY DARK. THE LITTLE RADIO was barely on. She was almost listening to it, A Whiter Shade Of Pale, from the bed, raising and lowering the sheet ever so gently for a breath of air. The door was locked. She could hear them in the corridor, her boys, pacing up and down, just the two of them. They might have been whispering or bickering in her name, preparing to report back to her, to betray her with their sun-drenched dream of tomorrow. She wouldn't have blamed them. She heard them knock at her door, then knock again. There could be no reply because she wasn't in her own room at that time. She closed her eyes and felt a cool rain of content, or at least of resignation, on her face. How long, she asked, before they came knocking at Walter's door? Now Oona's imagination invoked this or that scenario of defence or defiance – she quickly dismissed them all as unworthy or unnecessary. She reached out automatically to turn off the radio, but then she changed her mind. Although Walter was snoring beside her, she refused to hold that against him.

## ❧ REGATTA ❦

CALLUM WAS MOVED by what he saw that evening. He was touched by its power and glory. It might have been the arrival under marine escort of a mythological hero, or a state funeral at sea.

'Oi, you – yes, you – don't stand there gawping.'

But Callum did. He stood outside a little gatehouse on the slope below Government House and gawped at the whole scene. Perhaps he was easily moved – he felt the sting of emotion at the back of his throat. His rifle he held awkwardly at belt height as if he hadn't quite come to regard it as a weapon of war. Behind him and to one side on the drive the early cars approached the gates, but Callum ignored them for a few seconds longer with his back to the house and his eye on the view. The shadowy fronds in the grounds below were draped with coloured bulbs. In the thickening twilight the headlights bobbed like Chinese lanterns as the guest limousines climbed the driveway among trees, attracting winged insects while distancing birds. From beyond the headland, the flotilla entered the harbour with a chorus of horns that carried mournfully from ship to shore like the cries of fifty elephants adrift on a floe. Callum counted twenty – no, twenty-five vessels – and all on a painted sea. At their head, the carrier was lit up like a small airport. There was a guided missile destroyer. The frigate and a submarine came after. There were the supply craft and speedboats and yachts and launches, camp followers of independent means or flag. Each one made a noise. Every porthole shone a light.

256

Then the fire tugs spouted like whales around the aircraft carrier in plumes of cyan, magenta and gold.

'Oi, you –'

Callum felt a sharp blow to his shoulder. What was it? A gun? A hand? He wheeled round, still smiling.

'Are you deaf as well as fucking dumb?'

'No, sir –'

He had the spray of another man's saliva on his face.

'Just tell me, will you – what is it about you that makes me *notice* you, Kennedy? Eh? Eh? Because I don't want to notice you, do I?'

'No, sir.'

'No sir is right, sir. Now, shift your arse over there –'

They had opened the gates and lit the torches lining the upper drive. Now the jets from the sprinklers on the terraced lawns picked up the glow of the torches. There was a black Jaguar waiting outside the gatehouse. As Callum approached it from behind he recognised her – she was watching him in the passenger side mirror. He circled the car and crouched beside the driver as the man flashed his pass – he held up two party invitations for Callum to check. Callum wasn't interested in Farquhar and his credentials. It was the female beyond the steering column who held his attention. Hadn't he seen her in a white coat with or without blood on it? No, wait – he had seen her twice in a white coat. The driver raised the clutch.

'One moment, please –' she said, leaning across in her red dress to confront Callum crouched at the driver's window. 'I know you, don't I?' She was struggling to recall something. 'I saw you –'

'That's right, miss.' Her party dress had thrown him for a short time. Now he saw it as plain as day. She was offering him water on a desert highway. She was considering an above-elbow amputation in a room full of flies in a house in Crater. 'If you say so, miss –'

257

'No, no –' she said distractedly. 'I mean I saw you in a dream.'

Her middle name – was it trouble, or something like it? She was always trouble, Callum told himself, handing the invitations back to Farquhar with an informal salute. 'Enjoy your evening, sir.'

'No, wait –' She had her hand on the driver's arm now.

'Are you all right, Hildegaard?'

'Yes, perfectly, thank you –'

There was a queue of cars waiting behind. Callum met her eye once more and saw it happen. He saw her struggle to suppress what she had fought so hard to recall only a moment ago.

'I tried to warn you –' she whispered passionately, as if she had just surfaced from deep sleep. 'You had a koala bear in your arms.'

THE DEMOCRATS AND PARLIAMENTARIANS gathered on the lawn. Nolan skirted them with his jacket slung over his shoulder, crossing from the VIP car park towards the gazebo. There would have been journalists and lobbyists in their number, to say nothing of cultural attachés and consular bachelors with lovers and concubines in tow, plus the odd secret agent or mole. They reached out to one another easily with their goblets. They embraced formally under the banyan tree or drew each other close in a looser rite of captivated laughter, of cultivated gesture, of elbow lightly held and cheek softly grazed in the charming light. Ben Nolan put his jacket on. In a summerhouse that was also a bar he took a glass from a silver tray, then leaned on the balustrade in order to take stock. As cocktail parties went, it was a considerable affair. Nolan didn't expect to recognise any of them gathered under the twinkling boughs. Still the cars came. Backlit by driveway torches, a pirate crew of shrill children dodged juddering sprinklers in their fancy dress of eye patch and bandana or scarf and painted moustache. Abruptly the sprinklers died. The pirate children abandoned their game. Looking up at the big house, Nolan saw the bows of fiddles rise and fall from a dip beyond the brow of the slope as the musicians began their warm-up. He took another glass from a tray and climbed the lawn until he reached a terrace in front of the portico. The swimming pool had blue lighting below its surface and a scaled-down orchestra perched on chairs at its side. Reflected in miniature along and across the pool's short reach, the floodlit front of Government House floated on the placid surface like a pink frost. Two fez-toting bearers flanked the great doors beyond the pillars. As he passed inside the house and gave up his empty glass, Nolan was met by the discreet murmur of civilisation with entitlement.

'A very good evening to you, sir –'

He was reluctant to speak. Every platitude hurt. He didn't want to articulate, to be articulate – not now, not tonight. He dropped his olive pip into a vast display of orchids at the foot of the staircase. In a yellow music room done in the Chinese style he found Mathieson with Sonny beside him. Nolan saw it all with a particular vividness. There was a mothballed fireplace lurking darkly behind his friends – it had the picture tiles from Canton on both sides, and the priceless vases on the mantelpiece above. Sonny inspected him gravely from her position of colourful strength in front of the plundered artworks. Her organdie pyjamas were a charismatic green. She held her glass up high, a tiny pink handbag tucked under her arm. A chatelaine of trinkets tinkled at her waist as she offered Nolan her cheek.

'Big do,' he admitted conventionally.

'Impressive do,' Mathieson came back. 'All very Gatsby –'

'Sad do, too,' Sonny added, reaching out a hand. 'How are you feeling tonight, Ben?'

'Oh, I feel good – full moon fever, probably.'

'Whatever you feel – it must be in the cards.'

'Ah, yes, the cards – I was beginning to think it was in the gin.' Nolan cast around for a bearer, sweeping two glasses from a passing tray. 'Won't you join me, Duncan?'

'Don't tempt me,' Mathieson said, smiling gloomily.

'But have you met him yet?' Sonny asked solicitously.

'Who? Oh, yes – the man who almost saved my wife.'

The violins began to play. Outside, the air was enlivened by the scent of night flowers and paraffin lamps. Nolan stood at the crest of the rise, music stands at his back, and scanned the scene below. Was it Sulaiman? Yes, he rose slowly from the direction of the gatehouse like the founder of a religion, surrounded by children with balloons. Two kiddies seized his hands and swung on them. The rest skipped behind a tall woman who marched up the hill in front of their group, her fan fluttering at her throat like a humming bird. Nolan didn't go down to meet them. There was no need. The tall woman strode up to him as if she knew everything.

'I say – are you press, by any chance?' Her skin, tight across her cheeks, hung slackly below the chin. 'Only, he doesn't speak much English, you see. Do you, dear?'

Here she gripped Sulaiman's wrist and pulled him forward. The children ran off. The fisherman's shirt was buttoned at the neck. He wore no tie – his black suit was much too short in the arm and leg.

'I say – are you people press?'

She had collared two English language reporters and an amateur ethnologist. No, they had collared her. They were very interested in the case of Sulaiman, humble fisherman, modest hero and reluctant role model in a difficult and dangerous world. Didn't he have a son of teenage years? Did he smoke or drink? Did he have any message for young people today? The orchestra played on. Nolan backed off. Suddenly Hildegaard was beside him in a red dress he knew well.

'Hello, Ben –' she said, warmly enough.

It was to be a political evening, after all. Nolan saw that now. It struck him as crucial he air any private grievances before the official fireworks went up.

'Is this a queue?' Hildegaard went on, nodding at the fisherman and his entourage.

They had spoken, the two of them, since her enforced stay and subsequent rescue in the eastern desert. Farquhar had seen to that. How humiliating it had been in many ways for Nolan to discover the headstrong nurse was a spy – no, a double agent, effectively – in her spare time. And to think he thought he knew her as well as anyone.

'Official business?' he asked harmlessly, proposing an unspoken toast and finding he had two empty glasses in his hands.

'No, not really –' she said. 'Actually, I came to pay my respects.'

'Of course – you were corresponding with my late wife, weren't you? At the end, I mean?'

'Dear Ben –' She shook her head and smiled at the sky with the absence of amusement required of her.

'Dear Hildegaard –' he said, sardonic but not sarcastic. For how might he reasonably be expected to *fascinate* the British agent in her Campari dress? 'To the spy who loved God –' he moved, waggling two empty glasses at her. 'But how would that *work*?'

SHE WATCHED HIM GO DOWN to the summerhouse, his two empty glasses dangling from his fingers. She told herself again and again she had done nothing wrong – not in respect of Jacinta Nolan, at least. She eased through the knot of pressmen, apologising for interrupting their quest for truth, and introduced herself in Arabic to Sulaiman at their centre. After a rapid exchange they were alone with each other, traversing the lower lawns slowly towards a bower of fairy lights.

'I'm sorry to have to bring this up tonight,' Hildegaard confessed above the hum of a nearby generator.

'It doesn't matter,' Sulaiman insisted courteously.

It was a lie. Everything mattered, but nothing made sense.

'Is this your son?' she asked, holding up a college identity card.

'That's Isa,' Sulaiman confirmed. 'That's my son.'

'We know he's in Sheikh Othman somewhere. Or Al-Mansura, perhaps –'

'What will happen to him?' Sulaiman asked.

'There's an underground cell that operates from that area – an NLF unit. Do you know a doctor called Aziz?'

Sulaiman shook his head below the fairy lights. 'Please – tell me what will happen to my son.'

'I don't know what's going to happen. All I know is they plan to lift the ban on the NLF.' She watched him look away and narrow his eyes until he found it – the strip of sea between land and sky. 'It's what people want, isn't it?' she added.

'Is it?' he said. 'Who wants it? Tell me right now because I really don't know who asked these people to act on my behalf. Who chose the NLF? Did I? I don't believe so. I don't believe I chose them any more than I choose you standing here beside me today. They didn't ask me. They claim to represent me. They pretend to know what I want. Only God knows what I want –'

'We want to find your son, Sulaiman.'

'What will become of him?'

'Will you help me find your son before it's too late?'

Just then the music stopped – within seconds it was replaced by an aerial whooshing sound and a chorus of gasps from the scattered guests. As Hildegaard and Sulaiman turned to face the floodlit house the first few rockets went up quickly one after another and exploded over the party scene. Some pyromaniac had deliberately targeted the night. The whole sky fell apart, the colours running down in streams of red, white and blue that diminished beyond the trees and dried up altogether above the flotilla and the harbour. Hildegaard looked at Sulaiman for his answer. She watched him turn away and nod at a sea on fire. It was hard, all in all, not to assent in some way.

THE GUESTS GATHERED AROUND THE SWIMMING POOL beside the orchestra. They had set up the microphone on the far shore in front of the pink pillars. Nolan was there. Everyone was there. The high commissioner ambled forward from the portico in his white dinner jacket, a bow tie hanging off-duty around his neck. As the applause fell away, he unfolded his script.

'Permit me to be uncharacteristically brief –' he began, glancing up from his text and smiling affectionately.

A ripple of amused approval ran around the swimming pool.

'In the short time since I took up office in Aden, it has been my privilege to meet many fine men and women drawn from across all our communities – men and women who are working hard to make a success of the changes taking place here. These changes, let me just say, are as necessary as they are inevitable. It is almost one hundred and twenty-eight years, ladies and gentlemen, since British interests seized these barren rocks in order to protect our supply routes from lawless forces. Cynics might argue that little has changed in over a century at the mouth of the Red Sea, but I am not, let me be clear, one of those. Because, you know, it *has*. Everything has changed, my friends – everything *is* changing. And we are charged, each of us as individuals and citizens, with helping to make these changes *work*. A timetable for the withdrawal of British troops from Aden garrison is largely in place. It is no longer a case of if, ladies and gentlemen, but when. My solemn duty, which I am determined to carry out to the best of my abilities, is to implement our timetable in the interests of lasting peace and prosperity for all the people of Aden. To that end, it is my business to inform you that a ban on the National Liberation Front, which we had introduced to uphold the rule of law here, will now be lifted – effective midnight tonight.'

They waited in silence as if around an open grave. They didn't know what to do. After someone called out hip-hip-hooray from the back, they cheered and clapped with respectful restraint. Preparing to ad-lib, the high commissioner folded away his notes.

'But, you know, ladies and gentlemen – history to my mind is a lot more than the dry dates we take away from school. At the risk of sounding irreverent, I venture to suggest history in its making is all about individuals bumping into one another – often much too hard. Extraordinary times must throw up extraordinary achievers. That is clear. What about the rest of us, friends? They also serve who only stand and wait? Maybe. But we are honoured tonight to have with us a man who didn't just stand, who didn't wait. This is no soldier with a gun. This is a man who heard a cry for help on the darkening waters. He knew what he had to do and he didn't hesitate to do it. Ladies and gentlemen, I believe you know the tragic circumstances. This man has just told me that anyone else would have done what he did, insisting he just happened to be nearest at the time. So be it. For his exemplary citizenship and outstanding courage, which are an inspiration to all of us, it gives me the greatest personal pleasure to recognise and honour Sulaiman –'

The high commissioner broke off here to consult a note.

'To recognise and honour Sulaiman Ali Hassani.'

They ushered him from behind the columns of the portico. He stood at the microphone with hands folded neatly in front of him, his untailored attire a basis for whispered commentary around the pool. After the photographers crouched at the base of the microphone in a good-natured scrum, things happened pretty quickly. Sulaiman felt the medal descend around his neck on its ribbon of satin. He wasn't concentrating – not fully. Instead his attention focused on the young photographer kneeling at an obvious remove from the pack. As the flashbulbs went off, Sulaiman was blinded repeatedly. And yet there could be no mistake – the young photographer was his son. Isa had a moustache now. He was hiding behind his Rolleiflex. Sulaiman's heart galloped. When he heard them applaud from the far shore he tried his best to smile. The photographers were leaving. Look – they had forgotten a bag. One of them had left his grip behind. It was a sports bag with zip. There it languished at the edge of the pool with a hand grenade inside it. Sulaiman imagined he heard a bomb tick in the absence of all proper sound. He threw down the microphone stand and swept up the grip. The bag exploded just as it broke the surface of the water in the swimming pool with a heavy splash. The water sucked itself down before rising in a turbulent column above the pool. For a few seconds there was a keening in the air, backdrop to an abandoning of handbags and musical instruments. Then the water came back down. The medal ceremony was over.

EVERYONE AGREED – IT WAS A MIRACLE no one was killed. All the guests were shocked and damp. There was a diplomat's spouse from Malagasy who could no longer quite see. They had rounded up the accredited photographers. These few had emptied their pockets and their grips, but it was much too late to point the finger. The young photographer had been just that, they said – he was young. Yes, he had a light moustache. No, he had said nothing, nothing at all. He had a good turn of speed, clearly, having run for the trees when the

265

bomb went off. His ruthless professionalism marked him out, some suggested – he hadn't lingered to review his handiwork.

The lawn was deserted. Callum Kennedy stood beside the pool and tracked the lights of the last ambulance as it went down among the trees with the big boats at rest in the harbour beyond. Although their emotional significance was obscure, the distant warships were unforgettable to the young soldier. On the one hand he recognised them as just another part of the military build-up. They would have spoken to him, in that sense, directly. But there was something else, something spiritual, if only he had known what that meant. It was natural Callum should look for transcendent meaning in his hilltop vision. Anything so lovely to behold must offer a glimpse of heaven, he reasoned. The big ships would go home soon. Callum would go with them. Where to? The young soldier didn't know home as such. Home was a proud father on the quayside. It was a sister with a flag and child. They existed, didn't they? They would make themselves known to Callum when the time came. Meanwhile, he had a nurse's warning to contend with. He couldn't shake the thing off. In the pool the water was still again. The lamps went out below the surface. A music stand protruded indignantly from the shallows while a violin floated face down like a baby at the deep end. All around the violin, someone's tarot cards clung to each other like leaves in a fountain.

## ❧ NO SMOKE WITHOUT FIRE ❦

THERE WAS A FLINTY TRIANGLE OF POTTERY under his pillow. In the middle of the night they came for him. They placed a hand over his mouth, then wound a towel around his head and frog-marched him to the washrooms where the odours of carbolic and piss helped to orientate him. It was obvious to Callum what was happening long before they whisked his underpants off. When they trod on his toes, they probably didn't mean to do that. He was bent over a sink, head between the taps. It didn't occur to him to shout for help. He didn't struggle or kick. No doubt he had it coming to him. In any case, they would have found a way to silence him PDQ. He heard a scuffle and a grunting. Was there a skirmishing splinter group close beside? He let out a whimper. He had to – they had forced his hands too high between his shoulder blades. He felt his legs begin to shake before he was sick against their clinging towel. When they opened the taps on his head he thought he would have to drown slowly inside the towel arrangement. Increasingly now he expected to shit himself, but the burning sensation was just a prelude to a deeper feeling. At least he could no longer hear their panting. There was only the water.

The first one he felt plainly. After that it was hard to tell. It was hard to tell how many there were because each one felt the same as the last and the next. They would have been surprised and gratified to learn how alike they were, Callum decided with practical insight. He felt easier now – there was little left to learn about ease. What hurt him most was the sense of personal betrayal. It must have been Taylor who got the ball rolling. It must have been Taylor who made them doubt him. No smoke without fire, boyo. No, Callum couldn't see why men – the body of men – should care about him in this way or that. No one had cared before tonight. What had he done? Why were they so taken with his case? It was their successive escalations of intimacy he found hardest to understand.

Weren't they finished yet? No, they were still going in and out. It didn't take long, really – four minutes, tops, during which Callum thought about the friend who had betrayed him. He held Taylor in front of him and made himself forgive. His hurt began to lessen. He had little choice but to forgive – there was no one else to look up to.

At last he felt himself slip from the sink. He cracked his knee on the tiles as he slumped, but that was OK. They must have switched on a light. Callum glimpsed the light on the other side of the towel. Ah, peace – they had shut down his taps. He shook off the towel he had come to *know*, and found himself on his hands and knees. What did he see first in the unflattering light? He saw his big, strong buddy – the one who should have protected him. It was a difficult encounter that debased them both. Its import would bind them together until the waters covered the land. Callum shouted, but no sound emerged. Taylor, however, was necessarily redeemed. He lay curled up on his side, his hands tied to a pipe, below the dripping head of a shower. Although they had gagged him with what looked to be his own vest, they had chosen not to blindfold him. In his underpants he looked a little underdressed for an audience of this type. He had made himself as small as possible in a puddle. He was still banging his head on the tiles when Callum reached him.

NOTHING WAS DONE AND NOTHING WAS SAID. Their shame was a hand at their throats. Because Israel was prosecuting a short war to the north, they were kept busy protecting two hundred Aden Jews from arsonists and murderers. Taylor was resentful, to put it mildly. He resented the idea that an unpleasant washroom incident – or his response to its squalid fall-out – might define him more tellingly as a man from now on than the deadly conduct of a counter-insurgency programme. Mainly he resented Callum whose fault it was.

'Don't you know anything, Kennedy – I mean anything useful? They want to force me to choose between you and them, that's all.'

He lifted his bucket and ran up the steps, Callum close behind.

'Taylor, listen to me. I'll put in for a transfer. I'll do it tomorrow. No, tonight – I'll be doing you all a favour.'

The Arab cheering died away. They were inside the library of a synagogue on fire.

'There aren't going to be any transfers, soldier boy. Do you read me? Look – over there. Jesus. Over there –'

From the carpet to the ceiling the long, high wall was lined with tall, dark books. Around each shelf and every spine the thick, black smoke leaked in silent discharges heavier than air.

'My God –' Taylor whispered. 'She's going to blow.'

It was impossible for Callum to know what to do. If he directed the contents of his bucket at the smoking volumes, he would almost certainly ruin them. If he didn't, they would burn. Although the wall was preparing to explode, it was important to think things through as far as possible. Callum put down his pail and ran to the wall and selected a book – any book. He pulled it out and opened it, turning from the shelf. Hot, Yiddish book – its words meant nothing to the young soldier. Over there was his burly buddy, gaping in disbelief.

'Listen, Taylor – would you rather freeze to death at the North Pole or die of thirst in the desert?'

'What? Which frigging desert?'

'We don't have to report them. We don't have to do anything.'

'Come away from that wall, Private Kennedy.'

'Not until you explain it to me –'

'Get back here, you bloody fool.'

'Not unless you can tell me why the other men hate me as much as they obviously do.'

Two things happened to Callum at more or less the same time. First the contents of Taylor's bucket hit him full in the face or chest, then the wall directly behind him exploded. Each volume must have waited for the agreed signal. As books, they would go down together. Their outraged roar was tremendous. For a split-second, Callum was actually on fire. Soon he landed at Taylor's feet, black smoke issuing from his shirt. He took a second bucketful at his back. As the bulbs of the chandeliers popped one by one like firecrackers overhead, all the glass and the filaments came down like summer rain.

'Are you all right, you bleeding idiot?'

They were sitting on the steps of the synagogue, surrounded by hissing hoses. Below, the chanting crowd waited behind a cordon of soldiers and fire engines. Everywhere men ran, some with buckets, others like looters carrying off treasure. From step to step the water ran in filthy streams towards the sandals of satisfied onlookers, their faces pink in the sacrificial light.

'What you think of me – have you any idea how important it is to me, Taylor?'

He couldn't say it – that wouldn't have done at all. He wanted to tell his friend he loved him, simple as that. It should have been an easy enough thing to manage, but Callum didn't know how. He had the crazy idea the worth of any human instinct or feeling must reside in the number of blows a man was prepared to take for it. In fact, he had known it from the earliest age – he had just forgotten it.

'What,' Taylor said, 'made you think I would ever let you down?'

'I don't want you to have to choose – I mean between me and anyone else. We don't need to say anything about it –'

'Yes, we bloody do.'

When Callum heard those four small words he was content. He was shivering, but he wasn't the least bit cold. When he looked back he saw the roof of the synagogue collapse. As the sparks shot up, the excited citizens roared their approval.

'I want to thank you, Taylor.'

'Listen – no one gets away with what they did.'

'No – I mean for chucking that bucket of water at me.'

'You? I was aiming at the bookshelves.'

'And now it must be time for you to tell me –'

'What? Not the North Pole and the blinking desert again?'

'Who you saw, Taylor. It's time to tell me who you saw.'

'I think all that can probably wait, don't you? First I think you'd better tell *me* something.' Taylor's teeth when he grinned were very white against his sooty skin. 'That precious library book you can't stop hugging – are you sure you signed it out properly?'

## ✦ Exodus ✦

UNDER THE BENEFICENT EYE of the morning sun, Basim Mansouri stood on a downtown balcony and extended both hands, palms up in the messianic manner, above the throng. From the shady square directly below, they assured him God was great, and chanted deeply felt slogans until he calmed their excitable natures with an indulgent paddling of arms. God was indeed great, Basim acknowledged with an increasingly impatient flapping of his hands, but certain other, far more controvertible, truths – the principles of economics or political science, for example – demanded just as much respect in the pursuit and practice of government by revolution. Only let us crush *utterly* all FLOSY opposition, he beseeched God *sotto voce* as he breathed in the sunlit air. Yes, it was good to speak freely again on a range of topical issues after so long without a voice.

'Dear friends –' he began as a thousand men settled themselves in picnic mode on the flagstones around a bust of Ghandi.

He waited for them to stop chattering. He saw no veiled woman down there in the square – no doubt the women had been detained elsewhere by the business of living under colonial occupation.

'Dear friends – this is indeed a historic day.'

271

In no way did Basim mean to suggest the day was special simply because he had been released from detention and was therefore free to address them, Pope-like, from a balcony of noble calling. It was a historical overview, or big picture, at which he hinted. In this he was contextualising helpfully for the benefit of biographers or journalists – the others would have to keep up as best they could.

'The last political detainee in Aden has today been released, and all freedom of association restored –'

As the appreciative murmur rose up all around, Basim nodded with due solemnity. Ah, yes – he could see the soldiers at last. They had gathered in maximum shade around the Indian consulate at the entrance to the plaza. The sun climbed higher. Basim pressed on. It was in the best interests of brevity, honesty and longer-term political cohesion he cut to the chase in a statesmanlike way.

'Now is not a time for factional strife or recrimination, friends – FLOSY against NLF, NLF against FLOSY. This is not the time to settle old scores. No, no, no. We must bury our petty differences the better to focus on our shared destiny, which is a glorious one –'

OH, HE WAS VERY POLISHED AND CONVINCING, Taylor conceded, cradling his trusty rifle outside the shuttered visa hatch of the Indian consulate. Although he hadn't the first idea what the speaker was on about, the British soldier judged the balcony tone conciliatory. That was important. It meant there was little danger of the rabble being roused. Taylor would have admitted to mixed feelings about such a possibility at this difficult time in his own life. If it must come, let it – there was nothing like a good riot to clear the air.

Wait – the speaker had stopped, a heckler having silenced him with a question from the floor. The interlocutor stood up, extremely agitated. He was probably an *agent provocateur* from FLOSY, Taylor decided with a mental nod in the direction of today's briefing, sent to spoil the NLF's tea party. And what was that? Oh, no – was that the dreaded Nasser-word spoken in anger?

Taylor's ears pricked up. He too was angry and a little confused. It wasn't just that he had been witness – no, party – to a degrading act in a barracks washroom in the all too recent past. He had been further unmanned by love and affection. Again he had to ask himself why. Why had Suzy Wong seen fit to downgrade his marriage offer to a guileless gesture of sympathy? So what if it was just that? Taylor counted himself sympathetic, unless provoked inordinately. He was happy to be guileless. Since when was the constant heart otherwise?

Wait up – there were the genuine stirrings in the crowd now of discontent. Familiar with the signals, Taylor made ready to defend his few ideal values of honour, duty and loyalty. He eyed his nearest comrades and asked which ones he was ready to die for. More and more of the FLOSY malcontents were on their feet now. It seemed tempers shortened disastrously whenever Nasser's name was bandied about in a public place. That was Taylor's experience, at least. The Cairene colonel – he was incorrigible.

'MY FRIENDS, ALLOW ME TO ADDRESS your perceptive questions in due course. The value of grass roots opinion cannot be overstated.'

Bingo – there were any number of FLOSY activists down there in the crowded square. They constituted a significant rump, Basim suspected. Let them be flushed out now like weevils.

'History, however, won't wait. The humiliating defeat recently inflicted by Israel on Egypt will have repercussions for many years to come. And Aden is scarcely immune. For how could FLOSY's stock here fail to nosedive when its sponsor sustains such a blow? Could it be Colonel Nasser is fallible after all? Many of his crack troops were tied up in Yemen opposing the monarchist and reactionary elements so dear to Saudi hearts. They had their work cut out, to be sure. No doubt they would have been better deployed further north against the rabid Zionist dog. But this is exactly my point, friends –'

He watched as the umpteenth disaffected FLOSY supporter got up, pressing ahead more quickly now with his address.

'An end to factional infighting, I say. Let us pool our resources and our complementary strengths. In so doing we avoid diluting our common purpose, our just ambition –'

Now the umpteenth apologist for FLOSY attracted another and another until, pretty soon, half the square was on its feet. Basim let his voice tail off tellingly. He saw the soldiers draw themselves up in ranks like good sports waiting to applaud the visiting team. Soon the FLOSY walkout gathered pace, the dissenters turning their backs on the balcony and advancing among NLF jeers towards the consulate in the deep shade. They were a disciplined bunch, Basim noted – it was impossible to know whether their departure was orchestrated or not. Suddenly their first shouts went up. Soon the air was alive with the strongly held opinions of the FLOSY *refuseniks*. At this point the NLF lot began to rise and shout, their fists punching the perfect sky above Ghandi's pate. Louder and louder cried the rival factions until their partisan injunctions seemed to merge into one glorious chant.

*God is great. God is great.*

It was a statement of fact, stirring and soothing at the same time thanks to a delicious quality of absolutism. It was impossible, Basim decided, not be heartened by their faith in an idea.

THERE WERE SEVEN BUSES IN ALL with about thirty, mostly old and young, in each bus. Some two hundred weary Jews got down at the airport and milled about in the sun, their black clobber soaking up

274

heat with a vengeance. Few sang the song of exile and return. They were unlikely to kiss the tarmac here today or tomorrow, a sergeant was heard to say. And although Callum understood precious little of religious bigotry in its global application, his personal perspective on persecution, deepening daily, gave him unexpected insights.

It was the young girl waiting alone who caught his eye. She sat on her suitcase with her feet off the ground and her back to the wall of the terminal building. Behind her, beyond the glass, there was the traffic of cardboard boxes on trolleys, but she herself sat more or less still. She might have been a miniature secretary, recently bereaved and awaiting dictation. She had her hands on her lap. Her head was in shadow. It was impossible, given the glare and the deep shade, to discover what her face looked like, far less what lay behind it. How old was she – five or six, perhaps? She must have been roughly the same age as Amy, sitting so still in her Sunday best, or her Friday or Saturday best, or whatever it was. That wasn't important. What the young soldier found affecting as he rapped the arse of an empty bus to send it packing was the unstoppable sense he had that she was all alone – all alone in the world. He crouched in front of her in the hot light as she scuffed her heels against the hard shell of her suitcase. How he wanted to befriend her, to make her feel wanted or valued. So close was his identification with her he would have been willing to swap places with her if called on to do so. What was it about one soul's cry and not another's that triggered urgently in him a fidelity to the simplest ideals of service and sacrifice? This soldier's loyalty and allegiance – what had they to do with countries or kings?

'Hello, little girl – what's your name, I wonder?'

She regarded him with an almost complete absence of curiosity from within her deep pool of shade. As Callum perched beside her at the edge of her suitcase she wiggled further away along its length.

'Everyone has a name,' he insisted gently, holding out his hand.

She didn't take his hand, so he picked up her fingers and shook them gamely.

'For instance, my name's Callum –'

He gave her back her hand. It occurred to him then she might not even speak English.

'You do speak English, don't you?' he said. 'Everyone speaks it, don't they – a bit?'

And when she got down from her brave suitcase their positions were reversed. He was in deep shade while she was in full sunlight. Now he had become her – his identification with her was complete.

'Are you going to kill me now?' she asked.

'Oh, no,' he said. 'See – I haven't even got my rifle.'

She looked at her shoes, her black plimsolls with the little holes in them to let her feet breathe.

'Won't you at least give me a piggy-back, then?' she said.


NOW THE WHINE OF JET ENGINES was constant. From a plastic seat just inside the glass wall of the terminal building, Oona could see the black body of the runway. There was a Comet 4B on the apron in the MEA colours that would take her to London via Beirut, Rome and Frankfurt-am-Mein. Below its belly and at the tips of its wings, the jet's farewell lights were already flashing.

Oona watched them roll the steps towards her plane. Beyond the big jet, the props of the smaller Aden Airways planes began to turn in anticipation of a local exodus. Oona had heard the weary Hasids murmur in family groups around their parcels tied neatly with string. She had seen the Beatles in their coats of many colours on the cover of a newsstand magazine. There was a grave young soldier roaming the terminal with a sad little girl, a circus gibbon, on his back. How extraordinarily vital were Oona's impressions – her last impressions. She kept observing and observing because she hated to think about what was happening. It was funny – she was being cast out with the rest. She sat apart. She made no common cause. She had her own history to relate if anyone cared to listen. No one did. There were so many places to go, so many people to see. Everyone was peripatetic these days. They were all running towards happiness.

As they called her flight, Oona became aware of the music. She picked up her coat and handbag, enjoying the sweet harmonies that carried over the heads of perfect strangers like a summer breeze in a park. She saw Jimmy first, then Philip. They were strolling towards her in matching shirts with acoustic guitars around their necks. How touching and professional – it was as if they wanted Oona to believe they sang only for her. She hardly knew whether to laugh or cry. She couldn't remember making all that many mistakes in her youth, but from the later years she recalled only failure. Her boys – how young they were, and how blameless. They might have been serenading an empty ballroom as the sun went down on her last request, on their callow grins, on their Michael Row The Boat Ashore.

She heard a cry. Someone was searching for someone else inside the terminal building – but not for her. Oona looked at her boys for the last time. Alleluia – she would kiss them and make them glad.

BEFORE HE TOOK HER ONTO HIS BACK, Callum gifted her a shard of pottery as a token of something between them. He had wanted to give the fragment to Amy, for her expanding collection, but this was an emergency in many ways. Amy would understand – as she grew older she would understand all of it. Meanwhile, Callum was getting desperate. He had lifted a little girl on his back and carried her from group to group in search of a mother or father. He thought it would be simple. But each time he put down her heavy suitcase it was the same story. Although everyone agreed she was the prettiest little girl in the world, and very familiar looking, no one could place her. Try over there, they said – no, over in that direction behind Mendoza. It was hopeless – not one of them belonged to her or she to them. Poor Callum was sweating. He would have to desert her soon and report to his sergeant. And she had said nothing. She had asked him for a ride and then closed the shutters again behind her eyes. What was wrong with her? He had put to her relevant questions. She clung to his neck, legs locked around his waist. Although there was very little of her, Callum felt her get heavier and heavier as his own head grew lighter. Like a cruel monkey in a dream of flight she burdened him with her impossible weight as he went from trolley to trolley.

'Please help –' he called out finally. 'Listen to me, please.

He stood on an unused check-in desk with a crying child clinging to his shoulders. The exhausted silence was a dark sea below.

'Does anybody know this little girl?'

Callum thought he must faint. He thought she might be trying to kill him with her arms. He saw the sergeant check his watch beyond the glass wall. There was a woman out there with the sergeant. The woman was pointing at Callum like a mother in the sun.

'Please – someone must know this little girl.'

He brought her down beside him on the counter and held her hand and scoured the sea below. He heard a cry from the back near the glass doors of the terminal building.

'Ruth! Ruth!'

A man was wading through the crowd as through icy water, his arms raised high. At first Callum couldn't hear him over the tannoy.

'Of course we know who she is. What on earth is going on here? This is our beloved daughter Ruth, our only child, whom we love –'

278

'I looked everywhere for you,' Callum blurted out. 'Where were you? I couldn't find you anywhere.'

'We were here. We were just outside the doors. What on earth are you doing up there? Please – they're calling us now. Our flight is boarding now.'

Ruth's father lifted her down, dragging away her suitcase as the crowd opened up for them. The crowd inched towards the runway pushing baggage trolleys piled high. She was in her mother's arms now, carried on a dark tide towards the glare. Callum watched her go. There – he saw his gift jut in her hand. He saw a mother seize a precious gift and discard it. That was nothing – Callum knew Ruth would turn and wave goodbye at the end. She had to. He heard the sergeant bawl his name. He was likely to fall – he felt it coming. And when she turned at the doors to the runway and saluted him, smiling in her mother's arms, he fainted and pitched into the sea.

## ❧ THE COLOUR OF THE SKY ❧

'SHALL WE VENTURE OUTSIDE? I DON'T SUPPOSE the women are remotely interested in our sort of technical team-talk, major general – do you? No, indeed –'

So saying, the high commissioner preceded the serving officer through the doors to the portico where the bombed-out swimming pool had been drained. The two men left their breakfast coffee cups at the foot of a pillar outside Government House.

'Tell me, major general – are you, by any chance, a gardening man?'

The dew was upon the lawn. As he went down from terrace to clipped terrace beside the career diplomat, the officer commanding British troops in Aden sighed deeply within.

'Not as such, sir,' he said, brushing a persistent fly from his lips with a swagger stick.

Without its rays, the morning sun was a pale smudge in a white sky welded to the water of the harbour beyond the towering palms that marked the lowest point of the grounds.

'Pity – I could have shown you a thing or two of interest here.'

They had stopped temporarily on the beaded grass. As the high commissioner stooped to examine a canvas shoe stained darkly by the dew, the major general seized his chance.

'A growing number of our regular patrols are being ambushed in and around Crater, sir. We're seeing skirmishes, mostly – no loss of life at this point. But it can only be a matter of time, surely. And weapons continue to fall into the wrong hands.'

The high commissioner had removed his wet espadrilles. Now he tucked them under his arms as he descended barefoot beside the uniformed officer towards the summerhouse.

'Things fall apart, do they not, major general?' he suggested at last. 'The centre cannot hold. And what's all this I've been hearing about the federal army boys acting up?'

'No backbone, sir – they lack discipline, I'm afraid. I'm not sure the feds can be relied on one hundred per cent from here on in.'

'Good heavens, man – as bad as all that, is it?' With this the high commissioner plucked an oleander sprig from a solitary bush beside the few wooden steps of the summerhouse. 'But what exactly is their beef, tell me?'

'Their beef, sir?' The officer smiled patiently and waited as the high commissioner passed the pink flowers back and forth below his nose. 'There are accusations of tribal favouritism in the ranks –'

'Oh, are there really, major general? Then we must endeavour to do something about that, don't you think?'

280

The high commissioner dropped his wet shoes on the boards of the summerhouse and tossed the oleander blossoms negligently over the balustrade.

'No perfume, you see – not a whiff or whisker. Still – expecting anything to flower at all out here is asking for a small miracle.'

THERE WERE FOUR MEN IN EACH LAND ROVER. Taylor was in the rearmost vehicle as their little convoy approached the federal army barracks located on Queen Arwa Road. The cloth bazaar, colourful excrescence of the highway, took over the kerb and pavement at the spot where the incident happened. If the plan, as Taylor understood it from the day's briefing, was to develop a more visible presence in order to reassure the feds they were on the right side, then the plan was misconceived. As their convoy neared the gates of the barracks, mutinous feds opened fire on it from the roof of the building with an incontinent machine-gun. It was an outrageous way to let off steam. Luckily for Taylor his vehicle lagged behind the rest. He ran across the road to the bazaar, his rifle raised the way a whooping Apache or Navajo on horseback might have raised it, anticipating bullets at his back. There was pandemonium amid the bolts of material in the aisles directly opposite the barracks. Taylor brought down a trestle table, took cover behind it, and rammed home his magazine. When he raised his head to take a peek he counted seven dead soldiers – they sat, riddled with bullet holes, inside the front Land Rovers. An eighth, having dived forward through the windscreen, lay asleep on the bonnet while his comrades reclined in their seats, mouths agape. There was a sheepish quiet now of which the dead men were focus. Nothing and no one stirred in the aisles of the bazaar. There was no traffic on the road. Just then Taylor became aware of a hissing at his elbow. An ancient Indian gentleman knelt beside him with his eyes opened wide and his arms full of saris of every hue. He had bitten through his lip. The blood ran from his chin. He offered Taylor his saris with a motivation that was uncertain. Then the first stationary Land Rover exploded on Queen Arwa Road, slick flames shooting up immediately to roughly the height of a telegraph pole.

THE HIGH COMMISSIONER PACED THE PORTICO in the crepuscular cool, his big house lit up behind him like a ship.

'Tell me about Mitchell −' he said. 'He's a colourful character, by all accounts.'

The major general hesitated among the pillars. The grounds of Government House, spread out in the gloaming, had rarely looked so lovely to him. The harbour lights far below were rogue stars in a breakaway heaven.

'He's a bloody good soldier, sir. He's calling for reprisals.'

'After what happened today? He's not the only one −'

'It's clear Lieutenant Colonel Mitchell wants to cut a dash with the Argylls in Crater.'

'But squeamish politicians continue to stand in his way?'

'Politicians and journalists −'

'Ah, yes − those journalists. He wants − how did they put it? To *sort the Arabs out*.'

'It has the merits of a strategy, sir.'

'Don't tempt me, major general. Our objective now is to get out of here with as much ordnance as we can reasonably manage and as few casualties as possible.'

'I'll try to remember that, sir.'

'And to leave a working government behind, naturally −'

'Of course, there are plenty of other options available to us. We have six battalions to deploy here in Aden besides Mitchell's lot.'

'Exactly – so have a word with him, will you?'

As the high commissioner turned his back on the twinkling bay and the lawns they heard the crunch of a slow-moving insect caught below his espadrilles.

'Sir?' queried the major general, intent on clarification.

'With Mitchell, damn it – just tell him to keep the place as quiet as possible.'

THE BRIEFING, WHICH KICKED OFF EARLY, lasted for six minutes. Callum had begun to hurt now on the inside. In his imagination, he had begun to bleed from the gut. He told himself it was only natural in view of what he had seen and done these past few weeks. In the room the air was bright and clear. It was a textbook briefing set-up – there was the easel out in front with the enlarged map on it. Now the officer hefted his pointer to summarise.

'Our tactic is to isolate Crater. By launching a series of scouting patrols we aim to pinpoint guerrilla locations before sending in the main force.'

'Question, sir –'

'Fire away, sergeant.'

'The main force, sir –'

'Us, sergeant – the main force as well as these scouting patrols will be made up of Argyll and Sutherland Highlanders.'

'Very good, sir.'

'I hope so, sergeant – for your sake. Any more questions?'

Yes, sir. I mean no, sir. I mean why am I burning up inside, sir? As Callum glanced behind him from the front row he had a couple of questions he thought relevant to the conduct of the war. Why are they standing at the back, sir? Why stand when the seats are empty on either side of me? These seats offer a perfectly good view of your chart, sir. Won't you make them sit here, sir? Funny – when next he studied the map, Callum thought he glimpsed his own face made up of topographical data. Did no one else discern it – the extraordinary concatenation of factors or things?

'Are there any more questions? No? Carry on, then, sergeant –'

THE SNIPER FROM 45 COMMANDO LAY on his stomach on the crag above Crater. He had been there all morning. In fact, he had been there since the morning before. In a perfect world there would have been more shade. There was only the black rock below and the sky above with the all-seeing sun in it. The sniper's face was black with boot polish. Once every hour he drank from his blackened canteen and thought about his father who had taught him to be patient with the highborn game birds of England, to squeeze a trigger knowingly as if he were crushing the bird's heart. But by now it must almost be time. The sniper brought his weapon closer and nuzzled the warm rest plate attached to the comb of the stock. He used the new Mk 32 telescopic sight that brought the mosque effortlessly within range. At last he saw what he had been looking for – a worshipper with a gun. The man had just become a legitimate target because he was fielding a lethal weapon as he quit the house of God. The sniper from Royal Marines 45 Commando squeezed the trigger of his rifle knowingly. He heard every highborn game bird of England break cover with its cry. He saw the man's arms fly up. The body fell down. All the other worshippers fled, leaving a corpse and a rifle on the steps of heaven.

THE YOUNG ARAB WAITED ON A ROOF IN CRATER. He had built an extension to the water tank out of flattened cardboard boxes. As he knelt inside his cubbyhole, knees bleeding, the enemy's weapon to hand, he thought he must die of thirst before dark. He couldn't get to the water inside the tank without giving away his position. He shivered inside when he considered how easily a sniper's bullet might penetrate his flimsy enclosure. It didn't bear thinking about. Instead, the youth thought of his father who had taught him to respect every fish in the sea, to issue his line yard by yard as if playing out his own life hand over hand until the end. Although he was close to tears the youth smiled fiercely. He wasn't scared – he was excited. The patrol would arrive soon. He had observed it already through a telescopic sight. He planned to wait until the patrol came close enough to see it with his own eyes – it would have been the act of a coward to fire blind. Now he rested the barrel of the enemy's rifle on the wall. He took off his glasses and laid them aside. It was understood he should target the officer – without their officer, the rest would be all at sea. That was the theory. But when he looked again using the sight, Isa found himself reluctant to shoot. Their officer was much too visibly a target. An act so flagrant, so obvious – wouldn't it curse the young man forever? In the end, his was a type of cowardice or loss of faith. Isa knew it himself. There was no time to debate his new target. He lowered his chin and closed one eye and fired his rifle. He heard the fish cry, saw a soldier fall. The young Arab shook uncontrollably for about ten seconds inside his outpost. Before he fled, he snatched up his glasses and thanked God for choosing him.

CALLUM SHOULD HAVE KNOWN THE BULLET was for him. Had he seen it coming, he could have stood up in the jeep and plucked the missile from the air. He didn't see it. Its effect on his physiology was devastating. No body armour could have shielded him from it – the 7.62mm round of sniping type and quality, with lead-antimony core retained by a full metal jacket. The propellant behind it inaugurated a pressure of eighteen tons per square inch very rapidly within the

285

rifle's barrel. By the time it left the rifle, the bullet was spinning on its axis at something over 2,500 revolutions per second. Pretty soon it struck Callum's collarbone. It was still spiralling cruelly as it took a deflection there, going on to rupture his lung and penetrate his heart before crashing through his lower ribcage. He realised right away what was going on. For a short time he told himself he should have practised harder for this moment in order to get more from it – then he dismissed the idea. There was precious little ceremony – no bells, no doves, no rippling fields of barley or rye. Instead, there was a nice silence. He was lying in the streets of Aden with their faces bearing down on him from a great height. Were they smiling? For the final time Callum asked which of them would have been prepared to die for him. He had an idea he would know very soon. He had the idea he would know everything. He didn't. He kept his eyes peeled, but it was no use. He didn't even know the colour of the sky.

IT WAS LEFT TO TAYLOR TO MAKE SENSE OF WHAT HAPPENED. He couldn't. Although he was happy to accept that those who die young must be beloved of God, he viewed such preferment as inadequate compensation in the instance in question. He was bumping along in an armoured personnel carrier at midnight, determined to honour in his head the idea of his friend. All around, they were singing –

> *Up the hill and doon the glen*
> *See them march the Scottish men*
> *See them marching home again*
> *To the barren rocks of Aden*

Taylor couldn't recall Callum's face. It was tragic – he couldn't remember what his buddy looked like. He jumped up from a bench and knocked a singing sergeant down and threw open the hatch and howled at the night until they dragged him back inside. To invoke his own sniper's bullet – it was the least he could do for a friend. He was there with Lieutenant Colonel Mitchell the night they took back Crater for the first and last time. No one spilled his blood that night – no, not so much as an Arab. It was Mitchell's night. There was a method, after all, in his madness.

# 6 |
# Sulaiman

'What are you? Blind? Open your eyes –'

## ❧ DOG EAT DOG ❦

THERE WERE PLENTY OF MADDENED MEN IN SHEIKH OTHMAN that night. Sulaiman was just one of them. He had spent the longest and darkest hours of factional aggression inside the monkey enclosure at the local zoo in the scattered company of a limping lion, the cheetah of disdain, multiple aloof foxes, an anxious ostrich, and at least one dozing python. Against a backdrop of urban explosions the primates ignored Sulaiman completely, swooping from wall to wall inside the cage, hurling themselves repeatedly at the mesh with their hysterical protests. Although the monkeys covered their ears with their paws, the noise was too great. It went on all night until the men had killed each other outright in the streets of the township and on its rooftops – NLF and FLOSY – or entered the last waiting-room of the chosen with a promise in their heads of heavenly Catherine wheels to come. The final mortar went up and came down in the hollow just before dawn. The tired monkeys fell silent, then slept. Sulaiman watched and waited as the night shed its silvery skin. He had a book, chosen carefully from the few abandoned at home by Isa, for his pillow. His pillow was *The River Of Adventure* by Enid Blyton. At some time it had been a bridge of understanding between the father and his son.

Three cocks crowed. The inner streets were the preserve of dogs and goats come to reclaim the world with a reckless hunger. Seated at the foot of the minaret with the rising sun at his back, Sulaiman surveyed the ragged thoroughfare in front of him – it stumbled like a beggar from the mosque to the botanical gardens and back again. Not a living soul walked the earth. On either side along the length of the street, the smoke rose, cool and thin, from human habitations and former cars. No smoke rose from the charred corpse stretched out beside Sulaiman on the steps of the mosque. The dead man had smouldered for a while and gone out in the night. Within their black sockets, his eyes were as white as flowers – it was impossible to know whether they had looked on life, until as recently as yesterday, using the NLF or the FLOSY model of a glorious future. When Sulaiman made to close the dead man's eyes, an eyelid broke off in his fingers. At last he heard the reassuring splutter of a diesel engine. The first truck showed its colours from a side street strewn with personal and household effects too random to encourage classification. The truck hesitated, struck perhaps by its irrelevance or inadequacy, a federal army ensign hanging limply on its bonnet.

'Hey, old timer – what the hell are you doing there?'

'Nothing. Can't you see? I'm reading a prayer book –'

'Go home, please – there's nothing to see here.'

'What are you? Blind? Open your eyes –'

'That's all right – everything's under control now.'

'Under control, you say? Where are the British troops?'

'There are no British troops here. Go home, old man –'

'Won't you at least jump down to recover this corpse?'

'That's OK – it won't run off. Go home now, please.'

'Yes, I will – I thought the mosque would be open.'

'Forget the mosque. Look – there's nothing to see here.'

'OK, OK – I get the message. Just let me read for a bit longer and then I'll go home straight afterwards.'

He was crazy enough to mean exactly what he said. He waited for the two trucks to finish their brief tour of a stunned settlement, saluting their departing mirrors with his book raised. He was alone again with the dogs and goats. He opened his book on his knees. He turned up the first page and smoothed it down with trembling hand and read the words. He rolled the first two words around his mouth until he was ready. Then he spat the words out.

*Poor Polly!*

In the troubled silence the puny plosives ricocheted like gunfire from street to deserted street. Sulaiman looked at the sky. He heard an infant cry miraculously at an unseen window.

*Poor Polly!*

How obsessed he had become. How crazy could it get? He was searching for his only son – a boy content to kill his own father with a bomb beside a swimming pool above the sloping lawns. Sulaiman had stopped worrying about wooden boxes with or without severed heads inside. All that was too trivial for words. It was the unfinished business with his son that ate at his heart and consumed his reason.

He left the corpse and the steps. Head down, his open book in front of him, he advanced from doorway to doorway with a progress slow but sure. In fact, he had never been so certain about anything. Pace after pace he read aloud for the benefit of a stricken township on the day after its factional bloodletting. As he turned the pages of his book he was observed from shuttered windows, becoming quickly a target for curiosity in the aftermath of fear and dismay. He looked to be a type of village idiot, he imagined, with an English novel. Still he travelled the pockmarked boulevard up and down until a veiled woman crept from a doorway and gave him water. He stumbled on, refreshed. One by one they emerged like sleepwalkers and set about cleansing their street as the sun climbed higher and the ditches ran free of blood, ran all the way to Aden and the sea. Sulaiman didn't stop. He read his book chapter by chapter for anyone to hear. When he had all but completed the last page, he lowered himself, spent, on the steps of the mosque and felt at home beside a corpse. He closed his eyes and prayed for new strength. Soon he began to slip sideways towards the step – his step. He was about to let go and give up the ghost when he heard the voice, cold and quick, of logic.

'Have you taken leave of your senses?'

Isa stood on the bottom step, head wrapped in a scarf. Was it a late instinct for reconciliation or a renewed contract with contempt, Sulaiman wondered, that made the boy sport his old glasses above his new moustache?

'Me? I might ask you precisely the same question. I had to find you, Isa – that's all I know.'

'Must you make a complete fool of yourself in the process?'

'Is that what concerns you? I am not ashamed of who I am.'

'Good. But why come sniffing around here? It's not safe –'

'Oh? Tell me – what exactly does safe look like these days?'

Isa led the way. The sun took up position overhead. Immediately they were in a maze of whitewashed alleys, a labyrinth of light. The youth took them this way and that until Sulaiman thought he must be lost in a desert of doors, windows and telegraph poles, each one the same as the next. The squat date palms were as giant pineapples in the sand. Isa marched them more and more briskly like an angry lover who forges ahead. All the time the sun was above, unblinking eye of a vast portrait that followed them from lane to dazzling lane. There was a commotion not far off. Sulaiman heard it distinctly. It might have been around the next corner or the one after that – the intolerant laughter of children above a persistent drumming on tins. All of a sudden there was a mature ostrich up ahead. At a crossroads of transfiguring light it loped, disoriented, in circles before pausing, foot raised speculatively in the air, to release a stream of excrement. First the confused bird bolted. Then the near-naked kids appeared.

Isa didn't break step. He had far too much on his mind. Had he turned and waited every now and then he would have seen Sulaiman scatter the shredded pages of a book from street to street and corner to corner in order to mark the route. With each page lost, the father felt himself draw closer to what the son must be thinking and feeling as they went deeper and deeper into the light. Why not? There was so much new knowledge to explore together and so many insights to uncover. Too late, too late – at least one of them should have been one hundred per cent dead by now.

'This is Aziz,' Isa explained curtly in the presence of an injured colleague or comrade.

In a dark courtyard the wounded man sat on a stack of cement bags against a wall beside a trellis of etiolated leaves. He glanced up briefly as a woman bandaged his chest.

'Down below –' Isa murmured. 'We can talk there.'

They were in a low-ceilinged basement at the rear of the house. There was little to see or take in – just the rough concrete walls and two rope-strung beds without mattresses on either side of the stairs. As the father waited for the darkness to recede, the son unwound his headscarf in the shaft of light that came down from a tiny window of frosted glass set into the wall just above ground level.

'Look at me, son. Can you imagine what it feels like to stand in this room with you?'

'How could you do it? How could you come all this way just to hunt me down like that? At a time like this –'

'Tell me *why*, Isa –'

'Don't you get it? I thought I'd never set eyes on you again.'

'You mean you *hoped* you'd never clap eyes on me again –'

For a moment neither spoke. It would have been impossible for each to recognise the other's deepest desires in the shallow basement of understanding. Now Sulaiman took up again quietly.

'I only came here to make sure. Let me see – a dead father is a useful thing to have. You know where you stand with such a father. You can make it all up – just who you are or where you came from.

295

You can be whatever you choose to be, no strings attached. Let me hear you deny it. Let me hear you say it wasn't you beside that pool outside Government House. It was someone else, wasn't it?'

They waited for each other, a curtain of weak sunlight between them.

'You have bred me. You have bred me, a monster. I don't need you, father. I don't want you around –'

'Wait. Stop there. Don't say another word.' Sulaiman took two paces through a wall of light and kissed his son. 'You have brought down the sky,' he whispered.

What he had to do from now on – suddenly it was clear to him in all its terrible detail. Funny thing – his every hope and prayer and dream had brought him inexorably to this special time and place. He heard the cultivated accent from above.

'And who is our unexpected guest, Isa?'

Aziz stood on the stairs, his hands behind his back, with a clean bandage visible at his chest.

'I am the father of this brave and beautiful boy,' Sulaiman told him.

Aziz nodded slowly. Still his hands were behind him. 'But what is it you *want?*' he asked.

'I want to stand with my son. I want to stand alongside Isa –'

Aziz looked from the father to the son and back, then brought his handgun around carefully.

'And who is your enemy?' he asked Sulaiman.

'Why – my enemy is the enemy of my son, of course.' Here the father smiled at nothing and no one – at nothing except a gun, and at no one but himself. 'Let me go now and return later,' he said. 'If I can find you again in this rat hole I am worthy of your regard –'

'Return alone?' Aziz said, wincing as he tucked his Luger away.

296

'Alone?' Sulaiman said, as if any alternative was laughable under the circumstances. 'Would a father betray his beloved son?'

HE LAY IN A DITCH OF RUNNING WATER a short distance from the road at the appointed hour and waited for her to come. He heard a solitary car approach – how lyrical the note of a lone engine under certain atmospheric or temperamental conditions. Sulaiman listened until the engine's noise died. In his head, its note carried on. When he opened his eyes Hildegaard knelt above him. She reached down with one hand and helped him up in the peachy light of evening.

'Aziz is there,' he said immediately, dripping water.

'The boy as well?'

Sulaiman beat himself with his arms as if to test the currency of various physical sensations – no, to assert or confirm his existence. 'I have found Isa, yes –' he said. 'We will be together again.'

'I'm so glad about that,' Hildegaard told him.

'Oh, don't worry –' Sulaiman insisted mildly. 'I know very well you don't really care about my son. But your doctor is there, slightly damaged, perhaps. He is absolutely there –'

As he began to sway, silhouetted against the red sky, Hildegaard draped his arm across her shoulders and turned to face the road and the rising moon.

'Will you show me?' she said. 'I mean – could you find it again if you had to?'

'Tomorrow, maybe,' he said. 'Or the day after, perhaps – once they've recaptured the animals and returned them to their cages.'

'Their cages?' Hildegaard said.

On a desert road at around dusk she opened the door of her car on the passenger side. In the distance below the burgeoning moon, the lights of Sheikh Othman were coming on in sparse clusters.

'They have set free the zoo there,' Sulaiman explained, shaking now. 'They have let loose all the animals.'

'Have they, really?' Hildegaard said, lowering him into the car gently. 'That is so seldom a good sign in my experience.'

## ❧ THE LETTER 'K' ❧

AS SOON AS OONA HAD DEPARTED, THEY DECAMPED. Aden's Rock Hotel would be their last address locally. They had terminated their evening performances at the Crescent Hotel for contractual reasons. And because Ken had decided not to sign up for their mini-tour of Australia, Durbridge resolved they should all learn to cope without the vocal and other talents of the hotelier's son. So few came to dine at the Crescent, anyway – the days of the dinner-dance, it seemed to all concerned, were numbered. At around the time the Caledonian Society cancelled, hugely ahead of term, its Burns Night event – an action that spoke volumes – Philip set aside doubt the better to give Australia its chance. He knew little about it as a landmass, as a last refuge in case of atomic war. It was the head of a terrier barking at empire from the foot of a map, or from the back of the atlas. It was just a few days off now. The whole prospect of new horizons made Philip think harder about everything that had happened thus far in his young life. It was the end or the beginning of something – Philip couldn't decide which. He considered and then rejected the idea of marking the moment with a modest tattoo in the form of either bird or beast. Something had to be done – this impulse he felt strongly. Then he glimpsed the bigger picture. He was simply acknowledging for the first time the fact of the rest of his life.

To give these landmark preoccupations expression, he went out to buy a present for Ken. He had no fixed idea about what might be

298

appropriate to current conditions of unrequited love – conditions he downgraded necessarily to those of a mutually sustainable affection. Rather he acted on the basis of what his mother would have done – when it came to emblematic gifts, his responsibility should be to his own aesthetic discrimination and morality. The lacquered jewellery box was lined with scarlet satin. Its clockwork mechanism animated a plastic ballerina on a small mirror to the strains of Brahms' lullaby. It was perfect for keeping precious things in, Philip decided. And he couldn't deny it – he had always had a soft spot for that melody. He exchanged the ten bob note his grandmother had sent him inside a birthday card with a Spitfire on it. But when he tendered the cash it wasn't quite enough. Just when he started to think his gift strategy, like the sentiment it grew from, would have to be downgraded, the stallholder, connoisseur himself of hopeless causes, took pity on him. Philip bought a lacquered jewellery box and transported it directly to the Crescent Hotel in case his resolve should leave him.

'Is Ken about at all?'

The painted lady behind the all too familiar reception desk was unknown to Philip. The lobby felt subtly different to him – product already of social history. How easily things were capable, given half a chance, of resisting or rejecting memory, he decided. If you didn't cultivate them daily in the mind they might revert, in the way of a neglected garden, to a wilderness or desert.

'He certainly should be, darling. He should be right here, right now, because he's due to take over from me at any minute.'

The relief receptionist tapped the counter with her magnificent talons and smiled.

'Oh, well –' Philip said. 'I think I'll wait for a bit if that's OK.'

'Of course it is, petal. Let me just dial the room and invite him to pull his finger out, in a manner of speaking. The naughty scamp –'

There was once an era in which Philip would have climbed the stairs two at a time and surprised his friend without even knocking. Now he sat, the chaste petitioner, and waited with his gift beside the hiccoughing fountain he was hearing for quite possibly the last time. Suddenly the fountain stopped working. It halted there and then as if someone had pulled the plug on historical events in the lobby of a three-star hotel. How affecting and meaningful – to Philip it seemed the lights of a Christmas tree had been switched off thanks to a war. He had a sudden vision – reviewed today, as experienced originally, from a bend in the stairs – of Oona encircled by umpteen suitcases and a broken snare drum. He picked up a copy of *Films & Filming*.

TWO FLOORS UP, THE TELEPHONE WAS RINGING on the mat below the wash hand basin. Ken could see himself in the triple mirrors of the dressing table. He turned away to study the phone with a vacant expression, but the mirrors drew him back as they often did. He was naked on his hands and knees on the bed with Adrian Durbridge in the background. The telephone stopped ringing. On the candlewick bedspread the tiny radio played Puff The Magic Dragon. Although the reception was uneven, and the song came and went rather in the humid air, Durbridge thought it best to turn up the volume.

PHILIP COULD SMELL IT. NOW THE RECEPTIONIST was painting the tips of her fingers with an aromatic nail varnish remover a few feet away from him in the lobby of the Crescent Hotel in Aden.

'Goodness me –' he protested cheerfully.

'Let me try him again,' the receptionist said. 'Remind me – is it business or pleasure?'

'Not to worry,' he said. 'If I can just leave this here with you –'

He placed a parcel, wrapped in white tissue paper, on the desk.

'Best write his name on it, I would have thought, pet –' advised the receptionist, inspecting the denuded nails of one hand.

Philip accepted her blue ballpoint and set to work on the tissue paper, but his graphic design was interrupted almost immediately by an expansive voice from the stairs.

'Hello, tiger – come to visit young Kenneth?'

At the desk, Durbridge fairly oozed a type of sleek satisfaction. Although his hair was slicked back with water or tonic, that wasn't in itself proof of physical intimacy, Philip told himself, thinking hard.

'Is he up there, then?' he asked casually.

'Only, I can't get no reply,' the relief receptionist interposed.

'Really?' Durbridge said. 'Ah, yes – sorry about that. He was in the middle of singing me a song, you see –' He looked at Philip and winked. 'Very sweet, very sweet –'

In the upstairs corridor he hesitated, his gift in his hands. Was it a longing for decency, a yearning for universal dignity, which forced him to give Ken as much time as possible? Circumstantial evidence was everywhere around. Philip watched a column of ants march up and down the wall beside the door in parallel lines like black stitches between the ceiling and a crumb of something on the floor. He had seen the hair, freshly combed, at the ear of Durbridge, and his wink, of course. But the clincher was waiting inside the room. You didn't have to be a private investigator or a Belgian detective. Philip smelt it distinctly in the humid air. It wasn't Ken, quite, or Durbridge. It was the scent of warm semen on a candlewick bedspread.

'Blimey – is that a present for me?' Ken asked with a toothbrush in his mouth.

Later, Philip would describe it as being not unlike drowning, or how he imagined drowning to be. He saw his recent past, or certain parts of it, parade in front of him – key images, at least, of profit and loss. For example, he saw two colourful flip-flops drift apart wilfully on the surface of the Red Sea.

'I'm sorry −' he said, shaking with anger and self-loathing. 'It's actually a present for my Mum.'

'You mean you plan to *post* it − or did you intend to lug it all the way around Australia with you?'

'I don't know − I hadn't thought that far ahead.'

'Would you like me to give it to a guest flying back?'

'Flying back? Flying back where?'

'Back home, silly − they could post it in London for you.'

'Oh, no − I don't think that will be necessary.'

'Suit yourself − but we use the airport method all the time.'

'Do you? And will you be using it this Sunday?'

'Sunday? How Sunday, my dear boy?'

'Isn't that when we jet off and leave you? For good −'

'Just you try and stop me, tiger −'

Ah, *tiger* − there it was again. From the bed, the radio gave out only static. Looking down at the present in his hands, Philip had an urge, more powerful than desire, to open it, to open the lacquered box and have the music strike up now and forever.

'I'm not going to play the drums any more, Ken −'

There was a short delay during which the young man beside the triple mirrors spat toothpaste into the sink.

'I'm not really a drummer,' Philip went on. 'It's obvious, isn't it? Why pretend? I don't actually feel like a drummer. I don't even look like a drummer when it comes right down to it.'

'I could have told you that.'

'Could you?'

'Oh, sure − you're much too good.'

'Really? Then why didn't you?'

'Why didn't I what?'

'Why didn't you tell me, Ken?'

It was pointless to go on. He left quickly, his precious box under his arm, without any reference to love. At the bottom of the stairs he delivered his only true farewell to the silent fountain and the relief receptionist with her freshly painted nails.

'Did you find him?' she asked brightly.

'He'll be right down, he says –'

'He must think he owns the joint,' she said.

'Goodbye, now,' Philip said, fleeing the scene. 'Good luck –'

There was one thing left to do. The beggar without legs was on his wheeled platform. He was still there – he would always be there, Philip saw. The beggar rolled backwards and forwards outside the bus station on MacKenzie, trying his luck, soliciting with his stumps. He stopped in his tracks, his silk tie over his bare shoulder. Pinning Philip's offering to the ground with his elbows, he tore at the tissue paper and opened the lacquered box with his teeth. When he saw it was empty, he slammed the lid down and tossed the thing aside and rolled away. Why do that? He might have swapped it for something else. It was inconceivable a beggar should act that way. Philip took up the rejected gift. They were all staring at him now from the bus station. Again and again he consoled himself – his spurned offering was of limited practical use to a cripple on castors. The first thing he saw when he lifted the lid was a sliver of silvered glass. The mirror – it was broken. The plastic ballerina was redundant. Suddenly there was the sweet music. In the profane sunshine the lullaby by Brahms was like a prayer for rain. Over and over again it played until Philip lowered the lid of the box. They were applauding him now from the bus station. When the beggar came back and started to remonstrate, waving his stumps wildly, Philip refused to give up his box. He had

303

the idea he might carry it with him it for the rest of his life. Looking back from the corner of MacKenzie he saw a cripple rock back and forth inconsolably. Then someone picked up the tissue paper with the letter 'K' on it.

## ☙ INTERREGNUM ❧

'FUNNY – I DON'T THINK YOUR ENGLISH HAS SUFFERED at all,' she said out of the blue as to a long-time friend while loosening the knot of her shawl.

Although the heat was as intense as ever they were wrapped up like two explorers at the North Pole. No one troubled them. In the ruined zoo an opal light ran from the leaves of shell-shocked trees, exiles of the nearby botanical garden, labelled in English, Latin and Arabic. On one or other side of overgrown pathways, the signposts pointed this way or that without meaning. Only the indignant trees were reliable. Around the lake no flamingo stooped where once they gathered superbly, or roamed the shallows alone. The lake itself was shrinking, drying up. There was nothing left alive in any cage – not a boa or a budgerigar.

'You and me – we are old soldiers, Hildegaard. Survivors of the great hunger –'

Which hunger? She let that one go. Beside her, Aziz breathed in passionately as if he had discovered a modern Eden in a clapped-out zoo. Into his charged platitudes she read the delusional nostalgia of a bitter man and the self-deprecating irony of the cynic from Beirut. But there was something new – a caustic idealism that touched her inside as their dialogue moved freely between languages.

'Ah – but what could you possibly want with me now?' he asked suddenly, changing tack, or shifting ground, like a good guerrilla.

As she looked out across the lake Hildegaard thought fleetingly of her hospital rounds in the days before she took off her cross. She moved on quickly to the so-called abduction episode in the desert by a *wadi*. There was Hannan, the seer – her eyes were windows to her heart and soul. Hildegaard considered Aziz, too. She imagined him during the unpleasant period of detention that was probably fresh in his mind even now. How like a dream it all seemed at the edge of a shrinking lake in Sheikh Othman. Hildegaard had to force herself to remember why she had come.

'Do you despise me very much?' she began, surfacing.

Aziz didn't look at her. They were sitting side by side in a holed pleasure boat left high and dry by the receding waters.

'What's that?' he said distractedly. 'Oh, I don't waste my time. Instead, I review the question of how you reached me in my lair, and whether it matters. Does it matter?'

'Do you still carry a gun, doctor?'

'Ah – happy days, nurse. Innocent days –'

'The war is over, Aziz.'

'A war is rarely over. Didn't they teach you that in spy school? No – my war is just beginning. The task now is to eliminate FLOSY in the name of the NLF. As for peace – if or when it comes it will be worse than the war.'

He shrugged mechanically, wearily, beside her. She was looking for an opening, looking for her chance.

'But you know all this, Hildegaard,' he went on. 'We know you see everything from the top of the hill. But not for much longer, eh? Call it war or call it peace – where will you go next, nurse? What will you do next? Already we see far too little of you –'

'Have you heard the news?' she said.

'We make the news,' he said.

Just then she felt the pungent breath of the lake on her face. She tasted it on her tongue as she lowered her shawl.

'No –' he said quickly. 'Leave it on, please. You don't think we get our fair share of madmen out here?'

'Aren't you pleased?' she asked. 'Doesn't it satisfy you when the high commissioner suspends all parliamentary activity and invites you to form an interim administration?'

'Oh, I try to leave all that constitutional posturing to those more worthy. It's a kind of masturbation, surely, at the hand of history –'

So saying, Aziz hauled himself out of the boat. Where the water had been there was only the fetid mud now. As he went down to the provisional shoreline Hildegaard took her chance.

'And just how is the constitutional Basim Mansouri, I wonder? Still playing with himself in the corridors of power?'

He stopped then. She watched him turn around. Slowly he came back, his eyes on the sloping ground between them.

'Listen to me,' he said, rocking the stranded pleasure boat with his foot. 'Basim Mansouri will doubtless make his own outstanding contribution to history should destiny happen to knock even more loudly at his door. It's a door he is always ready to open as wide as possible, as you know –'

'But you haven't seen him?' she said. 'He hasn't sent for you, as it were, at this time?'

'If I didn't know you better, nurse, I might be tempted to think you were mocking me.'

'I had always understood you to be ideological bedfellows, that's all.'

'You know –' he told her. 'I have never really been one to put my faith in systems.'

'Systems of belief?' she said. 'The handmaidens of oppression?'

306

'Political systems, ideological or religious systems – by which we mean tyrannies, of course.' He had been rocking their pleasure boat absently in the mud. Now he pushed the boat away and turned his back on her and faced the sick lake. 'And you, Hildegaard – do you still put your faith in faith?'

'For such a small word it casts a long shadow.'

'But how could you *possibly*, after all – having been where you've been and seen what you've seen?' Abruptly he spread his arms and described the wasteland on all sides. 'Look –' he urged. 'They have drained the stinking waters of heaven. And this is what we fight for, I tell you – capitalist against communist, communist against himself. We fight for this mud. Look – not a bird in the sky.' He spun round and yanked up his shirt, and she saw a bloody bandage there. 'They will break us in pieces, Hildegaard. Who? Them. They will crush us all, one by one, in the name of freedom and justice. Tell me – what is freedom if not what I want for myself, and what I will do to you in order to get it? Yes – to you, nurse. Of course, the ones who *make* a revolution never live to see it grow old. No, no – first these idealists are replaced by ideologues. Then comes the turn of the opportunists banning this, banning that – banning God, Hildegaard. And Basim? He is simply making such a journey in reverse. He knows nothing of what people want. Even so, his first instinct is to stop them having it. How could he know what we want? He is alone, like you or me. At night he dreams first of himself. Soon his dreams embrace everyone who will *owe* him something tomorrow – a nice statue, perhaps, or a bust on a plinth in a minor plaza or park. In these dreams he feigns solidarity with a million starving souls in every corner of the world. Oh, yes – his dreams are global or universal now in their scope and reach. Each night he dreams, a hero – no, a cut-price messiah – but in the morning he wakes up alone.'

'And waits, like you and me, to be crushed?' Here she got down from the pleasure boat, and he followed her from the shallow recess of the lakeside towards the noble trees and the blasted landscape of the zoo proper. 'I don't think so, doctor. No, I can't really see that happening, can you? One more insignificant thing for the record – I don't believe him even *capable* of dreams, or of dreaming.'

'Look – Basim Mansouri will do anything to get what he wants. I mean *anything*. This man will stop at nothing to lift the prize. You, of all people, should know that, Hildegaard.'

'And you, Aziz? What will you do, and how far will you go?'

'To get what I want?'

'What you deserve –'

She took her time. There was a season for everything. To hurry at this point would have been a mistake. Soon they were nearing the monkey enclosure with its sad tyres hanging down so still. Nothing stirred – any breeze was confined to the lake and the shore.

'Over there –' Hildegaard said suddenly. Behind the cage was a monkey with its fingers hooked on the mesh. 'Isn't that wretched? I do believe it wants to get back in.'

Aziz banged on the wire until the animal withdrew with a cry – it loped off in the direction of the botanical garden. Aziz continued to shake the cage with both hands. Then he spoke out quietly.

'What is it about you, I ask myself again? What is it that makes me think of you fishing and fishing – always fishing? Were there just one creature left in all the sea you would find it. You know – I never made the mistake of underestimating you the way Basim did.'

'You fool, Aziz. You consider yourself an idealist, yet you don't even know what you want. I'm not convinced you believe in *anything*. What you want, in fact, is nothing. And that's what you'll get –' She saw him touch his forehead to the mesh. As she went on he closed his eyes and banged his head slowly against the cage. 'You allowed him to use you, and when the time came he cast you aside.'

'Really? I'm not sure I recognise the picture you paint. History, I venture to suggest, is mine. I have my modest portion of it —'

'Does he honour, I wonder, the memory of the prison hours you spent together — comrades standing shoulder to shoulder against the cruel inquisitor? Ask Basim exactly how he fared in detention, why don't you? Or do you imagine all men are made equal by your dirty little revolution in the sand?'

'Always fishing — fishing and fishing. What for, I wonder? What could you possibly want with me *today*, Hildegaard?'

'Would you care to be a spy for the British, doctor? There — that is really all I'm asking here.'

It was almost over. Look how far she had come without falling. She had done what she came to do. The race — it was nearly run.

'They have sent me here to find out one little thing — whether or not you are willing to turn. Do you understand me? Of course you do. They want to know if you would be prepared to represent their interests — their best interests. I told them — yes, there is some merit in what you propose. But is he bitter enough, they asked me — or is he, perhaps, *too* bitter to make a top spy? I said I really don't know, but I can find out for you easily enough.'

He opened his eyes and looked at her and shook his head. 'What did I tell you? A war is never won —' He lowered his hands from the cage and turned away towards the gate.

'Take your time,' she said. 'Think it over, by all means, then let me know what your answer is.' She waited for him to stop, but he carried on walking away. 'You know — Basim always said you were born to follow, Aziz.'

He stopped there. He had his back towards the shattered gate.

'Follow what, exactly, Hildegaard? Are we not, all of us, in the same boat looking for a star?'

'Do you forgive me?' she said. 'I think that's what I came to ask.'

Now it was over. She watched him raise his face to the grey sky. 'You?' he said.

He pulled his scarf tighter around his head. As he backed away through the gate, Hildegaard wondered if she would see him again.

### ❧ FUNERAL OF A FRIEND ❧

TAYLOR TOOK MATTERS INTO HIS OWN HANDS. Although he had never spoken to the chaplain before that time, he decided a man of the cloth ought to know his right from his wrong.

'It has to be done here, padre. It has to –'

On the sandy football pitch the chaplain drew him closer with a sinewy arm as dark as wet wood. They had turned their damp backs on the setting sun and a goalmouth yellow with sawdust – here the sportsmen warmed up, or down, with a disciplined demonstration of sit-ups and press-ups.

'Have you spoken to the CO about this?'

Taylor nodded, eyes lowered, kicking the sand over with a boot. 'He told me the body would have to be repatriated. He said it would normally go home except in exceptional circumstances.'

'So, are there any – exceptional circumstances?'

'I don't rightly know, padre. I mean – I don't know what counts as exceptional to the CO. It seems to me the business of catching it in the neck while doing your duty is exceptional enough, really, in any circumstances. That's where he bought it, sir – in the neck. Just here –' Taylor slapped his own shoulder as hard as he could, then glowered at the man of peace. In the ravishing light of evening, the

310

chaplain's dog collar looked grimy. 'I mean – how exceptional does it need to be?'

For a few moments they pursued their own shadows across the uneven surface. Up ahead, a ragged ribbon of sawdust described the halfway line of the pitch.

'I understand there's no family –'

'There's no family, no, because the *army* was his effing family.'

An unscripted breeze animated the uppermost layer of sand or dust and sent it scudding across the field towards an empty goal.

'I'm sorry, sir. It's just that – well, he didn't have anyone at all.'

They were standing, heads bowed, at the halfway line. Now the chaplain took his turn at configuring, or reconfiguring, the sawdust with the toe of his sandal.

'The thing is –' Taylor said finally. 'I feel responsible because I know he looked up to me. For better or worse, he looked up to me. I wouldn't normally mention it, sir. You understand that, don't you?'

He had to turn away then and consult the sympathetic sky. He could feel the desert, its relentless presence – right now it was in his eyes and on his teeth. Over there, seven men outlined in gold by the setting sun were doing star-jumps as if death had yet to be invented. Yes, that must be it – they were guiding the sun towards the landing strip. Taylor breathed in harshly and exhaled. He spun round ready to go on, to see the job through, to make the whole thing count, but the chaplain, hitching up his baggy shorts, headed him off smartly with his decisive little cough.

'That's quite all right, private. Let me just see what I can do –'


THE LAUNCH LEFT PRINCE OF WALES PIER at break of day, making straight for the open sea. Their haste was official – a war was taking place in the locality, and the morning's affair was, strictly speaking, a distraction, or a sideshow. Taylor looked at the chaplain who had stuck his scrawny neck out for him and done him proud. There was a bond between the two men – it was forged as much in their strong silences as in the laconic exchanges between them. The chaplain was dressed all in black. His new dog collar was a startling exception – it had the ability to fluoresce in the murky half-light. No one spoke to comment on the business of the day. They might have been a detail of ghosts going forth first among bunkered freighters before leaving astern the great warships asleep in the cradle of the bay. As the sun rose inch by inch above the horizon, Amy waved a posy of poppies at it. Beyond the calm of the deep water anchorage the salty breeze was only moderate. It was a perfect day for a funeral at sea. As the light grew in confidence, the swell prevaricated – it was either pink or gold. Suzy Wong looked at Taylor. Taylor saw the chaplain rap the sweating glass of the wheelhouse. Three miles out from Prince of Wales pier, the note of the engine fell away. For a moment the boat drifted respectfully in a rosy hush. Then the skipper poked his head around the doorway of the wheelhouse.

'Here?' he asked.

'Here,' the chaplain said.

They set to work without consulting further. Callum's body was already wrapped in linen sheets bound with rope. They had only to weight him down carefully with the two rods of Sheffield steel. They didn't bother with a plank or platform. After they laid the bundle on the deck, they stood in their small group while the padre spoke the time-honoured words and they listened to his sad speech. The padre kept his speech brief. The psalm, which he sang alone and without musical accompaniment, was short enough, too, for the unbeliever or the hard of heart. Taylor didn't speak at that time. It fell to Suzy Wong to say goodbye on behalf of all of them.

312

'We didn't know Callum for very long –' she began, resting her hands on her daughter's shoulders just in front. Her voice, when she spoke again after a short pause, was clear and strong. 'We liked him very much – didn't we, Amy?'

The child nodded gravely above her koala bear and her flowers. She was frowning – perhaps she was growing anxious now about the business of casting her few poppies on the sea.

'It seems to me,' Suzy Wong said, 'that many young men think they know everything, whereas, in point of fact, most of them know next to nothing. But Callum wasn't like most young men – not at all. His death only convinces me more – one day he would have come to know everything a man must know, and then we would have had someone very special to call our friend. *Adieu, adieu* – he was one of us, wasn't he? No – he was the best of us. He was in the same team as the angels, Amy. He will always walk with us, at our side –'

The padre backed off as Taylor and the captain lifted Callum's body and laid it head to toe against the gunwale. In the event, it was hard to tell one end from the other – they simply rolled the bundle over the side of the boat after Taylor counted to three. There was a splash, good and solid. As they peered over the side the white parcel disappeared below the surface without a second thought. For almost a minute they watched as the powerful bubbles rose up and burst all around Amy's scattered poppies. After Taylor nodded at the padre, the skipper went back inside the wheelhouse and started the engine. Then Amy did something unexpected – she dropped her koala bear into the sea right beside the boat. Taylor banged on the wheelhouse roof, but just then Suzy Wong raised a hand. Mother and daughter waved their salutes side by side from the deck as the launch circled once in tribute. They left Amy's koala bear floating face up among the poppies, turning one by one to confront the mist-shrouded land.

313

He had such a short time to make her love him. As soon as the chaplain had steered little Amy astern, Taylor put his arms around Suzy Wong from behind. He didn't want to speak – to speak was to begin to lose or win. How much he would have given simply to hold her like that, to plough the deepest currents with her at the prow of a ship with no crew and no tomorrow. Up ahead, the harbour boats were camped around the volcano like a besieging army boastful with reckless promises and resplendent in the colours of war. To Taylor, the view said all or nothing. How alike the two things were capable of looking in the shifting light of emotion.

'Please –' he said. 'Tell me you'll make me happy.'

'Not here –' she whispered. 'Not now.'

'It has to be now – don't you know we'll be gone in about three weeks?' He pulled her closer, spurred on by a perception he had of love running through his fingers like sand. He could smell the land now with its wanton perfume. Still she didn't say anything. 'Did you hear what I said?' he asked her.

'I heard you, Taylor, but I can't marry you.'

'Why not, Suzy? Tell me again, please –'

'I don't love you. No – I don't love you enough.'

'Ah, that's better – you don't love me *enough*.'

Was he was gripping her too tightly? When he felt her begin to resist him he had the urge to hold her all the closer in the face of her silent protests. Instead, he let go of her altogether.

'You have to go back now,' she insisted with her practical brand of wisdom. 'You must return to where you belong, Taylor. You are not the same as me. You are not even like poor Callum. You belong. But Amy and I – we have only each other to make life worth living.'

He didn't understand her at all. Why not? It should have been the easiest thing in the world to understand her.

'You have me, Suzy.'

'Please – you're such a dear friend, Taylor. I've never wanted to say those dreadful words because they mean –'

'Goodbye?'

She didn't deny it. Instead, she gripped the throbbing rail with both hands. '*Assez* –' she said. 'Enough. Let me try to describe what is happening between this woman and this man.'

Now she lifted up her voice – it reached Taylor torn apart by a freshening wind.

'He discovers her suddenly, unexpectedly, in the tropical night. Quickly they become lovers. He has never known anyone quite like her. How could he? In the morning she is no longer a stranger, but still she fascinates him so far away from home. *Et voilà*. Everything is different. Everything is new. But not for her –'

She was talking to the sea now, or the shore. Although her hair lashed her face cruelly she made no effort to restrain it. Taylor did that for her.

'She too is far from home – it's true. But nothing has changed for her. Nothing is new. Can you see it, Taylor? The world is so old. But now he falls in love with her, this man. Can it really be so? He asks her to marry him. Why? He wants to keep her, exotic flower, in a sunlit room. He wants to hold her, strange beast, in a rattan cage.'

'No, no, no –'

'If only he *would* hold her. If only he *would* keep her –'

'I don't understand you. I don't want anything to be new, Suzy. I want everything to be old, old, old.'

'Hold me now, Taylor, because I'm frightened. All my life I've lived in a cage.'

He turned her around then and wiped her cheeks. He loved to see her as she really was, with greying hair tossed about by the wind.

315

'I want to take care of you, Suzy. This is Taylor, remember?'

When he drew her near, her head fitted the curve at his throat.

'And feel yourself cursed forever? No, no – we'll take very good care of each other, Amy and I. We know exactly who we are. Better take a closer look inside your heart, Taylor –'

Then he saw it. He need never hold her in a special way, or let her go, again – not ever. How angry he felt – angry but relieved. He was angry with her for letting him believe he could ever have made her happy. He was disgusted, too, at his relief. It appalled him and made him forget how to act.

'Go ahead –' he said, wild and free. 'Go ahead and take care of each other famously.'

Did she sense the change in him? She pulled away considerately.

'I can't possibly know who you are, Suzy. Only you know who you really are. Is that it? Ten to one I don't deserve you anyway. Or maybe you're just too proud to let the little girl have a proper life, a decent life. Wake up, Suzy Wong. Wake up and say yes. It's not too late. Let me help you – please.'

'Be careful what you wish for, Taylor. You might find you get it.'

It was so wrong, so unfair – when she smiled he wanted to hurt her again and again.

'It's all my fault,' she insisted decorously. 'Yes, I may be proud and stubborn. I certainly hope I am, for Amy's sake. But this is my life, my darling Taylor. Not even you can take it away from me.'

After they tied up he lifted Amy from the deck and set her down on the pier beside a stack of swordfish heads attracting bluebottles. The chaplain was there, too, with Suzy Wong. The mother took the daughter's hand. She gave the padre alone her most gracious smile of farewell before turning from the sea to face the bustling quay.

'No, wait –'

316

Was it an error to call her back? Taylor couldn't help it. He had in his hand a charred library book she might mistake for his parting gift. Never mind. Never mind.

'I did love you —' he called out. 'I have loved you, Suzy — in my own way.'

Love was a matter, now, of historical record. They had stopped side by side, the mother and her little girl. The mother turned first.

'Soon you won't,' she said, swinging her daughter's hand back and forth. She looked fondly at Taylor, as if to fix the image of him in her head for the rest of time. 'Soon you won't love me at all,' she persisted softly. 'Already you begin to hate me a little.'

Turning away again, she drew the little girl very close. Together they looked to the barren hillside beyond the pier and the quayside. Watched all the way by Taylor they were lost finally to view among the uniformed school children disgorged by three buses.

'We'd best be getting back, private —'

The chaplain's hand was on Taylor's shoulder.

'I know that, padre, and I want to thank you for everything. We did the right thing out there, didn't we?'

'It was the right thing to do.'

'I believe so, padre. Look — I forgot to give him his book.'

Taylor held up the Yiddish library book blackened by fire.

'We'd best get back to barracks now, private.'

They heard the horn sound as the launch inched away from the pier. When the skipper hailed them from the wheelhouse door they returned his salute. Then the sea boiled around the screws, and the ensign opened like a hothouse flower in the smoke.

'It's a funny thing, though, padre —'

'What's that, Private Taylor?'

Already the chaplain was unbuttoning his dog collar at the back.

'Callum always wanted to learn how to swim.' Here Taylor stole a last look at the beautiful, dangerous bay. 'Perhaps now,' he said, 'he'll get his big chance.'

## ❧ Requiem for a Donkey ❧

IT WAS INCREASINGLY IMPORTANT in these dog days to be vigilant. Hildegaard took to wearing vermilion lipstick while more and more she framed her dark glasses with a headscarf of cerulean blue. Such an exuberance of taste and toilet was ironic – she was living, by and large, incognito, and shifting from room to room along Murder Mile as more and more flats fell vacant in Ma'ala. It was Farquhar's idea she limit the use of her own car in favour of a government sedan. A Volkswagen was conspicuous, he argued. Its everyday employment was dangerously complacent. It was overly frivolous for a spy, he had warned her, giving up the keys to the Zephyr.

She stood before the latest in a long line of mirrors, weighing up her appearance with the harshest objectivity. Her look was anything but complacent. Her faith was a sham – perhaps it always had been, she argued, weeping with reserve at a stranger's mirror in a second-floor flat without air conditioning. How could she honour God and be a good spy? These were mutually exclusive pursuits, she accepted unequivocally for the first and last time, having long since dismissed as impractical, or unsympathetic to the secret agent's calling, certain popular ideals of public service and civic duty. She was pretty much alone in a dirty world at a difficult time. To be, effectively, a double, not a single, agent – why did she plump for such an option if not to have her cake and eat it, or to please all the people all the time? No, it was a ridiculous state of affairs, a travesty of selfless devotion. She had probably been hedging her bets from the start.

In the mirror she mocked herself now without mercy. She had no clothes on. Her mascara of disguise had come unstuck. It slipped down her cheek like topsoil in a flood. What a senseless waste – she had practised and practised to get her maquillage right. Now it fell from her face towards the cross glinting impossibly at her breast and burning there like a lump of phosphorus. Hildegaard badly wanted to remove her crucifix – again. She yearned, one last time, to take it off. She put down her bottle of London gin, acquired at exorbitant cost in deteriorating market conditions. Off came the cross. She was quite naked. As she looked around the charmless room Hildegaard saw nowhere designed for storing small items over long periods. She had so few things to call her own. When, finally, she threw the cross into her suitcase and collapsed on the mattress she was subject to an overwhelming nausea brought on by warm gin. In between dreams that threatened, wave after wave, to crush her, she had a powerful urge to be underwater – in the sea, but underwater.

She woke up two hours later with an unexpectedly clear view of the road ahead. The kitchen thermometer said eighty degrees. The shower water came through in the usual tepid trickle for a couple of minutes before drying up. That didn't matter. Everything would be all right, Hildegaard decided, scrubbing her old make-up off with a towel before gathering up swimsuit, dress, sunglasses and headscarf. Having checked and approved her revised look in the mirror she was almost ready. She had only to choose between cars.

In a back street below, the black sedan was busy absorbing the afternoon heat. Hildegaard forsook the Zephyr in favour of her own car. She was on her knees beside a Volkswagen, but not to pray. She was examining the chassis for the giveaway wiring and telltale putty of the improvised explosive device. On the Ma'ala straight the lights were at green. They always were, these days. Although she carried her security pass, Hildegaard didn't need it. The few British soldiers she saw ignored her. Perhaps they recognised her car. Where were they all? They were somewhere else, thinking of distant sweethearts and a gentle rain that fell. Hildegaard removed her scarf and let the wind seize her hair. The sky was a casual blue. Such a sky might last forever, she thought, discarding sunglasses so as to enjoy the eternal qualities overhead. As she left Steamer Point she began to sing –

> *Were you ever in Bombay,*
> *Where the folks all shout 'Hooray,*
> *Here comes Johnny with his three months' pay',*
> *Riding on a donkey?*

> *Hey! Ho! Away we go,*
> *Donkey riding, donkey riding –*
> *Hey! Ho! Away we go,*
> *Riding on a donkey*

She sang all the way to Gold Mohur and the ocean. She didn't ask why she sang, far less why she sang in English. She couldn't see how an obscure sea shanty might pop, fully formed, into her head if not as a result of subconscious forces acting on childhood memory long suppressed. That was perfectly OK, Hildegaard reasoned – she was simply getting in touch with her imagination, too long denied in the interests of her unusual career, using doors or corridors that had been closed off to her for the best part of a young lifetime. She was still singing when she slipped below the surface of the ocean and let out her breath, sinking far enough to kneel on the sandy bottom. It was enough, it was plenty – she only wanted to stay there for as long as she could. Twenty-five seconds? Thirty? Although the recognised

320

way to survive and thrive underwater was, manifestly, to hold one's breath, Hildegaard had to expel all her useful air in order to stay at the bottom. Her actions marked a watershed, or a turning point, of sorts. She baptised herself, to all intents and purposes, in the Gulf of Aden. The sun pinned her brilliantly to the sand. She kept her eyes open all the time down there, the better to see what was happening.

ON THE FINE SAND BETWEEN THEM STOOD a large plastic canteen. When Sonny pressed the little button she released the pale mixture of vodka and orange squash, plus the last slivers of ice.

'Chin-chin,' she said gaily from her blue and red towel, handing Nolan a cup in the shade of their beach umbrella. 'To happy – no, happier – times, Ben.'

As she waved her own beaker overhead in a toast, Nolan caught a glimpse of the grey pinpricks under her arm where she had shaved that morning.

'To *much* happier times,' he commented drolly. 'Enough of sun, sea, sand, surf and other, mostly overrated, things beginning with an 'S' – we're all going home at last.'

'Correction –'

Mathieson chipped in from just beyond their oval shade. Supine on the sand, his tartan trunks parading massively below the relaxed curve of his stomach, he raked his heels across two thousand former shells made powder by the ocean. Between his tanned face and the sun he held a straw hat with which he fanned, every now and then, the freckled skin drawn loosely across his chest.

'Some of us are refusing to leave, Ben.'

Nolan smiled at Sonny. Sonny shrugged helplessly in return.

'Oh, don't mind him –' she advised. 'He's become so tiresome and boring since he gave up the booze.'

After Mathieson protested affectionately, Nolan turned his back on the shade and confronted the dazzling sea. From behind, Sonny was telling him about KL, where they planned, Mathieson and she, to try their luck, but her voice failed, for the most part, to penetrate the exclusion zone of memory surrounding Nolan. As he narrowed his eyes the sunlight exploded on the water. He thought he saw the contours of his wife's body as she went down to the surf for the last time. How terrible and lonely, Nolan acknowledged again and again as he stared, to be contemplating that final swim. Just this side of the shark net the Gold Mohur diving board platforms rose from the sea like rusty scaffolding, potential infrastructure of new dreams. From the towel behind, Sonny laughed lightly in expectation of a modest happiness. Nolan nodded empathetically. It was then he recognised the woman emerging in her bikini from the sea. She was waist deep and wading strongly towards the shore, skimming her fingers across the surface of the water. She looked downward at all times, as if she was fascinated by what lay below. As she stepped from the surf she wrung the ocean from her hair.

'Hello, Hildegaard —'

The water ran down her thighs and fell in flashing beads from her knees to the sand at Nolan's feet. He held up his towel but she didn't take it. 'You know Hildegaard, I think,' he remarked, without looking at his friends. 'You must have met her at the Port Trust – or at the high commissioner's party. Yes, at the *bomb* party —'

'Of course, of course —' Mathieson came back, sprawling on his side and flapping his hat. 'Not every civil service bash goes off with quite such a bang, my dear.'

'It's a wicked world,' Hildegaard admitted quietly.

'Wasn't it just awful?' Sonny said, shaking her head.

'Would you two excuse us?' Nolan said, getting up.

He took Hildegaard's arm and then let go, and they set off side by side along the edge of the surf towards the far-off gatehouse that marked the limit of the beach club compound.

'Are you all right?' he asked at the height of the silence between them.

'Of course,' she said to an empty sea. 'Everyone's leaving, Ben.'

'It's rather pleasant,' he told her, 'in a funny way.'

'All the traffic lights,' she said, 'are stuck at green.'

'What will you do, Hildegaard?'

'I don't know – study my options, I suppose.'

'Let me see – will it be nursing or espionage?'

'Haven't you overlooked a third possibility?'

'If I have, please excuse –'

'Knowing God, perhaps?'

He didn't speak because he wanted things to sit easily between them. There was something new in her voice, he told himself. There was something new in her acceptance of him, or in their acceptance of each other – to Ben Nolan it felt like rest after toil.

'Actually, there's a fourth option,' she told him in the shadow of the gatehouse. 'I could just tick none of the above and start all over again and give myself a second chance –'

'Do you know what a blue moon is?' he asked her.

'Not really,' she said.

'Isn't it when you get a second full moon within a single month?'

'That's nice –' she said.

'We should probably think about heading back now,' he said.

'What about you?' she said. 'What do you want?'

'Oh, the usual, I guess – to be a man. Or to be content with who I am, perhaps – I'd probably settle for that.'

'Take me home, please, Ben –'

323

'Absurd, isn't it? Sometimes I do believe my innermost thoughts and deepest impulses have been appropriated by someone else.'

'So, take me home, then,' she said.

'No, I won't,' he said, laughing. 'Luckily, I don't even have my own car.'

'Pity,' she said, smiling. 'Fortunately, I have mine —'

After they made their way back and Nolan had gathered up his things – red towel, white shirt, blue flip-flops – Mathieson reached up towards Hildegaard from the sand.

'Best of British —' he said with a dry little wink.

'All the best,' Sonny added with a suggestion of strong emotion.

'The same to you,' Hildegaard said, shrugging off the trademark inadequacy of words.

They drove in silence, hot currents swirling around their heads, until Hildegaard sang her song, her ghostly sea shanty, with her wet dress drying on her body and her hands at ten-to-two on the wheel.

*Were you ever off Cape Horn,*
*Where it's always fine and warm,*
*And seen the lion and the unicorn,*
*Riding on a donkey?*

*Hey! Ho! Away we go,*
*Donkey riding, donkey riding –*
*Hey! Ho! Away we go,*
*Riding on a donkey*

Leaning out on the passenger side, Nolan smiled – he had never known her to sing. The sky was blue through and through. There was no flaw in it – not the slightest hint of trouble or danger.

'Shall I drop you at the lights?' Hildegaard said as they neared Steamer Point and the heavier traffic.

'No – the roundabout, please,' Nolan said.

When the lights changed unexpectedly from green to amber she laughed, dropping down through the gears. She was remembering a party she had been to once on a roof. Ben Nolan was there – Aziz, too. It was a party in honour of Basim Mansouri, journalist without rival and propagandist for a fair future. Before the reluctant Marxist went among them with his soft drink, Nolan took it upon himself to get drunk. Oh, he was brave and clumsy. He danced out of time, his eyes a little closed, his mouth a little open, as Hildegaard recalled it, until she hurt him. She was very sure, back then, of what needed to be done. Now she wondered exactly what had been won and what had been lost. Up ahead at the crossroads and the red lights, a short queue of cars waited behind a donkey cart piled high with fragrant coriander. Hildegaard breathed in the aroma. Then it struck her – the correspondence between the beast of burden at the lights and the phantom song she had just been singing. Was it a donkey, a mule, or an ass up ahead? Hildegaard didn't know – she only knew it had to have a role. At first she thought the cargo of coriander might burst spontaneously into flames. Then she imagined an insurgent waiting below the pungent leaves to kill her without her make-up of disguise.

'What does it all mean and where will it all end?' Nolan asked with a random philosophical focus that was, at bottom, positive.

The donkey brayed and bolted. There was a beast on the loose. Why? How? Hildegaard jerked the handbrake on. There were loud complaints, very reasonably, from cars or trucks stationed on either side of the junction as, from left and right, two big vehicles swerved to avoid the frightened animal in their path. There was a donkey at large. Hildegaard saw it run this way and that before it was hit by a packed school bus and flew up in the air like a toy. The lights were at amber and red. The lights changed to green, but the car in front didn't move. The car was stuck, its engine running. By the time the door fell open and the driver jumped down and ran around behind, headscarf streaming, Hildegaard had wound her window up to the top. She had recognised Aziz before she had quite *seen* him. Now, as she looked into his eyes through the glass of the window, she didn't know what to expect. She found no clue in his eyes, nothing. First there was the signature moment of celestial calm. Then Aziz broke the window with a violent blow from his gun. Hildegaard raised her hand to her cheek. Briefly she wondered why a man armed with a gun and intent on murder would need to break the glass at all. Aziz crouched beyond her door with his arms extended stiffly. His pistol, gripped by one hand supported by the other, he directed at her jaw. Around his knuckles, which must have been damaged slightly by the breaking glass, the blood welled up in dark droplets.

'Well –' she said. 'Do you forgive me or not, Aziz?'

When he cocked his favourite pistol she wasn't scared at all.

'You shall have your answer, Hildegaard –'

She tasted blood on her lip. The glass must have cut her face.

'Goodbye, now, nurse. Remember this –'


TO NOLAN IT WAS LIKE A BOND FLICK at the open-air cinema. He imagined the projector might jam at any time, and the sound wind down as from a gramophone hit by a power cut. Leaning forward on the passenger side he watched Aziz divide his attention between the muzzle of his gun and the eyes confronting him calmly through the shattered window of the car. Nolan couldn't really see Hildegaard's eyes. Even so, he was convinced of their calmness. A sudden change came over Aziz – a glimmer of something, some deep feeling, made its presence felt momentarily within the dead pools of his eyes. As he watched the fingers tighten around the gun at last, Nolan let out an involuntary whimper, a yelp. Beside him or just in front, Hildegaard sat perfectly still. All this took several seconds only. First there was a brief exchange of words. Then came the click, amazingly loud in the local hush, as the gunman pulled the trigger on an empty chamber.

'Goodbye, then, Aziz —' Hildegaard murmured with something resembling tenderness.

Nolan watched the flawed assassin walk away fast and then toss his gun inside his waiting vehicle. When he hit the gas and let out the clutch the car lurched forward with a shriek, then skidded violently from side to side until the driver's door closed of its own accord. The lights were stuck at green. The road ahead was clear. From the cars behind came the resentful honking of horns. They had dragged the dead animal to the side of the road. From beside his aromatic cargo the donkey man remonstrated furiously with the driver of the school bus. Hildegaard released the handbrake and found first gear. There were some small glass cubes in her lap. At the edge of the windscreen as they crossed the junction Nolan saw a schoolgirl's face pressed up against the window of the bus.

'Is here all right?' Hildegaard asked soon after the lights.

'Here?' Nolan cleared his throat and tried again. 'Here couldn't be better —'

She pulled over just before the roundabout.

'I mean —' he went on. 'I could probably do with the walk.'

She wasn't looking at him. She was looking straight ahead.

'The good doctor, eh?' he said. 'You know — I never altogether warmed to him.'

Still she said nothing. She leaned across from behind the wheel and opened Nolan's door for him.

'Shouldn't I see you safely home or something?' he said finally.

'What you said before –' she said. 'You really shouldn't worry, Ben. Of all of us, I think you must be the one most like yourself.'

Much later, when he considered what she had said, Nolan saw its potential to mock him. He couldn't believe she would do that to him – not any more. Leaning in now from the side of the road, he was reluctant to say goodbye. He didn't see the point. He hoped she might feel the same way about that. He hoped she might see things pretty much as he saw them. What she had meant to him all along – it struck Nolan he had yet to discover it.

'You've cut your face,' he told her. 'Just here –'

'I know –' she said. 'Thank you, Ben – I expect I'll live.'

He offered her his towel again. Smiling, she refused it again. As he watched her drive off in a cloud of dust, Nolan heard a siren lay down its requiem for a donkey. He climbed the hill towards Hedjuff, towards a better version of himself. Anything was possible, wasn't it? Nothing was wasted. In fact, everything was connected. Nolan's flip-flops, for example, were exactly the same blue as the sky.

## ⤞ THE SILENT VALLEY ⤝

THE ORPHAN WITH THE SHAVED HEAD WAS a clever enough kid. Sitting cross-legged opposite him on the courtyard floor beneath the shrivelled vine, Sulaiman wondered what kind of country or world the boy would grow up to inherit. This kid made no mistake. When Sulaiman held out a round, the orphan took it from him and tossed it without hesitation towards a mound of .303s on the cloth between them. There was nothing childlike about the boy's actions. He was bored already with the game. He knew which bullet went where on the cloth just as he recognised the weapon to which every precious round belonged. He was light years ahead, martially speaking, of the old timer who sat opposite him. He was expert, for instance, in the manufacture of firebombs from bottles. Liquor bottles he disdained – they had been known to rebound entire from the doors of houses. Canada Dry's soft drinks bottles were the very thing. Comfortable in the hand, economical in terms of petrol used, they had increasingly found favour as the calling card of factional intent. Their glass was, so it seemed, not too thick. Their narrow necks were easily plugged with a fuse of torn bed sheet. The smart kid from the back streets of Sheikh Othman had found nineteen such bottles, many with straws in them, for the cause. Behind the favoured bottles the rifles leaned against the courtyard wall like artificial limbs of diverse specification.

There came three knocks, carefully weighted, on the door to the lane. Sulaiman rose immediately on his haunches. The child merely sat, staying the novice opposite him, raising his finger to his lips like a sage. They heard it again – two knocks this time. The boy sprang up. He had to jump to release the uppermost bolt. Two men came in. The kid closed the door and leaned his back against it, hands on hips like a hero. The first man bolted the door. The second rubbed the kid's scalp with one hand while unwinding a headscarf with the other. Sulaiman awaited instructions with a couple of rifle rounds in clenched fists. It was clear as day to him. With or without the scarf, the second man's identity was obvious.

'No one else here?' Isa asked his father.

Sulaiman shook his head.

'There's empty bottles needs filling,' growled the first man over his shoulder as he crossed the gloomy courtyard.

'What with?' Sulaiman said. 'I don't see any juice –'

'That's because you don't know where to look for it,' Isa called out from the steps to the basement.

'Hey, there, grandpa –' The first man pulled a folded bed sheet from below his grubby singlet and tossed it in the general direction of Sulaiman. Then he motioned towards the kid. 'Twenty fuses,' he barked. 'Twenty good ones, mind –'

The kid snatched the bed sheet from Sulaiman's hands. Isa was at the top of the steps with a sloshing jerry can.

'Aren't you going to introduce me to your comrade?' Sulaiman asked him.

'I'm not sure that's necessary under the circumstances,' Isa said, setting down the petrol.

There came three taps on the door to the alley. No one moved. They heard two further knocks – now the kid was at the door again. Soon there were ten men, including Aziz, in the courtyard. The kid was extra – he was passing his strips of cotton to the first man one by one. The first man wound each length of cotton in turn around his middle finger to make a stopper or a bung. The other men took up their rifles. There was an examination of carefully oiled bolts. Some men drew a four-by-two strip of cleaning cloth through this or that barrel on a yard of rope to honour the gunsmiths of Egypt or Russia or England. How respectful was their handling of these weapons. In the busy silence they insinuated their bullets lovingly into magazines and took them out again and counted them solemnly, wordlessly, as if each round was a gold tooth on a square of chamois.

Sulaiman crouched with his back to the wall. Between his knees was the British rifle Isa had chosen for him. As he ran his fingers up and down its cold dark metal and its smooth warm wood, Sulaiman wondered how many lives – lives unseen, lives unknown – the rifle had ended. Not that he harboured the slightest intention of killing a *stranger* with it any time soon. Instead, he observed his gifted son at work. The quick-witted and highly committed youth was welcomed in all four corners of the courtyard. He knew every chore of war. He was indispensable to their leader in his preparations for the briefing to come. He was equally at home with the gruff rank and file. How Sulaiman resented them. He resented them all with a bitterness he could taste. As he observed his son he was forced to conclude that Isa loved them – yes, *them*. His love, naturally laconic, was deeply felt. It was like a brother's love. There was a hard-won beauty in the son's unqualified fellowship with the taciturn platoon. That was how the father experienced it. There was a fierce pride in what they did for each other. There was a latent courage in the face of the risks they would soon take together that made Sulaiman long to cry out – 'He is mine. He is mine. I have loved him. I have loved him too.'

Aziz unveiled the plan. It was getting dark now. The kid had lit the lamps and stationed them either side of two pillowcases hanging from a wire. On the pillowcases was drawn a precise sketch map of the idea. It was an unsophisticated tactic that had to do with tit-for-tat murder or internecine arson in downtown Sheikh Othman after dark. Given that various FLOSY strongholds had been pinpointed on the Al-Mansura side of the township, three tenement buildings, forming an isosceles triangle on the pillowcases, had lately become key targets in the very shadow of the botanical garden. How simple it must have seemed to the silent warriors – they kept their counsel after Aziz had concluded his briefing. Sulaiman, however, voiced the doubts of the amateur.

'The other units you mentioned – the ones made up of our NLF comrades,' he began thoughtfully. 'How the devil will we recognise them if we're not allowed to identify ourselves one unit to another or, for that matter, one man to another?'

It was Isa who spoke up first. 'Weren't you listening?' he asked patiently. 'You won't need to recognise the other units because each unit has its own objectives and targets. Each NLF unit consists of six men in pairs –'

'Six men in pairs?' Sulaiman said. 'But we number ten, all told, do we not? I don't count the child, of course.'

'Three teams of two,' Isa said. 'If those six men fail to return –'

He left his sentence unfinished and shrugged negligently.

'Ah, very good –' Sulaiman said. 'You mean their empty shoes can quickly be filled by the remaining feet?' Here the novice smiled apologetically for the benefit of the whole company. 'No, no – I was afraid I might shoot the wrong chap out there, that's all.'

A caustic silence greeted this unwarranted confession. Sulaiman hung his head with new humility. It was as if it had just dawned on him – he had all but volunteered, uninvited, for a perilous mission. That was the look he was after. So far, so good – it was precisely an impression of willing incompetence he needed to give out from now on. They had to consider him eligible – no, expendable – when the magnificent six were called up. They had to damn him by choosing him – they had to. Now Aziz exerted his tired authority.

'In the experience of most, my friend, the question of who to kill becomes rhetorical or redundant when the moment of truth arrives. There can be no room for doubt at such a time, don't you see?' The leader smiled encouragingly at this point for the sake of their newest recruit. 'Was there anything else on your mind?'

'No, no – not a bit of it,' Sulaiman said, gratified. 'I suppose we get down on our hands and knees to pray now, do we?' He looked at all their closed faces. Were they laughing at him inside? They had written him off as the babysitter – the one who would stay behind with the kid. 'Shouldn't we pray, though?' he went on gravely. 'We really must introduce God to Marx, surely, and vice versa. How else will they know each other when the time comes to shoot?'

For a moment, only brave or foolish insects stirred in the light of the lamps. Then Isa spoke up again coolly.

'Between God and party there can be no confusion. There can be no confusing the two. Is not the one a stooge of America and the patron of reaction everywhere?'

It was a most timely expression of a widely held prejudice. In the deepening dark they were audibly impressed. Then Isa cut through their mutterings with a further insight.

'The new recruit goes with me tonight –' He waited until their murmurs, momentarily redoubled, fell away to nothing. 'The new recruit is my father.'

There ensued a private silence – a silence made for two. No one else was in it. Sulaiman nodded first at Aziz, then located his son in a region where light gave way to dark. No night was dark enough to hide the father's black love.

'We will be together, Isa,' he acknowledged hoarsely. 'In point of fact, I never once doubted it.'

ISA KNOCKED AT THE SHUTTERED WINDOW. It was past midnight. What time was it exactly? That didn't matter – they would await the signal from Aziz. In the urban gorge Sulaiman hugged the wall, his breathing much too loud, with the vapour rising from the bottles at his waistband. Beneath the black *chador* his rifle was a deadly splint at his side – it offered neither comfort nor reassurance in respect of the business at hand. To end it soon was Sulaiman's only desire. For so long he had thought of little else. Now the door opened noiselessly. Beyond the doorway, the interior of the house was unlit. As son and father entered and threw off their cloaks, the woman stood behind the door, saying nothing, with the wide-eyed infants at her skirts.

'Go now, please,' Isa hissed at her.

Up on the roof, the son hauled himself across the surface using his elbows and stomach with the rifles held out in front. The father came behind him with the cherry-cola bottles. Kneeling side by side behind the low wall in the shadow of the water tank they paused to get their breath back. Sulaiman closed his eyes and waited. Almost immediately he felt Isa's hand on his shoulder.

'Over there –'

Below them stretched a descending terrace of rooftops with, just beyond it, the dark void of the botanical garden.

'Can you see it?'

Sulaiman looked. He looked very hard. He had never surveyed the land so minutely – only the sea. He examined the first roof, the nearest one, and dismissed it. He studied the second, then the third. There was nothing – nothing to speak of. On the fourth roof he saw the hillock of sand and a sleeping concrete mixer and a motorcycle without wheels below a canopy of bougainvillaea. The small moon cast harsh shadows across the illusory tableau. How suggestive the night – from where Sulaiman looked it was easy to impute the most sinister motivation to a pile of sand. Then he saw it.

The house in question was less than a hundred yards distant. It was, Isa's manner suggested, within killing range. The son eased his rifle very slowly over the wall. As he nuzzled the telescopic sight his breathing became shallower and more rapid. There was altogether too much excitement in his breathing – Sulaiman would have stifled it there and then and drowned in the gorgeous silence. Not yet, not yet. He heard the action of Isa's bolt, so quiet and confidential. He glimpsed again the telltale glow of a cigarette cupped by a hand in a bivouac of uncertain material. The FLOSY fabric was too thin. The cigarette glowed fatally pink for a moment through the tent – then there was nothing. There was only Isa with his British rifle.

'Wait up –' Sulaiman whispered. 'What about Aziz? What about the signal?'

'Let this be the signal,' Isa replied. 'Aziz will follow. Look – this one is already dead. Very soon they will be a man less.' Here the son took his cheek from the rifle and turned from the wall and nodded. In his eyes, Sulaiman saw the light of understanding. 'Now it begins, father. To the unknown we submit. Before we get to that house you will know how to do it – what you came to Sheikh Othman to do. Can you remember how many rounds you have?'

'Five rounds.'

One bullet, however amateur or inexpert, would be sure to do the trick at close quarters.

'Five bullets – the same as me, father. Are you ready now?'

'I am ready.'

'You won't let me down? You know I count on you tonight –'

'I won't let you down, son.'

Isa's shot rang out. Immediately they were on their feet, a bottle each and a gun in hand. They saw the orange flame shoot up before they heard the explosion. Was that Aziz down there? They couldn't know. There was a conflagration of petrol bombs somewhere. They had no time to admire the pretty colours. They heard another bang, then two more, and the world was a far brighter place. One behind the other they plunged down the stairs and entered the lane. What a transformation – already their narrow street was busy with howling citizens who ran. Why so many? Why so soon? Their numbers were outrageous. They were moaning and running in the direction of the botanical garden. Had they been waiting, Sulaiman asked, behind their locked doors? They must have been waiting for a signal to run. Up ahead, the sky was on fire. Now the father scrambled to overtake the son. He had to go ahead in order to turn and look his son in the eye. The people parted for them like a zip opening up in the night. As they pursued each other with weapons held high, father and son heard the machine gun's appalling stutter. They both heard it in the same instant. Isa cursed it loudly. Small wonder – he knew it had to belong to the other side. The machine gun made a dreadful bloody racket before stopping as suddenly as it started. Look – there was a man on fire now. He was absolutely alight and stumbling brilliantly towards them to be hugged. Which team did he bat for? Impossible to know whose side he was on. He was quite definitely dead when he pitched forward at Sulaiman's feet. Then the machine gun took up again, and Isa went down with a little cry of astonishment.

Petrol ran away around a broken Canada Dry bottle. The night was full of muted screams. Sulaiman pushed the door, but the door wouldn't budge until he clubbed it with his rifle. He threw down his weapon and hooked his arms under Isa's arms and dragged the boy inside. It was dark in there – too dark to see. As he kicked the door shut behind him, Sulaiman heard a kind of laughter. It was no joke. He struck a match – a match made for arson and murder. When he held the flame low he saw his son was laughing.

'Five bullets, father – I reckon just one will be enough now.'

The flame reached Sulaiman's fingers. The light went out.

'Let me see –' cried the youth. 'Let me look.'

Sulaiman struck the second match. Isa's stomach loomed, shiny and red.

'You see, father – they have practically seen me off. Your work here is almost done. You have only to end it.'

The boy let go a cough. There was liquid or fluid in it.

'Finish it, won't you – what you came here to do? Careful now – you'll burn your fingers there. Quickly, please – there isn't much time. Will you go to the valley, father – the Silent Valley? Will you go to the mast – the radio mast? That's where you'll find them – my books. My books. Will you promise me, father? I want you to have them. I don't think I'll need them. Oh, no – not yet. I'm not ready yet. Let me find my glasses first. Only promise me, father –'

As the third match flared, Sulaiman saw the youth's eyeballs roll up inside his head and come down again. There was a simultaneous seeping of blood from his nose and ears before his voice came back through a frothy veil.

'Did you find my glasses? I can't feel your hand. Let me feel your fingers, father – very tight, very tight. That's it. That's it. No, no – don't let go, please. Won't you finish it now and then close my eyes and kiss me? Oh, I can hear blood. I can hear the blood –'

The match went out. There was a little cry in the darkness, and a whisper.

'I can't hear it, Dad. I can't hear it any more.'


HE MUST HAVE SLEPT. WHEN HE WOKE UP, he found the door was open to the deserted street. How so? Had someone waltzed in and gone out again while he dreamt? He gazed at the body beside him. The body was still there, sticky black blood all around it. It was too early for flies. The body was cool, but not cold, when Sulaiman lifted it up from the ground and laid it out on the table. After he drew the tablecloth up and over on both sides he closed his son's eyes, kissed the bruised eyelids, and stepped over a rifle in the doorway.

Outside, the light was pale, the air still. Where were the people? Where had they all gone? There was only the last of the smoke and a silence. The burning man lay face down in the lane where he had fallen. The cherry-cola bottles were broken or empty. Sulaiman left them behind and wandered in the botanical garden among the old trees and watched as the sun popped up between their noble trunks.

How comforting to discover sundry sturdy succulents on a day like this one, the bereaved father thought. He was the only man left alive anywhere. Wait – he heard a faraway noise, rhythmic, repetitive. As he set off gladly in the direction of the noise it enveloped him like a breeze, growing steadily louder and more insistent with each step he took. What on earth was it? It was a chorus of reason, the sound of many people chanting. Sulaiman stopped to listen and to watch. He could see it now through the leaves of the trees – a dark tide running from right to left with no end in sight. As they progressed in a slow and dignified stream the citizens clapped and chanted with a single voice. Sulaiman advanced willingly towards them now. By the time he emerged from the trees they had filled up a street. They were the older and younger women, mostly. They were women without their veils. They had with them the smaller children and a few older men, all of them singing and chanting for an end to bloodshed. Sulaiman fell in with them unhesitatingly. Although he had never heard a song quite like theirs, he sang it as if he had always known it.

Up ahead was the town's mosque. As the procession slowed and the chants died away, Sulaiman glimpsed a man on the steps of the mosque at a height just above the crowd. When the man waved his arms, the women began to settle on the ground like exhausted birds. Sulaiman pressed on towards the front of the throng. He picked his way through the dark forms until he reached the head of the flock, enticed by the steps – his steps. He rested there in the shadow of the minaret. As he studied the many faces around him he began to cry. No one would have known he was crying. No tears came down – he just shuddered and his shoulders heaved for a few seconds. Then he saw the kid with the shaved head dash forward towards the saviour on the steps. The clever orphan from the streets of Sheikh Othman ran into the man's open arms. With the tearful child in his embrace

338

the speaker raised his megaphone above the heads of the crowd and made his appeal.

'My name is Basim Mansouri —' he boomed. 'Let me show you the face of our glorious future.'

## ❧ KINGDOM COME ☙

TOWARDS MIDDAY SULAIMAN RETURNED to Bir Fuqum, hitching a lift around the bay as far as Little Aden where he got down from a pick-up, the songs of peace still ringing in his ears, and thanked his host like a visiting stranger. Everything looked different. The whole world was new. Glittering with fresh purpose and promise, the silver towers of the refinery rose above the scene like lords of light. The air itself was blinding – Sulaiman found it hard to look on life with the naked eye. He was dead on his feet. The thing that kept him going was his unspoken promise to his son. All morning it had driven him closer to a valley called Silent Valley, to the canyon that cut through the rock from town to village, between the refinery and the open sea. To finish his business – it was all Sulaiman's ambition. He had some unfinished business in a cold canyon pierced briefly around noon by a migrant sun. Let him sleep first – sleep but not dream. High above him as he lurched through the defile was the famous radio mast, the ultimate focus of his intentions. From the roof of the chasm the mast climbed unseen towards heaven. For now, Sulaiman resisted its pull, its magnetic reach, and trudged onwards towards his village and the sea. As he left the gloomy gorge and saw his home bask again in the remorseless light he tasted death again on his tongue. But there was something different after all – the prospect of peace, tired and dirty, at the last. Where the door of Sulaiman's home had been there was only an aperture that loomed larger and larger in his imagination as he went. What did the dismal hole offer, he asked, if not a privileged access to the inevitable end?

Heart on fire, he drank from the tap outside his house. Beyond the gaping doorway he found a form of chaos. The place had been turned over ruthlessly. Sadness upon sadness – in the face of further provocations Sulaiman was strangely unsurprised. It was the elusive eighth box, he decided immediately, which had inspired their brutal investigations. His living quarters being small, there was nowhere in them to conceal something like that successfully. There was little, in fact, to root through, but they had done their best – witness the torn mattress and the far-flung drawers of the tallboy. Sulaiman righted the table and picked up Isa's favourite chair, ruined reminder of the dead son. Now the father surrendered to his unspoken promise, the call of unfinished business. There could be no sleep before the end. What he lacked was a spade or some other digging implement. Any garden trowel would have stood in perfectly. Instead, Sulaiman was obliged to call on the faithful blade they had press-ganged so cruelly in the conduct of their vandalising searches. As he rescued his knife from the ripped mattress the first tears came down without apparent context. How disheartening it was to survive an only child. Oh, look – in the rubble of nameless possessions beyond the torn mattress lay Isa's transistor radio, silent and crushed to death.

Outside the house, he confronted the Silent Valley with knife in hand. Had they watched him quit the village they might have taken him for a somnambulant killer or an avenging ghost. Soon he was in the deepest shadow of the gorge where the colder air was king. The sky was a bright incision in the dark cloth above. Sulaiman climbed towards the inspirational slash using bare hands and feet. His shoes he carried inside his shirt, his blade between his teeth. As he made his way up the face of the cliff the black rock helped him as much as it could. Sulaiman would happily have stretched out on its tolerant ledges. At last the rock felt appreciably warmer. Nearer and nearer Sulaiman drew to the crest of the cliff. Victory – he saw the girders of the radio mast hurl their lengthening shadows across the bay. Far away below the cliff the warships awaited the end as, rotors turning lazily in the sunshine, three helicopters hung in the blue afternoon.

ACROSS THE BAY, ON A WINDING DRIVE overlooking the harbour, Basim Mansouri climbed impressively towards Government House with one elbow on the armrest of a black saloon. He had a German car. He had his local driver. He had every expectation of a glittering future. His official duties were unlimited in scope. All his tomorrows egged him on. He had declaimed before a host of angry women for half the morning, and now it was time to shift down a gear and don an estate agent's hat. His valued client in this latest geopolitical role was a people's putative republic.

Through the sleek, contented trees the black saloon rose towards a deserted gatehouse. Call it good or bad timing, call it serendipity – it was a historical snarl-up. Although the big gates were open there could be no possibility of entry for Basim's car until the three Crown Daimlers, descending in a self-conscious convoy from the house, had themselves passed through the gates, or been reversed, or removed from the drive altogether. There ensued a stubborn standoff between chauffeurs awaiting partisan instructions. All the brake lights were on as Basim leaned forward with the satisfied smile of the dialectical materialist vindicated. How gratifying it was to see historical events shaped by the clash of social ambitions, precisely as they were meant to be. To back three Daimlers up the hill would have made no sense at all – far more practical to reverse one limousine rather than two or three. It fell to Basim, in the face of their vehicular impasse, to be the magnanimous conqueror. He gave the necessary command. His driver reversed, pulling over at the shady margin of the drive below a fig tree. Three Daimlers issued noiselessly from the gate with their blinds drawn down and the Union flag on their bonnets.

Outside the house a drained swimming pool was the playground of lizards. Basim stroked first one fluted column then another as if to confirm their architectural bona fides. Gazing now across cascading lawns he got from his saliva the piquant savour of a destiny fulfilled. How mouth watering were the seaboard views from the neo-classical villa enjoying vacant possession. Sighing with a profound content as he backed through the doors, Basim had his first whiff of distemper.

'Excuse me, please —' he called out in the spacious hall.

'Up 'ere —'

There was a workman, a genuine Adeni by the sound of it, on a gantry raised high against the wall. The curving staircase below was festooned with his spattered dustsheets.

'Would you kindly update me on what's happening here?' Basim requested crisply.

The local craftsman lifted, one in each hand, his paintbrush and tin pot.

'I am reworking to my own 'umble specification,' he explained humorously, 'the ceiling of the Sixteen Chapel at Rome.'

'Are you, really?' Basim said. 'And who is likely to reward this reactionary endeavour now that the high commissioner no longer lives at this address?'

''Ere — what's your game?' asked the man. 'As a matter of fact 'e's already paid me 'andsomely. Proper gent, 'e is. Well, *was* —'

'Ah, yes – very civilised,' Basim commented. 'Rather moving, in its own way.' Now he took time to examine the vaulted ceiling high above. 'And what particular shade is that, may I ask?'

'I don't know, do I? What's it look like to you? The same as last time, 'e tells me – not too light and not too dark.'

'Things are so rarely black or white,' Basim conceded. 'But do find out what it's called and let me know, won't you? They used to say the devil was in the detail –'

'Did they just? And who might *you* be when you're at 'ome?'

'I, sir, am the minister responsible –'

'Blimey – for the devil, or for painting and decorating?'

'For *presentation*,' Basim explained, his smile invisible from above. 'Behold –' he urged, arms thrown wide below the chandelier. 'Your brand new Ministry of Information.'

ACROSS THE FACE OF THE ROCK ABOVE Silent Valley the shadows continued to lengthen as Sulaiman circled the radio mast, his knife in his hand. There was no obvious place to start digging. The earth itself gave no clue. The four feet of the mast were embedded in grey concrete set into the rock face above the valley. Sulaiman widened his investigations, touring the plateau in arcs around the mast until he reached the edge of the chasm on one side. Still the fruitful ground eluded him. It was at the rear of the apron, a stone's throw from the mast and the cliff, that he found what he was looking for – a barren sward of hard-packed soil like the scab of a wound in an otherwise unlikely setting. There was nowhere else to try. Four marker stones made of the digging zone a rhombus or a squat diamond. Was that the sign? Had they dropped from the sky, these significant boulders? Too large to lift or drag, they described an expanse of softer ground about the size of Sulaiman's boat.

He began his sacred work at the centre of the favoured terrain, attacking the parched dirt with his knife, stabbing the earth in small jurisdictions before scooping it out with bleeding fingers. Although the sun was sinking steadily, the work was torrid. As the perspiration mingled with the dust among the hairs of his arms and muddied his wrists, Sulaiman sized up his trench and lashed out again and again with his knife, spit drying at the edges of his mouth. As the low sun kissed his forehead he thought himself a lunatic prospecting for love on the roof of the world. In his mind, he was hollowing out a grave. He was digging a grave for his gifted son. It was too thick, the earth. It was much too dense, Sulaiman decided despairingly. Then he hit something shiny or hard, and the blade of his knife snapped off.

Isa's bicycle was at the top of the cache. Sulaiman scraped away the dirt between its spokes and raised it high and shook it at the sun. He bounced its tyres, laughing first then crying, on the rock and laid it down on its side, its wheel turning with a comforting clicking note that diminished. Isa's books were next. Sulaiman recognised many of them. There were the moralising tales in English of the children's variety, plus familiar school texts the father had covered with brown paper jackets to protect them from the sun. The books resided now in their exposed stacks several volumes deep, no proper steps having been taken to safeguard them. It was as he raised the books up one by one that Sulaiman discovered a football at the bottom of the pit. It was the only item left down there now – a football, evidently, in a polythene bag. No, it wasn't quite round. It was surprisingly heavy. As he retrieved it from the dig and brushed the earth from its outer covering, Sulaiman ditched the idea of a football, so uncharacteristic of his bookish son, and glimpsed instead a rogue's gallery of leering faces or bobbing heads. It was grotesque. He saw Isa's face with its bruised eyelids, then Kanoo's with its string of shiny beads. He saw the orphan with the shaved scalp – the face of the future. All their heads were parted from their bodies. Sulaiman tore open the plastic bag and poured out the unlikely legacy of his son. The magnificent

344

bust should have been safely tucked away inside a plywood box, but it wasn't. It would have fitted perfectly inside the eighth box in place of Kanoo's fleshy head. For a moment Sulaiman stared, fascinated, at the precocious football on the roof of the world. Soon he began to laugh. Inching closer on his knees, he cupped the bust in his hands. What a turn-up – he was gazing into the unseeing eyes of a beautiful youth. He was staring at a life-sized head cast in bronze and dating from impossibly long ago. How the eyes bulged with the promise of earthly pleasures. To the amateur eye the bust looked authentic, the hair plastered to the intelligent forehead in sensual curls. Could ever such perfection be faked? No, never – it had to be as old as the sea, Sulaiman reasoned with a little shudder. Such physical grace might easily be priceless. So much cruel beauty might well cost the earth.

IT WAS COOLER, THE DAY BEING NEARLY DONE, and the light was blue now in Silent Valley. Sulaiman had descended, Isa's bike at his side, by the track of loose stones that unwound from the rock above Little Aden. The books he left buried up there with the broken knife. He was sick of shadows as he pedalled, his damp shirt billowing, his plastic bag swinging from the handlebars of Isa's bike, towards Bir Fuqum, his home. His unfinished business was virtually concluded. Soon he would rest. Outside his house he drank again from the tap, then abandoned the bike and went directly to the water and found his boat still there. Yes, it was there. Who would take it and tear the heart from him? He had little else to cherish besides the bequeathed bicycle. He carried a priceless bronze artefact in his plastic bag, but for how much longer? He pulled on the rope and fell inside his boat with his antique cargo. When he jerked the cord the engine started first time as if nothing had happened in the world for days and days. Sulaiman faced about, steering west to east in the Gulf of Aden. He might have looked to his left across the busy anchorage and seen the warships blush pink and the aircraft carrier bristle with able bodied salutes as the high commissioner went on board. Sulaiman didn't hear the band strike up – he was far too far out now, and the breeze was mostly to the shore. Cutting his engine he drifted slowly towards the fish with his priceless bundle at his feet. Above the desert the sky turned indigo and gold with a sudden glory that spread from cloud to cloud and ran from one side of the world to the other. Sulaiman acknowledged it and let go. He dropped his priceless package on the water and pictured it sinking all the way to the ocean floor. Taking up his net he stood in his faithful boat, his back to the land, and felt the promise of peace run through his body – flesh, blood, and bone. The sea was calm, the sea was full – Sulaiman laid his net on it.

Made in the USA
Columbia, SC
14 November 2017